Green River Rising

BLOODSTAINED KINGS

Tim Willocks
BLOODSTAINED KINGS

Random House New York

Library of Congress Cataloging-in-Publication Data

Willocks, Tim.
Bloodstained kings / Tim Willocks.
p.   cm.
ISBN 0-679-45009-2
I. Title.
PS3573.I456558B57   1997
813´.54—dc21   97-1523

Random House website address: http://www.randomhouse.com/

Printed in the United States of America on acid-free paper

24689753

FIRST U.S. EDITION

Book design by Carole Lowenstein

And the LORD said unto Satan,
Whence comest thou? Then Satan
answered the Lord, and said, From
going to and fro in the earth, and
from walking up and down in it.

Job: 1.7

CONTENTS

Part One
COLD DAY IN HELL

A Plantation Farm on the Mississippi Delta.
Twenty Years Ago.

See the fatman. See him run.

See his legs—massive in their strength, in their flight—plunge and flounder and suck through the muddy deltan ooze. Feel the clinging weight of that melted clay, that driven rain, that night; that steaming dark. Know the spasms in his gut as he feels the gaze of the great grandfather spirit: appalled by the horror the fatman leaves behind him. A brilliant shard of lightning cleaves the sky. It floods the midnight campo with incandescent witness: the fatman is there.

He is running. He is running.

But the earth cannot stop him, nor her gods, nor the gone dead souls that grieve upon the wind. For he cannot be killed, the fatman. No. Not this night. He cannot be stopped. And the pounding of his vein and blood, the pressure in his skull, the encoiled writhings of his bowel come not from fear. As the futile thunder dies, enraged, the screams return. The screams of a woman. They seek him out across the harrowed field. But these screams too—of a pain too wide and deep for human knowing—these screams too must stumble and fall unheeded. They do not pierce the fatman's heart. They cannot stop him in his course. He will not let them, though he could. The blood on his hands—and flung in splashed, diluted gouts across his gale-drenched coat—is not his own. For now the losing of blood is the work of others: others past; others yet to come.

And still he pounds; and plunges and sucks.

His left arm holds a bundle of sodden rags pressed hard into his heaving chest. The arm is thickened; it is clenched; yet in spite of all the violence of the world, its embrace is tender. So tender. A wooden fence looms front: raw hickory posts held fast in barbed wire lacings. With his right-hand fist the fatman grabs the stave that blocks his way and wrenches and uproots it in one; for he is strong, is the fatman. He tramples down the twisted wire and is gone. His feet, encased in dirt, now pound a blacktop road. From up ahead come yellow beams: a vehicle in the rain. A car.

The fatman's lips are beautiful. They're full. They smile.

The woman's screams have vanished on the wind.

The car pulls down and over, alongside his massive form. A pale face, young and thin—a man—smiles back. Unknowing. Without knowledge. Unpossessed of truth. The young gaze falls on the bundle, ragged and drenched; his mouth gapes wide. The fist that wrenches hickory staves enfolds around his neck, a fist so large the fingers almost reach the thumb across the nape. Rolling whites of pale young eyes are speckled of an instant with the stars of tiny vessels bursting red. The car heaves and rocks to the hammering of convulsion, of flailing, panicked limbs. The smell of shitting and death. Another soul sighs its passing, slipping through the fatman's strangling hand; yet throughout all, the muscled cradle of his arm is tender still.

The pale one, thin and young, is dragged—and stomped for measure—into a watery roadside ditch. It was not his destiny either, then, to be a bearer of witness.

Is that the scream—the distant, vast and bottomless scream—that the fatman catches on the wing? Windblown far—as far as this—as he treads the pale one down?

It matters to him not.

His embrace is tender. He runs no more. The vehicle shelters his bulk within and roars; and carries the fatman, and his bundle, hence. Whither he knows not, nor yet does he care.

For though he knows not why, he loves her whom he carries.

He loves her dear.

ONE

HATRED had desiccated Lenna Parillaud's soul and she knew it. The thought sickened her. As she drove toward the Stone House beneath an April blue sky she tried to tell herself that her thought was not true; but despite its desiccation—or maybe because of it—her soul replied otherwise. It was the truth and worse than merely truth: her hatred was her destiny; it was that which she was meant to be. Yet where once her hate had been a wrathful deity, calling for horizons blazed with fire and cities cracked in sunder, it was now a squirming creature that clung to her back, its arms coiled around her neck while its sour breath in her ear droned a litany, the words of which she no longer cared to comprehend. Lenna was tired of listening to it, tired of carrying it; yet who else could or would? The hatred was hers and hers only. Today—even though today she needed it—she wished the hatred might find itself as weary as she.

She was driven most places by her bodyguard, Bobby Frechette; to the Stone House she always drove alone. Now that Clarence Jefferson was dead, Frechette was the only person left in her life with whom she felt she stood on level ground. The possibility had crossed her mind that it was Frechette who had killed Clarence Jefferson and burned his corpse on a pyre in the swamps. He had done worse things on her account with her knowledge and blessing, and yet others without them. Frechette was one of few who could have taken Jefferson down. His contempt for him, though silent, had been clear enough. But even if Frechette had never understood it, he had accepted her need for Jefferson's foul embrace and he would not have taken it away from her without her command. Frechette did not know the secret of the Stone House. Now that Jefferson was dead no one knew except her, not even its keepers; not even its wretched occupant. The Stone House was the receptacle—the squat gray cathedral—of her shame. Through the windshield it now appeared in the middle distance: a featureless box in a featureless landscape.

Lenna no longer enjoyed these visits, if she'd ever convinced herself that she had. They were a ritual she could not avoid; the first of each month, every month, for over a dozen years. Again she pushed herself to admit a disagreeable truth: without these visits the months would contain nothing of meaning at all. She wondered what else she might have brought into being if she'd committed to some other endeavor the vast energies consumed by her hatred; yet she could not imagine what that endeavor might be. She wasn't blind. She didn't lack for intelligence or insight; on the contrary she had grasped the essence of the world and its workings with a ferocious acuteness of perception. Yet that world was a dark one, filled with malice and pain. She knew that another, brighter, world existed—one in which some were lucky enough to expend their strength in the generation of something more beautiful than themselves—but she knew the existence of that world only as a person leafing through an atlas knows of the existence of far-away lands and glittering seas. She would never go there, nor had she ever been; or, rather, she had been there but in another time, so long ago that it seemed a lost dreamscape, dimly remembered and beyond the power of all her striving to visit again.

She drove a black four-door Mercedes, tooling it one-handed around a broad curve in the blacktop. To either side of the road swept broad fields of marsh grass, yellow as wheat in the spring sunshine and flat—as only the Delta could be flat—as far as the mighty levees that marked the blue horizon and kept the Big Muddy at bay. The black alluvium had once produced a rich yield of cotton, tobacco and maize, but in the thirteen years she'd been keeper of this land she'd returned it to the caprices of the wind and rain, and now the marsh grass had taken it back. She would not profit from this dirt and had no need to. A twelve-thousand-acre oil lease in south-central Louisiana, a pharmaceutical company, a casino license, and a decent chunk of New Orleans, plus other real estate in Florida and Kentucky, bloated her assets week in, week out with more cash than she cared to know. She would never spend a fraction of it; would not have known how to. The land here, at least, could become what it knew itself to be, even if she herself could not.

6

She turned off the blacktop onto a dirt road. At its far end stood a windowless building constructed of concrete blocks threaded with steel. The gray walls were pale and streaked with the workings of sun and rain. Though its shell was of concrete, its heart was of stone, and so to Lenna the Stone House it remained and always had been. The Stone House was built on one side of a large tarmacadamed yard. On another, adjacent, side stood a suburban frame house with a garden, a garage and a pickup truck. The gap between the two buildings was open to the fields. The fourth side of the yard was closed in by a grove of silver birch trees. In the frame house lived Harvill and Woodrow Jessup.

The Jessups were brothers, originally Mingo County backwoodsmen from northern Mississippi. As a young man Woodrow had trained as a psychiatric nurse in Tupelo, but the company of his coworkers, and what he'd regarded as "big city life," hadn't agreed with him and he'd thrown it in and gone back home to raise livestock and run a still. Harvill, by a decade the younger of the two, was of borderline subnormal intelligence. Neither had ever been married or, as far as Lenna knew, showed much interest in human sexual relations of any kind at all. They'd worked for her at the Stone House since it was built and, in their way, were as dependable as Bobby Frechette. They too owed her their allegiance. Their house did not exist in the records of the parish or those of any utilities company. Neither man was known to the IRS or any other agency, public or private.

Before the brothers had been picked to work here, Harvill—fourteen years ago and aged sixteen—had butchered his widowed mother "like the last shoat of a long winter," as Woodrow put it. Thanks to the intervention, on Lenna's behalf, of Clarence Jefferson, Harvill had never been punished, or even charged with this crime. Harvill never left the property and didn't seem inclined to, and whatever feelings he harbored about his adolescent matricide he kept to himself.

Woodrow's needs weren't much greater than his brother's. A drinker in his youth, he'd been born again since his mother's death and favored the Old Testament over the New. Once a week he drove down to a mall on Route 51 and bought supplies and took in a movie at the multiplex. His passion was in breeding dogs, German shepherds, the litters of which he was allowed to sell once a year under a false name and out of state. He also raised hogs. As Lenna pulled over in the Mercedes and got out, two of the last batch of German shepherds, which Woodrow had held on to, came bounding toward her with ebullient, throaty barks. They were still a little under a year old but already big, going on massive: long-haired, mostly black with slashes of gold. Lenna smiled and held out her hands to greet them. The dogs were still too young to have much meanness in them—Woodrow would train them in that capacity to a pinnacle of savage obedience when the time was right—and they danced around her waist in a low cloud of dust. One of them stood on its hind legs and threw its paws on her shoulders, licking her throat and slavering on the jacket of her black Karan pantsuit. Lenna grabbed two handfuls of dense neck fur and wrestled him back and forth while he rolled the whites of his eyes with joy. At the sound of a guttural shout both dogs spun away from her and bounded toward a big, lugubrious man with an easy stride.

He was dressed in clean white overalls and burnished oxblood Red Wings. At the man's heels—a heavy black shag of fur swaying from its belly and chest with each step—padded a cool, bleak-eyed monster that made the average wolf look like a muskrat searching for the nearest hole. The man was Woodrow Jessup. The dog was the pups' father; his name was Gul. Gul cast a single brief glance at the pups and they quietened down and fell in behind him. Woodrow nodded his long face at Lenna.

"Hope th'animals din't bother you there, Miss Par-low."

"Par-low" was as close as Woodrow ever got to Parillaud. Lenna didn't mind. Gul, though he knew her well, stared up at her with neither a pant nor a blink. She knew better than to hold that black gaze for too long. She realized that she'd never heard Gul bark; then found herself hoping that she never would. She turned back to Woodrow.

"They're growing fast," she said.

"Oh, they've a ways to go yet." Woodrow nodded at one of the pups. "Seth's paws're already bigger than his pappy's. Give him another year, he'll be full growed into 'em."

"That's frightening," said Lenna.

Woodrow didn't smile. He raised his hand and Seth jumped up and took his wrist in his jaws, growling with fake menace.

"Not yet," said Woodrow. "But it will be."

He cuffed Seth down and looked over to the heavy steel door of the Stone House, then at Lenna.

"Smilin' Boy's ready in thar if you are, Miss Par-low," he said.

Lenna nodded. The good feelings provoked by the dogs vanished from her chest. As they walked over to the steel door Woodrow pulled a set of keys from his pocket. He unlocked the door and slid it open on bearings so well oiled they murmured. Inside, a walkway led off between crates of farm implements stacked to twice head height. The crates were dusty. The room was illuminated with harsh white strip lights. Woodrow turned to the dogs.

"Sit."

Gul sank back on his haunches. A moment later the younger dogs followed suit.

"Now, stay."

Woodrow went inside first and Lenna followed him through the maze of crates. They stopped at a second door set into a blank wall. Woodrow opened it and they stepped through into an antechamber: six feet by eight, matte steel walls; a ten-foot ceiling with a light set behind a metal grille. The antechamber was hot. At the far end was a third door set with a peephole. On the wall next to the door was housed an intercom. Woodrow closed and locked the door behind them. Despite the heat Lenna felt a chill. Woodrow went to the intercom and pushed a button.

"Harvill? Coming through with Miss Par-low! You ready?"

A pause. The intercom crackled with a voice. "Ready, Wood."

Woodrow opened this door and stepped back. On the other side stood Harvill Jessup, shorter than his brother by four inches, but heavier, barrel-chested, open-faced. At his feet stood the German shepherd bitch Dot. She was black and gold like the pups and didn't have her mate's psychopathic eyes, but the fear of God was at her disposal even so. Harvill squared his shoulders and half bowed and smiled at Lenna, and Lenna thought: *"Like the last shoat of a long winter."* She smiled back at him.

"Mornin', Miss Parillaud," said Harvill.

He seemed proud to have gotten her name right again.

"Morning, Harvill."

Harvill stepped through into the antechamber.

"You need anything, I'll be right here," said Woodrow.

Lenna nodded and stepped past Harvill through the door.

Inside, a single huge room stretched away to the far wall. There were no windows in the walls, and no other doors, but shafts of sunlight fell through the space in two intersecting cones from a pair of skylights, one set into either slope of the tented roof. Between Lenna and the rest of the room a giant cage wall of inch-and-a-half steel bars sprouted up from the tiled floor toward its bolted fastenings thirty feet above. The bars were set five inches apart and in the center was a locked gate. Behind the bars, in the middle of the room, was a shack: a mildewed clapboard shack with a corrugated iron roof, a one-room dwelling of the kind a sharecropper might at some time past have called his home, or might call home still. The shack had been transplanted wholesale, and with meticulous craft, into the concrete chamber, where it stood on a specially constructed timber platform at the common focus of the intersecting cones of sunlight. The single door to the shack was reached by a short flight of steps up to the supporting platform. Between the shack and the cage wall sat a man on a padded rubber armchair. He looked at her.

Lenna walked up to the bars and sat down in the chair left for her on this side. She crossed her legs and folded her hands in her lap. The man was fifty-six, fifteen years older than she, and his face was bloated and pale. His torso, clothed in a clean blue denim shirt, was similarly swollen; his legs, in jeans and rope-soled deck shoes, were wasted reeds. Until his forties he had been a handsome, vigorous—even vainglorious—man; these days, when he stood up, he looked like a boiled potato penetrated by cocktail sticks. Right now he couldn't stand at all: Harvill had bound him to the chair with leather straps around his chest, wrists and ankles. The strapping was not because the man was likely to harm her—even though at this very moment he was no doubt willing her slow mutilation and death with whatever imagination was left to him—but because it increased the depth of the humiliation and helplessness that she required from him. From those depths, which could never be deep enough, his gray eyes stared out at her with the still, dead malevolence of a lizard.

Lenna imagined that her own eyes, staring back, looked much the same. His name was Filmore Eastman Faroe and he was still—though only she and he knew it—her husband.

"Hello, Fil," said Lenna.

Faroe said, "Magdalena." He paused, then opened with, "You never look any older."

"Remind me to give you my workout schedule," said Lenna.

Faroe's voice was flat and uninflected by emotion. This was a side effect, like the bloating of his flesh and the stiffness of his features, of the neuroleptic tranquilizers that he had been given, in enormous quantities, for over a decade. A week before Lenna's scheduled visits, the Jessups routinely withheld the drugs and Faroe's central nervous system was allowed to recover from the stupor in which it was generally maintained. On the morning of her visits he was strapped into the chair and given an injection of the amphetamine drug methedrine—pure speed—to boost his dulled consciousness to the frantic level of a Super Bowl quarterback about to make a big play. In that heightened and overstimulated state he would endure her presence for as long as it pleased her. When she left, Faroe would remain in the chair—alone; immobilized; chemically hypercharged so as to dwell more acutely upon his fate; and soiling himself as his bladder and bowel found necessary—until the following morning, whereupon he would be returned to a state of tranquilized oblivion and released from his strappings to stumble about his cage—a slurring, retarded zombie, more vegetable than man—for a further three weeks.

Perhaps it was only the drugs that prevented him from going insane.

Before he'd been involuntarily exiled to this chamber, Filmore Faroe had seen his name make the lower end of *Forbes*'s list of the four hundred richest men in America. Now, this was his life. Lenna Parillaud had designed and constructed it for him; and thus did she maintain it.

She stared at him now and couldn't think of anything to say. These meetings had changed for both of them over the years. Faroe no longer foamed and ranted and shrieked in the eye-bulging, speed-stoked frenzies of rage and despair that had characterized the beginning; and Lenna no longer shrieked and laughed back, while lifting her dress to show him her pussy and torment him with pornographic inventions. When that had paled—and it had taken a long time—she had shown him videos of herself engaged in sweating, grateful congress with Clarence Jefferson. And Faroe's lips had bled and his nails had peeled the skin from the palms of his hands and he'd pleaded to be killed there and then, and she'd told him: *Never. Never. Always it will be like this.* When that too had lost its savor, Lenna had taken to reminding Faroe of how the great kingdom that he'd built and won was now hers, and of how, under her direction, it was making more money than even he ever had, and of how also, while all those activities he had loved continued and thrived in what once had been his world, he himself could only sit there in his rubber chair—at the epicenter of all he'd created— and piss in his pants while she smiled.

Now, like two junkies who could no longer remember why they'd ever taken smack in the first place, and had long ago lost the buzz, they sat staring at each other through the bars in mute and mutual disgust.

Finally, Faroe asked, "Have you fucked any niggers lately?"

In his eyes she saw a glimmer of the reptilian intelligence that had once put him among the most feared corporate hitmen in the South. His pathetic attempt to initiate a dialogue was a measure of how low she had brought him, and her answer of how low she had brought herself.

"You enjoy that one, these days, don't you, Fil?" she said. "It really turns you on."

The lizardy eyes blinked.

"Harvill's seen you, you know," said Lenna, "trying to reach your dick to jerk yourself off after I've gone. If you like I could ask him to do it for you."

Faroe dropped his gaze to the skin of her throat and the suggestion of cleavage. The creases at the corners of his eyes deepened. His gaze lost focus and grew glassy.

"For want of a nail the shoe was lost," said Faroe. *"For want of a shoe the horse was lost."*

Lenna had heard this before, as she had heard all of his limited repertoire before. According to Woodrow, Faroe, during his one night a month on speed, could sometimes be heard moaning and rocking in his straps as he bellowed the nursery rhyme from his chair, over and over again throughout the early hours. Perhaps it gave him some comfort. She let him finish.

"For want of a horse the rider was lost. For want of a rider the battle was lost. For want of a battle the kingdom was lost." Faroe looked back at Lenna, the glaze clearing. *"And all for the want of a horseshoe nail."*

Lenna stood up. Already, she'd had enough. It was getting difficult to breathe. She asked herself, as she had many times before, why she didn't have Faroe killed and the Stone House plowed beneath the ground. It would have been easier and safer than keeping him alive. She looked past Faroe to the ancient tin-roofed shack, poised on its platform like a surrealist installation amid the gray concrete and yellow sunlight. Her gut tightened. Somehow her instinct insisted that while Faroe was alive there still remained a lingering possibility, however remote, of some kind of completion, of resolution. What that was, she did not know and she couldn't make any sense of it; she just knew that if she killed him, then she too would remain here in the Stone House

12

forever. She turned away from the wooden shack, and away from Faroe without looking at him.

"Goodbye, Fil."

As she walked away Faroe said, "I loved you, Magdalena. Never forget that."

Lenna stopped. He had played this role before, the noble penitent enduring a cruel and unjustified punishment. She despised him for it. In part she despised herself too, for the pretense of love, sustained over flesh-crawling years, that she'd used to seize his power. Yet she'd done what she had done, and without trying she suddenly recalled something Clarence Jefferson had once told her. *"Consider those deeds that history writes most bold, Lenna,"* he'd whispered in his honeycomb voice. *"Hatred is the blackest ink. Not love."*

Lenna looked back at Faroe over her shoulder.

"But remember I never loved you, Fil," she said. "That's the difference between us: you could never fake it. I could."

Without waiting to see his reaction Lenna walked out through the antechamber and between the stacked crates and out into the yard. There the air felt good. She breathed deeply, a hand pressed to her chest. She dropped the hand as she heard Woodrow Jessup cough behind her.

"You okay, Miss Par-low?"

"I'm fine," she said.

"Thought I'd wait till you'd finished your bidness before giving you this. Hope that's all right."

He handed her a sealed white envelope. The back was blank. On the front was handwritten *Lenna*. Lenna felt a convulsion through her spine. She recognized that elegant and extravagant hand.

"Where did this come from?" she said.

"Fella brought it this morning, a stranger." Woodrow nodded at the letter in her hand. "I asked him, he said he didn't know what was in there or who it was for, he just had to deliver it here by hand. Said them was his instructions. Declined to give his name or who'd sent him, then drove off. Didn't even get out of his car, but maybe that was on account of the dogs."

"What did he look like?" asked Lenna.

"Old guy, sixty maybe? Lean as a whip and all turned out in a suit and tie. I don't think he was up from the City, though."

"Why not?"

"Well he was polite, for a start-off, and I'd say smart, but not slick, you know? Straight as a string, that was my feeling. Calm, too. His eyes put me in mind of a certain kind of old-time horse trader you see back home, or maybe a lawyer. I don't know exactly where, but he was country for sure."

Lenna frowned and looked again at her name on the envelope.

"Would've cost us a fuss to stop him leaving, Miss Par-low. I calculated you wouldn't want that."

"You did the right thing," said Lenna. "Has anyone else been around?"

"No, ma'am."

"Anything strange at all?"

Woodrow shook his head. "Things as quiet as always. The dogs would've picked up any snoopers."

Lenna nodded. She raised the envelope. "You and Harvill forget this ever happened."

"It's forgot."

"You did well. Thank you."

Woodrow blushed and shuffled.

"Anything else happens you call me right away. Okay?"

"Sure thing, Miss Par-low."

Lenna walked over to the Mercedes and got in. She put the envelope on the seat beside her and drove away. Now that she was alone the dread that the letter provoked was so intense she was unable to think. She swung off the dirt road, fishtailed in a billow of red dust, straightened up. A mile along the blacktop she jammed on the brakes and stopped. She opened the envelope and took out a single sheet of paper. The same elegant handwriting met her eyes.

As she read them the words seemed to bypass her consciousness and open a channel to an underground sea of emotions that she could not name and which she had thought long dead. Halfway through the letter she started sobbing. Then the paper fell from her hands. And Lenna clung to the wheel and gave herself up to the roar of forces so immense she would not have believed her body could contain them and still live. Yet if she did not believe, it was because she had known them before but had forgotten, and so she wept: as she had not wept in twenty years.

Time passed. The sounds of her grief escaped from the car and drifted away to lose themselves among the whispers of the marsh grass. After a while the car fell silent.

When the forces had finally passed, Lenna put her hands over her face and made things dark. For a while all she knew was the wetness on her palms, the quieting shudder of her breath, the flicker of yellow shadows upon the blackness she squeezed from her eyes. More time passed, in an emptiness so crystalline, so utterly void, she would have stayed there forever if she could. Then into the void came fear, at first of nothing in particular, just fear itself. Then came something worse: hope. With the hope came the knowledge—the horror—that if she failed, then all this—*all* this and worse than this—awaited her again.

Something wiser than herself shut it down, blanked it out. Her breathing steadied. She took her hands from her face and blinked. Ahead of her she saw again the April blue and the shifting yellow-brown sea divided by a black strip of pavement. She found she couldn't remember what she'd just read; rather, she could not afford to remember. Not yet. She had to act, and to act she had to shield herself from its contents—and from the terrors of the void it might provoke—until she was ready.

Lenna snatched up the car phone and punched the buttons. It was answered, silently, after the first ring.

"Bobby?" she said.

"Tell me what's wrong," said Frechette.

Frechette's voice, at the same time mellow and alert, calmed her. She took a breath; her strength flowing back. She felt her jaws grind until her head ached. At last she had something worth going to war for. She let go of the bite.

"I'm fine," she said. "I'm on my way back. Call Rufus Atwater. Have him run a check on a guy—a doctor—called Grimes, right now. Tell him I want to see him as soon as he's done."

"I need that name again," said Frechette.

Lenna reached down and picked up the letter. Patches of it were wet, the ink blurred. Without rereading she scanned the paragraphs until she focused on the words she needed.

"Grimes. Eugene Cicero Grimes."

"Dr. Eugene Cicero Grimes," said Bobby Frechette. "You got it."

Lenna hung up. Then she folded the letter, put it in her jacket.

She thought: *She's alive.*

She felt the crumbling edge of hope open up beneath her feet. *What if it's not true?* She hauled herself back. *Later.* She crammed the thought down and slammed the lid. Then Lenna Parillaud gunned the Mercedes to life and headed back to Arcadia.

TWO

CICERO GRIMES raised his head a couple of inches from where it lay pillowed on his forearms and opened his eyes. Lethargic motes of dust drifted about his field of vision. Beyond the motes a filth-strewn terrain undulated away toward the far wall of the room, which, in its turn, was blackened by the scorch marks of fire and smoke. The sight was wretched but familiar. Grimes dropped his head back down and waited for a thought that was worthy of the mental effort required to process it. Experience suggested that he would have to wait a long time.

He was sprawled in a loose tangle of his own limbs on the hardwood floor of his living room. The radiant heat hammering into the back of his skull told him that the sun had risen high enough to pour directly through the casement window facing out onto the street and that it was therefore sometime after noon. From deep inside his chest he heard a groan.

Grimes had been more or less unconscious for about thirteen hours, and had the option been open to him he would have stayed that way for thirteen hours more. To have slept would have been better still, but sleep was a state that implied a degree of comfort, a repletion of cortical centers, of which his brain no longer seemed capable. From time to time he would surface from his third-rate oblivion with the unwelcome knowledge that he should drag himself to his feet and act like a man. Instead he would pray for the oblivion to return, and if luck was with him, he would drift back into the haze of half-remembered dreams and sweat-drenched squirmings for which he was so grateful. Now, with the sun tormenting him from the far side of an indifferent cosmos, he knew there was no point; and so he waited, with the patience of one for whom time possessed neither meaning nor value, for the arrival of the thought with which he would begin this, his day.

When the thought finally came it was not a product of his own impoverished intellect but, if he remembered correctly, of the fearless metaphysician Arthur Schopenhauer. The human personality, claimed Arthur, was not something to be glorified or exalted but, on the contrary, a gore-encrusted dungeon in which the futile horror of existence was placed on display as squalid and mindless suffering and, occasionally—in a few select specimens—as tragedy.

Grimes was by now far too intimate with his own bespattered cell to flatter himself with the idea that he belonged among the company of the select and tragic few. He was, he knew, merely a scumbag; clinging to the driftwood of his own self-disgust on a far-flung beach of despair. Indeed, it occurred to him—as he lay there on the floor amid a debris of half-empty pizza boxes, squashed cigarette packs, unwashed clothes and sundry other trash—that if he'd ever laid claim to the nobility of despair, he had finally lost even that delusion. The shingle upon which he now sprawled was beyond the ocean of anything so grand as despair. Today, in the aftermath of Schopenhauer's reassuring description of the human estate, Grimes discovered that he did not even pity himself. This startled him: he was even losing his capacity for self-loathing. He was becoming a shriveled bag of basic life functions, burdened by a consciousness that knew the desire—but lacked the will—to bring itself to a dignified end.

These reflections were sufficiently humiliating to drag Grimes up as far as his knees. He rested his forehead on the bare planks. Then he mumbled a few words to Jesus, most of them profane, and stood up, blinking, on his hind legs.

The sun was an evil but he could not close the window blinds against its rays. Grimes had torn them from their hangings during one of the black rages that periodically broke through his torpor to destroy whatever was closest at hand. The broken blinds were somewhere in the ankle-deep garbage that formed the shallow pit from which he had just risen. Grimes stood in the pit and wondered what to do next.

He lived on the second floor of an old New Orleans firehouse and had called it home for eight years. In the eighties the fire department had abandoned the building for modern premises and it had stood disused until Grimes had found it and taken out a lease. The living room was large and distinguished by a tarnished brass pole that ran through a hole in the floor to the former engine room below. The engine room contained a heavy bag, which in health Grimes had pounded for thirty minutes a day, and a set of iron weights; both weights and bag were now as idle as he was. Behind the living room were two bedrooms and a bathroom. He'd decorated and furnished the place without any concern for aesthetic integration or style: he sat on the chairs; he placed things on the two scarred tables; the shelves supported books; the kitchen area was small and rarely used. Across the rear half of the room the walls and ceiling had been damaged by fire. This created an atmosphere that reminded Grimes of newsreel footage of postwar Berlin. To date he'd made no attempt to repair the damage. Grimes had known good times here and bad. He had listened to music and sipped whiskey and talked through the night with friends. He had made love here: with women he had loved, with women he had not. And he had been broken here, too, on the wheel of his own psyche.

At this moment he regarded this place—his place—as his prison and his tomb. The door was open; he was a free man; yet he went out for no more than a few minutes a day, walking to the store to buy cigarettes and juice and a few items of fresh food that usually went bad before he got around to eating them. Then he would walk back home, climb the single flight of stairs and slam the door behind him for another twenty-fours hours or so of mindless isolation. He kept his telephone unplugged. He had no TV. He never switched on the radio. Occasionally he listened to music; but too often it reminded him of things he would rather forget.

He had not worked in months and could not imagine doing so again; in fact it scared him that he had ever been capable of any such activity. Grimes was a doctor: originally a surgeon; latterly a psychiatrist. Somewhere in the haze of memory he knew his work to have been something infinitely valuable to him: the passion and the labor of his life. There had, it seemed, once been such things. But then was then and now was now. It was as if his hands had died on him, for it was in his hands that his passion and his labor had resided. He had betrayed that passion and that labor, before himself, even if before no one else; the details of the betrayal itself had milled and sifted into a dust of futile regrets, long since blown away across the barrens of melancholia.

Grimes avoided alcohol and was under the influence of no drugs other than those deranged neurotransmitters generated by his own unstable brain. He could have named some of them. He could have speculated at length on the nature—biological, psychological and spiritual—of his affliction, and even prescribed sage advice on how to treat it; and from time to time what was left of his observing ego did just that. But his heart preferred not to hear. Something in his soul insisted that he endure this dark passage to its end, whatever that end might bring, and wherever that end might be.

Grimes stretched. His body felt perpetually poisoned. He did not know how many pounds he had lost, but his clothes were baggy on his frame. Whenever it was that he'd last been hale he'd weighed one-ninety-five and could bench press two-twenty. He was still an inch and a half over six feet and strongly built, but he felt as if his spine had lost several of its vertebrae. He was thirty-eight years old and he felt seventy and he no longer cared. He had given up the fight that had depleted him more with every punch he'd tried to throw. This was where he was and where he would be until he found himself somewhere else. Today, like yesterday and the days and months before that, he would do nothing: not a relaxed, take-it-easy-and-recharge-the-batteries nothing, but utterly nothing. An infinite nothing. Until the end.

He would do nothing—he would strive toward nothing—with the same extremity of purpose that he had brought to the other driven journeys of his life. And while Grimes stood there—and as he knew he would later lie there prone, shot through and steeped to the marrow with content-free psychic pain—he realized that he was in a place he'd never been before, a place where no one else had been or ever could be: for it was his alone and his to know alone. He was no longer anything: man or melancholiac, psychiatrist or psychotic. He simply was; and this he could not escape. He had stripped himself of everything that he felt himself to be; he had sought his own nothingness, an extinction more profound than a bullet through the head; and at the outermost rim of that nothingness, he now found—in spite of all—that he was. Like it or not, he was.

With that discovery—that he *was*—Grimes felt a tremor, a stirring: something that distantly reminded him of the heartbeat of excitement. Then it was gone. The sun once more punished his eyes; his poisoned limbs tested their ability to hold him from the floor; the pit in which he stood beckoned him sweetly.

And then the doorbell rang.

For a moment Grimes did not react. He had been out of contact with the outer world for so long that the attempt at communication implicit in the sound of the bell seemed hallucinatory. Then the ringing came again, this time the thumb or finger pushing longer, with more insistence. Grimes went over to the window and threw it wide. Humid air and jagged street noise gusted over his face. He leaned out over the sill and looked down.

Standing on the pavement by the door was a thin man in a gray summer suit and a flat straw hat with a striped band—a boater—the brim of which hid his face. He held his shoulders square. In his left hand was a briefcase, the leather smooth with age. Grimes waited. The thin man took a step back from the door and looked up. His face was lean, a healthy lean, and had seen a lot of sun. The eyes—blue—were both frank and shrewd. Grimes guessed he was in his early sixties. His voice, when he spoke, had a rural edge and was from out of state. Alabama, maybe. Or Georgia.

"Good afternoon," called the thin man.

Grimes started to speak but found his throat hoarsened through lack of use. An incoherent rasp emerged. He nodded, coughed, tried again.

"What do you want?" said Grimes.

The thin man absorbed this lack of courtesy as if it were something he expected. "I was hoping to speak with Dr. Grimes," he said. "Dr. Eugene Grimes."

"Who are you?"

"Holden Daggett. I'm an attorney."

Grimes thought about that. "Does that mean I've got a problem?"

Daggett didn't blink. "Not as far as I know. I'm not here to serve any papers on behalf of any court—federal, state, or civil. I've been instructed by a client to deliver a letter to you."

"A client," said Grimes.

Daggett nodded, then glanced briefly down the street before calling up again. "Can I come inside?"

Grimes studied the clear, shrewd eyes a moment longer. He pulled his head back inside. He felt it again: the rumor of a heartbeat. And something else: a sinister premonition, a tinge of fear. Before the premonition won out over the heartbeat he left the window and went to press the button on the wall by the door. With a buzz and a clank the lock on the door to the street below was released.

From the top of the stairs Grimes watched Daggett close the steel-plated door behind him and tread across the unopened mail carpeting the corridor. Daggett climbed steadily, the flat crown of his straw hat cleaving a straight line, and reached the top of the stairs without panting. Grimes felt a pang of envy. Daggett glanced him over. Grimes, suddenly aware of his appearance, shuffled. He'd slept in his black suit, which was consequently badly crumpled and, here and there, dusted gray with patches of cigarette ash. His white shirt was limp and enfilthed. He wasn't wearing any shoes or socks. Grimes asked himself why he'd let this stranger in to see him this way. *Because you have no pride,* he answered. Anyway, Daggett didn't have to hang around any longer than he was inclined to.

Daggett, his face revealing nothing of what he felt about Grimes's appearance, held out his hand. As Grimes shook it he noticed a small raised spot with a crumbly surface on the skin of Daggett's left temple.

"As a rule, I don't visit unannounced," said Daggett. "But you're not an easy man to contact, Dr. Grimes."

Grimes said, "The way I like it is the way it is."

To Grimes's surprise Daggett smiled at that. He nodded back down the stairs toward the scattered envelopes. "I tried to schedule a meeting with you. There should be a couple of letters from me down there."

The premonition returned and stuck Grimes in the craw. He swallowed it down.

"But not the letter you've brought with you," he said.

Daggett shook his head. "That one I'm obliged to deliver by hand or not at all."

He glanced over Grimes's shoulder through the door into the living room. Grimes looked too, as if with fresh eyes. Now postwar Berlin seemed a romantic notion. The room looked like an Iberville crack factory that had been fire-bombed by a rival gang. Again, whatever Daggett thought of what he saw, he kept from his face. Grimes made a note never to play poker with him. He coughed.

"I had a fire here, a while back."

"So I see," said Daggett, evenly.

"Please, come inside, then," said Grimes.

"Thanks, but that's not necessary," replied Daggett. "I have a plane to catch."

He opened his briefcase and took out a white envelope. On the front, written with a lavish hand, was the word *Grimes.*

"This is all I came for." Daggett paused. "I don't mean any offense by this, you understand, but I'm obliged to ask you for some kind of identification. To prove that you are indeed Dr. Eugene Grimes."

Grimes looked from the envelope to Daggett. "Maybe I don't want the letter."

"If you want to burn it without opening it, that's your privilege," said Daggett.

Grimes hesitated.

"I came a long way to give it to you," said Daggett. "But I guess that's no concern of yours."

Grimes fumbled in his jacket pockets and found his wallet. From the wallet he produced his driver's license and gave it to Daggett. Daggett glanced from the photo on the license to Grimes's face and back again three times. Grimes wondered just what the hell he must look like these days. Had he changed that much? He absently raised a hand and found, as if it didn't belong to him, a matted growth of beard on his neck and jaw. Christ. Daggett handed the license back and held out the envelope.

Grimes took it.

"You don't need any kind of answer to this?" he asked.

Daggett shook his head. "My only instructions were to deliver it."

He closed his briefcase and held out his hand again. "Thank you for your time." For a moment the frank blue eyes were illuminated with an unexpected warmth. "It's been a pleasure to meet you."

For a bizarre instant Grimes felt choked. Daggett appeared to mean what he said; and Grimes wanted to believe him. He thought: *man, you are a long ways further gone than you know.* He pulled himself together, blinked.

"You too, sir," said Grimes.

They shook again. This time Grimes felt as if the firm dry hand were squeezing his heart. Daggett let go, nodded and turned to the stairs. Grimes didn't want him to leave. With something close to shame he felt a craving for company sweep over him.

"Mr. Daggett?" said Grimes.

Daggett turned back.

"I couldn't help noticing." Grimes pointed to the spot on Daggett's temple. "If I'm not mistaken that's a basal cell carcinoma, a type of skin cancer."

"This little thing?" Daggett touched the spot. "I had a physical a month ago. My own doctor didn't mention it."

"They're easy to miss," said Grimes. "They grow slowly but it will get worse if you don't get it treated. Cure is guaranteed."

"I'll take your advice." Daggett squinted at him. "You're from somewhere up north, am I right?"

"Chicago," said Grimes.

"Tough town, or so they say." From his breast pocket he took a card and gave it to Grimes. "I live in a little Georgia 'gator hole you won't ever have heard of: Jordan's Crossroads, on the Ohoopee River."

Grimes took the card without reading it.

Daggett said, "You ever find yourself in the middle of nowhere, come say hello." He smiled. "Not much to do on a Saturday night 'less you're a moonshiner, but the Ohoopee River bottomlands are pretty, especially in spring. If you like that kind of thing."

"I do," said Grimes. "Thanks."

He slipped the card into his wallet with his driver's license. Daggett's eyes flickered up and down Grimes's body: the bare feet, the dusty black suit and unkempt beard.

Holden Daggett said, "Take care, now."

"You too."

Grimes watched Daggett descend the stairs and close the door behind him without looking back. For a moment, from both within and without, Grimes felt engulfed by a great silence. He felt more lost than ever. And yet the brief contact—the press of flesh, the meeting of eyes, the sound of voices, his own not least—had breathed an oxygen into his blood, a whiff, and no more than that, but he felt roused from his anesthetic torpor. He turned and went back inside.

At the kitchen table Grimes cleared himself a space by scraping an armful of debris onto the floor. The letter in his hand felt heavier than it ought to. On the front, his name: Grimes. Nothing else. Grimes found a cigarette, lit it. He sat down at the table and opened the letter. Inside were three folded sheets of paper and an American Airlines plane ticket. Grimes unfolded the papers but avoided the last page: he didn't want to read the signature until the end. By halfway through the first sentence he realized he wouldn't have to: he could hear a voice—rich as burnt toffee—smiling as it whispered in his ear.

> Dear Grimes,
> If you are reading this, then I must be dead; and who knows—maybe even buried. Congratulations. You must have done me proud. But even so, I worry about you: I wonder, as I write this in a dead-man's hand, how you're going to get by without me when I'm gone. And I can't help wondering, too, if you ever think of me these days?

Sure you do.

So let me tell you the score: this is my last will and testament. Good words. Testament. Will. Words that don't come cheap. And the way things are between us, you and I, there's only one way to spend them: on you. I believe the proper title is "beneficiary."

Are you laughing yet? Then listen to this.

I'm going to give you the chance to be the instrument—the hammer—of an apocalyptic justice. I say again: apocalyptic.

Now, I hear you laugh.

But I also hear you ask, through the tears rolling down your cheeks, just how the fuck I'm going to do that. It's simple: I'm going to give you the anvil upon which you may forge that justice. The anvil has been twenty years in the making and it's mine. It grieves me that I left it too late to see the iron glow red and the sparks fly high. But so be it; and if these be the times—then you must be the man. The story goes like this.

Once upon a time there was a lawman who understood the way of things human. He knew that men of power were drawn by inexorable and extravagant appetites toward the possibility of their own ruin. He knew that they robbed the people they were meant to serve, and bribed each other, and corrupted the laws which even they had made and with whose keeping they were entrusted, in every way imaginable; that they fucked children and animals and whores; that they ordered the deaths of those who stood against them. These men stood high in the land; yet they were scum.

Now, the lawman, he was powerful too, both in their ways and in other ways that they would never comprehend. He did his share and more of killing, and of torture, and of other evils as vile as any a man might set his hand to; and he put into his pocket the coin of those who believed themselves his masters. But this man—perhaps, it sometimes pleased him to think, this man alone—this man knew the inner nature of what he did and he asked no absolution, either of God or of himself. And though his appetites too were ruinous and vast, they could not bind him. He saw beyond such desires to the possibility of a deeper gratification—a delirium of ruin and destruction, a pandemonium, a festival of anarchy that would shatter the foundations of and tumble to the earth that city of corruption whose sewers and alleys he knew so well, and better—so much better—than did they.

So during the course of his journey this man—this lawman—became a gatherer of witness; a collector of irrefragable testimony and of evidence beyond refute of every stripe. He gathered papers and statements, photographs and films, databases and disks. He taped the voices of the guilty. He stole wholesale their secret crimes. A corpus delicti of fabulous proportion. And he stored it. He stored it all and waited for the moment when senators and congressmen would tremble at the call; when judges would be gunned down on their doorsteps by wiseguys who'd bought their homes for them and knew they knew too much; when old family names would be smeared with their own feces and the bloated scions thereof dragged off to jail. Louisiana meltdown: a billion-dollar blow-out and a million years of Texas Steel for those who thought themselves beyond all reckoning.

Such was the lawman's dream.

Are you still laughing, Grimes? I hope so because it's all yours, buddy. That's my bequest to you. You are going to start the hurly burly on my behalf. But walk softly: they're already out a-looking. Truth to tell, there must be panic on the streets. Somebody knew it was out there, my anvil; with any kind of secret somebody always does. You know that. While I was alive those few bravehearts that dared to sniff too close died—badly, I confess—but now I'm gone the dogs will be off the leash and panting for blood. All you have to do is collect my bag of tricks and expose its contents before the dogs pick up your scent.

You need to know where to find my goodies. I'm only going to tell you part of it. The other part you have to get from somebody else: a woman; in fact, a girl. She's nineteen years old. Her name is Ella MacDaniels. You'll find her at 175 Willow Street. Treat her right, Grimes. Besides you she's the only person in the world I give a shit for. She knows me as Charlie. Look after her. The dogs will be on to her too, sooner or later, and she's no part of all this, except that she's part of me. Just tell her Charlie wants her to take you to the Old Place. You got that? The Old Place. In the basement there you'll find two suitcases; inside them you'll find my trove. Don't waste it on my erstwhile colleagues in the police department, or on the federal authorities; the one bunch would sell it and the other would bury it. It's the media you need if you're to bring them to their knees. That's where the power lies. Take it to *The Washington Post*, then buy yourself a TV and watch the fun.

So that's it, Grimes. Good luck to you. By the way, you may be wondering what that airline ticket is for. I'm a fair man and I wouldn't want you to feel you didn't have any choice in this matter. The ticket is your choice. If you decide not to accept my legacy, take the ticket and run; get out of town and don't come back; ever. But listen close, and believe me, son: do it soon. Do it now.

If you do accept, trust no one except yourself.

Good luck, Grimes. It's going to be a cold day down there in Hell, so wrap up warm.

Yours always,
Clarence Seymour Jefferson

Grimes stared at his hands. To his surprise they were steady. His mind was vacant. His body was seized by an overpowering desire for sleep, an intense muscular fatigue grinding in deep between his shoulder blades. He realized what his body was telling him: you can't deal with this, buddy. Do yourself a favor and pass out. He looked over to the shallow grave dug amid the trash on the floor. No bed of flowers, no leafy bower, no woman's arms had ever looked so inviting. His brain shambled into low gear. *They will be coming,* the brain said, *and you know it: the Captain says so.*

Grimes had known Captain Jefferson for little more than twenty-four hours and yet no other hours of his life had been scorched more indelibly into his being. A little over six months before, Grimes's older brother, Luther, had looted the Louisiana Mercantile Trust bank of a small fortune; Captain Jefferson, in pursuit of said fortune, had seized and imprisoned Cicero Grimes, here in this very room. And here the Captain had interrogated him; with mercy neither offered, asked nor given. Tooth and claw, head-to-head, they had ravaged and wrestled each other back and forth: from interrogation to torture, from torture to odyssey and from odyssey to a final, pain-soaked standstill, somewhere in the unmapped breach between life and death.

It was this experience—and Grimes's revealed experience of himself; of the things he would rather not have known—that had left him suspended in the psychotic melancholia from which he was only just now beginning to stir: with Clarence Seymour Jefferson's last will and testament clutched in his hand.

Grimes put the letter down and picked up the airline ticket. It was an open one-way flight, first class, to Buenos Aires. Grimes recalled that in his youth he had found comfort in the dictum that in an absurd world one had a duty to live an absurd life. But this wasn't absurd; it was ridiculous. Between the thin cardboard leaves of the ticket he found another piece of paper. He opened it. On it, in Jefferson's florid hand, was written:

P.S. Give my best wishes to your daddy.

Grimes felt a rush of fear.

Jefferson was a man born for games, a Russian roulette addict, who forced others to play along with him and usually left their corpses in his wake. Now, from beyond the grave, his swollen corpse had spun the cylinder and placed the gun to Grimes's skull. For himself, Grimes was too far retarded by his own melancholia to care if a bullet lay in the chamber or not, but the reference to his father was like being dropped into an Arctic sea. After six months of stagnation Grimes suddenly felt horribly alive. He put a hand over his eyes and squeezed the bones of his face. Bristly hair rustled under his fingers; and from the midst of the terror spreading through his entrails came a greater fear: he couldn't let his father see him looking like a bum.

Somewhere, he recalled, he had another black suit less shabby than the one he was wearing. If he was lucky he'd find a half-clean shirt too; maybe even a tie. George liked ties. George was his father. And George might be in danger.

The good times—the times in the pit—were over.

Cicero Grimes took his hand from his eyes and stumbled to the bathroom to find a razor.

THREE

RUFUS ATWATER was thirty-two years old and a prosecuting attorney for the city of New Orleans. He'd chosen that career rather
than private practice for two reasons. First of all, while God had
given him brains he had also whipped him with an ugly stick: pale orange hair, an overfreckled lopsided face with too much forehead and
chin and not enough lips, and muscles like knots in string no matter
how much he hit the gym and drank those bullshit drinks. People
didn't like to hire ugly lawyers, and for the same reason he would never
sit behind the D.A.'s desk. Second, he recognized that he had a strong
natural inclination to be unpleasant, and prosecuting enabled him to
probe, threaten, humiliate and imprison people, with the arms of the
law wrapped around him and without being shot at like the poor saps
in the police department. So far he'd remained basically clean. Okay, so
he'd folded five hundred here and a grand there into his hip pocket,
but they were fucking tips, virtually an insult to the intense ambition
that underpinned what passed for his dignity. When Magdalena Parillaud had contacted him to investigate the disappearance of Clarence
Jefferson, Atwater's antennae, developed over years of rooting into
others' lives, told him he was finally being offered a seat at the biggest
game in town.

Atwater had just finished listening to a tape recording procured
that very morning by Jack Seed. He switched off the machine, pulled
out the earpieces and looked over at Jack, who was slumped beside
him in the driver's seat. They were driving north in Seed's Chevy Impala and the late afternoon sun spilled around the oily contours of
Jack's head into Atwater's eyes. Atwater put on his Wayfarers. Jack
displayed his gold tooth in a smug grin.

"Well?" said Jack Seed.

"What did you do?" said Atwater. "Bug her pussy?"

Jack laughed, pleased. "No, man. The Mercedes. I wired the Mercedes. She got quadraphonic sound in there. I put one of my specials in the front-left speaker."

"If Frechette finds it we'll have a long way to paddle home."

Seed snorted. "Frechette couldn't find his own black dick in daylight. Anyhow, the beauty of it is, I can disable it, the bug I mean. Like right now, it's switched off, man. Frechette can sweep that vehicle with an electron fuckin' microscope, he won't find a signal 'cause there isn't one. See I figure what's the point of having the car miked twenty-four hours a day? She doesn't sleep in the fuckin' thing. But today I also figure it's the first of the month, maybe she's gonna visit this weird concrete hangar deal with the hayseeds and the dogs again, so I switch it on and there you are, she's on talk fuckin' radio."

"You did good, Jack."

"What do you figure she was doin' towards the end there? Jerkin' herself off? Man, that must've been some monster fuckin' dildo."

"The lady was upset," said Atwater.

"You'd be surprised what people get up to in cars. I could tell ya some things. And dogs? Man, guy I did a job for one time? Lab technician at a private clap clinic, up in the Garden District? He told me ten percent of the women check in there for a once-over got dog sperm up their snatches. Can you believe that? Ten percent. Jesus, I was shocked. I mean four-five percent, sure, why not? But ten? And these are high-class babes, not pigs. See, the clinic do what he called 'high vaginal swabs' . . ."

"Thanks, Jack, I got the picture."

"Well, this technician guy's wife was getting her high vaginal swabs from a washing-machine salesman just sold her a brand-new . . ."

"Jack," said Atwater. "I need to think. Gimme a break."

Jack shrugged, not offended, and stared out the windshield. Atwater picked up an envelope from his lap and pulled out a stack of grainy black-and-white photos.

Atwater didn't mind Seed's inexhaustible anecdotes on human sexual behavior. They were the obsession at the core of his genius. His motto was: "If you can get an eight-by-five glossy of a married guy—with kids at private school and pulling three hundred G's a year—down on his knees, sticking his thumbs up a Chinaman's ass, with a stainless steel drinking straw ready in his mouth, you can get a shot of just about anything." Seed had been eager to display the said picture; Atwater had declined.

Seed's real name was Jack Santini. He'd learned his trade in the CIA but the Agency had been forced to retire him quietly after one of Noriega's army colonels in Panama interrupted Jack in the midst of doing unspeakable things to his wife. Jack had killed both the colonel and the wife with his bare hands. With his severance pay Jack Santini had set himself up in New Orleans as a private investigator, but at the prices he felt his expertise commanded, business had proved nonexistent. Then he'd hit upon the brilliant idea of changing his name. "You know? Like Archibald Leach changing his name to Cary Grant." Reborn as Jack Seed—"Your secret is safe with me"—he'd never been out of work since.

Atwater had previously employed Seed for the City when a result was particularly vital; for instance during the D.A.'s reelection campaigns. Jack had always delivered and his discretion was absolute. If he ran his mouth off with Atwater it was because he saw him as a fellow pro and, Atwater speculated, because the pressure of keeping all those secrets to himself must have been just too intense. On this job Jack was working for Atwater privately. His fee of two thousand dollars a day was being paid, via Atwater, by Parillaud. As Atwater sifted through the stack of photos that Jack had had taken of her, the irony of this financial arrangement gave him considerable pleasure.

The sequence of photos showed Parillaud getting out of her black Mercedes, talking to a bony-shouldered *Deliverance* type in white overalls with a bunch of evil-looking dogs, then entering what looked, as Jack Seed had said, like a concrete aircraft hangar but was probably some kind of warehouse . . . A second hillbilly emerging from the hangar . . . A few more shots of the hayseeds playing with their dogs . . . Then Parillaud coming out again.

"How long does she spend inside?" said Atwater.

"Ten, twenty minutes. Takes nothing in, brings nothing out."

Atwater studied a shot of Parillaud in a black pantsuit walking toward her car. Her blond hair was pulled back into a tight knot. The picture had been taken from some distance and her features were a little blurred, but Atwater could remember them well enough. His lip curled. He did not like his employer. Not to put too fine a point on it, he thought she was an arrogant slut rich-bitch whom he'd like to have put on the street to give blow jobs to vagrants. In the photo she looked thirty; in the flesh thirty-five; in reality she was forty-one. In addition to having great tits—whether surgically maintained or not seemed irrelevant to Atwater—she was able to make deals that took up inches in *The Wall Street Journal* and referred to her assets in terms of "units." A "unit" was rich supercocksucker talk for a hundred million bucks. To make matters worse Atwater would have liked to fuck her. His gut dislike of her somehow stoked up her sex appeal, whereupon his unrequited lust made him hate her all the more, which made the hard-on he couldn't use even harder. It was a spiral of bullshit he didn't understand.

In contrast to Parillaud, Atwater's own wife was twenty-eight and, since the second kid, looked like a sack of potatoes. Atwater actually liked his wife but fucking her had demanded a lot from his imagination for a long time. Since Parillaud had hired him Atwater had often thought about her while fucking his wife; sometimes he imagined Parillaud going down on the vagrants in the street; and enjoying it. Atwater had sworn to himself that if he ever did get the chance to slip it to Parillaud, he would turn it down and walk away. He wouldn't give the bitch the satisfaction. He would tell her, Sorry, honey, you're just too fucking old. Atwater shook himself; he was turning into Jack Seed. He went on to the next photo, which was a blowup of Parillaud accepting a white envelope from the older of the two hillbillies. Atwater tapped a thumbnail against his teeth. He would have given a lot to see inside that envelope. It had to have something to do with this guy Grimes he'd spent the morning running through the computer.

Jack Seed glanced at the blowup and read his thoughts.

"So what did you get on this Grimes guy?"

"Nothing worth a shit so far," said Atwater, still looking at the pic. "He's some kind of shrink, specializes in addiction."

"Drugs? Maybe she's developed a sweet tooth," suggested Jack.

Atwater shook his head. "Not her. You need blood in your veins to get into hard drugs and she'd don't have any."

"She's so ice fuckin' cool, what'd make her crack up the way she did this morning?"

"I don't know," said Atwater. "But I want to."

Atwater shuffled through the photos; he'd seen them all. There was a frantic tension in his belly that he didn't like. The train was starting to move and if he wasn't careful he'd get left standing at the station with nothing more than his fee. Another fucking tip. Atwater wanted more. Much more. He wanted a house in the country, a walk-in closet full of foreign suits and a speedboat and a couple of teenage girlfriends. He closed his eyes and ran it all through his mind for the hundredth time.

Thirteen years ago Filmore Faroe had driven his Porsche into an oak tree—on this very road—with his wife sitting in the bucket seat next to him. Faroe, no seat belt, had left the best part of his face stuck to the tree trunk; Lenna Parillaud had broken an arm and some ribs. A stupid commonplace fuckup; no foul play suspected or looked for. Parillaud had inherited the plantation estate toward which Atwater and Seed were now driving, plus the rest of Faroe's vast fortune. Instead of spending her time shopping and getting her hair coiffed by overpaid faggots—like most other women in her position would have done—Parillaud had taken back her maiden name and launched a series of aggressive corporate raids and takeovers that had stunned the good old Louisiana boys who believed that the state and its riches belonged to them by divine right. Respected, if not liked, Parillaud had become an accepted force. Things had gotten more interesting when the state legalized gambling: Parillaud had gone after a casino license and certain parties had tried to dissuade her.

According to Jack Seed, the remains of the four men sent to do the dissuading had been found, chained hand and foot, in a bayou pig pound. They'd been eaten alive by hogs. Atwater had a momentary vision of the four guys watching each other writhing in the mud and pig shit and screaming while the porkers tugged them apart. Death by hogs was a recognized trademark of Captain Clarence Jefferson, a giant vice cop and law-unto-himself known in the wrong circles as the Three-Hundred-Pound Shithammer. Six months ago Jefferson had disappeared without trace, and a lot of folk were starting to soil their underwear. Atwater, never having had any dealings with the Captain, wasn't among them. Atwater guessed that that was one reason he'd been hired by Lenna Parillaud.

"You did some work for Clarence Jefferson, didn't you, Jack?" asked Atwater.

Seed nodded. "Enough to have some idea what everyone's looking for. Remember the guy felching the Chinaman's ass with the stainless steel straw? That was your local senator's eldest son. The Captain's got the negs. He also had me track down some bank accounts in the Cayman Islands set up by representatives of a cartel who'd won drilling leases in the Gulf. Accounts are controlled by the state governor's wife. And believe me that's just the tip of a very large and infected dick. I tell ya, that shit ever gets out, Court TV'll have to franchise ten new channels."

Atwater pursed his thin lips. Jefferson was what you might call an enigma. The evidence he'd accumulated on the corruption of others had allowed him to do more or less what he wanted. Yet materially, at least, he had lived simply and as far as anyone could tell strictly within the limits of his salary. He'd owned a modest home not much bigger than Atwater's and an Eldorado, and that was all. Sure, a man like Jefferson could have stashed millions where even Seed couldn't have found them; but if he had done so he'd never spent it so as you could tell: no stocks and shares; no racehorses or real estate; no gambling; Hawaiian shirts rather than foreign suits. Atwater had traced Jefferson's life all the way back through his career with the police department and a spell in the air force to a private school he'd attended in Atlanta from the age of twelve. There the trail had ended. Atwater had been unable to discover anything about his family or his childhood. It was like he'd just appeared at puberty from another planet. But, again, it would not have been beyond the Captain's ingenuity to alter his own past.

Atwater said, "I never met Jefferson."

"Then you oughta be happy. Dealin' with the Captain is like fuckin' a rattlesnake with AIDS, without a condom. Cross J. Edgar Hoover with George Foreman, stir in a four-figure IQ and the worst bits of the snake, and that's the Captain."

"You're talking like he's still around," said Atwater.

He peered over the top of his Wayfarers. It may have been his imagination but Jack's skin looked a shade paler.

"You holding out on me, Jack?"

Jack squeezed the steering wheel and rolled his shoulders. His earlier bonhomie had evaporated. He didn't answer. Atwater waited. Finally Jack grunted and reached into the glove pocket of the car door and pulled out another of his photographs. He handed it to Atwater.

The photo showed one of the hayseeds carrying something into the concrete hangar. Atwater squinted at the blurred shape between the hayseed's hands.

"What's he carrying?" he said.

"Lunch," said Seed. "It's a tray, with a coupla plates and a Styrofoam cup."

Seed fished out a magnifier, something like a jeweler would use, and placed it flat on the photo. Atwater shifted the lens over the tray and squinted and convinced himself that Seed was correct. He looked at him.

"You're saying they got someone in there?" said Atwater.

Jack Seed nodded. "I reckon that place is a high-max jail. For one."

"Why didn't you tell me this before?"

" 'Cause I know my limitations," said Jack. "And I don't want to mix it with the Shithammer."

Atwater's mind reeled. Jefferson was dead. He said, "She's got Jefferson in there?"

Seed said, "Who else would be worth the effort?"

Atwater pulled out a pack of Kools and stuck one in his mouth. Seed held a flaming Zippo across the seat for him. Atwater dragged deeply.

"So Parillaud's hired us to find out what happened to him even though she's got him locked up."

"That's a blind," said Jack. "She wants the Captain's treasure but she can't sweat it out of him, which doesn't surprise me."

"I thought Jefferson couldn't be taken."

"Plenty've tried over the years. Was like the Captain had a charmed life. The worst ones always do. Physically he was the strongest guy I ever even heard of, but when you come down to it he's just a man, and if you got pussy in the picture anything's possible, especially rich blond pussy. And Christ, even I never seen a pussy worth a hundred million bucks."

Atwater was in turmoil. He couldn't work out if all this was good news or bad. So far he and Jack had kept their investigation strictly between themselves; that, and Atwater's lack of any personal history with Jefferson, had enabled them to be discreet. They'd come across the footprints of other interested parties hunting for the Captain's hoard: the Mafia, who'd always given him a wide berth; the governor's people, total losers; a couple of stiffs from the Bureau in Washington, D.C., who'd gotten themselves mugged and hospitalized in a strip club in the Quarter their first week in town; and certain City cops who, while not in principle unhappy to see him go, were shitting blue-serge bricks at the prospect of exchanging their uniforms for striped pajamas at the Angola State Pen. There was panic in the air but Atwater, being essentially outside the frame, had kept his head. As far as he could tell the other parties didn't know he and Jack were in business on Parillaud's behalf. The question arose: should they go into business on their own?

Atwater said, "Okay. If Parillaud wanted to she could hire the U.S. Marine Corps. And if Jefferson breaks out—which can't be beyond him—he'll be in a very bad mood. Then there's you and me: brains to burn, but no muscle. In other words, we can't compete with these characters on their own ground."

"I'm glad you got that much worked out."

"But we can pick a side and make ourselves worth whatever we're worth to whoever's willing to pay. Am I making sense?"

"You can make whatever sense you want, man, just drop this 'we' business."

"Fortune favors the brave, Jack."

"But not the stupid. Look, Rufus, I like you. You got poke, and poke'll get you far in this life. But you haven't put the time in on the street. You don't appreciate the temperature down there."

"I deal with scumbags day and night," said Atwater, stung.

"That's different. By the time you see them they're surrounded by cops and steel bars."

Atwater felt himself flushing. What Jack said was, to some extent, true. To reassure himself Atwater recalled his diligent practice in the use of firearms. Just last week he'd put five holes through a seven-inch card at thirty-five feet in six seconds. It had made his day. He'd never killed a man, it was true; or, he had to admit, even shot at one; but he could if he had to. He was prepared for it, mentally and physically. He'd kept the seven-inch card as a souvenir.

"Jack," he said with renewed confidence. "I know I'm not a tough guy the way you and the Captain are, but there's an angle here, a big one, I feel it. Like why the fuck would she snatch Jefferson in the first place? He must've had something on her, something mega."

"That's her problem, and if you stick around, yours too. It's time for us to collect our paychecks and back off. Remember: no one knows we know he's in there. If he ever gets out—and I wouldn't put it past him—I don't want him *ever* to find out we left him in there. I don't plan on inhaling no pig shit for nobody."

Seed clammed up and brought the Impala to a halt at a pair of elaborate wrought-iron gates set into a twelve-foot red-brick wall. A hundred yards or so beyond the gates the road ran under a leafy tunnel of live oaks and Spanish moss. Atwater got out and went to an intercom set into one of the gateposts. A pair of video cameras peered down at him from the wall. Atwater pressed the intercom.

A deep voice answered, surprisingly clear. "Identify yourself."

It was Bobby Frechette. Atwater didn't consider himself racist. He worked with plenty of black guys, and women too. But if he didn't like a black person for any reason, that person, reasonably enough to Atwater's mind, became a nigger, just like someone with no hair might become a bald cocksucker. Faggots, it had to be said, were a case unto themselves. Frechette was unquestionably a nigger, and nigger that he was, he was giving them this "Identify yourself" bullshit even though he had to be watching Atwater, whom he knew well, scowling up at the cameras.

With the Kool still in his mouth, Atwater said into the speaker, "Mr. Rufus Atwater to see Miss Parillaud."

Frechette didn't reply. A moment later the iron gates started to hum open, and Atwater got back into the car. As they drove without speaking underneath the arched branches of the trees, Atwater sourly pondered Jack Seed's words. Jack was over forty and too comfortable in the life he'd made for himself. He was happy to work for tips. Atwater had to turn him. The leafy arbor above ended and the road passed through the middle of an extravagant expanse of flawlessly kept lawn.

Two white marble fountains, a rose garden and artfully placed trees and flowering shrubs decorated a wide esplanade leading up to Parillaud's mansion. It was called Arcadia and had been built in 1872 by Filmore Faroe's great-grandfather, a carpetbagger and opium addict from Baltimore, who'd swooped in during the last days of the Civil War to prey on the shattered local gentry. On Atwater's first visit, when his mind had been swimming with visions of becoming Parillaud's most trusted and indispensable counselor, he had been stunned by the mansion's beauty. There was a phrase that had always appealed to him: *éminence grise*. Yeah, he'd dreamt of being Parillaud's *éminence grise*, shaking and moving on her behalf from behind her throne, maybe even slipping her a length from time to time. Now that he knew from her manner with him that it had been an impossible fantasy, and an embarrassing one at that, he regarded the approaching mansion with the loathing of frustrated envy. They'd never find Jefferson's secret fucking files whether he was alive or not, and even if they did, they'd never profit from them. The power the files represented would be vacuumed up by the gaping mouth of Parillaud's wealth and he, Atwater, would be paid off, given a snotty thank-you-oh-so-much and packed off back to the City like a Mexican dishwasher after the guests have gone home.

Now Jack Seed wanted to run out on him too. Seed halted the Impala on white, evenly raked gravel outside the Palladian entrance. Atwater shoved the door open and flicked out the butt of his cigarette. From the rear of his belt he pulled off his Galco SOB pants holster with its Glock 9 mil and put it in the glove compartment. As his right foot touched the gravel, he hesitated, removed his Wayfarers and turned back to Seed.

"Jack, what if we sprang the Captain from that high-max jail?"

Seed's eyes narrowed, flickered away for a moment, then returned to Atwater.

"I warned you about fuckin' with rattlesnakes."

"You virtually said it yourself, man. If he knows we left him in there, we're high on his shitlist. But if we sprang him . . ."

Seed looked away again.

"A friend in need, Jack. He'd owe us."

Seed tugged on his mustache with a finger and thumb.

"I don't know I want him to owe us."

Atwater squeezed Jack's shoulder. "Think about it while I'm inside. Will you do that for me?"

Seed nodded sullenly. Atwater slammed the car door shut behind him and walked up the steps to the house. As he approached the door it was opened by Bobby Frechette. The big po-faced nigger was wearing a charcoal-gray suit that made Atwater's look like he'd made it himself. Atwater stepped through into the hall, his shoes clicking on the marble tiles. In the thin amber light coming through the stained glass of the dome high above him the hall seemed gloomy. This was a dead place. Frechette stared at Atwater without blinking and Atwater found his own gaze focusing on the knot in Frechette's tie. Frechette made a gesture with his hands that meant he wanted to frisk him. Normally, Atwater submitted. This time something in him rose against it.

"What kinda game you trying to play, Frechette? You know I never carry a piece."

So far Atwater had kept his eyes on the tie. He risked a glance up at Frechette's face: it was impassive and unperturbed. In the cast of the cheekbones was a built-in contempt that Atwater knew he would never be able to answer. He dropped his eyes again.

"Just routine, Mr. Atwater," said Frechette, softly. "No disrespect intended."

"I don't care whether it was intended or not. I'm your boss's lawyer, not a fucking hit man."

Frechette still had his palms raised at waist height. He didn't move. Atwater fought an urge to raise his arms and submit to the search. He nodded past Frechette.

"Okay. You go and ask Miss Parillaud if she wants me frisked. She says yes, then okay. I can wait. My time seems cheap enough around here."

This time Frechette did blink. He scanned Atwater's suit for bulges. And with that Atwater felt the elation of a petty but significant victory.

"Miss Parillaud's in the study," said Frechette, and turned to lead the way.

Atwater followed. He felt several inches taller. As he walked down the hall he reflected on how all this super-rich shit could get to a guy like himself. It was weird. On his own territory Atwater was taken seriously. He yelled at gold shields and medical examiners and precinct captains when they fucked up; in the holding cells he eyeballed killers from an inch and a half and told them how he'd guarantee them cellmates who'd fuck them in the ass till they shat blood unless they made a plea. And in the courtroom he could more than hold his own against his flabby, overpaid opponents. But the minute he stepped through the door here it fell on him like a shroud: an awestruck timidity induced by the distilled presence of sheer and outrageous wealth. He felt like he'd been trained from birth, without knowing it, to kneel before all that this hunk of marble, teak and gold leaf represented. A good rule of thumb among criminal lawyers declared that it was more or less impossible to pocket an after-tax income of over five hundred thousand bucks a year without knowingly breaking the law. Yet here in Arcadia, Atwater felt himself permeated with a sense of wealth's rightness. It was as if even the walls and the floors knew that anything this rich must be right. How could this much money come together in one place and be wrong? *"Be still,"* it said, *"and know that I am God."*

Atwater made himself think about the tape of Parillaud sobbing and the photos, and the way he'd faced down Frechette. He managed to wrestle the awe down to manageable proportions. He wasn't going to be pushed around anymore. Frechette had had her chance to take him into her confidence and she'd dropped the ball. All this high living, soaking her brain day and night, had made her soft and careless; Frechette too, for all his routines. Jack had proved that today with his bugs and telephoto lenses. And Atwater himself when he'd stared Frechette into dropping the body search: that could prove handy. Yeah. They were complacent. They were weak. And Rufus Atwater was honed and ready.

Frechette opened a door and spoke into the room beyond.

"Rufus Atwater, ma'am."

"Show him in, Bobby."

Frechette showed Atwater his cheekbones again, then stood back to let him pass. Atwater walked into the study. The louvered shutters were drawn across the windows and the room, paneled in dark woods, was dimly lit. Behind a desk the size of Atwater's bedroom, and probably worth more than his house, stood Lenna Parillaud. She was dressed in what looked like the same black suit as in Seed's pictures and her face was in shadow. He noted, with gratitude, that for once she wasn't displaying much cleavage. Somewhere in the room a clock ticked. Atwater told himself not to let this Vincent Price shit get to him. He nodded at the shadowy face with what he estimated was just the right balance of respect and self-confidence.

"Miss Parillaud," he said.

"Rufus," she said. "Come and sit down."

Atwater felt a slight weakness in his legs. She'd never called him by his first name before. As he walked over to the chair on this side of the table she pitched her voice over his shoulder.

"Thanks, Bobby."

Atwater heard the door clunk shut behind him. He sat down in the chair. His hand drifted toward his pocket. He stopped it and put it in his lap.

"You may smoke if you want," said Parillaud.

"Thanks, I'll be fine," said Atwater.

He crossed his legs, then wished he hadn't, but thought it would look bad if he uncrossed them again. Parillaud stepped closer to her side of the table and he got a good look at her face. He felt a moment of shock. In the time he'd known her she'd never had a tan; in fact her face was always unnaturally white, as if she used some kind of foundation. Right now her face looked pale with something more than powder: she looked drained, and her green eyes had circles under them, and some wrinkles at either corner he'd never noticed before. She was five-six—maybe five-seven—in height and had a ripe but firm figure. He'd noted that when she wanted, she was able to give the impression of being more vulnerable than she could possibly be, a please-Daddy-just-for-me deal that she'd probably been using to get what she wanted all her life. At other times she was rude to the point of almost stamping her feet. Spoiled scum. Today he sensed that at least some of her vulnerability was genuine.

"What did you find out about Dr. Grimes?" she asked.

Atwater always got the impression that speaking softly didn't come naturally to Parillaud, that the silky lilt was something she'd cultivated. Her natural voice probably had a harsher, coarser edge to it. A hint of that edge leaked through now. She was trying to appear calmer than she felt. That was good. Atwater took the pack of Kools from his pocket.

"Think I'll have that cigarette after all," he said.

Parillaud pushed a crystal ashtray across the table and waited while he lit up. Atwater looked at her through the smoke. For once he felt on top of her. It was a feeling he liked.

"In the time I had I didn't turn up anything that seems significant," he said.

"Tell me anyway."

Atwater spoke without reference to the notes he had in his pocket. "Grimes is thirty-eight years old, lives alone in an old fire station in the Irish Channel. He has no criminal record and no service records. Qualified M.D., University of Chicago. Did postgrad training there in general and trauma surgery, then disappeared to Central America— Nicaragua or Salvador, maybe both—for a couple of years."

"Why?"

"I believe he did some kind of aid work during the fighting there— I guess Red Cross–type stuff. I'm waiting to find out more on that. He returned to the States around eight years ago and gave up surgery, completed another residency program in psychiatry, this time at Tulane. I'm told it's not so unusual for medics to change specialty in mid-residency, but it's unusual to complete a whole program and then start over again. Now he specializes in treating drug addicts, mainly heroin."

A shadow of anxiety—a question—flitted across Parillaud's face. Atwater paused but Parillaud said nothing.

He went on, "Far as I can tell Grimes is respected but considered something of an outsider in professional circles."

"Why did he come to New Orleans?" she said.

"I don't know. Since there wasn't much to show on him I ran a cross-check on his family. He's got a brother named Luther, a real bad actor: Vietnam war hero of the psycho category, later spent time in Angola State for nearly killing two guys in a fistfight. His whereabouts are unknown. Their father, George, lives in Algiers, might be the reason Grimes settled down here. George is an old commie union guy, worked as an organizer for the American Federation of Labor during the fifties and sixties. He's got a long record of arrests, all for union stuff, including one jail term of eight years in Illinois for assaulting a cop during a strike. Clean slate for the past thirty years."

None of his findings had suggested any connection to Clarence Jefferson, but he didn't say so. He leaned forward to flick his ash.

"I'm afraid that's about all I got, Miss Parillaud."

Parillaud was still standing. She clasped her hands together. The movement was executed casually enough but Atwater got the impression it was intended to stop her hands shaking.

"You've been very thorough," she said. "I appreciate it."

Atwater puffed on his Kool to lay down a little smoke. He chose his words carefully.

"I presume this is something to do with our looking for Captain Jefferson's little library," he said.

"No," she said, just a beat too quickly. "It's another matter. A personal problem."

Atwater looked at her and thought: *You lying, pasty-faced bitch, I am going to see you on your knees after all.* He waited for her to ask about progress on the Jefferson investigation. If she didn't ask, Atwater's mind would be made up.

"I need to speak with Dr. Grimes in person. Face-to-face," said Parillaud.

Inside, Atwater smiled. His face he twisted into an expression of concern.

"I'm sure he'd be happy to. I hope it's nothing serious."

"As I say, it's personal."

"Of course. I don't mean to pry."

"I want you to escort Dr. Grimes out here to see me, this evening. Now. As soon as you can find him."

The smile vanished from Atwater's inner face. He had other plans for tonight. She read his hesitation.

"I ask you because I know you're thorough and utterly discreet. You are also capable of the appropriate delicacy."

He had to hand it to her: she even managed a shadow of the little-girl-lost smile that he guessed had swung some of the biggest deals in recent times her way. Even as he had the thought, he felt himself blushing with pleasure and heard himself saying, "Sure, Miss Parillaud, whatever you want."

She nodded. "Then I'll see you later, with Dr. Grimes. Thank you, Mr. Atwater."

She stood there waiting for him to get up and leave as if he'd just finished shining her shoes. She was amazing. Atwater wanted to say, "Yes sir, no sir, three bags full." Instead he stood up and stubbed out his cigarette in the ashtray.

"I'll get right on it," he said.

"If at all possible I'd like Dr. Grimes to come out here voluntarily. Don't push him. Ask him politely and promise him my gratitude."

"And if it's not possible?" said Atwater.

"Then use your judgment. Just make sure you bring him to me."

"I can't guarantee I'll find him tonight."

This time the real voice broke through her self-control.

"Then let me know the situation and keep on looking, Mr. Atwater."

Her eyes drilled into him. Tiger eyes. To his shock Atwater felt physically afraid. He took a pace backward and blustered, "Anything you say, Miss Parillaud."

With that Atwater nodded goodbye and left. In the corridor stood Bobby Frechette. Atwater shrugged his jacket and walked past without speaking. He felt the nigger walk behind him all the way to the front door but declined to flatter him with a backward glance or a word of goodbye. On the way down the wide portico steps toward Jack Seed's Impala, Atwater reflected on Parillaud's strange mood. His hunch was that the Grimes angle was an avenue going nowhere. Maybe it was just what she said it was, a personal matter. Maybe the letter she'd gotten that morning said she had breast cancer or something. Why, then, a psychiatrist? And why get Atwater to run a check on him for her? He remembered the lie in her voice. No, he had to treat the Grimes development seriously, cover it properly. In the meanwhile Jack could set the ball rolling. Tonight. Atwater's gut was clear about that. He couldn't wait. There was something building. He had to press on tonight; but he couldn't spring Jefferson from the concrete prison by himself. Atwater opened the Chevy door and climbed inside. He looked at Jack.

"Well, Jack? Are you willing?"

"What if it ain't Jefferson in there?" said Seed.

"You reckon it is."

"I know, but what if it ain't?"

Atwater said the first thing that came into his head.

"Then we'll leave not a trace behind us."

It was only after he'd closed his mouth that he understood what he'd said. He was a prosecuting attorney, solemnly pledged to defend the law. Now he was suggesting murder, at the very least of Parillaud's hayseeds. Suddenly it was real: a line he'd never dreamt of crossing before. Inwardly he gulped. Once, back in high school, he'd climbed to the top of an Olympic diving board and gotten as far as standing on the edge. He hadn't looked down at the water far below. He hadn't needed to: it had filled him from top to toe with a shimmering terror. It had been all he could do to climb back down the ladder—to the jeers of his buddies—without throwing up. That was how he felt now: he didn't want to look down. He was about to backtrack and qualify what he'd just said when his eyes focused on Seed's face: Jack was looking at him like he was Vito Corleone. Atwater closed his mouth.

Then Jack said, quietly, "I'll need some boys."

And with that Atwater felt a zing go down his spine and spiral up through his belly. He felt light-headed. This was it, man, this was what it felt like to go from marijuana to heroin. All his anxieties dissipated in the rush of power and daring. He, Rufus Atwater, was a fucking nightmare on wheels. He had the law's steel gauntlet on his fist and his fingers in that rich bitch's cunt. For the first time he understood where Jefferson had been coming from: his word meant life or death. Goddamn. And shit. Dead *or* alive, the Captain was yesterday's man. Now Rufus Atwater was in the catbird seat. Atwater suppressed the urge to take a deep breath. Instead he smiled, thinly, at Jack.

"Cash is no problem," he said. "One way or the other I'll square it. Just get me whatever it takes."

Seed started the engine and pulled away from the house.

"But no mob guys," added Atwater. "Independents."

Jack Seed sniffed and ran the back of a finger across his nostrils.

"Two hayseeds and four dogs," mused Seed. "Two extra guys?"

"Make it four. I want to be sure. Guys who won't be missed if we take casualties."

Atwater barely knew where his words were coming from, but he liked it.

"I know some Cubans," said Jack. "Ex-army. Got pissed off with Castro."

"Good. I want to go tonight."

Seed nodded. "I guess if we waited till morning we'd realize just how far out of our fuckin' minds we are."

They were racing now toward the tunnel of oak trees that would take them to the wrought-iron gates. Atwater's heart raced too. He looked out through the window. To the west across the manicured lawn the sun was one half of a dull yellow disc and the sky was shot with red.

Seed said, "What's the deal with the shrink?"

Atwater turned. "What's that?"

"The shrink, Grimes."

Jack was right, thought Atwater. Now more than ever he couldn't afford to neglect a single detail. Anything could mean anything. The car darkened as they barreled under the moss-hung trees.

"You just get those Cubans lined up," said Atwater. "Dr. Grimes I can deal with myself."

FOUR

ICERO GRIMES looked at his father, George, across the polished aluminum tabletop, and in spite of himself, and of all that was dire upon his mind, he smiled. They were sitting in a diner built in an old railroad car that served basic French and American food without the obsequious bullshit usually attendant on eating out. Grimes smiled because he liked the way his father attacked his steak, slaking it down in big chunks with too much mustard and too little mastication. It wasn't something funny, or something that anyone else would likely have smiled at, it was just something that Grimes liked seeing. George leaned back to wipe his mouth on his napkin and glanced at Grimes's plate, its own steak abandoned half-eaten.

"You look like hell, Gene," said George. "Oughta get the rest of that beef inside you."

His father had named him after Eugene Debs, the man who ran for the U.S. presidency from his jail cell. Cicero was a kind of nickname Grimes had picked up as a kid, not for any quickness of mind or skill in oratory, but because Cicero Grimes had been the name of the villain in a Paul Newman western. Personally, he liked Cicero but he also thought it was kind of foolish. With most people he used his given name.

"I'm fine, Dad," said Grimes.

George grunted. He had dressed up to come out in a dark blue poplin suit, a white shirt and a red Slim Jim tie. He had a full head of iron-gray hair, shorn, as it had been for over half a century, in a no-holds-barred marine's crop. His eyes were as gray as his hair, and deep set in a wide, big-boned face. His hands, which gripped his knife and fork as if they were crowbars, sported knuckles like walnuts and were bound across their backs with thick tendons and heavy veins. Grimes's hands were built along similar lines, but his fingers seemed only half the diameter of his father's. George had spent decades hauling meat carcasses and stacking crates, and even now took work down on the docks when he could get it. The thousands of tons of dead weight he'd gripped and lifted over the years lived on in the dense forearms and the hunched bulk of his shoulders as he leaned across his plate.

"You've been lying low, then," said George.

"That's right," said Grimes.

"Sure you haven't been sick?"

What was he supposed to say? Yeah, Dad, I've been contemplating suicide for six months but I was too fucked up to get it together.

Grimes said, "Doctors don't get sick."

George let it go. He nodded.

"Mind if I smoke?" asked Grimes.

"They're your lungs."

Grimes lit a Pall Mall. George finished his steak, mopped up the blood and gravy with a piece of bread and washed the bread down with a mouthful of Dos Equis. He looked around the restaurant. It was early evening and the place was only half full, mainly with youngsters practicing their cool, guys in T-shirts and tattoos, girls wearing lots of Lycra and nose studs.

"This place has changed," said George. "Used to be a regular working man's diner."

"It's okay," said Grimes. "It would've closed for good if they hadn't taken a step upmarket."

"I ain't saying I don't like it." George raised one eyebrow. "It's expensive for my money but the women're a hell of an improvement, I'll say that much." He nodded from Grimes's suit and tie to his own. "Must think we're a coupla stiffs, though."

"What, us?" said Grimes. "Harvey Keitel and Robert Mitchum?"

George laughed. "That's Luther talking."

Grimes grinned and nodded. The sadness in his chest was reflected in his father's eyes. Luther, Grimes's eldest brother and George's eldest son, had died six months ago. Grimes had been there. Some of the best moments in Grimes's life had been when the three of them had sat in a movie theater together, or around a TV, and watched hard men with gentle eyes perform feats of derring-do. But that was when they'd all been much, much younger.

46

"Luther loved them movies," said George.

Grimes looked away, his throat constricted. Luther's death was the main part of his having spent the last months lying on the floor. Grimes looked back as he felt thick fingers squeezing his arm.

"Hey," said George. "Luther wouldn't make any apologies for himself if he was still around. Neither should we for us."

The constriction got worse.

"Yeah," managed Grimes.

George, realizing this wasn't the time to get into it, flicked his eyes across the aisle at a woman in a short dress made of fake silver chains and not much else. Under the dress she wore a snowy-white bra and pants. George looked back at Grimes.

"The great thing about being my age," said George, "is you can look and enjoy without feeling pain." He smiled. "God, the grief it caused me. Don't imagine I would've missed it, though, not for a gold clock."

Grimes was grateful for the change of subject.

"I believe Aristotle said something along the same lines."

George pounced. "Socrates," he said.

"Socrates, then," said Grimes.

George leaned forward, his eyes bright and his index finger raised, as if he were imparting a secret of great value. Grimes knew the gesture well.

" 'Men do not become tyrants in order not to suffer from the cold.' " George smiled grimly. He paused to let the aphorism sink in.

The pause was unnecessary. Grimes was already uncomfortably aware of the letter in his inside pocket. It was as if his father had picked up on its contents, on Jefferson's "men of power," on the ghost of Jefferson himself hovering over Grimes's shoulder.

"That's Aristotle for you," said George. "*The Politics.* Those old boys knew a thing or two."

Grimes felt willing to accept advice from any quarter.

"Did they ever work out what to do about it?"

George rolled his shoulders with gusto. This was his life.

"Why, fight the bastards toe to toe, what else? That's the history of the world, ain't it? And history's a long way from over no matter what they try to tell us in *The New York* goddamn *Times.*"

Grimes felt his heart sinking. He was insane to have come to his father hoping for help with this matter. The best he was likely to do was to make himself look feeble and, if his luck held, avoid a violent argument. He felt like a middleweight climbing through the ropes with John L. Sullivan. He'd outboxed him before but the victories were always Pyrrhic, which is to say that George, battered into the canvas though he might be, always won the moral high ground. George's psyche was dominated by the fight for universal justice, as he saw it. He hadn't officially won a war since 1945 but he didn't seem to mind losing as long as he left some blood on the floor. Blood wasn't what Grimes wanted.

"You're right, Dad," he said.

He decided not to show him the letter and felt better; but the scorpion Jefferson had slipped into his pocket was still scuttling around: *"Give my regards to your daddy."* What the fuck had he meant by that? Had he written to George too? Was the Aristotle a signal rather than telepathic coincidence? George wasn't usually that subtle.

"Dad," said Grimes. "Has anything out of the ordinary happened these past couple of days?"

"You mean besides you taking me out for dinner?"

"Yes. Anything. Telephone repair guys, door-to-door Bible salesmen, stray cats . . ."

George thought about it. "No," he said. "Why?"

"No reason."

George grunted and gave him a look. Grimes ignored it.

"I was planning to go away for a while," said Grimes. "Overseas. Wondered if you'd like to come with me."

George stared at him while picking a piece of meat from between his teeth. Grimes found himself floundering in the gray steel-trap gaze.

"I thought maybe South America." Grimes started to go under. "Or Europe."

George pried the meat loose and swallowed it.

"I don't have a passport," he said.

"Oh," said Grimes. "How about we drive somewhere then? Wyoming, maybe. Or the old town, Chicago."

"Why, you want me to catch pneumonia?"

Grimes sighed, swamped by the awareness of his own incompetence. "You never were big on vacations, were you, Dad?"

"I never could see the point of traveling a thousand miles in order to do nothing."

A brief picture flashed into Grimes's mind, of a younger George, standing, shirtsleeves rolled, fists leaned on the kitchen table while he told a bunch of union guys what they had to do to stop the strike from crumbling, infecting them with his conviction that the only way to do the right thing was his way. Grimes turned away and tried to catch the eye of the waitress. He wanted the check. He felt the clasp of the veiny hand again. Grimes looked back into the trap.

"Just tell me the score, son," said George. "And I'll give you my best advice."

Grimes looked at George for what felt like a long time. The busy sounds of the diner faded into silence. The gray eyes looking back at him had suffered, greatly; enjoyed, greatly. With a sense of burden heavier than his own worst fears and more precious than his best lost dreams, Grimes felt the vast magnitude of his father's care for him. Yet he saw more than just that, something dangerous and inspiring, the source of Grimes's awe. He saw, and did not doubt, that behind and beyond that immeasurable care there stood a higher court, and it was to this authority that George Grimes submitted his soul, and not to love. It was to his conscience alone—that which *knew with* himself—that George was fatefully, perhaps helplessly, fidelitous—whatever it was that his conscience might know and whether or not another court should judge it right or wrong. It was this, Grimes knew, that made him a rare and dangerous man. George lived alone in a drafty shotgun house, wore a thrift shop suit and a Slim Jim tie and was seventy-three years old. It had been a long time since he'd issued an order, and longer still since anyone had obeyed him, Grimes included. Destiny, and time, had made him weak. Yet to Grimes he was, still, a king; a king from an age when giants strode a wider earth than this.

Grimes reached into his pocket and pulled out two sheets of paper and handed them to George. While George put his glasses on, Grimes put out his cigarette and lit a second and watched as his father read with a concentration so complete it took him close to radiance. With rapid small shifts of his head, back and forth, George absorbed the words and flicked to the second page. Halfway down he paused, showed the page to Grimes and pointed out a phrase with his finger.

"What's that say?" he said.

"*Corpus delicti,*" said Grimes. "It means the body of facts relating to a crime."

"I know what it means. Just couldn't read it."

George read on. When he got to the bottom of the page he looked over the rim of his glasses at Grimes.

"Where's the rest of it?"

The last page, the one containing Jefferson's instructions as to where to find his suitcases, was still in the envelope in Grimes's pocket. He'd separated it from the others before leaving his apartment.

"The rest you don't need to see," said Grimes.

In the pause that followed he prepared himself for George's reaction.

"I never thought I'd have cause to call my own son a sneaking bastard." There was no humor in George's voice; rather, it simmered with imminent rage. "But that's what you are."

"You said you'd give me your best advice."

"Then I'll need to read the goddamn rest of it."

Heads turned, including the waitress's. Grimes waved her over. He looked at George: age had mellowed him, considerably, but from a starting point of such hard-wired belligerence that it sometimes didn't seem that way.

"We'll talk on the way home," said Grimes.

George glared at him, read a stubbornness the equal of his own and folded the pages back in three. He handed them back as if he'd rather ram them down Grimes's throat, then took off his glasses. The waitress arrived.

"Everything okay?" she said, uncertainly.

"Terrific," said Grimes. "We'd like the check, please."

As she went to get it George stood up and said, "I'm going to the bathroom. I'll see you outside."

After the air-conditioning the atmosphere in the street was muggy and close. Grimes, waiting, took off his jacket and draped it over his shoulder. The street lights were on, the mid-evening traffic a steady drone. The old Ward 15 district had improved a lot in the last decade as interesting people who didn't have any dough, followed by less interesting people who did, had colonized the neighborhood. Grimes couldn't see the harm in a few craft shops and restaurants. He looked up at the sky and saw clouds and wondered if it would rain later. Then his father stepped down from the railroad car behind him and they started on the four blocks back to the shotgun house where George lived.

The first two blocks passed in silence. As they moved away from the main drag, the traffic got quieter. They were close enough here to smell the river. Grimes felt his father smoldering as he stomped along at his shoulder.

"Gene," said his father at last. "I know you haven't got the . . ." A fleeting sensitivity to Grimes's feelings caused him to hesitate; then, as expected, he pressed on anyway. "I mean, I can understand why you wouldn't have the stomach for a thing like this."

"Thanks, Dad," said Grimes.

"You're a young guy, a professional man after all. You got a life." He added, belatedly, "Dammit, there's no shame in that way of thinking."

"I'm not ashamed," said Grimes. "I'm just worried. I don't want to be tortured by psychopaths."

Grimes felt that the fact he'd been tortured before, by his late benefactor Clarence Jefferson, gave him the right to come out against the pastime. Of that experience—that utter humiliation—he was indeed ashamed, irrationally so. He'd spoken of it to no one, and intended never to do so.

Grimes added, "And I don't want to die."

George was silent for several paces, then attacked from a different angle.

"This here is a great country," he said. "You know why?"

Grimes didn't answer.

"Because we've always had the guts to take the truth."

"I can't believe this," said Grimes. "You've spent most of your life telling anyone who'll listen that we live in the corrupt kingdom."

"Exactly. Am I in prison for that? No. You think I think the guy who don't agree with me should be? No. Let him fight his corner and may the best man win. But the scumbags who put their hands in our pockets every day and fuck us with their lies and hypocrisy? You bet I want to see 'em in chains. The reason we're bleeding from open wounds is people look around and see a bunch of assholes they wouldn't put in charge of a hot-dog stand running their fucking lives for them. It's like it's not their country. In the old days it was even worse, even easier for the scumbags to hide under the rocks of their phony prestige. Now we can drag their asses in front of the world and make them drop their pants. We can show 'em that maybe—just maybe—this is our country after all."

"Dad," said Grimes. "I'm not an asshole and, believe it or not, I have been listening to you for thirty-odd years. I know the kingdom is corrupt. I know that the judge sending homeboys up to Angola State Pen snorts his coke with his after-dinner mints. I know we're ruled by grifters and thieves and men without honor. But listen to me: I don't care."

George wouldn't look at him.

Grimes said, "Whatever debt I owe, to you and the things you believe in, I paid off long since. I live my life, I ask no one's favor and no
one pulls any strings for me. If this town, or this whole state, wants to
sail to hell on a paddle steamer, that's fine by me. We've gotten the
world we deserve. I'm not going to get my balls cut off trying to
change something I don't give a shit about."

George stopped under a street light. Grimes stopped too. He could
sense his father on the verge of an explosion he'd witnessed many times
before.

"Then let me deal with it," said George.

"No," said Grimes.

With a titanic, and uncharacteristic, effort of self-control George
turned away, his thick shoulders clenched, his head bent forward. Beneath the bristly gray hair on the nape of his neck the muscles contracted into two thick straps. His voice, when he spoke, crunched like
gravel.

"I want this thing, Gene. I mean . . ." He shook his head, as if he
amazed himself by the violence of his desire. "I want it."

Grimes slipped his hand under George's left arm. Beneath his fingers
the sleeve of the poplin suit was stretched tight.

"I don't want you to die either," said Grimes.

George turned his face, looking up over his shoulder, and said, "Die?
You don't know what the word means."

Grimes had expected a lecture, a fight, a withering attack on his own
gutlessness; he hadn't expected this. His father's eyes were haunted by
a desperation Grimes had never seen. If it had been in George Grimes
to stretch his hands out to anyone and beg, his eyes said that now was
the time he would've done it. Instead of opening outward, his hands
bunched into fisted lumps of bone and ground against each other,
knuckle to knuckle, pulled tight into his chest. And because it wasn't
in him either to exploit the pain he was feeling, George turned away
again.

Grimes felt stranded. He knew that if each generation hadn't produced its share of Georges, then the world would be an uninhabitable
place. But he couldn't let an old man rush off to tangle with scumbags
high and low. He squeezed the thick arm still in his hand.

"Let's go home, have a drink," said Grimes.

George's body seemed to unstiffen a little. His voice evened out.

"I read a lot, you know that, always did," he said. "So I get up in the mornings and shave, eat and do some chores, take a walk, maybe see if they're hiring down the waterfront, get a paper and come home. That gets me as far as ten A.M."

Grimes brushed away an image of his own squalid timetable. He listened.

"Now, I don't plan going blind or, worse, watching TV all day, so I read, mainly guys I've read before, reread it, find the stuff I missed last time around. And one of 'em says, 'Death closes all.' " Now George looked at him. " 'But something ere the end, some work of noble note, may yet be done, not unbecoming men that strove with Gods.' "

Grimes, at his core, trembled—with guilt, sympathy, adoration and Christ knew what-all else. Then a voice in his head said: *How dare you lay that old-time-master shit on me at a time like this. These are cars driving past, not horses. You can get someone killed in this town for two thousand dollars, elect a judge for twenty and stick your dick in anything you can name, breathing or not, for a hell of a lot less than that, state and city tax inclusive. There are no gods to strive with anymore, old man.* Then another voice said: *That old man fought the Japanese, Taft-Hartley, Joe McCarthy, the FBI and John F. Kennedy and was teargassed at Selma when the great unwashed of the campuses thought KKK was a hallucinogenic drug. He's earned the right to quote whoever he wants to.*

George stopped the dialogue for him by saying, "Forget it, son. Let's go have that drink."

He disengaged his arm and started to walk away. Just like that.

Grimes felt a surge of anger. "Hey," he said.

He caught up with him, fell into step.

"Forget what? I ask you for some advice because a turd the size of China has been dropped in my lap and you tell me to let you deal with it. Am I supposed to relax now? It's all okay, my dad's handling it for me?"

"That's my advice, you don't want it, don't take it. And if you didn't want to hear it you shouldn't've shown me the goddamned letter in the first place."

"All I asked was if you wanted to take a trip with me."

"You wanna run like a gelded dog, that's your business."

Grimes had done his share of battlefield surgery, under fire, in the Nicaraguan highlands and in the killing fields of Salvador. George knew this. Grimes didn't feel that it was worth reminding him.

Grimes just said, "If they do come looking and don't find me, they'll come for you."

"They'd be doing me a favor. Just don't let me know where you're runnin' to and you'll be safe."

The shamelessness of this blackmail took Grimes's breath away.

"And you had the gall," said Grimes, "to call me a sneaking bastard."

Eyes front, George sniffed. "I apologize for that."

Grimes didn't know whether to laugh out loud or grab his father by the throat and strangle him. He suddenly realized he hadn't felt this alive in months. He was walking and talking and waving his arms instead of lying belly-down on a dung heap. As he decided to keep this revelation to himself he saw a car—in the street lights he couldn't tell what color or make, maybe a Nova—parked on the corner of his father's street. In the car were two white men, thirties, one in a sweatshirt, beard, the other in a sport coat, reading a paper. The men appeared entirely uninterested in, indeed oblivious to, Grimes's and George's noisy approach.

Grimes's inclination to laugh, along with his fragile sense of well-being, disappeared under a gut-tide of paranoia. He resisted the urge to stare at the men or point them out to George. George walked past the car, with no more evident awareness of its passengers than they had of him, and crossed the cobblestone street to the opposite sidewalk. Grimes kept the pace and tried to look natural. He had no experience of feeling out this kind of situation. Almost without exception all the countless cars with guys in them that he'd walked past in his life had been nothing more than cars with guys in them. That left him with only his most primitive instincts to guide him and at the moment they were heavily prejudiced toward anxiety, suspicion and fear. If a little girl holding a balloon had turned the corner toward them, Grimes would have suspected her of signaling to the characters in the Nova, now thirty feet behind his back.

With that he thought about the girl in Jefferson's letter, something he'd so far avoided. *She's nineteen years old.* Grimes couldn't recall her name. Ella? The idea of predators moving in on her as well disturbed him, in fact it turned his stomach, but at least he didn't know her, couldn't feed his guilt with pictures of her face. It was entirely possible that she was a fiction, that Jefferson's letter was one last postmortem black joke, dashed off to amuse himself while Grimes had been squirming at his feet on the living room carpet. Jefferson had that kind of mind. The girl's address was probably a heroin-supply depot manned by Vietnamese gangsters loaded with Mach 10's and even more paranoia than his own: Dr. Grimes knocks on the door, and it's goodnight Joanna. Then Jefferson would have another funny story to tell his buddies in hell; or "up there," as he'd put it.

The ponderous machinery of his mind stalled on a sudden thought: the girl Ella was Jefferson's daughter. Who else could she be? Why else would he care for her?

George said, "Come on in."

They'd reached George's house: a narrow front door with a single window frame to the left. Inside, the rooms were stacked in a straight line, one behind the other, like compartments in a train. Parked outside, for all the world to see it now seemed, was Grimes's Olds 88. He beheld its strident conspicuousness with pain. He should trade it in for a Nova soon, or a Hyundai. George climbed the step and opened the front door and Grimes followed him inside.

The door opened directly into the living room. George closed it behind them and without switching on the light went straight to the window and peered out, back down the street.

"You made those guys too?" said Grimes.

George stood back from the window and pulled the curtains. Without the yellow light from the street the room was pitch-black.

"They've gone," said George from the darkness. "You can turn the light on."

Grimes did so. In the sudden brightness he felt foolish.

"For a moment I thought those guys were out for us."

"They were," said George, with grim satisfaction.

"How do you know?"

"Experience. Organizing for the union I spent twenty years lookin' over my shoulder. Company goons and Pinkertons? Hell, I been set up, beaten up, tapped, tailed and photographed more times than Billy-be-jiggered. Why, I was carrying you on my shoulders more than a time or two, but you were too young to know all that."

Grimes threw his black suit jacket over the back of the sofa. His shirt, he discovered, was wet through.

"So what do we do?" he said.

"I guess that's up to you," said George.

"Don't start," said Grimes. "We're not going to get ourselves killed just so you can relive the good old days. These are bad new days. Decide now: Wyoming, Chicago or, if you can't take the chill, Florida. I need the bathroom."

"You know where it is."

Grimes went to the bathroom and took a grateful piss. He closed his eyes. His father was worse than insane. The old days were thirty years gone; he was out of touch. The guys in the Nova were probably scoring grass or conducting some other petty illegality. That's why they'd given off a vibe. George was showing off. It was natural enough. He just had to get him out of the City for a while until this whole thing cooled off. During his long horizontal meditations Grimes had promised himself a hundred times that when he got well he'd leave this stinking burg. He'd only come here in the first place to be near the old man. Grimes didn't want to die down South. It would be nice to see snow again, feel cold once in a while. The girl? Ella? She'd survived nineteen years without him. And anyway, if he knocked on her door he was only guaranteed to heap her with the same bullshit he was trying, even now, to get out from under himself. He flushed the toilet and went back to the living room.

George was pouring Wild Turkey into a pair of glasses. As he handed one to Grimes he seemed calmer. He raised his glass and grinned.

"Old times," he said.

"Old times," Grimes raised his drink, "you old bastard."

Grimes drained the shot in one and gasped, his eyes watering. George picked up the bottle and poured refills.

"I spoke some harsh words back there, Gene," he said. "Will you forgive me?"

"Not till we're deep down in Florida."

"You know, I was thinking on what you said about Chicago."

Grimes raised his glass again. "Chicago it is, then."

"Chicago," said George.

They drank again and Grimes started to feel positively human.

Then, for the second time that day, the doorbell rang for Cicero Grimes.

Grimes put his glass down and glared a warning at his father.

"I'll get it," said Grimes.

"Wait," said George.

He disappeared down the corridor into the back of the house.

Grimes paced in agitation. He decided not to peek through the curtains. From the depths of the shotgun house he heard some muffled snaps and clicks. The bell rang a second time. Grimes waited. He slipped his jacket back on and wondered if he still looked like Harvey Keitel. He didn't feel much like him. When George returned he, by way of contrast, was carrying two automatic pistols. Grimes was no gun aficionado but he recognized them: a Luger 9 mil and a Colt .45. George held out the Luger toward him.

"Locked down and loaded," he said. "Took this one from a Jap army captain on Tarawa. Had to crawl under the roots of a coconut tree to smoke him"—he hefted the Colt—"with this one."

Grimes held out his palms, refusing the gun. His felt his saturated shirt drag against his lats.

"Take it easy, Dad."

"Please yourself."

George stuck the Luger into the back of his pants. This time whoever was at the door rapped on it with his knuckles. George slid against the wall behind the door, the .45 held loose and easy, no theatrics, and nodded to Grimes. Grimes walked over and opened the door.

Standing on the step was a gangly redhead in a double-breasted suit a size too big for his bones, all freckles and Adam's apple and milky eyes. Despite the milk there was something in the eyes that was feral and shrewd. Grimes rarely took an instant dislike to someone; when he did the feeling was usually mutual. Perhaps that was why the redhead's smile seemed unnatural and forced; or maybe he just had that kind of smile; some people did. The more they tried to be likeable the more they made your flesh crawl.

"Evening," said the redhead.

He showed Grimes a leather wallet with a photo ID card in it.

"Rufus Atwater, deputy prosecuting attorney."

He said it as if he were a papal emissary, as if Grimes was meant to kneel and kiss his ring. Grimes held his hand out for the wallet.

"May I see that?"

A beat, the redhead not so much peeved as wounded, then: "Sure. Can't be too careful these days."

An upstate accent with a tinge of the City. A poor boy made good. Grimes didn't allow this to provoke any feeling of kinship. He studied the ID card. Like most such cards it meant as much or as little as you were inclined to believe. Nevertheless, it didn't have MURDER INCORPORATED emblazoned over it and Grimes felt a little easier. Grimes handed the wallet back and did a quick sweep of the street. The redhead appeared to be alone; but then he would.

"What can I do for you, Mr. Atwater?"

The redhead smiled his pally smile. "I'm looking to speak to Dr. Eugene Grimes."

"This isn't his home."

"I know that, sir. I guess I should say that I'm here on behalf of a private client, not the D.A. I showed you my ID to reassure you that I'm an honorable man."

"An honorable man," said Grimes.

"Only thing in this world that counts for a damn," said Atwater. "Least, that's the way I see it."

The words *Murder Incorporated* started to appear, faintly, beneath the beads of sweat on Atwater's forehead.

Grimes said, "I'm glad you said that. I'm Dr. Grimes." He didn't usually call himself Doctor, but in certain situations it gave him at least the illusion of a certain protected dignity. He held out his hand. Atwater shook it.

"May I come in, Doctor?"

Through the slab of wood to his left Grimes felt the presence of his father, loaded down with what were almost certainly illegal firearms.

"I'm afraid my father's taken ill," said Grimes. "Something he ate. I'd rather not disturb him."

"I'm sorry to hear that."

"You said you were here on behalf of a client."

"That's right. Miss Magdalena Parillaud. I'm her special counsel, exclusive. You may have heard of her."

Grimes had some vague memory of having seen the name in the business section as he threw it in the trash. The words *rich* and *reclusive* swam into his mind.

"Howard Hughes meets Barbara Stanwyck," he said.

Atwater looked about to say "Barbara who?" then thought better of it. "Miss Parillaud would be grateful if you'd come visit her," he said.

Grimes felt queasy. This was it: the first strands of Jefferson's web, but from a direction he couldn't have imagined.

"Why?" said Grimes.

Atwater's face writhed, strangely, as if he thought it a stupid question and wanted to say so.

"I don't know," he said.

The naked sincerity of this answer made Grimes feel better. He almost asked if Atwater had tried any big cases recently.

Atwater recovered. "She said it was personal. I presume some medical situation. She needs to see you tonight."

"So it's an emergency medical situation," said Grimes.

"I don't know that I could say that." Atwater shuffled, then leaned forward, with a guys-like-you-and-me shrug. "You know these big-money types, Doc. Want what they want when they want it. Neurotic, all of 'em. But you'd know all about that stuff. She'll pay for your time, naturally. I can take you out there, her driver can bring you back. This time of day it's a thirty, forty-minute run." Atwater smiled. "We can talk, you know?"

Even given his dire situation, Grimes could think of nothing more revolting than a forty-minute conversation with this creature. Atwater had probably been the school sneak, the type who'd turn his parents in for smoking grass then sue them for the emotional trauma. Grimes's mind ordered him to make a decision. If they had hold of him, then at least his father was out of the frame. That alone would halve his adrenaline levels. If he was going to end up with his dick wired to a mobile power generator then it was going to happen. And anyway, a million-airess was unlikely to have too many strangers buried in her basement. There was no point asking why she needed a city prosecutor to fetch her a doctor; he didn't want to see Atwater's face writhing again as he tried to invent an answer.

"Where's your car?" asked Grimes.

Atwater, relieved, jerked his head over his shoulder. Behind the Olds 88 was parked a green Monte Carlo in need of bodywork.

"Give me five minutes," said Grimes. "I'll follow you."

Atwater's underdeveloped lips twitched with disappointment. He struggled toward his own decision, then said, "Sure. Why not?"

Grimes nodded and closed the door on Atwater and the street. He looked at his father.

"You want me to come with you?" said George.

"You've got a bellyache, remember?"

George pulled out the Luger from under his jacket and offered it for a second time.

"Driving out into the country alone, I'd take it."

Grimes shook his head. "I'm not going to shoot a prosecuting attorney."

"Attorney my ass."

This provoked an idea and Grimes seized it: give his father something to do, cool him down.

"I want you to check him out for me while I'm gone. Ring the D.A.'s office. Take his license plate."

George grunted as if to say he knew a bone when he was thrown one.

"And what are you gonna do?" he asked.

"Play innocent. I don't know anything about anything. No guns, no fear. Just a psychiatrist called out to see a crazy millionaire."

"Not so crazy that she can't run an empire founded on slave labor and greed."

"You would know something about her, wouldn't you?"

George's eyes narrowed. "All I know is her husband was Filmore Eastman Faroe, and that he was a bastard and the son of bastards. Klansmen and fascists to a man, going all the way back to the first burning cross. Only times Filmore Faroe ever paid a decent wage was to thugs with ax handles and riot guns. Thank Christ he left no children. If there ever was a line deserved to end, it was his."

Grimes was barely listening. He didn't have time for a politics tutorial.

"I'd better go," he said.

George stuck out his hand. His face, to Grimes's surprise, was grave with barely controlled emotion.

"Good luck, son," said George.

Grimes took the hand, returned its grainy dry squeeze as best he could.

"Hey," said Grimes. "I'll be back in two hours. Don't worry."

George nodded once. Grimes let go of his hand and went to the door, opened it. Outside, the Monte Carlo's lights came on and the engine turned over, came to life. Grimes looked back at his father and smiled with more levity than he felt.

"And don't shoot anyone."

Grimes climbed into his Olds, the Monte Carlo swung out ahead of him and they pulled away in convoy across the cobblestones. As he turned the corner at the end of the street Grimes looked back and saw his father standing on the doorstep, watching him go. At the last moment George Grimes raised his hand in farewell. And Cicero Grimes had the crazy thought that he would never see George again.

FIVE

B Y THE TIME Grimes followed the rear lights of the Monte Carlo through the humming iron gates to Parillaud's walled estate he had just about managed to beat into his mind the idea that he was a doctor visiting someone who needed a psychiatrist. That and nothing more.

Throughout the journey he'd threatened, bullied and cajoled himself to believe that he'd never heard of Clarence Jefferson or any of his works, great or small. He would give his opinion as best he was able on any other subject under the sun, but of that one he was ignorant and ignorant entire. Grimes concentrated on the road as it swung in a wide curve beneath a canopy of trees. Wide, gnarled trunks flickered by in the swinging beam of his headlights, and the occasional drooping skein of Spanish moss. Live oaks. The road straightened and in the glare of the beams Grimes could see Atwater's pencilly orange head bobbing around in the Monte Carlo up ahead. He wondered what the prosecutor's angle was. Some kind of informer. Anyone who could afford trees like this in their front yard had to have connections everywhere. *Trust no one*, Jefferson had said. That much Grimes would remember of the goddamn letter and no more. *You know nothing*, his mind roared. Not "I may have heard of him" or "We met once at a Birch Society taffy pull" or "I know someone who went to college with his sister." Nothing. Sustained denial. Controlled paranoia. The flanking trees disappeared abruptly and Grimes felt his eyebrows rise.

A garden the size of a city block unrolled before him. No wild blooms or unruly bushes here but, rather, a frozen mosaic of perfectly balanced flower beds and sculpted shrubs and symmetrical ambulatories as smooth as satin ribbons. Illuminated fountains threw arcs of golden liquid into the night. White marble statues meditated over lawns trimmed with nail scissors. At the top of the garden, its great facade artfully lit and shadowed by hidden spotlights, loomed an Italian Renaissance palazzo that would have sent Cosimo de Medici to the nearest realtor on his knees. From a dozen or more high arched windows came the glimmer of chandeliers hanging from the eighteen-foot ceilings. The main entrance, centrally placed, was by way of a broad flight of steps narrowing into a classical portico dressed in white stone.

The Monte Carlo stopped with its engine running at the foot of the steps. Grimes pulled in beside it and switched off the ignition. He got out and looked up at the entablature capping the two columns mounted either side of the steps. Engraved on the frieze beneath the cornice was the word ARCADIA. Grimes took it to be the mansion's name, chosen in a period when irony probably wasn't in vogue. He looked over as Atwater called from the open window of his Monte Carlo with the forced pallyness that Grimes had already grown to dislike.

"Quite a pile, ain't it?"

Behind the leering grin the redhead's face was strained and preoccupied and shiny with sweat. He looked at his watch.

"Listen, Doctor, I've got other business to attend to." An obsequious shrug. "That's the life, you know? Just go ring the bell. And, hey, don't let it get to you. Remember, their shit stinks bad as yours and mine."

Atwater withdrew into the car, backed out and drove away.

The sound of the Monte Carlo faded and died, leaving only the quiet splash of the fountains in the heavy evening air. Grimes stood before the portico of Arcadia feeling curiously abandoned. The squalid teeming of New Orleans—and of the rest of the world itself—seemed infinitely distant from this place. It was more than its geography, miles from any other habitation. It was a distance of heart and spirit too, expertly engineered, and beautifully so, at a time when the City was not thirty minutes away but a full day's ride. He wondered what kind of mind had conceived and demanded such a distance—had needed it— and what kind of mind needed it now. With a tingle down his spine he realized that from this Olympian remoteness it would be easy to believe oneself capable of anything: not merely in the sense of being able to bring anything about, but of being able to germinate the want of anything, and to believe that anything justified. For all the controlled and geometric precision towering above him—and laid out behind him like the lid of a jeweled casket—this was a receptacle of infinite boundaries, a monument to the paradox of reason and desire. Grimes imagined a human consciousness—any human's consciousness—sprawled within and groping ever outward toward ever more disparate cravings, cravings to which no one would ever say no but only: "This is how much it will cost." If that consciousness had been his own, raised and confined here throughout a lifetime, what would it—what would he—have raised his head and bellowed out for in the restless heat of the night?

Perverse desires stirred in Grimes's subconscious. He shrugged off another tingle. The splash of water on white marble was all the answer the evening gave him.

The question for the moment was irrelevant. He could dwell on it further in Chicago, shivering from the wind instead. Tonight he would say no to whoever waited inside, and no matter what the blandishments he was offered.

Grimes mounted the steps and rang the bell and waited. He buttoned his shirt and straightened his tie. His suit was crumpled but it was linen, and black. Thank Christ he'd shaved and smartened himself up for his father. Cicero Grimes, vagrant on call. The door was answered by a lean black man three inches taller than Grimes. That made him over six-four; and maybe a hundred and ninety sinewy pounds. He had planed cheekbones and a scimitar nose, and in his eyes a Moslem hauteur as old as the stone beneath his feet. His suit was loose-fitting and just expensive enough to soften the man's natural menace into quiet intimidation. Whoever the guy was, he wasn't the butler.

"Eugene Grimes," said Grimes.

The black didn't smile but he held out his hand.

"Bobby Frechette."

Grimes shook the hand, the fingers surprisingly long and delicate. On the first two knuckles Grimes spotted the raised calluses of someone who trained seriously on the wooden punching board. A karate man, then. Grimes warmed to him a little.

"Come in, please, Doctor."

Grimes walked into a large hallway, from the center of which a wide staircase splayed upward into a first-floor balustrade. Set into the roof was a dome paned with stained glass. Frechette stepped back a pace from Grimes and opened his hands toward him.

"If I may, Doctor," said Frechette.

Grimes realized he had to be frisked. He nodded and raised his arms. A moment of vulnerability, primitively felt, but Frechette didn't take advantage of it as he might have done. Just a man doing his job. As the long hands fluttered over his limbs and flanks Grimes thought about the embarrassment he'd saved himself by refusing his father's Luger. Frechette straightened up.

"Thank you, Doctor. Will you come this way, please?"

Grimes followed Bobby Frechette down a broad corridor hung with several million dollars' worth of paintings. Grimes wasn't too hot on the fine arts but he could recognize a Picasso and a Dalí as readily as the next man. He remembered being puzzled by news stories of art treasures being stolen and sold to wealthy collectors who, presumably, would only ever look at them alone. It didn't square with the theory of art as consumer status symbol. As he walked through Arcadia his puzzlement was answered by the voice of that uninhibited consciousness he'd imagined outside. *"I want it,"* said the voice and the want was all that was necessary. It justified itself. It was not even necessary that the painting be looked at at all; it had only to be possessed. The words echoed in his mind again, in a different voice: his father's. *"I want it, Gene."* George hadn't gotten an awful lot of what he'd wanted out of his life, and he'd never been one to complain, but his voice had trembled when he'd said that. Another echo hit him, from Jefferson's letter: *"inexorable and extravagant appetites."* And Rufus Atwater: he wanted too. Exactly what, Grimes didn't know. Grimes himself hadn't wanted anything in what seemed like a long time, other than to lie alone in his hole, but he wasn't judging anyone. He had known his own appetites *"ruinous and vast"*; Clarence Jefferson had stretched him on their rack. Now Jefferson's ghost had him stretched upon another: the letter. Grimes almost stopped midstride.

The letter was still in his pocket.

Suddenly it felt like a slab of radioactive waste strapped to his chest. He should have burned it, eaten it, tossed it away. It just hadn't occurred to him. If Frechette decided to find and take the letter, Grimes doubted there was much he could do to stop him. A yard in front of him Frechette turned left into a second corridor. Grimes followed, then with a burst of elation thought: Why not? Just hand the letter over, free of all charges, liens or conditions, and let Miss Magdalena Parillaud do whatever she would with the information. Then he could forget the whole damn thing and go back to his want-free life.

As quickly as his spirits had risen, they collapsed. He was already contaminated by what he'd been given. He was doomed to be the keeper of the forbidden truths. The only person he could count on to sustain the secret was himself. If Parillaud used Jefferson's hoard to make some unsavory people unhappy, they might decide to take it out on Grimes. He'd always be waiting for another knock on the door. And there was the girl, Ella. *Look after her, Grimes.* He couldn't dump the girl in this too. If he couldn't be his sister's keeper, he could at least not be her executioner. His mind stepped back to the solid ground of his original strategy.

Trust no one. Know nothing.

Frechette stopped and knocked on a heavy door.

"Come in," said a woman's voice.

Frechette opened the door, held out his arm to usher Grimes in.

Be cool, Grimes told himself, and went inside.

The room was large and well proportioned, lined and shelved by dark, lustrous hardwoods. Light from concealed sources illuminated the corners of the ceiling. It was furnished with a gloomy antique elegance as a study, or a library. A woman stepped out from behind a desk topped with green leather and walked across the room toward him.

She had blond hair, shoulder-length and wavy; the color may have come from a bottle, Grimes could never tell. On first impression she appeared slight in build, with an almost-shyness in her body language that had to be contrived given her circumstances; or maybe not. People often felt guarded with doctors, especially shrinks. They sometimes had the fantasy, hilarious to Grimes, that psychiatrists were mind readers with the power to penetrate their deepest secrets at a glance. She had a heart-shaped face, unnaturally pale, and a sullen mouth painted with dark red lipstick. The light in the room wasn't bright enough for him to make out the color of her eyes: as they stared straight into his own as she came across the floor, they appeared quite black, with a shifting light at their center as melancholy as the moon on empty water.

Grimes guessed her age at mid-thirties but it was hard to be sure; she could have been an old thirty or a young forty. She had a quality of frozen youth about her, as if something in her had been prevented from growing up the way it should have. Grimes had observed a similar quality in young old-soldiers, and in a patrolman he'd once treated, who'd been drenched with the brains of his sergeant when they'd pulled up outside the wrong convenience store at the wrong time. The killer had escaped without the shock-paralyzed youngster even calling base for help—a professional failure the shame of which would haunt him forever. It was strange that Grimes should suddenly recall that particular case and for a moment he wondered why, then returned to the present.

Whatever Parillaud's age she was a fine figure of a woman; not his type, but fine. She wore an ocean-blue dress, calf-length, with a high neckline and long sleeves, smooth contours. It was made of an iridescent material, some kind of silk maybe, and looked very old. Grimes liked it. Somewhat to his disappointment he liked her too, and immediately. Liking people invariably made life more difficult. As she got closer he saw that the wide black pupils were surrounded by a rim of green iris. She held out her hand.

"Lenna Parillaud," she said.

"Eugene Grimes."

"Thank you for coming, Doctor. I appreciate it."

Up close he saw she was much less slight than he'd thought, her body fuller and more densely packed. Her hand was larger and stronger than he'd expected too. The fragility he'd sensed wasn't in her body then, but in the eyes, in the moon on empty water.

"Would you like to talk here or in the sitting room?" she said.

He liked her voice too. It was soft and pitched low, but with a strand of barbed wire wound through it that he could imagine snapping taut if she ever decided to say "Fuck you."

Grimes said. "Whichever suits you, Miss Parillaud."

She tossed her eyes around the room, frowned.

"I've been stuck in here for hours. Let's move."

"Fine."

She opened the door and they went into the corridor.

"You can call me Lenna if you want, Doctor," she said.

Grimes could have said "Call me Gene," but he didn't. He wanted to keep a formal distance; and as it happened he liked the way she said *Doctor*. She gave the sound a sexual undertow; or so his company-starved brain imagined. They walked back down the corridor, almost side by side but she half a pace ahead, her heels clicking on the marble tiles. She looked at one of the paintings in passing then threw her chin back over one shoulder, glancing up at him across the blue shimmer of her dress.

"Do you like beautiful things, Doctor?"

The word *beautiful,* as she said it, was clogged with boredom. Or indifference.

Grimes said, "The things I find beautiful, I like. Doesn't beauty define itself?"

"I want to know your definition," she said.

"I don't have the brains to invent one but I can steal someone else's. The one I like best is 'aptness to purpose.' "

She thought about it. "I like that too." She shrugged, looked away. "By that score this place doesn't make the grade."

For reasons unknown to the part of his mind that he remained in control of, Grimes said, *"Et in Arcadia ego."*

Lenna stopped with her fingers on the gilt handles of a double set of doors. She looked at him again.

"What's that? Virgil?"

She said it casually, as if to show that she could flash a big-balls education too, and Grimes cursed himself. He'd never read Virgil in his life, and certainly not in Latin, but he'd asked for it.

"As far as I know," he said, "it's the inscription on an anonymous gravestone, I don't know, someplace in Europe. But I could be mistaken."

"A gravestone?"

She smiled and for a moment the sullen melancholy of her face was almost banished.

"You're funny," she said.

"Then excuse me," said Grimes. "I don't mean to be."

"It's okay for a doctor to be funny. In fact it's good."

Grimes had no answer for that one. Lenna flung the doors open and they entered one of the rooms he'd seen from the road: high ceiling, a flickering crystal chandelier supplemented by discreetly placed lamps. The room was furnished and decorated in the same late-nineteenth-century style as the rest of what he'd seen of the house. It was immaculately laid out but it didn't feel as if anyone lived here; it was a room that hadn't been animated with laughter or conversation in years. It had the feel of a stopover on a package tour of the historic South, or of standing in an antique dealer's window. Grimes decided it wasn't his problem.

"Sit down," said Lenna.

Grimes glanced at the sofa, then chose an armchair, not too low, not too soft. Lenna Parillaud remained standing.

"A drink?" she asked.

"Nothing, thanks," said Grimes. "What can I do for you?"

Lenna turned and paced two slow steps away from him, the palms of her hands pressed against each other.

"What do you want most from life, Dr. Grimes?"

Grimes wished he could smoke. There was a jade ashtray on a small table by his chair but he wanted to preserve all the professional poise he could muster, or at least the illusion thereof. It was his best defense: an armor plate with a compassionate surface constructed, of necessity, through his years of confrontation with madness and pain.

"That's hardly what I drove out here to talk about," he said.

Her hair bobbed as she nodded. She turned her head slightly, offering a pale and oblique profile from which she couldn't see him. In the candlelight the gesture was deliberately theatrical, but effective: she looked genuinely haunted and drawn. Her lashes fluttered as she dropped her eyes.

She said, "It must be hard for you to believe that I could want for anything."

"That's not so," he said.

She held the profile. "Really?"

In the way she stretched the word—mournful and slow—there was a muted desperation to be heard. The desperation hammered on the door of Grimes's better instincts. He stomped them down. *Tell her to cut to the chase so you can issue your denials and leave.* Grimes felt caught between his formal role as a psychiatrist and his undercover status as a hapless loser hoping not to get his balls cut off by swine.

"Yes, really," he said to her back.

Lenna turned her eyes on him, full, frank, momentarily shocking. Her words shocked him considerably more.

"Clarence said you weren't a man to be pushed around."

Grimes was grateful he was already sitting down. *Clarence?* What the fuck had that cocksucker told her? And how? And who else had been given Grimes's name besides her and Atwater? It was like it had been announced on the radio.

"I'm sorry, Miss Parillaud," he said. "Who?"

His voice sounded more convincing than he'd dared hope, but the easy—almost contemptuous—familiarity with which she'd said *Clarence* disturbed him. He concentrated on not being the one to break eye contact.

"Clarence Jefferson," she said.

"I'm afraid I've never heard of the man."

He managed to hold her gaze without blinking. A slight pursing of her lips. Lenna flopped her head back and stared at the ceiling, debating. She closed her eyes.

"Why, should I know him?" said Grimes.

"I don't know if you should or not," she said. "That's the trouble."

She opened her eyes again. She walked to an armchair matching the one Grimes sat in and pulled it over so that it faced him at an angle from an arm's length away. She sat down, leaned her elbows on her knees and looked at the floor. She let out a long, quiet breath. As something of an expert in the field himself Grimes recognized the sigh of someone close to despair.

"Doctor," she said. "The only person I trust is Bobby Frechette. I would like to trust you. The rest of the world, I don't need to."

"Anything you might say to me is confidential," said Grimes.

"That's not what I mean. Fuck."

Lenna slammed the palms of both hands on the armrests of the chair. A flash of tantrum. Grimes took it in his stride. She hadn't looked at him since she sat down; she didn't still.

"Excuse me, Dr. Grimes. I'm having the second-worst day of my life."

Grimes-the-psychiatrist was intrigued by what might be the first-worst day; the other Grimes, the one who wanted a quiet life, didn't want to know.

"Just say what you need to," he said. "If I can't handle it, I'll let you know."

Lenna rested her elbows back on her knees, grabbed two fistfuls of hair from which she suspended her head and spoke into the space between her forearms.

"If you're lying to me about Clarence—and, shit, I can't tell—and I threaten you, you'll clam up. If Clarence has lied to me about *you*—and he lied to me for decades, except when it hurt me more not to—then I'm making a fool of myself—which is fine—and maybe endangering you in the process—which isn't."

"Don't worry about me," said Grimes, stoutly.

He realized he was beginning to dislike himself.

Lenna said. "Either way, unless you do know what I'm talking about and you do help me, I'm fucked, Doctor. I'm completely fucked."

By the minute Grimes was more convinced that whatever was the detail of her hidden agenda, it was personal, painful and intense; not political, not money, not "the anvil of justice." He stamped a cold heel on the throat of his rising sympathy. *Trust no one. Be professional. Neutral and calm. Just keep lying.*

"If I knew what this was about," he said, "I'd try my best to advise you, but I don't."

He felt like a rank scumbag.

Silence. Her face was hidden by her arms and the shadows they cast.

"Without making any assumptions you might find offensive," said Grimes, "I should tell you that it's no secret I have a special interest in drug addiction. Maybe your Mr. Jefferson was aware of that and was trying to recommend me."

"Captain Jefferson, not Mister. He was a policeman. In vice. Clarence was the king of vice, anointed and crowned by his own hand."

"It's possible," said Grimes, then hesitated.

He saw Lenna's shoulders tense. He shouldn't give her any threads to pull on; but it was a deception too clever to resist.

"It's possible, if vice was Jefferson's business, that he came to me at some point under an alias. You'll appreciate that in my line of work that's not unknown. A police officer, more than most, might want to protect his identity if he had a problem."

Trust me, I'm a doctor, Grimes thought as he lied. He played his card.

"So tell me, what does this man Jefferson look like?"

No image, human or otherwise, was so readily and forever available to his mind's eye than the face and form—the very breath and brash aroma—of the fatman: Clarence Seymour Jefferson. As Grimes congratulated himself on his cunning use of the present tense, the mounting dislike he felt for what he was doing became a full-blown contempt for his own guts.

Lenna kept her gaze on the floor and so did not see whatever was inscribed on Grimes's face. She took a gulp of air to steady herself. Her voice shook, fluctuating between anger and disgust.

"What he looks like now, I wouldn't like to know. Or maybe I would. He's been missing, presumed dead, for six months."

Grimes knew it for a fact and didn't have to presume anything. He'd run a sixteen-inch Bowie knife into Jefferson's belly and left the body to burn in a swamp-country cabin on the banks of a bayou a hundred and thirty miles to the west. He didn't speak.

Lenna pushed herself on. "If you'd ever met him you wouldn't forget him."

Grimes blinked, again relieved that she wasn't looking at his face.

"Big man. Fat man. Strong man."

Her words came out in short blurts, as if she couldn't trust herself with more than two at a time. Within their larger sound, of anger and disgust, hummed the threnody of an awful tenderness. Grimes was able to hear the hum because in a dreadful portion of his own heart he, too, knew that same tenderness: awful because it was hated and shunned, dreadful because the very fact of its existence was beyond his comprehension; for the object of that tenderness was Clarence Jefferson.

"I'm sorry," said Lenna. She took more air.

"You're doing fine."

"Yeah. So. Clarence was around Bobby's height and twice his weight. White guy, fifty years old. Yellow, wavy hair. Lips like Cupid's bow, smiled a lot, with a honeycomb voice. His eyes were . . ."

She stopped, and Grimes was glad.

"Anyway, you would remember him," she finished.

"I guess I would," said Grimes. "I don't."

Grimes waited.

Behind her arms Lenna nodded, slowly.

"Forgive me, Doctor. I've wasted your time."

Grimes almost let out a breath. His stratagem appeared to have worked but it had to be followed through to completion. Much as he didn't want to, realism demanded that he express the natural curiosity of an innocent, and ignorant, man.

"My time's no problem," he said. "But I must ask you: if this man's been dead six months, how did he communicate the idea that I might be able to help you?"

Another silence.

"You're not obliged to answer," said Grimes, hoping that she wouldn't. "It's just that for me this has all been a little bizarre."

Lenna let go of her hair and dropped her arms. She raised her head and looked at him. Her eyes were dry now, but he saw that damp tracks marked the powder on her face.

"You think I'm crazy," she said. "I mean insane, paranoid delusions . . ."

"No."

"I wouldn't blame you. You must have heard this kind of crazy stuff a million times."

Again, the desperation to be heard, this time barely muted at all.

"You're distressed but you're not insane."

A pause. Then the psychiatrist in Grimes spoke out uncensored, and maybe other pieces of himself as well.

He said, "It's always hard to lose someone you're close to."

It was a dangerous slip. He watched Lenna's eyes rove over his face and wondered what was written there for her to read. Maybe, he thought, some ghost of the months—those same six months that Jefferson had been dead—that he'd spent upon the floor wishing he were not alive. Of what was the ghost he saw in hers? Had Lenna loved Jefferson? Of the psychosis of love Grimes could believe anything. Did he care who she loved? No. Not really. He just hoped he hadn't given her the thread that would unravel him.

Lenna twisted in the chair and reached into the sleeve of her iridescent dress and pulled out a folded piece of paper. She brushed a strand of hair from her eye, braced herself and unfolded it.

So: Jefferson had written her a letter, too. To be delivered on the same day.

Lenna glanced at Grimes. "This is from him."

She scanned the letter. It clearly caused her pain. It was clear too that she didn't intend to read the whole text and Grimes was glad. He already knew more than he wanted to. Lenna's eyes paused as she found the passage she wanted.

" 'Down there in the City,' " she read, " 'you'll find a man—a doctor—called Eugene Grimes. He, and he alone, can tell you all you need to know. But Lenna: don't push him. That boy just won't be pushed, believe me. So ask him to help you. And if he will not tell you, then ask him this: Is he yet the man he knows he is meant to be? Or is he, merely, the man he's too scared not to be? Put that to him, Lenna, then . . .' "

Lenna broke off suddenly and closed the letter into her lap.

Grimes did not ask her to go on. His stratagem lay like ashes in his mouth. He tried to quell a wave of rage at another elaborate ploy by that fat bastard to goad him into doing his bidding, to make him trade his fucking suitcases of porn pics and proof for an early and unmarked grave. Fuck him. Fuck the people. They wanted a cleaner world let them raise their voices and get it done. Then let them pay the bill. He owed nothing to no man. He had already given and he had already paid. He felt his fists clench; he loosened them. Use the anger, he thought, it'll look real. Professional anger.

"I'd have to say that whoever it was who wrote that letter is the person most likely to qualify for a straitjacket," he said. "As you said, I've come across that stuff before."

A strange calmness had come over Lenna Parillaud. Grimes wondered what else was contained in the sentence she hadn't finished: "put that to him, Lenna, then . . ." Grimes didn't dare ask. Lenna folded the paper and returned it to her sleeve. She seemed to have made some decision that required her to hold herself in.

"You came in your own car?" she asked.

"Yes."

It was over. Lenna Parillaud wiped her face and stood up. Grimes stood up too.

"It was good to meet you," said Grimes.

"You too."

"I'm sorry I couldn't be of more help. It seems you're the victim of a malicious game."

Lenna Parillaud looked at him. "If you knew how long it was since anyone had seen me cry, Dr. Grimes, you might have some small idea of exactly how malicious." There was less pupil to her eyes now, more green. "But I knew Clarence Jefferson, and you did not. He was a man capable of anything. And you're right: he liked games."

Grimes had had his fill of this place and more than his fill of the nausea induced by his own performance. He had not known it had lain within him to lie with such an expert, and total, lack of integrity, and he had used—he had *disgraced*—his profession in order to do so. He'd done it for his father? George had not asked him to do such a thing; George would have died screaming first.

The man he was too scared not to be.

The rage came upon him again, fighting down his shame. Fuck them. Suddenly the world and its brother were taking it upon themselves to tell him how to live his life. The fatman had been right about that much: from Grimes's earliest childhood recollections, being pushed triggered in him an almost psychopathic contrariness. He'd be pushed no more. It was time to go. He'd smiled sympathetically and lied softly for long enough. He glanced over at the double doors.

Lenna caught the glance. She walked over, the blue dress whispering about her body, and pulled the doors open. Grimes joined her on the threshold. Three paces down the corridor, hands folded calmly before his thighs, stood Bobby Frechette.

"Bobby will see you to your car," said Lenna Parillaud. "You'll send me your bill?"

"My what?" said Grimes.

He thought: another slip-up. The neutral professional he was supposed to be impersonating would have smiled graciously, rapidly calculated the biggest hourly rate he'd ever charged, and trebled it. But Grimes was past giving a shit.

"Your bill. For your time, Doctor."

"Sure," he said. "If you should want to talk again, call me."

This was insincere. If she was aware of it, he didn't care. He knew this mood now upon him. The mood said simply: Leave me alone or, one way or another, I will hurt you. Grimes didn't enjoy the mood but it did at least vanquish all anxiety. He glanced into the corridor. Even Bobby Frechette no longer looked like such a handy customer. Frechette sensed the violence in Grimes—as Grimes would have sensed it in him—and tensed, almost imperceptibly. Grimes stared at the bridge of Frechette's scimitar nose. Let him try to take the fucking letter from his pocket. Grimes had had calluses on his knuckles too, in his time. At that moment physical combat—win or lose and no holds barred—would have been a grim pleasure. *For Chrissakes, Grimes, just go.*

Grimes turned back to Lenna.

"Goodbye, Miss Parillaud."

He held out his hand and she took it.

To his surprise, she smiled. "You never called me Lenna like I asked you to."

The smile didn't make him feel any less sour. "No," he said. "I guess I didn't."

"Goodbye, Doctor."

Grimes nodded and walked out down the hall. As Grimes approached, Bobby Frechette relaxed and swiveled and led off in front. Grimes put a lid on his thoughts and contented himself with scowling silently at the big-deal paintings on the wall until they reached the main entrance hall. Frechette opened the door for him.

"Good night, Dr. Grimes," said Frechette.

Grimes looked at him and Frechette nodded. Frechette was a good man. The violence Grimes had felt a moment before now shamed him. He added it to the pile. He nodded back.

"Good night, Mr. Frechette."

Grimes stepped out over the threshold.

"Dr. Grimes?"

Grimes looked back into Frechette's eyes. There was something living inside them, too, that was ten thousand years old.

Frechette said, "In your shoes I wouldn't trust her either. But she means you no ill. You have *my* word on that. If you were able to help her—in any way—I'd be in your debt."

Grimes saw in Frechette's face how profound was his concern for Lenna Parillaud. And Grimes knew that he was being offered something that couldn't be bought, even here: a total loyalty.

"The best advice she could take is to sell this mausoleum and get a new life."

"I could tell her that myself," said Frechette.

"Why don't you?"

Frechette didn't answer.

Grimes said, "Do you know what's going on? What this is all about?"

Frechette shook his head. "There's a lot that Lenna keeps to herself. That doesn't mean she isn't true. She is true."

On instinct Grimes asked, "What did she do for you?"

Frechette's eyes narrowed as he debated how much he was entitled to give away. All he said was, "I was on death row. Lenna gave me her hand when no one else would."

Grimes didn't doubt that Frechette was a killer; but he did wonder if he'd been guilty of murder or not. Looking at the narrowed eyes it was impossible to tell.

Frechette said, "Without her I am *ronin*."

Grimes understood, as Frechette had somehow known he would. *Ronin* meant a masterless samurai: a warrior of supreme purpose who had lost his purpose for living.

Frechette said, *"You* are *ronin."*

Grimes said, "That isn't an honor I deserve."

Frechette said, "I believe otherwise, but only you can know it."

Under Frechette's steady gaze, and the lash of his own shame, Grimes's resolve suddenly collapsed. If Lenna was basically decent— and he believed she was—and if Jefferson had wanted her to know the score—which it seemed he did from his letter to her—then who was Grimes to stand in their way? He reached into his jacket for the letter Jefferson had sent him. His hand dipped into his pocket and stopped there.

The letter had gone.

His fingers felt the thin oblong card of the airline ticket; but no envelope.

Conscious of Frechette, Grimes suppressed his inclination to scrabble through his other pockets. He knew the letter had been there and now it wasn't. Only his father had known it existed. The man who had called him a sneaking bastard to his face had shortly thereafter stolen the letter from his jacket while he pissed: George Grimes, with his Pacific War sidearms, and his work of noble note.

Cicero Grimes cursed his paternity, cursed God and cursed his day.

Then an image blipped across his mind, of the blue tip of a cutting torch flame licking his father's eyeballs while faceless men laughed. Grimes felt a fear so intense he wanted to vomit. His mind cleared. He saw Frechette looking at him curiously. Grimes pulled his empty hand from his pocket.

"I have to go," said Grimes.

Frechette blinked. He had failed.

Grimes didn't see the use of explaining. He walked down to his car and turned the engine. There was no point wasting time to see if George was still home eating milk and cookies. Grimes had to find the girl before George did. The girl, Ella. *She's nineteen years old.* Jesus Christ. Ella. That was all he could recall. He ground savagely through the gears. He scowled all the way down the drive from Arcadia and into the vale of live oaks growing. *Her last name. Her address. Her last name. Her address.* Grimes kept scowling until the wrought-iron gates in the high red-brick wall were humming closed on his dust. He couldn't remember.

Grimes stamped on the gas and the Olds 88 screamed through the night between ghostly fields of marsh grass, swirling in a Dionysiac celebration of the freshening wind. He would remember. By the time he reached the City, he'd remember. He had to. Then maybe he would kill his goddamn father himself.

SIX

T HE RHYTHM FACTORY was driving its clientele to work full capacity on drinking, sweating, and letting the good times roll. As her face dipped in and out of the full glare of the lights Ella caught glimpses of their faces grooving on the sounds, funky and hot. It was her dancing they liked, she knew, more than her voice. For her it was the other way around; it was the voice that counted most. It was the voice that carried her ambitions and dreams. But if the audience dug her snaky limbs and the way she shook that thing, that was all right by her, at least for the time being. She could dance the way she did without effort—it would have been an effort not to—so she could spend all her concentration on her phrasing, on opening up the power channels to her diaphragm and the resonating spaces in the hollows of her skull, and on not ripping her throat apart. The voice would take years, she knew, and she was wise enough to be patient. She had the time: she was nineteen years old. Dancing gave her a platform from which to perform that maybe other, better, singers deserved; but in time the voice would come, and when it did she'd be prepared. She'd already be a veteran, a semi-pro. She'd be cool. *Shit, girl, you're already cool. They love you.* She closed her eyes and arched her head back in the hot blue dazzle of the lights and let her arms twist and float up on a surging wave of down and dirty funk—*mmm, who's playing that fatback?*—and they whistled and cheered and she knew they loved her. The band at her back caught the energy and moved up—always like magic to her—another invisible gear. Her fingertips, glossy red, came together high above her head and she swayed like a flame, held it longer than she had any right to, and the band, teetering, held it with her, then she fell, flaring her eyes and nostrils, lunging her head and shoulders and tits at the mike as she hit the final chorus and soared.

The band stopped abruptly, perfectly, and she stared down on the raucous applause without smiling. She never smiled onstage. Maybe later, when she was who she intended to be, she'd smile, but for now they could look up into her face and check her lips and think, Man, who the fuck is *she*? She was too young to smile and still stay sexy. A sexy smile came with age, Charlie said. Smile now and you'll look like a little girl looking for approval; but give them a fuck-you sneer, you'll make their dicks go hard and when they go home after the show to fuck their girlfriends, they'll be thinking of you when they come. Next week they'll be back for more. That had been Charlie's theory. She'd found it hard to believe, maybe even a little creepy, but it worked. Every Friday night at the Rhythm Factory they came and clapped and licked their lips at the gold ring through her navel and the way her nipples showed through whatever it was she was wearing. The Factory was small and no one much outside the neighborhood came here, but it was her neighborhood. She shared an apartment with two college friends three blocks down the street. She turned her back on the whoops and cheers and winked at Sammy, on bass. Sammy grinned and went to the mike stand.

"Ella MacDaniels," he growled. "Ella MacDaniels! Let's hear it, people."

Ella turned back to the audience. The club was in a dingy basement, with air-conditioning that hadn't worked right since 1979. At the back of the crowd along the far wall was a wide bar with shelves of bottles winking beneath blue bulbs. Standing, not leaning, by the bar was a man in a dark suit and tie. Ella had glimpsed him a couple of times during the set. He stood out not because of his clothes, though the suit wasn't sharp, but because he was old and white. Old brothers showed up often enough, to keep an ear on the scene and recall how much hotter it had been in their day, but white men never. And the old guy seemed to be looking straight at her. Then, so were eighty or ninety other people. Ella opened her arms wide and bowed low. Long cords of tightly braided hair fell to either side of her face. She threw them back over her shoulders as she straightened up and stood there, long and lean.

"That's all from us tonight," said Sammy, "but you got *any* sense at all in them heads of yours you'll hang in and sizzle some more with our friends from old Habana by way of Miami: Ernesto Ruiz y Los Halcones de la Medianoche! Ernesto Ruiz and The Nighthawks! Okay, let's hear it one more time for Ella MacDaniels!"

The band laid down an outro and Ella bowed once more and walked off backstage. She went straight to the tiny private bathroom by the manager's office and threw the bolt. After a show she liked a moment to herself, to enjoy the excitement, the glow of having been enjoyed. It was another thing Charlie had taught her: always take something for yourself, inside. Make it yours. Hold on to it for the times when things are bad and you can't remember what it's all about; for those times will come. Charlie had a way of saying things so that you didn't forget them. She missed him. He hadn't been there tonight, again. For the first year she'd played here he'd hardly missed a date, standing at the bar where the old man had stood tonight, in wraparound shades and slicked-back hair. Sometimes one of the more dubious customers had given him a strange look and Charlie had spoken to him, smiling and soft, and whoever it was would never show up again. She'd never been told why and on instinct she'd never asked. Now Charlie didn't show up either, hadn't in months, and she no longer expected him. The same instinct had warned her many times—ever since she was a child—that one day Charlie might just disappear from her life. Now that he had, she missed him. In fact she missed him bad. For no good reason in the world she felt less safe without him around.

Ella ran the cold water tap and splashed her face. The café-au-lait skin of her body, most of which was visible through the slashes in her outfit, was beaded with sweat. She cranked a yard of rough paper from the towel dispenser and wiped her face and arms. She didn't wear makeup; didn't need it. Just the ragged red dress, the ring through her navel and the diamond stud in her nose. Her features were fine-boned, delicate but strong, except for her nose, which was broad; in her heart of hearts broader than she would've liked. Reading magazines, she'd occasionally had forbidden fantasies of getting a job on it, raise and narrow the bridge just a little. But that was bullshit. She'd gotten the piercing instead and that she did like. She heard a clunking against the door. She crammed the damp paper into an overflowing trash can and stepped out into the corridor.

Ernesto and his Halcones were crowding and chattering their way between the narrow black walls of the corridor toward the stage, their arms loaded with instruments. She felt Sammy squeeze her shoulders from behind.

"You were smokin' tonight."

She smiled and he kissed her on the cheek. Sammy had four kids and ran a tow-truck service, but in his time had played with Mac Rebennack and been a session man for Allen Toussaint. He sneaked past her into the bathroom for his Friday-night line, his one reminder of more carefree days. Apart from a little spliff, Ella didn't do drugs. There'd been a doorman here one time with the hots for her, had pestered her repeatedly to try some coke as part of his pick-up jive. She'd told Charlie about him. Next time she'd seen the guy his arm was in a cast and he'd crossed the street to avoid her. She made her way toward the dressing room. There she'd smoke a Camel Light, drink a liter of Evian and get changed before heading back to the floor to catch Ernesto and, if he was as good as she expected, maybe dance some more. As she reached the dressing-room door she looked above the bobbing heads of the Latinos and saw the old man from the bar.

He looked flushed and bewildered, the muscles in his withered neck stretched with tension. This wasn't his scene, she could tell, and her heart went out to him a little. The old man caught her eyes. He called out to her over the chaos.

"Miss MacDaniels?"

Ella blinked. He was a total stranger to her and he didn't belong here, yet there was no threat in him that she could identify. She found herself nodding.

The old guy struggled along the wall, holding his buttoned jacket together as he scraped by. She waited for him. He stopped before her and unconsciously straightened his tie. That touched her too. His eyes were gray and honest beneath thick brows a darker gray than his hair. He smiled uncertainly.

"I'm George Grimes. Could I speak with you a moment?"

Ella couldn't work out what he was doing here. Was he from another club? He looked too out of place. An agent? No. He wasn't smooth enough.

"What's it about?" she said.

George Grimes lowered his voice a tone. "Charlie sent me."

Ella's gut clenched. She'd never met any of Charlie's friends; for her his life had been a closed book.

She said: "I need to change. Will you wait?"

"Sure," said George. "Right here?"

"If you can stand it."

"Oh, I reckon I've survived worse."

He smiled again, more easily, and this time Ella smiled back.

"Five minutes," she said, and pushed open the door to the dressing room.

The room was dingy and cramped and heaped with a dozen other people's junk. From amid it she pulled out a blue nylon backpack and dumped it on the table in front of a mirror smudged with phone numbers written in lipstick. From inside the bag she pulled out a pair of black lace-up work boots with Doc Martens soles, a black Lycra halterneck top that ended just below her rib cage and some matching leggings. Her jacket was in there too, but it was too hot in here to wear it. She peeled her dress off over her head, rolled it into a cylinder and shoved it into the bag. She put one hand on the table for balance and, with relief, tugged off her heels and bagged them. As she dressed she wondered what Charlie wanted and why he'd sent George Grimes instead of coming himself. Was Charlie okay? She raced the lacing of her boots, straightened up. She opened the door.

The corridor was quieter now. George, standing almost to attention, turned toward her. Behind him Sammy emerged from the bathroom. Sammy sniffed and tugged at his nose. He saw George and frowned.

"Ever'thin' okay, baby?" said Sammy.

George turned his head. Ella smiled and nodded.

"Everything's fine, Sam. I'll see you on the floor."

Sammy shrugged and ambled off. She jerked her head at George to invite him in.

"It's a dump but it's quiet."

George came in and she closed the door. There was one broken exswivel chair at the dressing table.

"Sit down," she said.

"Obliged."

George nodded and tested the chair with his hand before sitting. Ella pulled her bottle of water from her bag and broke the seal on the cap. She held the bottle toward George.

"It's warm but—do you want some?"

"No, thank you, Miss," said George. "You go ahead."

He waited while Ella swallowed a good half-pint. She suddenly wondered if it was unladylike and lowered the bottle. Funny, being ladylike wasn't something she often worried about. It's his age, she told herself, and he's a gentleman. He was even being careful not to look at her body, though she could tell he was inclined to.

"You know Charlie, then?" she said.

George shook his head. "Not personally," he said.

He paused and seemed to search for a way of saying what he had to say.

"This is what you might call a weird situation, Miss MacDaniels. I don't know how else but to come straight out with it."

Ella felt her insides roll over again. "Go ahead."

"Well, it seems like the man you know as Charlie is dead."

For a moment she didn't feel anything, then suddenly George was up and helping her to sit in the chair.

"Take some more water, Miss. Make you feel better."

Ella took another drink. She put the bottle down on the table and found her cigarettes in her bag. She lit one. Her mind was racing with thoughts too fast to hang on to. One of them blurted out.

"Are you a cop?" she said.

George shook his head. "No, Miss, not me, but Charlie was. His real name was Clarence Jefferson."

The name meant nothing to her. She suddenly understood better why Charlie had never spoken about himself. Her chest started shuddering and she knew she was about to cry.

"I'm sorry, Miss," said George.

Ella tried to stop the tears falling down her face but couldn't. She couldn't think either. It was as if she didn't know where the tears were coming from or why.

"Here."

George handed her a clean white handkerchief and she took it and wiped her face.

"I'm sorry," she mumbled.

"I'm sorry too," he said.

She looked at him and in his lined face saw genuine sorrow for her pain. In herself she was shocked. She hadn't known that Charlie meant this much to her.

"I know you need time to deal with this," said George, "but I don't know that we got it right now."

The tears dried up as the anxiety in his voice overshadowed his concern. She lowered the handkerchief.

"What do you mean?"

George looked away from her for a moment, then back.

"I don't mean to scare you, and I hope I'm wrong, but you may be in some danger."

Ella couldn't think of anything to say.

"Jefferson, that is Charlie, said to ask you to take me to the Old Place."

"The Old Place," she said.

For some reason, and amid everything else, she felt stupid for the way she said it.

"Yes. That mean anything to you?"

She nodded. Since she was twelve years old Charlie had taken her to the Old Place half a dozen times for vacations. The last time he'd asked her to go, she hadn't gone because she'd been dating Terrence, and for some reason Charlie hadn't wanted him to come along. Charlie had given her some cash and she and Terrence had gone to Jamaica instead. Charlie and her had only ever been to the Old Place alone. It was far away.

"It's in Georgia," she said.

Confusion descended on her like a blanket. She didn't know this old guy from Adam and here he was asking her to take him to Georgia. She needed to talk to someone. Sammy maybe, or one of the girls at the apartment. They'd just say the same thing she'd say to them: get rid of the old guy and call the cops. The old guy read the fear on her face.

"I know this must seem totally crazy, and scary too," he said. "It is scary. There's nothing I can tell you or show you to make you trust me. I could be anyone and I have no legal authority. But you're in something you haven't got much choice about. Charlie told us not to trust the cops or anyone else."

"How did he tell you all this?" she said.

"He sent a letter."

"Can I read it?"

"We ought to get moving."

She couldn't believe this guy. Her street head started to wake up.

"Moving where?" she said.

"The Old Place."

"Are you kidding? It must be nearly midnight."

By his sides, George Grimes clenched and unclenched his fists. It wasn't an aggressive gesture, more a nervous one. The old man looked frightened too.

"I'm not trying to scare you," he said, "but if we wait till morning I don't know we'll still have the option."

Ella stood up. "I need to talk to Sammy," she said.

"Don't, please." The urgency in his voice was reflected in his eyes. "The more people we pull into this thing the worse our chances. Theirs too."

"What thing? I don't know what you're talking about."

Ella could feel the tears coming back and she fought them. She'd come off the stage feeling strong, on top of everything she knew. She'd felt all woman with, if not the world at her feet, then at least a little piece of it. Now she felt scared, and a girl. Treat it like stage fright, she thought. To deal with that she always told herself: *The worst thing they can do is kill you:* to which she would answer: *Not true. They can boo you off the stage;* then: *In that case they can just go fuck themselves.* She took some deep breaths, something else she did before going on. She wrested back some control.

"Have you got Charlie's letter with you?" she said.

George Grimes had to think too long. By the time he nodded she knew he had it anyway.

"This is what we're going to do," she said. "There's a café across the street. We're going to go over there and have an espresso and I'm going to smoke another cigarette while I read the letter. Otherwise I'll have some of the guys come in here right now and take it off you."

The old guy looked at her and decided that she meant it, which was good because she did. Ella picked up her bag and slung it over her shoulder. She felt better. *Once you decide to do something, even something hard, you always feel better.* That was Charlie again. Or Jefferson. She didn't like it that she hadn't known his real name. It wasn't really like he'd lied to her, it was just, she didn't know what it was, she felt stranded. Or something. She looked at George Grimes again. Maybe that wasn't his real name either. Somehow she knew he was okay— crazy for sure, but she couldn't sense any malice in him. She stepped over to the door and he opened it for her.

"We'll take the back door," she said.

"Suits me, Miss," said George Grimes. "I had to go across that dance floor again I don't think I'd come out alive."

The back door was kept closed by a fire bar. Ella shoved it and the door swung open on a flight of wrought-iron steps running up from the basement to ground level. George followed her up the steps to a narrow garbage-strewn lot sandwiched between the backs of two old seven-story commercial properties. There wasn't much light, but thirty yards to their left the black slit of an even narrower alley could be seen, running at a right angle back toward the street out front. George looked up and down.

"This way," said Ella.

She led the way toward the alleyway. Maybe it was the walking and the sense of open sky above her but she felt clearer-headed. Half of what had happened in the dressing room was a blur in her head, mixed in with the stage lights and the pounding music and the crowd's applause. A double espresso at Carlo's, nice and quiet, and maybe she could work all this out.

They were twenty feet from the alleyway when a man emerged and looked at them and smiled.

Ella felt George's hand on her left arm, stopping her dead. The hand was firm and dry and reassuring. She could feel him standing close up, directly behind her. The guy up ahead was white and arrogant-looking. It was the smile, like he was Mr. Maximum Joe Cool, when in fact he was just a slob in a sweatshirt. He had the worst kind of damply curly beard that made him look even fatter than he was. Joe Cool lifted a hand-held radio to his mouth and said something.

She wasn't sure because of the traffic noise bouncing down the alley behind him, but she thought he said, "Chicken's in the pot."

Behind her she heard the old guy's breathing get faster. Suddenly she couldn't even remember his name.

In her ear she heard him say, "Don't turn around, Miss, if you can."

She almost turned there and then, but didn't. The hand disappeared from her arm. She missed it.

Joe Cool, still smiling, ambled toward them, shoving the radio into the pocket of his baggy off-white pants.

"Evenin', lovebirds," he said. "Where y'at?"

Ella's arms rippled with gooseflesh and she shivered. She didn't turn. She wanted to. She wanted to see the steady gray eyes and the heavy brows. George, she remembered now. George's eyes, the ones without malice. Joe Cool had rat eyes, bright and empty. They kept flicking between her crotch and her tits.

"Oh, Mama, do I like that dinky belly ring," he said.

"Whadda you want?" snapped George.

Ella almost jumped. The voice was steel-hard with don't-fuck-with-me attitude. She wondered if George had vanished and the voice belonged to someone else. She couldn't sense his presence anymore, but she didn't turn. Joe Cool stopped and put his hands on his hips and pushed his potbelly at them, all aren't-I-just-the-man-and-funny-to-boot.

"Oooh," he said. "Why, I wanna talk to you and your little lady, old-timer. No fuss, no mess, you just come along with me for a—"

"Let me see a badge," said George.

"A badge?" Joe Cool snorted in a short, ugly laugh. "Well, let me see what-all I got back here."

Joe Cool casually reached back under his sweatshirt, his eyes drawn back to the ring through her navel. As he started to pull his arm back out, Ella felt herself hurtle sideways across the alleyway. By the time her shoulder hit the dirty red-brick wall, Joe Cool was pirouetting into the garbage with blood-sprays coming out of him, back and front, and her ears finally registered the aftershock of two deafening cracks as they echoed and died between the buildings. There was a clatter as a silver revolver dropped from Joe Cool's hand. The back of his skull hit the pavement with a sound she'd rather not have heard. Ella turned her head.

The old man stood in a pale cloud of smoke aiming a funny, pointy-barreled gun at the body. He looked at her and raised his free index finger to his lips. Ella nodded. She didn't scream. She didn't feel like screaming, though she knew she was supposed to. The old man— George, George—flashed a glance back at the lumpen heap. Joe Cool wasn't moving. George turned back at her and made another gesture. He seemed to want her to get down. She nodded and went into a crouch against the wall. The bricks were clammy against the outside of her bare arm. George strode forward, his pistol never wavering from its target, and picked up Joe's revolver by the trigger guard. Next to the body was a plastic trash bag that Joe had burst open when he fell. George slipped the revolver inside the bag. Still ready to fire on the instant, he bent down, grabbed one of Joe's wrists and, with a strength that surprised her, hauled him across to lie by the same wall as Ella, ten feet closer to the black slit of the alley. Joe's belly wobbled, obscenely pale and bloody, from under his crumpled sweatshirt, but he made no sound. Ella discovered she felt nothing for him at all. *You're in shock.* All she could think of, with relief, was that at least the old man was on her side.

She watched George slide along the wall toward the alley. She awoke to the fact that Joe Cool must have spoken to someone else on that radio. She felt a flood of concern for George. He was near the alley mouth now, moving like an old cat. Just this side of the blackness he stopped and waited. Listening. Her ears had recovered after the shots. She tuned in. All she heard was the traffic noise, and some rhythmic thumping from inside the club. George suddenly turned to face her but didn't look at her. He crouched stiffly, then using one hand on the ground to steady himself he sat down, his legs pointing her way, and shuffled up close to what he thought was the right distance from the dark gap in the alley walls. What the fuck was he doing? George raised his right arm, the one nearest the wall, to full stretch and pointed his gun at the sky. Then again he waited, like that, for the longest seconds she'd ever counted. She wanted him to look at her but his eyes were resolutely fixed on some distant point far above and behind her head.

In a blink, George flopped backward from the waist. As his gun arm cleared the wall it snapped down into the gap, his face turning with it, and she heard three brief cracks, this time not so loud. On their heels came a muffled moan and clatter. George lay motionless, staring intently along his arm. Then slowly, the gun and his hand still invisible to her, he shuffled up onto his ass and clambered stiffly to his feet. Without a glance in her direction he disappeared into the gap. Ella crouched there alone for what was the longest wait so far. Another gunshot: Ella jumped and almost lost her balance. She stood up and looked back at the stairs to the club. Sammy. A telephone. Big guys who knew and liked her. Go for it.

"Miss MacDaniels, I'm coming out!" shouted George.

She almost ran anyway, but didn't. George reappeared with a second revolver dangling from his finger. He dropped it in the bag with the first and walked over to her, slipping his own gun into the rear waistband of his pants. He was just the way she needed him to be: cool as one of Sammy's bass runs and just as clear.

George said, "Go back to the club, right now, and forget any of this happened."

"What?"

"They must've followed me. I didn't mean to endanger you this way, I apologize for that, but if you go back now and say nothing to the cops, no one will be the wiser."

Ella found herself saying, "You can't do this."

"Yes I can. Just tell me where the Old Place is."

"I don't know the address. I just know the road there from Macon. It's near a town called Jordan's Crossroads."

George frowned. "I guess Jordan's Crossroads'll have to do. Please, Miss, go now. The shots may have been heard. No one will know you left your dressing room."

Ella, irrationally, was enraged.

"You just put me through the worst five minutes of my life, you old asshole. I'm coming with you."

And that was that and she saw that George Grimes, looking at her eyes, knew it.

"Miss," he said, "if we'd had more like you on Tarawa we'd have cleared the atoll in two days instead of three."

Ella had absolutely no idea what he was talking about, but it sounded like a compliment. George took her arm.

"Let's go."

Ella followed him into the alley. Twelve feet inside, a man in a sport coat lay huddled facedown in a gleaming black puddle. George nodded downward as he strode over him.

"This one kind of knew what he was doing. He just didn't expect I would too."

Ella's foot brushed the dead man's arms as she stepped over him. Again she felt nothing.

"Were they cops?" she said, hurrying to keep up with him.

"No. Cops would've shown a badge," said George over his shoulder. "I don't know who they are or who sent them."

They approached the end of the alley. Cars passed through her line of vision.

"We get out, we're turning right," said George. "My car's fifty yards down. Keep a coupla steps behind me."

And in a flash she was out on the street and blinking in a glare of lights and noise that seemed more dazzling than those in the club. After a few steps she realized that it was dazzlingly normal. The street was exactly as she would have expected it to be if nothing had happened. Her feet skimmed the sidewalk as if her boots had wings. She slowed, kept George a little ahead like he'd said. There weren't many people walking. The drivers that passed by didn't stare at anything except her ass, which was also dazzlingly normal. George stepped over to a battered sedan and opened the passenger door. As he walked around the hood she climbed in with her bag and slammed the door. It was all dreamlike and floaty, as if everything happened without her having to think about it. George got in behind the wheel and started the engine.

"You okay?" he said.

"Let's go," she said.

They pulled smoothly into the traffic.

"When we've made a few blocks, pull over at a phone booth," she said.

"What the hell for?" said George.

"I want to call Sammy at the club, to tell him I'm fine and that he's not to say anything about you or me to the cops when they show up."

George stared at her.

"We don't want Sammy thinking you've kidnapped me, do we? They'd have our descriptions then and we're kind of easy to spot, don't you think?"

"Jesus Christ," said George. He seemed impressed.

"Plus, Sammy's carrying a gram and he might want to get rid of it."

Suddenly, from nowhere, she started shaking from head to foot. A wave of nausea rolled up from her pelvis.

"Stop the car," she blurted, and grabbed the door handle.

George swung up to the curb, no dramatics, and stopped gently. Ella threw up into the gutter. She had nothing in her stomach, just a thin fluid. She felt George's hand on her back. She retched dryly once more and felt okay again. She pulled her head back in and slammed the door and as she settled back they were moving again.

"Nerves," said George. "Delayed reaction. Happened to me a whole bunch of times."

Ella looked in her bag for a cigarette. She wished she'd brought the water with them.

"You know," said George, "I didn't expect to enjoy traveling with you, Miss MacDaniels."

Ella lit the cigarette. It was good.

"If I'd had a chance to think about it, neither would I. I'd like you to call me Ella."

"Ella."

"Have I earned the right to read Charlie's letter yet?"

George grinned and shook his head. He reached into his jacket and pulled out an envelope.

"Jesus Christ," he said, in what sounded like wry admiration. "Jesus Christ."

Then he handed her the letter and she took it and held it in her lap. And before she opened it she wondered, to herself, how long it would take them to get to Georgia and if she'd ever again hear the crowd whooping it up at the Factory.

SEVEN

ICERO GRIMES made it back to the City without killing himself or anyone else and without getting arrested for pan-homicidal driving. He also managed to remember Ella MacDaniels's name and address. Fortified by these omens, he dared to hope that things might be looking up. On the edge of town he stopped at a gas station and called his father. As expected there was no reply. He drove on through light traffic. All he had to do was get his father under control. And the girl. He had time, he was sure: it seemed unlikely that Ella MacDaniels would go waltzing off with a stranger like George in the middle of the night. Maybe all three of them should go back to Arcadia and swap notes with Lenna Parillaud. Grimes had to admit he would feel safer with Bobby Frechette pitching for their team. Maybe Jefferson had made some deal with Lenna for her to look after his daughter. Why hadn't he told Grimes? There was no reading the Captain's mind. He was a riddler. As Grimes turned onto Willow he saw by a clock that it was getting on midnight.

He peered through the window to try to catch the street numbers as he passed. Up ahead his eye caught a ripple of winking lights, red and blue. A police patrol car was pulled up to the curb beside a milling group of spectators. The seven-story building rising behind the crowd looked to be industrial, not residential, and Grimes relaxed. It wasn't Ella MacDaniels's apartment then. As he drew closer he made out between the spectators a pair of legs splayed limply on the sidewalk and he cursed. It was probably a drunk passed out, or an epileptic, but it might be a cardiac arrest or a stabbing or something else he might be able to do something about. Grimes couldn't drive by a casualty without checking it out. He pulled over behind the patrol car and got out.

He peered over a shoulder and his heart sank: the guy had been shot. Grimes would lose valuable time.

"Please, folks! Give the guy some room!"

One of the cops was trying to keep the curious at bay. The other knelt beside the wounded man with a small white plastic case decorated with a red cross. The lid of the case was open and the second cop was sifting through it in an aimless panic. He looked as if he were searching for a cold beer. Grimes put his reluctance aside and shouldered his way forward. The first cop pointed at him with his nightstick.

"I'm not asking you to stand back, sir, I'm *telling you*."

Grimes looked at him and said, "I'm a doctor, Officer. Maybe I can help."

The second cop looked up at him from the sidewalk, almost grinning with relief as the responsibility for something he knew little about slipped from his shoulders. He was young and nervous.

"God bless you, Doc. Paramedics are on their way."

"What's your name, Officer?" asked Grimes.

Names relaxed people, made them more efficient. As the cop spoke Grimes got to work.

"Felton, Rod Felton," said the officer.

Grimes crouched by the wounded man and pressed his fingers into his groin. The femoral pulse was rapid and thready. The guy's blood-soaked shirt had been pulled up under his armpits to reveal two small puckered holes in his torso an inch above and below the right costal margin in the midclavicular line. Gut and liver. Bad news, the liver. Heavy internal bleeding, difficult to control. The man's chest heaved in fast, shallow pants. Plasma volume was the priority. As Grimes pulled the first-aid chest over he glanced at the guy's face. His head rolled from side to side, pillowed on a rolled-up jacket. Beneath a clammy lemon-gray sheen his bearded features were contorted and he murmured with pain. In the first-aid case Grimes found a bag of saline and a 16-gauge IV cannula needle. Gauge 18 would have been better. He handed a pair of scissors to Officer Felton.

"Rod, cut that shirt off for me, would you?" instructed Grimes. "I need to get to his neck."

"Sure thing, Doc."

While Felton hacked through the shirt, Grimes tore open the bag and inserted one end of a short tube, squeezed the saline through. The guy's veins were collapsed and he was in cardiovascular shock; Grimes didn't see a cut-down pack in the case. He would go for the subclavian. Felton pulled the bloody cloth clear of the guy's throat and shoulders.

"Good man," said Grimes. "Hand me this tube when I ask for it."

Grimes handed the drip bag and connecting tube to Felton, put the needle on the guy's chest and moved to position himself behind the guy's shoulder. As he did so he glimpsed a poster in a glass case on the wall nearby:

THE RHYTHM FACTORY
tonite:
from Miami!
ERNESTO RUIZ
and
THE NIGHTHAWKS

As Grimes's eyes swept by they were drawn back again by some subliminal recognition toward a second poster:

Every Friday:
ELLA MacDANIELS
and
CATDADDY

Beneath the title was a grainy reproduction of the head and shoulders of a young, unsmiling black woman with striking features. Grimes bit the inside of his lip.

Ella MacDaniels plus man shot down in street was an equation with only one answer: George Grimes.

Where was George? Where was the girl?

Later.

Grimes looked back down at the wounded man's heaving white thorax. His mind was totally clear, the information from the poster suspended for examination in an anxiety-free space. Medical action always did that for him: it cleared his mental field of all other concerns and coated his nerves with ice. To that extent it was paradoxically calming. He regretted that he was unable to attain this state in any other realm of his life. He lifted the guy's head and took the rolled jacket and pushed it lengthwise between his shoulder blades to enlarge the gap between collarbone and first rib. The guy looked at him with the muddy, panic-flecked eyes of the dying and Grimes knew then that he was one of the men from the Nova, and knew for sure that it was his father who'd shot him down.

"Anybody see what happened?" asked Grimes.

He picked up the needle and ripped it from its sterile package, his eyes and hands concentrating as he listened.

"He came staggering outa that alley there and collapsed in front of me," said a voice behind him. "I didn't hear a thing."

"There's another body back there," said Felton, "but he's dead as mackerel. Three in the body and one in the head. Last shot, muzzle to skin."

Grimes remembered the Japs on Tarawa. With his fingertip he found the spot he wanted: two centimeters lateral and inferior to the midpoint of the clavicle. The HIV risk briefly flitted across his mind; he banished it. He aimed the needle at the sternal notch and slid it in between the clavicle and the first rib. The guy was in too much pain to notice. The hub of the needle filled dark purple. Grimes went in a couple more millimeters, then held on to the needle and threaded the plastic cannula into the vein.

"I'll take that tube now, Rod."

Grimes smoothly withdrew the needle, put it on the ground by his foot and covered it safely with the sole of his shoe. He took the drip tube from Felton's hand and screwed it home. Holding the line firmly against the skin with his fingers, Grimes took the bag from Felton and squeezed, forcing the saline through as fast as he could.

"Is there another of these bags in there?" asked Grimes.

"No, that's it."

A siren approached. Paramedics. Grimes's role was nearly over.

"Pass me some strips of tape," he said.

While Felton rummaged in the white case Grimes looked at the wounded man. His waxy eyelids fluttered as he hovered on the edge of consciousness, and Grimes felt sorry for him. Whatever the guy was, or had done, lying on the ground with a bullet in your gut wiped clean a lot of slates. Pity had a habit of making good and bad seem unimportant. Still, Grimes had to know. He bent forward to the guy's ear and lowered his voice.

"You work for Atwater?" he said.

The guy's head floated up from the sidewalk, his panic-stricken eyes swimming for focus on Grimes's face.

"Who are you?" he whispered.

Grimes regretted having increased the wounded man's terror; but it had told him what he wanted to know. He gently pushed the guy back down, raised his voice again.

"Take it easy, sir. The ambulance is here."

A hand dangling three strips of adhesive tape appeared in Grimes's vision. He looked up into Felton's curious face.

"Thanks, Rod," said Grimes.

He took the strips one at a time and secured the drip tube as best he could to the victim's skin.

"What did he say?" asked Felton.

"He asked me who I was."

Grimes saw that Felton thought this a fair question. At least he didn't appear to have heard him speak of Atwater.

"Name's Tom Jackson," said Grimes. "Family doctor up in Kansas City, Kansas. I'm on vacation, would you believe?"

Felton felt a bond and relaxed. "Always the way," he said. "It's happened to me too."

"Never off-duty," said Grimes, nodding.

There was a commotion behind them as the paramedics clattered through with a gurney. Grimes was suddenly surrounded by two eagle-eyed men weighing up his work with a hint of territorial suspicion as they unpacked their gear.

"I got a subclavian in," said Grimes.

"Yeah," said one of the paramedics, as if this were second-best.

"This is Dr. Jackson," said Felton.

The paramedic said, "Yeah."

Grimes handed over the near-empty drip bag. He pulled over the first-aid case, found a sharps box and discarded the used needle. He stood up. It was time to slip away.

"Well, you guys know this business better than I do."

"Yeah."

Grimes nodded and started back through the crowd toward his car. He felt a hand tap his shoulder. He turned. Felton smiled at him.

"You were cool in there, Doc. Thanks."

"Couldn't have managed without you, Rod. Thank you."

"Where ya staying?"

"With friends, in the Garden District," said Grimes.

His lying was improving all the time. Before Felton could probe any more Grimes held out his hand.

"You keep safe now."

Felton shook. "You enjoy your vacation. And try not to scare the folks back home. This town's rep is bad enough as it is."

Grimes smiled and headed for his Olds and got in. As he drove away he saw the paramedics' trolley trundle its bleeding cargo toward the ambulance. Grimes felt his clinical calm slipping away. Somewhere inside the head of the man on the stretcher was Grimes's real name; his father's, too. Grimes couldn't bring himself to wish the man dead but the thought crossed his mind. His father was on his way to the Old Place, wherever it was; maybe with the girl Ella, maybe not. There was only one place for Grimes to go. He took a right at the next light and pointed the Olds in the direction of Arcadia.

EIGHT

THE VISIT OF Dr. Grimes left Lenna in a state of intense psychic and muscular agitation. If she'd been able to read him one way or the other she'd have felt better, but she couldn't. She considered herself a shrewd judge of character, especially of men, among whom she spent most of her time. She'd sat through a thousand negotiations knowing exactly what was going through the minds of her opponents, for all their dissembling and false smiles. That was her advantage: they could rarely read her at all. She imagined them whining to themselves in their failure: she was a goddamned woman, and who the hell ever knew what went on inside a woman's mind? Those old puffed-up self-important boys knew that while she could speak their language, they couldn't speak hers. Their gender was against them. They knew how to push each other but not her: were they being too aggressive or not aggressive enough? She could be as aggressive as she liked; and while their attempts at seduction were laughable, hers had them whimpering in confusion. Some had the sense to try to play it straight and treat her like one of them in a skirt but even they lost too because she wasn't one of them. Lenna wasn't one of anybody.

Neither, she sensed, was Eugene Grimes.

As she paced around the gloom of her study she followed that track. What was it that made her different, and if so, was it what made Grimes different too? Grimes was a psychiatrist. He knew all the nodding-dog tricks, the bland facade behind which his brain churned ten-to-the-dozen. Only at the last had he let something more leak out. But what? This angle would get her nowhere. She turned back to herself.

Her strength in the business deal, she'd learned long ago, was that she didn't really care whether she won or lost. Her opponents nailed some vital part of their inmost selves to the success or failure of the deal and therefore they were scared. No matter how deep down the fear might be buried, it was there. Lenna wasn't scared. She wasn't scared because nothing of herself was at stake. She ran her businesses the way she did because she had nothing else to do with her time and nowhere else to go. She worked out daily in the gym downstairs for the same reason: there was no one she wanted to look good for and she had no desire to extend her life span. If she'd enjoyed collecting plastic-surgery scars or meeting Hollywood actors or shopping or big-game hunting, maybe she would have done those things instead. None of them would have occupied her mind to the degree she needed in order to keep her monster at bay. The monster, she did fear: for it was at the core of herself and at the core of her ineradicable self-loathing too.

Maybe that, then, was why she hadn't been able to outguess Grimes: he didn't want anything; he didn't care. But this idea didn't help her: she did not know if Grimes was a liar or not. That was the drip of doubt that Clarence Jefferson—the liar's liar—had known would torment her. On balance, logic—based on her knowledge of Clarence's techniques—dictated that Grimes was an innocent, randomly picked to stoke her pain. Certainly Grimes was no Atwater, snuffling desperately at the trough of power. Her strongest doubt about the doctor lay in the accuracy of Jefferson's description of him, that Grimes was not a man to be pushed. She'd sensed that in the way he'd turned his pale eyes on Bobby Frechette. For a moment there she'd almost expected him to use the fists he'd held clenched by his sides. Jefferson had told her not to push but rather to wait. Yet the waiting—and the hope she dared not name—was peeling the lining from her guts. Lenna took Jefferson's letter from her sleeve and read it through for the hundredth time. Then she went to the desk and called Bobby Frechette.

Frechette came through the door a moment later and stood waiting in silence. His presence relieved the churning in her gut. Only once had she spoken to Bobby as if he were a servant, and Bobby had quietly, and on the spot, tendered his resignation. He protected her, but she could have purchased that protection from many others; she could have hired a private army if she'd pleased. Lenna valued Bobby because although he adored her, he was prepared to look her in the eye and tell her what she didn't want to hear. She had told him nothing of Jefferson's letter.

"Bobby," she said. "What did you make of Dr. Grimes?"

Frechette paused and Lenna waited.

"He gave me respect," said Frechette.

"Would you trust him?" asked Lenna.

"I'd trust him to be his own man. That's not the same thing."

Lenna nodded, wearily. This she already knew.

Bobby said, "Grimes has been to the floor of the pit."

"You know this?"

Bobby said, "Like I know you have."

He'd never said this to her before. Had he dug into the things she hadn't told him? Had the Jessups broken faith?

Lenna said. "What do you mean?"

"How or when or why, I won't know—for either you or him," said Bobby. "I know because I've been there too. If I was called on, I'd go there again. So would Grimes."

Lenna knew for sure now that Grimes had lied to her: in their different ways both Bobby and Jefferson had described the same man.

Frechette said, "This is part of the Jefferson business, right?"

Lenna read the worry in his eyes.

"It might be. That's what I need to know."

Bobby Frechette said, "Grimes is no fuck-boy for Jefferson."

Lenna flinched inside. In her way she'd been Jefferson's fuck-boy. No other punishment had been appropriate to the scale of her guilt.

"Lenna," said Bobby. He stopped, then, "Maybe it's not my place to say this."

"Don't insult me, Bobby."

"You should drop this whole thing right now."

"I can't."

"Whatever the Captain left behind, this blackmail shit, you don't need it. And if he had something on you and someone tries to use it against you, that someone will die."

"Did you kill Clarence Jefferson, Bobby?"

"No."

He held the moment so that she'd know he spoke the truth; and so she'd know, too, that he would've liked to.

"Whatever Jefferson was holding over you, I don't care," said Bobby. "Leave it to Atwater and the other scum. If they find it and come after you, fight them."

"Bobby, it's not about that anymore."

"Lenna, I see you." Frechette closed his eyes for a second. "No one else can. Believe me: you don't need them or any of their workings. You never did."

He paused and looked around the room that enshrouded them.

"And Grimes was right: you don't need this place, either."

"What did he say?" asked Lenna.

"He called it a mausoleum."

Lenna knew Bobby hated Arcadia. So did she; it was part of the punishment she'd agreed on with her conscience. But Frechette had never spoken to her with such emotion.

"What's wrong, Bobby? Are you expecting trouble?"

"No." Behind the high-boned face Bobby struggled with himself. "But I saw the tear marks on your face too. I didn't like it."

"Then help me," she said. "And forgive me if I can't tell you why."

This hurt him, though he would never say so. He stepped back inside his armor. A blankness glazed his eyes.

"I'll do whatever you say," he said. "To whoever you say."

Lenna turned and walked away, trying to find a line through the jumbled impressions in her mind. In the letter, Jefferson had told her to wait. By now she knew it all by heart: *"Put that to him, Lenna, and only that, then have patience and wait."* But she couldn't wait. She turned back to Bobby.

"I want to see Grimes again. Tomorrow."

Bobby remained impassive. He nodded once.

"Not here," said Lenna. "We'll go to him, to the City. And no Atwater. You're right. I'll pay him off tomorrow."

"That might not be that easy. He might figure he's got something to sell to someone else."

"Then we'll fight them, like you said."

The light came back into Bobby Frechette's eyes and he nodded.

"Thanks, Bobby."

Frechette closed the door behind him and Lenna went behind her desk. She searched in the desk drawer for the bottle of pills, found them. Her insomnia was entrenched. Twice a week she allowed herself a pill. Tonight she decided to take two. Anything to blank out some of the hours she would have to wait before seeing Grimes again. She knew in her gut that next time he'd tell her the truth. Or maybe that was just hope deluding her. Lenna tossed a pair of egg-shaped capsules into her mouth and drank from a glass of water. An intense exhaustion seized her from head to toe. Lenna put the glass down and went up to her bedroom.

By the time she'd showered and removed her makeup the drug was taking hold: a strangely plausible sense of peace. She'd wondered before how molecules could do this. Did it prove that all that she felt was just a dream after all? But because the drugged peace was so believable it was also incongruent with what she knew and therefore false. She looked at her face in the mirror: cleansed of makeup it appeared lifeless and parched. Another falsehood. She was drifting on a sea of falsehood. On that sea she walked through to her bed and lay down naked on the cover. Did she really care for what she cared for most—for *whom* she cared for most—or was that a falsehood too?

Lenna didn't know her name.

She had never seen her face.

She had never heard her voice.

The molecules stroking her to a false peace took her under and Lenna fell asleep.

When she awoke the first thing she was aware of was that she was cold. She shivered and clenched her arms across her chest. She opened her eyes and the bedside lamp glared at her. She blinked. Her head was muddy: no thoughts, no pictures, no dreams. The telephone next to the lamp was ringing. She realized that that was what had woken her, not the cold. She dragged the coverlet around her shoulders and grabbed the phone.

"Bobby?" she said.

"Sorry to wake you, Lenna." Bobby Frechette's voice. "Atwater's down at the gate. He wants to see you."

"Why?" she said. "What time is it?"

"It's quarter after one."

"What does he want?"

A pause.

"He says he's found Clarence Jefferson. He's alive."

The sleeping pills buffered this information to the extent that she did not scream her reply.

"Let him come up. I'll be down."

The line went dead. Lenna got to her feet and walked to the bathroom. She felt a little unsteady but her head was clearing fast. She stuck her head under the cold shower and felt clearer still. She massaged her face and head with a rough towel and went back to the bedroom. Her blue dress lay crumpled on the floor. She stepped over it and slid open the wardrobe door. On a hanger she found the black pantsuit she'd worn earlier in the day and pulled it straight on, without underwear. She slipped on a pair of black leather pumps. She looked in a mirror. Her hair was damp and ratty. She looked like a hag. She didn't care.

Atwater had found Jefferson. Alive.

Lenna went to the door and walked along the corridor to the broad first-floor landing. Beyond the balustrade she saw Bobby Frechette standing in the reception hall below. He looked more tense than she'd ever seen him. She saw his hand pat the small of his back where he carried his 9 mil Beretta. Then he heard her steps, soft on the carpet, and turned.

"Stay up there," he said. "I want to check this out."

Lenna walked past the balustrade and started down the steps.

"Why?" she said.

She was still feeling the cobwebbed floating effect of the sleeping pills. Bobby's caution seemed alien and irrational.

"Lenna, please just do as I ask. Atwater's brought that creep of his, Seed. They're driving a panel van and it bothers me. Just give me five."

Lenna scrubbed a hand across her face. She couldn't make sense of the idea that a worm like Rufus Atwater might bother Bobby Frechette. Even so, she paused with her hand on the banister less than halfway down the stairs.

There was a rapping on the front door. Bobby stepped into a short alcove to one side of the door. In there was a row of monitors relaying pictures from the various cameras set up around the building. Bobby reappeared, chewing his lip.

"So what's wrong?" she said.

"Nothing. Seed's sitting out in the van. Atwater's grinning at the camera."

She felt a sudden impatience. "Let them in then."

"I should've gotten some guys."

"Bobby, it's Rufus Atwater, for Christ's sake. Open the door."

Lenna started down the steps. Frechette patted his back again and opened the door with his left hand.

As gunfire exploded through the widening gap Lenna kept on walking, as if in a trance.

The Beretta appeared in Bobby's hand as he tried to slam the door shut, but the bullets lifted him backward and threw him in a bloody slither across the marble floor. As he hit the tiles the Beretta clattered from his fingers.

Rufus Atwater came through the door with an automatic gripped in both hands.

Lenna's immediate reaction was a gut pain at how bad Bobby would feel: not at having bullets in his body but at the knowledge of his having failed her.

Bobby Frechette spun on his back and slid through the blood toward his gun as Atwater bore down on him.

"Atwater!"

Her voice was big enough to fill the hall with echoes but it wasn't a scream. It was an order. It was enough to stop Atwater squeezing the trigger again but not enough for Bobby. Bobby kept going.

This time she did scream: *"Bobby!"*

But Bobby kept going still. When he was a foot short of the Beretta, Atwater started shooting again, pumping frantic point-blank rounds. Bobby Frechette took the bullets. He took them. Even as the slugs pushed him further and further across the blood-greased marble and Rufus Atwater pursued him, Bobby Frechette snatched up the Beretta. He turned. Above the gunfire she heard a sound that cracked her heart.

"Lenna!"

Bobby, his long, ravaged limbs wheeling convulsively, fired once.

The bullet shattered harmlessly through the stained glass dome.

Atwater cringed, then bent and pressed his automatic against the side of Bobby's head and fired. Two shots slammed.

The automatic snapped empty.

Bobby Frechette finally lay still.

Lenna couldn't see his face.

She found herself at the foot of the stairs staring into the barrel of Atwater's empty pistol. She didn't know how she'd gotten there. Atwater was staring at her with glazed, bewildered eyes. The pistol in his hand trembled. Heavy steps pounded up the staircase beyond the door. Jack Seed blundered into the hallway and stopped. He leveled a shotgun at the ragged body on the floor. His mouth opened.

"Jesus Christ," said Jack Seed.

He looked at Atwater. Atwater blinked. Sweat dripped from his nose. As if snapping out of a trance, he ejected the clip from his gun. It clattered to the tiles. Seed looked from the empty clip to Bobby Frechette's body.

"Fuck, man," said Seed. "That was a seventeen-round mag."

Atwater, trying to insert a fresh clip with shaking hands, didn't answer. In the doorway behind Seed appeared two Latinos. They also carried shotguns. For a moment there was an extraordinary stillness. And Lenna knew that whatever their business was, they wouldn't dare kill her.

Lenna walked across the hall, her pumps sticky in the shambles, and knelt down beside Bobby's body. He was crumpled facedown. She couldn't tell how many times he'd been hit. One side of his skull gaped open. She didn't turn away. Gently, she rolled his face toward her. It was splashed with blood but undamaged. His eyes were shut. She put her palm of her hand against one high-planed cheek. It was still warm with the fire that had burned inside him, the fire that had burned for her and for all that he'd stood for. Lenna shut her eyes too. She didn't cry. She wouldn't, not in front of these men who stood around her. Instead she felt the last of that dying fire; and hoped that it might find its way inside her.

Time passed. Then she heard a voice and opened her eyes. Suddenly she could see nothing, not even the blood on her hands. For a moment she was blind.

The voice said: "Get that black sack of shit out of my home."

Lenna stood up. Her vision swam back. She turned toward the door.

Filmore Faroe, his arms supported on either side by a third and fourth Latino, stood nodding at her with his bloated gray skull. His eyes shone.

"Hello, Magdalena," said Faroe.

Lenna didn't answer. She felt nothing: neither fear nor hatred nor grief. But she closed her right hand: to keep alive what she'd taken of Bobby's fire.

Faroe stretched the moment for as long as it lasted, then turned to the first pair of Latinos.

"Bring him in," he said.

The two men disappeared outside. Faroe stared at her again.

"You know, Magdalena, I thought about this moment many times. Many times. I thought of all the things I would say to you. Now that it's arrived, there's nothing that I want you to know. Not a thing. Isn't that remarkable?"

Again, Lenna didn't answer.

"But there's one thing I would like to know."

Faroe paused and the shine in his eyes grew blurred.

"How long was I in there?"

Without emotion, Lenna said, "Thirteen years."

Faroe blinked once, as if presented with a mystery beyond his comprehension. His mouth trembled. He took a deep breath and looked up into the grand vault of the hall. He composed himself. When he was ready he looked at her again.

"Thank you," he said.

Scuffling sounds, and muffled whimpers, came from the portico steps. The Latinos reappeared. Between them they manhandled Harvill Jessup. Harvill's mouth was covered with gray masking tape and his wrists were handcuffed behind him. There was a bullet wound in his left leg. Above the masking tape his eyes rolled. Faroe jerked his head and Harvill was kicked to his knees.

"Mr. Atwater?" said Faroe.

Atwater almost ran across the hall toward him.

"Mr. Faroe, sir?"

Faroe shook off one of the arms supporting him and took the pistol from Atwater's hand.

"Remove the tape, please."

Atwater ripped the gray tape from Harvill's mouth. Harvill spluttered and looked at Lenna with naked terror.

"They killed the dogs, Miss Par-low! Miss Parillaud? They killed 'em all!"

Without any appearance of pleasure, Faroe shot him in the head.

Faroe handed the gun back to Atwater.

"I'll be in my study."

Faroe walked unaided toward the corridor.

"Mr. Faroe?" Atwater coughed. "What do we do with your, I mean, with Miss . . . ?"

He ran out of words as Faroe stopped halfway across the hall and looked back at him. Faroe didn't look at Lenna at all.

Faroe said, "Why, take her to the Stone House, Mr. Atwater."

"I'm sorry, sir?" said Atwater. "You mean the hangar? The concrete hangar?"

Lenna had never found his eagerness to please quite so repulsive before.

"The Stone House is what my wife calls it, and thus it shall be known. She can direct you there if you get lost. Do anything you feel inclined to that doesn't endanger her life. Anything. Do you understand?"

Atwater's mouth gaped a little.

Jack Seed said, "Anything at all?"

"I'm not used to repeating myself, Mr. . . ." Faroe turned to Atwater. "What was that name?"

"Seed," said Atwater.

"Mr. Seed," said Faroe.

Seed nodded.

Faroe stole a glance at Lenna's face. What it told him, she didn't know. She didn't know what was in her to tell. Faroe turned away and continued into the corridor. He disappeared from sight. Lenna found the one called Jack Seed staring at her breasts. With a stubby finger and thumb he tugged twice on his fat, mustached lip.

"Well?" said Seed. "What are we waiting for?"

Atwater looked at her. Lenna stared back at him without feeling anything for him at all. Her right hand was still closed, still warm. Though Bobby Frechette was dead, his fire guarded her still. Let these animals do as they would.

Atwater said, "Take her to the Stone House, like Mr. Faroe said."

Seed came and stood in front of her. Lenna smelled his breath as he snapped a single handcuff bracelet around her left wrist.

"You handle her alone?" asked Atwater.

"Oh, I think so." Seed smiled. He patted himself on the belly.

"Good. I need your guys to clean up here. Leave the van. Take the lady's Mercedes." Atwater straightened his tie. "I've got some arrangements to talk over with Mr. Faroe."

Seed raised his eyebrows.

"You mean you don't want a piece of this?"

Atwater looked Lenna up and down, and curled his thin lips.

"I wouldn't give her the satisfaction. 'Bye, Miss Parillaud."

The bracelet jerked tight against Lenna's wristbones.

Jack Seed pulled her across the hallway and down the portico steps toward the awaiting blackness and—within that blackness—the Stone House.

NINE

ARK WAS the night and threatening rain as Cicero Grimes swung off Route 51 past the sign declaring PRIVATE ROAD—NO ACCESS and urged his Olds onward into the heart of Arcadia. During Grimes's childhood his father, with that special passion and daring that belongs to the formally uneducated, had read ferociously of the great texts. Grimes remembered his teenage amazement when George had found him reading *The Sound and the Fury* and declared it "a good book" and recommended he try *Light in August* too. Grimes had also felt a pang of shame at his amazement, for it implied that he thought such works were beyond the grasp of a working man. George could no doubt have taken advantage of the GI Bill and gone to college himself, but he'd gotten caught up in the union movement and decided that that was work of greater moment: or maybe of more "noble note." In contrast, Luther's taste had leaned toward *Guns and Ammo* and Mickey Spillane, but he'd become a soldier and to the war had gone, so in the end George had been appeased by them both.

The upshot of this was that Grimes possessed some vague notion of what the first Arcadia had meant to the Ancients. A rural paradise of mountain, forest and pasture where the pleasures of the flesh were innocent and many, and where the goat god Pan had ruled. Pan, it seemed, was later reincarnated as the Devil, but that was Christianity for you.

Lenna Parillaud's modern Arcadia would have been a disappointment to the Greeks and probably to Pan as well. Slap in the middle of the Mississippi Delta, it had never seen a mountain, or even a hill, and if it had ever known forests, they'd long since been cleared with ax and spade. The moon was only just on the wane and when it slipped out from between the clouds it cast an eerie light over great silver undulations of marsh grass, waltzing with the wind for as far as his eye could see. Grimes was no farmer but this land had to be prime; it was the whole reason for the state's original prosperity; yet he saw no sign that the soil was being exploited for profit. Maybe Lenna Parillaud was an eco-nut. If so, marsh grass was a strange species to protect. Or maybe the land was like the paintings on her walls and the fact of its possession was the only crop it was required to yield.

As Grimes hurtled along the narrow strip of blacktop, he wondered where his father was now and what he could do about it. A dialogue bounced back and forth in his head. *Do everyone a favor, Grimes: go on home and leave George to have his last mad fling. He doesn't need a second-rater like you trying to save him.* But he just gunned down two men on the street and kidnapped a nineteen-year-old girl. He's lost it. *Then call the cops and turn him in; that's the only sensible thing to do. No one could say you were wrong.* But it's my fault he's in this. He's an old man, I don't want him to die. *He made his choice, you make yours. What was that phrase? "Run like a gelded dog"?*

Grimes laughed. If he could have known his own mind as well as George knew his, he would have . . . Grimes found he couldn't think of what he would have done. But the world just didn't run for him along the straight iron tracks that it traveled for George. George might not like who was driving the train but he knew he was on one. Grimes felt more like a blind beggar wandering a land he could not see. In an absurd world the only rational option was an absurd life.

Then a quieter voice told him that at the rock root bottom of the matter it was none of these things, and simpler than them all. It was a deep thing, bred in his gut and his bone, and it was old—as old, perhaps, as this silver-drenched and whispering Delta—and thus begged no rhyme or reason, and it was this: if George Grimes was going to die, be it in a rage of guns or drooling spit in a bathchair, he—Eugene Grimes, his son—wanted to be there with him at the end. He wanted to be there to feel his spirit passing by and to hear the music in his dying breath; for somehow he knew in his inmost heart that the music would be sweet, and worth the listening.

And that was all.

And Grimes at last had something that he wanted.

With the wanting, his sense of urgency became greater, and he leaned on the gas. He was on his way to ask Lenna Parillaud—to whom he had lied—for help. He no longer even had anything to offer her in return: except that it was George who now had the information she needed. Parillaud had the resources to track George down. She could hire men and helicopters and spy planes and whatever else was necessary. It was even possible she knew where the Old Place was; there was no telling what had been in the letter Jefferson had sent her. He suddenly remembered that George had shot two men working for Atwater and that Atwater was working for Parillaud. His head spun. Maybe, yet again, he was doing the wrong thing. Bobby Frechette's face came to him. He had Frechette's word that she meant him no ill. For Grimes, that was word enough.

The moon above was smothered by a blanket of cloud and the landscape turned as black as ink. He couldn't see more of the road than his lights revealed and he slowed down. An intersection came into view, another plain black strip at right angles to the one he was traveling. He slowed almost to a halt and checked his memory. He'd followed Atwater on autopilot, it would've been easy to make a turn without registering it; but he decided that the route lay straight ahead. As he picked up speed across the intersection he saw, in the thick darkness a mile or more ahead, a white light moving in his direction. Before he'd worked out why, he'd switched off his headlights and hit the brakes.

As his tires smoked to a halt Grimes realized he was thinking like his father without even knowing it: he was now invisible. He hoped he'd seen the other driver's headlights first. The light ahead resolved into two bright dots and kept coming. It was past one in the morning; this was a barely used private road; Grimes didn't belong here. The chances were no one else did either. And the other car was moving fast. If Grimes didn't put his own lights back on, or move, there'd shortly be a loud bang and all his cares would be behind him. He jammed the stick shift into reverse and plowed back toward the intersection. Left or right? The other guy's blind side: left. Grimes spun the wheel counterclockwise and swung around into the left arm of the crossroad, straightened up, pulled back a dozen yards and switched everything off.

The other car approached, the roar of a performance engine. Cones of light. As the beams flooded the crossroads there was a squealing of brakes. A black sedan—a Mercedes—slowed to a halt at the center of the X. Grimes put his hand to the ignition key. Had he been seen? The Mercedes reversed back three yards and it was then that Grimes saw her.

The passenger windows front and rear were rolled down. Sitting in the seat, with her arms handcuffed around the doorpost between the windows, was a woman. At first Grimes didn't recognize her. Her hair was tangled and hung limply over her face. Across her mouth was a wide strip of tape. His first thought was that this was the girl, Ella Mac-Daniels, that they'd gotten to her and his father before him, and his father was dead. Then he recalled the poster at the club: Ella MacDaniels was black. In the driver's seat on the woman's far side he caught a glimpse of a man's face, a salacious mouth puckering beneath a heavy mustache. Then, as the Mercedes turned and accelerated into the opposite arm of the crossroad, the woman's head jerked back, and with it her hair, and Grimes saw that it was Lenna Parillaud.

Grimes sat and stared at the red glow of the taillights streaking away from him.

So. Goodbye to all that. Helicopters, spy planes and everything else. Grimes had been apprehensive enough about tangling with her and the forces she could draw on. Who the fuck, then, had the will and the means to do this to her? His fingers turned white on the steering wheel: Bobby Frechette was dead. He had to be. Frechette was not *ronin:* only death would have prevented him from allowing this to happen to her. Grimes turned the ignition key and the engine of the Olds grumbled to life. The red glow was just visible in the distance.

He told himself: you're not *ronin* either; not anymore.

Grimes drove across the intersection in pursuit of Lenna Parillaud.

As he was running without lights, all his concentration was absorbed by the task of not wrecking himself. The Mercedes itself was pushing the danger limit but at least its driver could see where he was going. Grimes rolled down the window to get a better impression of the road. The blacktop was fringed by a deep flood ditch on either side. Six inches out and he'd be tipped into it. He tried to gain on the red glow but without success. Several miles passed. The red glow didn't change; then it started to get closer. Grimes was gaining. Gaining still. He started to slow down. Up ahead the brake lights flared on in an added efflorescence; then the glow disappeared completely.

The Mercedes had turned off the road.

Grimes followed at a steady thirty, peeling his eyes for the cutoff. The darkness mocked his sense of distance. He must be close. There: an apron of shale leading into a dirt road. Grimes nosed into the turn. He could see nothing up ahead. He stopped, switched off the engine and listened.

Total silence.

If the Mercedes had been moving he'd still have been able to hear it, he was sure. Had the driver with the mustache heard him? Did he have a partner riding shotgun in back Grimes hadn't seen? Were they waiting for him with pump-actions? He couldn't afford to drive any further: they had to be close. Grimes got out of his car, closed the door quietly, went around to the trunk and opened it. Amid the jumble he found a four-battery flashlight and a tire iron. He stuffed them into the pockets of his suit, shut the trunk and started up the road in the dark.

He walked as fast as he could without running. He started to sweat from the effort but that was good. The sweating helped keep his mind off the gun blasts he expected to roar from the pitch dark at any moment. At least he was wearing black. He unfolded the lapels of his jacket to cover the patch of white shirt at his chest. Three or four hundred yards ahead he saw a pale yellow glow: the headlights of the Mercedes, pointing away from him. Silhouetted by the lights, and blacker than the surrounding dark, loomed a geometric hulk. Some kind of building.

As he got closer he slowed down. He could see the Mercedes clearly now. Both doors hung open and the car was empty. It was parked in a wide tarmacadamed yard framed on the far side by a family-size house and on the left adjacent side by a concrete building with the shape and dimensions of a large barn. Between the house and barn was a field. The family house was in darkness. The concrete barn had no windows in its walls but Grimes could see light rising skyward from what must have been windows set into the roof. The headlights of the Mercedes were trained obliquely on the front of the barn, set into the wall of which was a sliding metal door. There was no other entrance that he could see and the metal door was shut. The third, right-hand, side of the yard was closed in by a bunch of trees with pale gray trunks, faintly luminous in the reflected light. Throughout the yard nothing moved and Grimes could hear no sound above the thump of his own heartbeat in his ears. He headed for the line of trees.

They were silver birches. He slipped behind the nearest trunk and scanned the yard again. It was still silent but now, in the eccentric light and shadows thrown by the headlights, he could make out four dark heaps scattered about the yard. The farthest heap was bigger than the rest. Even at this distance Grimes recognized the limp density characteristic of a human corpse. The other heaps, he couldn't make out.

Grimes looked down. The ground at his feet was overgrown with knee-high grass and ferns. He decided not to risk the flashlight. Trying not to step on any branches or break his ankle, Grimes crept forward past a dozen more tree trunks, then peered out again at the yard.

The three smaller heaps appeared to be dead dogs.

Grimes swallowed and found his mouth as dry as adobe brick. He'd heard no shots: this small massacre must have taken place earlier on. Lenna and her captor had to be inside the concrete barn. He could still hear nothing, but the walls looked thick and the door heavy. Grimes turned away from the yard and squatted on his heels with his back to the trunk of the tree. The tire iron in his pocket jabbed into his side and he thought about the slaughter decorating the tarmac behind him. He closed his eyes and sifted through his options. He could run, that was always the first. His father had been kind enough to leave him the airline ticket to more peaceful climes. Or he could wait until whoever was in the barn with Lenna came out again and jump him at the door. Grimes remembered the plump pout of the guy's mouth and his gut soured with disgust. No, he'd have to go in clutching his tire iron and hope for the best.

Grimes heard a rustling sound.

With his eyes already closed as they were, he was tempted to leave them that way and let Death release him right now. The rustle got closer; he could feel the grass moving against his shins. He opened his eyes.

His first thought was that Death had taken him after all and was staring him in the face. But while he was willing to believe that Death might choose the form of a black wolf from eternity's nether regions, Grimes didn't believe that he'd show up bleeding.

The dog stood between Grimes's splayed knees and gazed into what felt like his soul. The dog's eyes—he knew at once that it was a male—were as black as the sea and twice as deep. If Grimes had ever believed that consciousness was the property of humans alone he now abandoned that idea in an instant. In the sea of this animal's eyes moved an unquestionable sadness and pain. Its face, which managed to suggest at one and the same moment both savagery and grace, was tapering and fine; and, somehow, as sad as its eyes. The dog was huge—its chest as wide as Grimes's own—and hung with a robe of long, dank hair. Some demon breed of German shepherd. On its skull, curving down obliquely from the crown into the root of its half-severed ear, was gouged a moist wound. From the base of the gouge came a glimmer of exposed bone.

Grimes found that he wasn't breathing. He breathed. He also found, and for some reason this didn't surprise him, that while he was frightened by just about everything else that had happened that day, he wasn't frightened of the dog. He figured he might as well play it straight up. If the dog decided to kill him there wasn't much he could do to stop him.

"Come here, pal," said Grimes.

The dog came.

He pushed his chest and shoulders between Grimes's thighs and lifted his muzzle toward his face. Around the dog's neck was a plain leather collar two inches wide but no ID tag. He opened his jaws to show a set of serrated yellow fangs, then a lilac tongue longer than seemed possible rolled out and flicked across Grimes's throat. Grimes didn't flinch. He slid his hands through the fur on the dog's flanks and the dog pressed its long throat against his chest and licked his face. And Grimes knew that to whomsoever the dog had previously owed its loyalty, he had now transferred it to him.

Grimes wasn't sure if that was what he wanted but he wasn't about to argue.

"Okay, wounded soldier," said Grimes. "We'll fix you up later."

If he was honest with himself he was as glad of the dog's company as the dog appeared to be of his. He disengaged himself and stood up. The dog reared up on its hind legs and slapped his paws on Grimes's shoulders. If the tree hadn't been just behind him Grimes would have fallen over. The dog was even bigger than Grimes had thought: the glittering black eyes were almost level with his own.

"Down, pal," said Grimes.

The dog dropped immediately to the ground and stood waiting and Grimes felt thrilled to be obeyed. He turned and looked across the yard: it was as silent as before.

"Come on," he said, and stepped out from the trees.

The dog padded ahead of him, big paws slapping the asphalt as if to show Grimes it was okay, he could handle himself. The dog went over to the human corpse and sat down beside it. Presumably it was his former master. Grimes followed. The man was as dead as he could get, with a shotgun wound in the midsection and a bullet hole in the side of his head. His eyes were half-open, the uprolled whites vivid in the shadowed face. It was ugly and strangely banal; as it always was. Grimes squatted and straightened the twisted limbs and closed the eyes. He did it gently, partly from respect, partly so as not to upset the dog, then quickly searched the body for weapons. In one pants pocket he found a clip of shells but no gun; he left the clip where he found it. He stood up and looked at the dog and at the bullet gouge on his skull. The dog looked back.

"Looks like you were the lucky one," said Grimes softly.

He guessed the dog had been stunned unconscious by the slug and left for dead. "Smart enough to hide when they came back, too."

Grimes walked past the dead animals to the Mercedes. The dog trotted ahead of him with a professional disregard for his dead companions and stuck his head, snuffling, into the driver's seat. From the depths of his chest came a low, primal growl, the kind of sound Grimes imagined a mountain might make as its entrails were torn out. Grimes wanted to swallow but couldn't find any spit. The dog sounded angry—raw-meat angry—with the mustachioed man.

"Down, pal," he whispered. "Sit."

With a hint of reluctance the dog backed off and settled onto his haunches. Again Grimes was impressed. He took a quick look around the car's interior. No guns. He ducked out.

"Heel, pal," he said.

With the dog at his right leg, he walked over to the sliding steel door. At its right-hand edge was a jagged twist of metal, the edges scorched blue. The lock had been blown open. These boys had come prepared and hadn't messed around. Grimes sensed a military ruthlessness at work. Kill anything that moved, blow the door, go in. He put his hands to the door and slowly increased the pressure until it budged. It moved the first inch easily and without much sound. Light spilled from within. Grimes's neck tingled again as the growl rumbled low and menacing at his knee. Grimes crouched and looked the dog in the eye.

"Listen, soldier, when we find whoever it is you've got a grudge against, you can have his dick for supper. Until then I want you to stay cool, okay? Like me. Cool."

The dog blinked once and Grimes took that to mean it was a deal. He straightened, and keeping his body behind the door, he slid it open another two feet. The dog smelled the air but held his ground. Inside was what looked like a warehouse space, lit by harsh white strip lights and stacked full of crates. Grimes stooped and slipped his right hand under the leather collar and let the dog pull him inside.

He was almost dragged off his feet. The animal's strength was shocking and he wasn't even trying. Grimes tugged back a little and the dog slowed. If it had been the dead man who'd trained him, he'd done so to perfection. Grimes allowed himself to be guided through a short maze of stacks until they reached a wall with a second door, also of steel and also breached by explosives. It hung partly open. Grimes looked into a short, featureless corridor at the end of which was a third door. This one was closed and showed no signs of damage. On the floor of the corridor was a pool of congealed blood. No sound came from within. Grimes walked down the corridor and put his eye to the peephole in the door. He expected it to be lensed so as to look outward, toward him; but this one was for looking in.

A warped perspective, a distorted cone of space, offered itself to his eye. The visual field was striped with blurred vertical lines, which he realized after a moment were steel bars. He was looking at a giant cage, brightly lit. Inside the cage, in the center of his view, was a massive dark brown box. Grimes struggled with the hallucinatory focus. No, he was right: the box was a building. It had a window in it, and walls built of logs. A shack or a cabin. At the edge of the cone, where the lenses distorted most, there was a blurry movement of something pink—fleshy pink—and closer to the intervening bars than it was to the cabin. The surreal picture was accompanied by utter silence.

Grimes looked down at the door's handle, a short matte stainless steel tube above an empty keyhole. It looked like the kind you had to lock deliberately. Either way he was fucked if it didn't open. He took the handle, twisted down and pulled. The door edged a couple of millimeters toward him. Grimes glanced down at the dog, silent and poised.

"We're in business," whispered Grimes.

Still holding the handle he put his eye back to the spyhole. The fleshy blur had gone. He pulled the door back a fraction more and the blur reappeared and came into focus. It was a naked man. With a mustache. He was swaying back and forth in a strange dance. His right hand was gripping his penis. As Grimes pulled the handle again to get a different angle through the lens, the edge of the door came open an inch from the frame and there was a sudden blast of sound from within.

"Fuck me then, maggot-dick! Pick your hole and stick it in!"

Lenna Parillaud, defiant. But Grimes heard horror in the voice too. There followed a burst of coarse laughter.

"Why, we got all the time in the world, Miss High and Mighty. Me,

I'm a big fan of all that good foreplay shit. Ain't that what you gals like too?" He laughed again.

Grimes drew back from the spyhole and pulled the tire iron from his pocket. He suddenly felt a monstrous anger battering on the inside of his forehead. A flood of adrenaline and other rage chemicals swamped his arteries and weakened his limbs and something inside him screamed for the spilling of blood. *Easy,* a calmer voice counseled. He breathed and nodded and his muscles steadied. He looked down. The dog glanced at him, licked its chops, and resumed its beady gaze at the crack in the door.

"Yeah," said Grimes, "me too. Let's go."

He snapped the door wide open. A dark snarling wind flew inside. Grimes charged after it.

Impression: unbroken bars; the cage door closed against them. A yell of surprise turning to fear. A pink ungainly movement to his right. A clatter. The gate to the cage. Keys dangling from the lock: the other side. Three paces to go. The dog already there. A deafening canine roar that seared the oldest synapses in Grimes's body. His hands swapping cold iron from right to left, arm through the bars, fingers on the key, twisting, wrenching. The door swinging out toward him. A black bolt of thunder past his leg. Grimes plunged into the cage.

He turned his head.

Impression: a naked man waddling away from a seated figure in black. Brown liquid leaking down his legs. Hairy arms stretching toward a crumple of clothes on the floor. On top of the clothes: a blued revolver. A face, a mustache: carved with total fear. The cold iron swapped again—left to right—and raised and thrown. The carved face already shrieking as the iron smashed bloody into hair and teeth and white-taut lips.

Grimes kept running.

Impression: a long black tapering snarl of skull, heaving and hauling beneath a juddering paunch. The naked man floundering as he fell with a piercing falsetto scream, arms still flapping for the gun as the dog wrenched free of his crotch in a shower of red. The nerveless hands slapping at the gun, fumbling, dropping. The black thunder scrambling on top of him for more, burrowing into the throat with dripping jowls.

Grimes bent down and picked up the gun.

Above a pair of busy, shag-furred shoulders he saw a gargling face.

Grimes crammed the gun barrel into one stretched and glazing eye and pulled the trigger.

After the gunshot there was a window of deathly silence. Then into Grimes's ears seeped the moist rummaging of serrated jaws.

"Down," said Grimes.

The dog ignored him.

"Down, goddamnit. It's over."

The dog stopped and stared up at him with what looked like reproach. Grimes was careful not to look beyond the panting jaws to what lay on the floor behind. He slapped his thigh.

"Come here, pal," said Grimes.

His bloodstained guardian reared up and leaned against his chest and smeared Grimes's throat with another man's gore. Grimes shut his eyes and gave himself up to blind trust and tried not to be sick. He put his arm around the dog and squeezed.

"Good dog," he said.

He opened his eyes. He was staring at an old log cabin—in a steel cage in a concrete barn—with a corpse at his feet, blood slaver on his neck and a multimillionairess on his hands. "Good dog" was as apt as anything else he could think of saying. After all, without the dog the dead guy would probably have reached his gun.

Grimes said it again. "Good dog. I owe you one."

He pushed the dog down and slipped the gun into his waistband and looked over at Lenna Parillaud. She was sitting in a strange plastic chair with two straps binding her wrists to the armrests and a third around her chest. She was dressed in a black jacket and long pants and seemed physically unharmed. She watched Grimes walk up to her with the steady green eyes he remembered from before. He started to unbuckle the straps.

"Are you okay?" he asked.

Lenna took a breath, held it for a moment.

"Yes and no," she said.

Her face was scrubbed clean of cosmetics. She looked less pale than before, and older; the wrinkles around her eyes more obvious, the skin dryer. Without the makeup, Grimes thought she looked better. Her hands were stained with dried blood. It didn't appear to be hers. She glanced downward to his right. Grimes felt the dog against his thigh.

"You've made a friend," she said.

"Don't be afraid," said Grimes. "So far he's on our side."

"He never seemed to like me."

"You know him?"

"Yes."

"What's his name?"

Lenna said, "He's called Gul."

Grimes liked the name as soon as he heard it. He tried it.

"Gul."

Gul barked once.

Grimes unfastened the chest strap and Lenna stood up in front of him. Her face was impassive. He couldn't read her. She seemed super-humanly calm—matter-of-fact—as if none of what had taken place around her was especially unusual. He put it down to shock.

"Why did you come back?" she said. She sounded as if she wished he hadn't.

"To tell you the truth, I'm looking for my father."

Her expression didn't change. "Your father," she said, flatly.

"George. He's missing."

Lenna didn't say anything and Grimes felt uneasy.

"It's a long story," he said. "I guess yours is too. Maybe we should swap them somewhere else."

"Bobby's dead. Bobby Frechette."

Grimes glanced at the dried purple-brown streaks on her hands.

"I'm sorry," he said.

"Atwater murdered him."

Grimes felt bad about Frechette but the bodyguard—the samurai—wouldn't have wanted him to waste time grieving.

He said, "We should go."

Lenna walked past him and stopped by the dead man. She looked down at him. Grimes didn't. Lenna looked up into Grimes's eyes.

"I would have left him alive a little longer," she said.

Grimes said nothing. He felt the revolver, heavy against his stomach. He couldn't say why he'd shot the man: whether to spare the guy a few final moments of obscene terror or to indulge the rage that had seized his heart in the corridor. It didn't really matter.

Lenna said, "He was called Jack Seed."

Grimes couldn't say he was interested. This place hummed with bad vibes. He wanted to get moving.

"Lenna," he said.

Lenna turned and walked toward the gate. Grimes followed, the dog

Gul trotting at his heel with every appearance of contentment. They left the building in silence.

Outside Grimes said, "My car's at the end of the road. Can you walk there?"

"Do I look like I can't walk there?" said Lenna.

"I was just trying to be polite," said Grimes.

"Give me a break," she replied. "Don't bother."

"Fine," said Grimes.

"Are you like this all the time?" said Lenna.

"Like what?"

"Like Mr. Psycho-Shrink, calm, cool and collected?"

That he gave this appearance was news to Grimes. Lenna's own calm astonished him. Since their earlier meeting her manner had changed, become brittle and spiky. But then a lot of other things had changed too. Whatever way she needed to deal with it was fine by him. It crossed his mind to wonder if this was a realer version of Lenna than the one he'd met before, but he knew that was bullshit. All versions were real in the end; even the most calculated pose.

"I'm just trying to get through the day," he said.

"You're so fucking rational."

"Look, you're upset," said Grimes. "Who wouldn't be?"

"Jesus."

Lenna turned and walked away. She disappeared out of the light thrown by the Mercedes and into the darkness of the road. Grimes shrugged and followed. He could hear her steps ahead but until his eyes adjusted he couldn't see her. She seemed familiar with this place and he wondered why. It was on her land. But why would a person maintain a small jail—containing an old tin-roofed shack—in the middle of that land? Now didn't seem like the moment to ask. He remembered the flashlight in his pocket and took it out and switched it on. With his path lit he doubled his pace and caught up beside her. They made it to his car without further acrimony by virtue of not speaking.

"What's that?" she said when she saw it.

"It's an Olds 88," replied Grimes, and added, "it's a classic."

He opened the passenger door for her. She got in without further comment. Grimes suddenly realized that somewhere during the walk to the car the black shadow had vanished from his heel. The dog, Gul, had gone.

Grimes shone the flashlight back up the road: nothing. He considered an impulse to go back and get him, then told himself this was no time to be a cornball. If the dog didn't want to leave his home turf that was his business. When Atwater and the others came back, as they would, they would kill him. Grimes wavered. *It's just a dog, man. You can miss him later.* Grimes walked around the car and got in behind the wheel.

"Where are we going?" asked Lenna. "And don't say the police."

"I don't know," said Grimes. "Does 'the Old Place' mean anything to you?"

"I thought I just told you to give me a break."

Grimes massaged his eyeballs. A cigarette seemed like a good idea. He found one and lit it. It tasted wonderful. His brain swam pleasantly. A name sprang into his head.

"Holden Daggett," he said.

"What?"

Lenna stared at him. Grimes dug out his wallet, searched the pockets and pulled out the card. He put the wallet away and shone the flashlight on the card. After he read it he slipped it into his breast pocket. He switched off the flashlight and turned on the ignition. The engine caught. He switched on the headlights.

"So where are we going?" said Lenna.

Grimes opened his mouth to answer and stopped. At the outermost edge of the beams he could see two points of light glittering in the dark. Without debating it he threw the door open and climbed out and shouted down the road.

"Gul! Make up your fucking mind!"

There was a pause and in the pause the dark clouds high above opened their arms and dropped a sudden drenching deluge all around them. Grimes made to get back in the car but it was too late: his clothes were already plastered to his skin. He squinted again. Through the layered silver curtain that the headlights made of the falling rain the two glittering points could no longer be seen.

Then, from the downpouring night, came a howl: a mournful *yoop-yoop-yaroo* that froze Grimes's blood and at the same time made him ache.

He waited a while longer, getting wetter. But Gul didn't show.

"Good luck to you, man!"

Grimes wiped a handful of rain from his face. He ducked back into the Olds. As he was about to shut the door a black shape, its body shining lithe in a dripping coat, padded unhurriedly into the lights and up to the car and slithered past Grimes into the rear seat.

Grimes could not remember when anything had made him so happy.

"Great," said Lenna. "You have any idea what a wet dog smells like?"

In the rear seat Gul shook himself. Lenna endured this in a silence more eloquent than words. Grimes slammed the door and reversed the car out onto the blacktop. Gul's breath was damp and warm on his neck.

"He saved our ass," said Grimes. "Show some gratitude."

"You didn't say where we were going," said Lenna.

Grimes changed gears and started back toward the highway.

"I've been told that it's pretty, especially in the spring. If you like that kind of thing," said Grimes.

"What is?" said Lenna.

"A place in Georgia," said Grimes, "called the Ohoopee River bottomlands."

Part Two

OHOOPEE RIVER BOTTOMLANDS

The fatman burns.

He waits.

And as he burns and as he waits, he remembers.

He remembers the cold of steel and the heat of flame; the crunch of severing sinew and bone; and the crackle of intolerable pangs through the skin of calf and thigh; the teeming multiplication of the microscopic forms that sought to feed on him and perished in the trying. And though he remembers these things, he does not remember cries or groans, yet such, he imagines, there must have been, for the pain was huge. The pain was huge and remains huge still. But his strength has seen him through, and his will; these things and, too, his burning.

For though the flames have long since played themselves away, his burning has not ceased. Now he burns within; from frustration and the need to know, from the impotence and impatience of the once-was-mighty, from the molten drip, drip, drip of what-might-be, from the endless wonderment of what-will-be? His left hand—his only hand—reaches forth from his fastness but he knows not—though he hopes—what it touches nor what that touch will bring. In any or all of the minutes of each hour passing by, in any or all of the sifting seconds of each month, a lesser will might have jettisoned its sanity and gone gratefully mad. But the fatman, blistered, scarred and bestumped though he is, will not permit himself that reprieve. He will pay in deposits infinitesimal the infinite debt that cannot be repaid until that moment of completion which renders all dues null and void. Until then he will not succumb, neither to the cowardly bleating of his organicity nor the sweet temptations of the psychosis. For there is a higher power than he or they. This he knows even if this he does not believe. He thought—this he admits—he thought he had transcended the human collective by smashing its most sacred taboos each after the other, in hecatombs and orgies needless and wild. Now his waiting, more than his burning, has shown him different. His manifold transgressions—his dancing beneath a pagan sun in the realm of human violence he thought he'd made his own—were nothing more than the curse that blessed: a glorious sacrifice before the altar of the power that condemned him.

At this the fatman laughs and his body shakes and the burning scalds him anew, and he embraces it for his own.

His own defiance makes him his mock of mocks.

And so: the choice stands before him. And in that choice is the knowing, if not the belief, before which he must kneel. His being squashes conscience and consciousness both beneath its heel, and demands at the last he keep the bargain struck without knowing while gestating in the womb he grew to loathe. His own malediction is upon him now. The full moon wanes. The light begins to glimmer through the trees. And the fatman harbors his strength, once mighty, and waits, and burns, as he has waited, and has burned, for the ones he loves.

The one and the other.

The twain.

And the mystery that accompanies them.

The mystery that offends, for he believed himself above it.

The last transgression: the love in which he holds them.

In his fastness.

TEN

T HE RAIN fell thick and hard, covering the highway with two inches of water and knocking thirty miles an hour off their top speed. In the passenger seat of the Olds 88, Lenna Parillaud slept. In the rear sprawled the dog, Gul, wet and stinking, in a similar state. Which left Cicero Grimes to peer through an opaque windshield and worry about what to do next. The interior of the car was stifling and getting worse by the minute as water and sweat evaporated from hair and clothing and condensed on glass and wood and Grimes's forehead. The Olds did not have air-conditioning. Grimes pulled out his pack of Pall Malls. They were too damp to get out of the pack. That decided him. Slugging through the rain at the speed of a mountain bike was an option only a panic-stricken loser would take. He was made of sterner stuff. And he needed a smoke.

When a blur of hollow light up ahead signaled some kind of roadside mall Grimes pulled over and drove into the parking lot. Lenna stayed sleeping. Maybe she was on something. Gul raised his head and looked at Grimes.

"Sleep," said Grimes, hopefully.

Gul closed his eyes and flopped back down. From the pouch in the door Grimes took out a road map and found their approximate location. They were a long way from Georgia but, as he suspected, not far from the cabin that Grimes leased near the Mississippi line. He used it as a retreat and as a quiet place where he sometimes took clients for detoxification. He hadn't been there for what seemed like a long time. He figured they could hole up there until the storm passed, dry out a little and recover some composure; or at least he could. He looked up at the lights outside: an all-night, all-everything gas station and grocery. As he opened the door Gul popped his head up again.

"Stay," said Grimes. "I'll be back."

Gul stayed and Grimes got wet again gassing up the Olds. He went inside the store. There he gathered up a quart of Tropicana and a carton of Pall Malls, and went over to the refrigerator. As he bent over to grab two pounds of rib-eye steak wrapped in Styrofoam and plastic, the gun in his waistband dug into his belly. He buttoned his jacket over it. He approached the checkout and smiled at the guy behind the counter and hoped that the cops weren't already on their way.

"Bad night out there," said Grimes affably.

"In here all the nights bad, buddy," said the guy.

Grimes nodded sympathetically, paid in damp bills and went on his way.

When they pulled up outside Grimes's cabin a half hour later the rain hadn't eased up any. The cabin wasn't remote—there was another house only fifty yards away—but it was quiet. Lenna still didn't stir. Grimes got out and Gul looked at him and waited until Grimes clicked his tongue before clambering out after him. While Grimes found his keys and opened the cabin door Gul roved off into the darkness to look for trouble. Finding none in the immediate vicinity he returned and as Grimes stepped over the threshold Gul followed him inside and shook himself down over the kitchen–living room floor. Grimes accepted this in good grace, switched on the electricity at the mains, emptied his groceries on the breakfast counter and put a pot of coffee on the stove. The place had that drafty, familiar-but-unoccupied atmosphere, but after the rain it felt as good as a suite at the Royale. Grimes found a raincoat in a closet and went to get Lenna from the car.

She awoke as he opened her door.

"Where are we?" she said drowsily.

Her eyes were blurred and drooping and Grimes decided she was on pills for sure. That was okay by him. He nodded over his shoulder at the cabin.

"Rest stop," he said. "It's my place. It's safe."

He helped her to her feet and spread the raincoat over her shoulders and took her inside. He sat her on the sofa and gave her a glass of orange juice. She looked around the minimally furnished room as if she were in a Mexican jail.

"You live here?" she said with pity.

"Sometimes," said Grimes. "Relax awhile."

Grimes went into one of the two small bedrooms, dumped the revolver and the contents of his suit onto the bedside table and stripped off his wet clothes. While Gul sniffed the place over, Grimes took a pair of jeans and a sweatshirt from a drawer and pulled them on. From a cupboard he took out his first-aid bag and carried it with his wet clothes through into the living room. Lenna had finished her juice and looked more alert. Grimes put the first-aid bag on the table. Lenna stood up.

"Do you mind telling me what's going on?" she said.

Grimes was getting used to her dry, confrontational style. It's just her manner, he told himself, it doesn't mean you're getting on her nerves or anything like that.

"I figured we needed to regroup and get our minds right," said Grimes. "Or at least *my* mind."

"In other words you don't know," said Lenna.

"I wouldn't say that," said Grimes.

"You're beginning to get on my nerves," said Lenna.

Grimes went to the dryer by the sink and threw his suit inside, turned the machine on at low.

"I'm going to dry my clothes, stitch the dog's ear back on and work out how we're going to travel six hundred miles without getting gunned down or worse. Then, if it's still raining, I may catch an hour's sleep."

"You're going to sew the dog's ear back on?"

Lenna stared at him as if he were mad.

"It would be easier if you left us alone awhile. He'll be less nervous."

Lenna looked grateful to be excluded.

"Is there anyplace I can wash off the smell of Jack Seed?"

Grimes pointed. "The bathroom's through there. You'll find a robe in there too."

Lenna walked into the bathroom and closed the door. Grimes felt relieved. He ripped open one of the packs of steak. Gul trotted over and sat down in front of him and licked his chops. Grimes took a sixteen-ounce steak from the pack and showed it to him.

"Stay there," said Grimes.

He walked over to the table and Gul watched him go with mournful eyes as Grimes put the meat on the table. From the bag he took out a syringe, an ampule of lidocaine and a suture pack. He drew up the lidocaine, opened a number-two catgut suture and clipped the needle into a pair of forceps. He picked up the meat again and turned to Gul.

"Okay, pal," said Grimes.

Gul ambled over as if to say he wasn't that interested in the meat after all. When Grimes let go of the steak Gul snapped it from the air and with a couple of strenuous gulps took it down in one. Grimes cleared disturbing images of the concrete cage room from his mind and sat down on a straight-backed chair. He took two handfuls of Gul's neck fur and pulled him between his legs. He looked into the dog's eyes.

"Listen," said Grimes. "We can't have you walking around with your ear hanging off like that. No one will take you seriously. I'm going to patch it back together. It will hurt but you can take it. Afterwards it will hurt a lot less than it does now. Okay?"

Grimes was glad Lenna wasn't around to see this and make him feel stupid. Gul looked at him for a while, then blinked.

"Good man," said Grimes.

He examined the wound. It was clean enough but there was some skin loss and there had to be some dead tissue along the edges. He opened a sachet of antiseptic and soaked a cotton ball. He dabbed at the wound and Gul pulled away and growled. Grimes pulled him back and tried not to look at his teeth.

"I know," he said. "I know. It won't take long."

Grimes finished cleaning the wound and picked up the syringe. Gul shied away again. Grimes pulled him back.

"Trust me," said Grimes. "It's local anesthetic. Now, hold still and take it like a man."

Gul settled down. Grimes stuck the needle into and along one edge of the wound, murmuring in what he hoped was a comforting fashion as he did so.

"You're a soldier, pal, a real soldier, and you saved my bacon back there. I won't forget that, no sir. We need you on this deal, you understand? Yes, we need you. We need somebody who knows how to handle himself. Christ. You and me are the only characters around who aren't totally fucking nuts. Good man, good man."

To Grimes's amazement and gratification Gul stood stock-still while he infiltrated both edges of the wound with local from each of its four corners.

"That's the worst of it over," said Grimes.

Gul gave him a how-can-you-do-this-to-me? look. Grimes murmured and petted a little more while the local took hold, then he took a pair of scissors, trimmed the dead flesh from the edges and put in eight stitches. Throughout it all he mumbled away in a low voice without really knowing what he was saying and Gul put up with it without stirring. While he worked, Grimes turned a few things over in his mind.

By the clock his father had a three-hour lead on them now and had probably missed the rainstorm to boot. They would never catch up with him. And that was presuming they were all heading in the same direction. For all Grimes knew the Old Place was in Mexico and George was halfway across Texas. Holden Daggett was the only link they had but Grimes thought it was a strong one. Clarence Jefferson must have trusted Daggett for many years to have given him the task of delivering his last will and testament. It made sense that Jefferson would not have used some sleazebag in the City. Grimes also figured that if the Captain had confided that much in Daggett, then the old attorney would probably know where the Old Place was too. If he didn't, then all Grimes would be able to do was sit and watch CNN for news of George Grimes, last of the desperadoes.

"It would be just like that old bastard, after all these years, to turn himself into some kind of national hero, wouldn't it, pal?"

Gul rolled his eyes up toward him without moving his head. Grimes snipped the ends of the last suture and put the forceps down. He examined his handiwork.

"Goddamn if you don't look handsome," said Grimes. "Come here."

He opened his arms and Gul clambered up onto his lap and licked his face. Grimes rubbed his flanks, shocked at how good it made him feel.

"You are an asshole," said Grimes, to cover his embarrassment in front of himself. "But at least you are now a handsome asshole."

"I guess that makes two of you," said Lenna.

Grimes looked up. Lenna was standing in the doorway wrapped in a white bathrobe down to her ankles. Her hair was wet and combed. The glassiness had gone from her eyes; instead Grimes detected a penetrating melancholy. She smiled but the melancholy didn't go away.

To Gul, Grimes said, "Down, pal."

He stood up, went over to the counter and opened a second pack of raw steak. He threw a slab of meat at Gul's feet.

"Eat," he said, roughly. "And be good."

"That was neat, what you did to the dog."

"Thanks."

Lenna walked over to the stove and poured herself a cup of coffee from the percolator.

"I was thinking, in the shower," she said. "That car contraption you've got outside is easy to spot, and Atwater knows about it."

"That little turd can't use the cops any more than we can."

Lenna said, "It's not that little turd I'm worried about."

"Who then?"

"My husband. Filmore Faroe."

The name triggered Grimes's recollection of what his father had said about Faroe. A line that deserved to end. Klansmen, union-breakers and fascists. Maybe Grimes remembered wrong—he hadn't been paying that much attention—but he thought George had said, or implied, that Filmore Faroe was dead.

"I thought he was dead," said Grimes.

"Officially he is. But Fil's alive and well. And probably very angry with us."

"What did we do?"

Lenna took her coffee over to the sofa and sat down.

"Look, I don't want you to be my doctor anymore, you understand? Otherwise this will be impossible for me. I don't want to have to deal with all that phony empathy bullshit."

"Suits me," said Grimes.

"You lied to me about Clarence Jefferson."

Grimes decided to take her at her word.

"In retrospect," he said, "that didn't do me much good. But I didn't ask you to invite Rufus Atwater into my life, or for my seventy-three-year-old father to have to gun down two of his men and go on the lam. I don't apologize."

"I don't expect you to. But you did know Clarence Jefferson."

"Clarence Jefferson was the Devil who always demanded his due. And always got it."

"How well did you know him?"

Grimes opened a dry pack of Pall Malls and sat down on the chair and lit up. Gul padded over and pushed his face into Grimes's crotch. Grimes put a hand on his shoulder and pushed gently.

"Get down, pal."

Gul obeyed. With the clothes dryer droning in the background, the rain drumming on the roof, Lenna curled on the sofa with her coffee and the dog yawning at his feet, Grimes was struck by a surreal sense of domesticity. Before he could get to liking it, he thought about Lenna's question. It wasn't easy to answer.

"I only ever spent twenty-four hours with Jefferson," said Grimes, "in a place he called Bad City. The why and the wherefore aren't important, at least not to you. To cut a long story short, he tried to kill me, and I killed him."

"You?" she said. "You killed Clarence Jefferson?"

For the first time since he'd met her, Lenna's face gaped with naked shock.

"I didn't mean to make it sound easy," Grimes said. "I stabbed him in the gut and left him inside a building that I watched burn to the ground. I guess I just got lucky."

"Luck didn't happen to Jefferson. He didn't allow it."

"Luck happens to everybody, especially a player of games. He wrote me a letter, a to-be-opened-in-the-event-of-my-death kind of deal. I got it this morning. Seems you got one too."

As calmly as she could Lenna said, "What did his letter say?"

Grimes observed the desperation graven on her face. It puzzled him. Why should a woman like her need Jefferson's *corpus delicti*? There no longer seemed to be any reason not to tell her.

Grimes said, "I presume you're aware of this bunch of evidence he stashed away."

Lenna nodded.

"His letter told me how to find it."

Lenna didn't even blink.

Grimes went on. "He said it would make life difficult for a lot of important people. And that some of those people—heavy people—would be looking for it. Jefferson wanted me to take his stash to the media. He suggested *The Washington Post*."

"And?"

"The idea didn't hold much appeal for me but I was stupid enough to tell my father, George, and he thought different. He stole the letter from my coat and now he's disappeared to find the stash himself."

"That's it? That's all?"

"Look, if I had the letter you could have the goddamn thing. You cannot imagine how small a shit I give for Clarence's fucking evidence or for anything you or anyone else might do with it. If we can find it before George—which I doubt, since I don't know where it is—it's yours, okay? I just don't want to see my dad being worked over by the likes of your Rufus Atwater."

The desperation on Lenna's face became more intense. Grimes felt as if he wasn't getting through. He tried to lay it out.

"We're going to Georgia to find the man who delivered me the letter, Holden Daggett, a lawyer. I'm gambling that Daggett knows where 'the Old Place' is, even if he doesn't know what's hidden there. With luck, Jefferson's stash of goodies will be yours. Then you can fight off your husband and make yourself another billion and I can forget I ever met you and go back to my life, which, I must tell you, was sweeter than I ever realized."

Grimes got up and paced. He stopped by the window and stood with his back to her. Anger was a waste of energy. He smoked.

"Dr. Grimes," she said behind him. "I care as little for Jefferson's stash as you do, believe me. But he said that you knew everything. I need to know. Everything."

He turned. The desperation in her eyes was as frantic as ever, only now it moved him to pity. He didn't know why. Beneath the strained steadiness of her voice he could hear a muted sob. Grimes went to the chair and sat down.

"You must forgive me," said Lenna. "I can't tell you all I know. Not yet. Even though I'd love to." She clenched her eyes shut. "I'd love to."

She collected herself, looked at him. "But I can't trust you. It's too important. It's too dangerous."

"Lenna," said Grimes. "The reason I found you in the cage is I was coming back to Arcadia to ask your help—to find my dad, goddamn him. I'm as fucked up by this business as you are."

"No you're not," she said. "With respect, you can't be."

And, with a chill, Grimes saw something terrible in her eyes and believed her.

He ran Jefferson's letter through his mind: the anvil of justice, the great apocalypse, the Old Place, the girl who knew where it was, the combination to the safe, the *Post*. He wasn't mistaken. Daggett was the only lead they had.

Grimes shrugged and said, "Jefferson didn't tell me where this 'Old Place' was. He meant for a girl to take me there."

"A girl?" Lenna put a hand to her chest.

"A young black woman. But my father got to her before I could. Jefferson said the girl was 'part of him.' I took that to mean she's his daughter, I assume illegitimate."

Very softly, Lenna said, "Did he tell you her name?"

"Ella MacDaniels," said Grimes.

More softly still, Lenna said, "Ella."

"She's nineteen years old. She's a singer."

Lenna turned her face away and seemed to struggle within herself for a long time. Then she looked up at him.

"She isn't Clarence Jefferson's daughter." Lenna said it as if the idea made her sick.

Grimes didn't answer. The chill returned to his blood.

Lenna looked upward and away: at some inner picture far, far distant in space and time. Grimes saw there were tears in her eyes. He waited. Lenna blinked the tears away and took a deep breath.

"When I met Filmore Faroe he was thirty-six, good-looking, charismatic, rich. And I believed, and I still believe, that in as far as he had it in him, he was in love with me. I'd blushed my way through the debutantes' balls, and I'd had a few dates with gawking boys, but I'd never had a lover before. I married him without really knowing why."

She paused and swallowed: and suddenly Grimes knew why she was so desperate.

Lenna said, "I was nineteen years old too."

ELEVEN

ELLA MACDANIELS drew back the hammer of the Colt .45 with her thumb and squeezed the trigger. The hammer snapped down with a dry click. She'd performed the action about fifty times now and her hand was starting to ache. She put the gun down in her lap and massaged her index finger and the web of her thumb. George glanced sideways at her from behind the wheel.

"Maybe you should rest that awhile," he said. "Blisters come up easier than you think."

They'd crossed Mississippi and had just cleared the outskirts of Mobile, Alabama, driving north on I-65. For a moment George's face was washed with ghostly light as a roaring semi hauled past them heading south, then his features fell into shadow again.

"Okay," said Ella.

She put her hand on the gun again, so the feel of it would become natural, but she didn't dry-fire it anymore. She'd never handled a gun before and the pleasure of it had disturbed her, though not badly enough to take the pleasure away. The Colt was beautifully made and beautifully imagined by whoever it was had designed it; she could see that; but the pleasure lay in something more than just its beauty. She'd touched other beautiful things in the world and none of them had felt like this, like this heavy black steel Colt. Now she understood why they were an evil and why people with sense wanted to control them, for the pleasure was forbidden and lay in the evil itself: in the evil of the power and in the power of the evil. Ella lifted the Colt and rolled her wrist back and forth to feel its weight. She thought about it some more.

She believed in opening her soul to the things she felt, in her heart and her gut and her body, without backing away from them. She didn't expect that all the things she might feel would be good things. She was a singer, and a true singer too, and anyone who sang the song truly felt the feeling inside it for what it was. If you didn't, you were a false singer, which was to say no singer at all. The music she thought of as hers wasn't all love and sex and sweet hearts broken and crying. It was mostly those things, sure, but she'd sung mean songs too, with hurt and hatred and spite in them, with the wish in the words and the music that someone would get hurt. And because she was a true singer and respected the song, she'd felt that meanness in her bones and she'd wanted someone hurt, not anyone in particular, but the million some-ones for whom the song was meant. Or maybe it was meant for no one at all, she didn't know, she just knew that the point was to feel it.

And so she opened herself to the song in the gun and it was one of the mean songs. That was its truth and that was the way she under-stood what she felt when she turned the Colt in her hand. Like the sounds she could make with her chest and throat it was partly in her and partly in the music and always in both; each one had some power over the other. She looked down at the Colt, blue-black, oily, dense and gorgeous in her fist. It made her hand look slender; she couldn't think of anything else that did. The Colt had given her slender hands she'd never had before. It was dancing with her. It was like the bad-ass guys she'd seen at the club and had wanted to fuck in an instant but hadn't because they were bad; woman-haters and crackheads and pimps, with girls stretching out before them to eternity, a stand-in-line-here for the previously-fucked-who-wanted-to-be-fucked-up-more. That wasn't her bag. She didn't have the time to be someone else's fool. The Colt was bad-ass all the way. If she hadn't been in the place she was in, she would have told the gun, No thanks, Slim, and never picked it up again. As it was, she would dance with it as far as she had to and no more. She wouldn't let it scare her off, but she wouldn't let it spirit her away.

She looked at George and the Colt didn't seem like such a bad-ass anymore. George was a dancer, she'd decided. For the first two hours of this drive through the night he'd tangled up her mind. She hadn't known where the fuck he was coming from. Then she'd realized that unlike just about everybody else she ran into he wasn't coming from anywhere except where he was. It had taken her that long to see that he was treating her like she was on the highest level he knew: his own. He told her straight, he let her make her mind up, and once she did he didn't try to persuade her otherwise. It was so right—it was so true—it was weird.

Like the gun, for instance: she'd asked him about it and he'd told her; then she'd asked him for it and he'd unloaded it and given it to her and explained what she needed to know. Was he irresponsible and crazy? she'd wondered. Then as she'd cocked the hammer to squeeze the trigger for the first time George had said, "The only reason on this wide earth for holding on to that thing is if you know deep down in your gut—I mean right down, below that ring you're wearing, not high in the stomach—that when the moment comes to kill a man you can do it right there and then without a quiver or a qualm. That's something you can know—and must know—before that moment comes. If not, you're a hell of a lot safer not to carry it at all. So you think on it for a while."

Now, as she looked at him, his skull gaunt and shadowy in the light bouncing back from their headlights on the road, he turned to her and said, "Well? Can you do it?"

Ella knew that if she lied to him George would know.

"Yes," she said. "I can do it."

"Good," said George. "We stop over at Mitch's maybe he'll let us loose off a few rounds so you can get the feel of the back kick."

"Who's Mitch?" she asked.

"Sorry," said George. "I been turning things over in my head, thought I'd told you. Mitch is an old union buddy, lives up the road a piece towards Greenville. Back in the sixties him and me organized a canning factory together was paying segregated wages, no safety standards worth a damn, the usual stuff. Under Reagan they kicked the union out again—same all over—but at least by then they couldn't go all the way back to the way things were."

George seemed to drift off for a moment, then caught himself and came back.

"Anyhow, I figure the cops aren't looking for us—that's thanks to you—and Georgia'll still be there come morning, so we may as well rest up a few hours. I need it even if you don't. Mitch'll give us a new car too. No point taking chances on someone tracing this one."

Ella filtered half of what he said through the gauze of what she knew to be her own ignorance. No one she'd ever spent time with had made her feel that she knew so little about the world, or at least its past. She knew her world well enough. But Tarawa, unions, segregation? Even

Reagan was a just dimly remembered comic figure from her childhood. She wasn't ashamed not to know these things, she was just excited to curiosity by the conviction with which George spoke of them.

"It's the middle of the night. Won't Mitch be surprised?" she said.

George laughed from his belly. "Hell yes, but not so he'll let us know it. I've tried to surprise him before."

"I have to ask you something," said Ella.

"Go ahead."

"Did you enjoy killing those two men tonight?"

"That's a good question." George thought about it for a long time. Then he said, "Ella, I haven't done anything—or anything that felt like anything—in a long time. In almost as long a time as you've been alive." George rolled his shoulders. "Now I'm doing something again and that feels good. You can't know how good. Killing those guys back there was part of that. Made me think I can still cut the mustard. That's a dangerous feeling. But I didn't ask those scumbags to follow me, make threats to you, throw down on us like they did. They took their life in their own hands. I guess their dying gave me more of a feeling of life, I admit, but I didn't enjoy the killing in itself. I didn't have time to hate them enough for that. It was just something I decided needed doing and I don't apologize for having done it."

He kept his eyes on the road ahead. He said, "You think that's cold?"

Ella thought about her own reaction to the deaths. It was as George said: the men had been there, and they'd meant them harm, and then they were gone.

"I don't feel sorry for them," she said. "Maybe I should, I don't know. Taking someone's life's not a good thing to do, I mean as a basic principle, but I guess it's all relative."

"Lot of folk these days talk about good and bad being 'relative,' as if they were telling us something new. That's why you're confused." He shrugged. "Seems to me good and bad've always been relative out there in the world, but they're not relative inside your own self, and that's the place it matters. You look inside and you draw your line, then you stand on one side or the other and you pay the price. Those guys died for money." He glanced at her face and body. "Or worse. Let their families feel sorry for them."

"What if your good is different to mine?" said Ella. "What if your good is my bad?"

"Then, up to a point, you live and let live," said George. "Beyond that you talk. Talking was my job, negotiating. I'll talk with the Devil himself to avoid a fight. But if you pull a gun on me you'd better know that I'm readier than you are: readier to die or go to a hospital or prison or anywhere else you want to lie down and be in pain. That's the difference that counts. They think life and limb's worth more than it really is. Their life, my life, whoever's. That's what makes them weak. That's why they're dead and I'm not."

George's lips and jaw stiffened into a grim and unrepentant sculpture.

"I got past all that sanctity of human life stuff a long time ago, when the bodies—friend and foe alike—were heaped as high as my shoulder and rotting while I watched."

Ella sensed from his voice, from the reverence and the fire, that this was the central memory of his life.

She said, uncertainly, "Tarawa?"

George nodded. "Right."

"Was that in Vietnam?"

George relaxed and smiled and shook his head. "By the time Vietnam came around the FBI'd had me pegged as an old commie agitator for ten years. They wouldn't have let me go there even if I'd wanted to, and anyway, I was way too old."

Ella said, "You must think I'm kind of stupid."

"No," said George. "When I was nineteen I didn't know much about what'd happened fifty years ago and ten thousand miles away. Hell, at seventeen I was so stupid I joined the Marine Corps *before* Pearl Harbor." He glanced at her. "That's when the Japanese air force attacked us without warning."

"I know that part," said Ella.

George smiled again. "You don't want to listen to an old man telling war stories."

"Yes, I do, really," said Ella.

She wasn't humoring him. She was on the adventure of her life with this guy, she wanted to know what made him tick. It might even save her life—or his. But then she couldn't imagine that he would ever need saving.

She pressed him. "I want to know. Go on."

"Well," said George. He shifted in his seat so he was more upright. "The island itself was called Betio, a pinprick on a map of the Pacific Ocean, part of Tarawa atoll. Now, I wasn't green. I'd been with Carlson's Raiders—Second Battalion—at Makin the year before, where we'd surprised a hundred and fifty Japs and left only two alive to tell the tale—and I thought I knew the score." He grimaced. "Jesus Christ."

Even though he'd said so little, Ella felt a lump in her throat. She didn't know why. Then she realized it was because George had one in his. He coughed.

"Anyhow, on Betio there were four thousand Japs waiting for us—Imperial Marines, man for man as good fighters as any ever wore a uniform—and they were dug in deep like only those fuckers knew how." He stopped. "Excuse me," he said.

Ella almost said, "What for?" then realized it was for swearing. "Don't worry," she said.

"The island was less than one square mile in area and we dropped three and a half thousand tons of high explosives on it. When we cleared the landing craft it seemed like we might as well have dropped popcorn. We waded five hundred yards through red foam. That first day my company took sixty percent casualties and I hadn't seen a single yellow face. That night, waiting, I wanted to kill more than I wanted to live, and when we got down to it, on the second and third days, yes, I enjoyed it too. We burned them in their hundreds and gutted them with bayonets and blasted and shelled and gunned them in their warrens and holes till the island stank to high heaven with their rotting yellow bowels. We killed all four thousand of 'em and I wished it had been four million. Later, when we dropped the bomb on Hiroshima, I wept. For joy."

"No," Ella heard herself cry. "You don't mean that. I can't go along with that."

"You're right not to," said George. "I won't argue. But they were an evil. I'm not talking individuals but what they did as a nation. They'd murdered millions of civilians—Chinese, Siamese, Koreans, Malays—and enslaved multitudes more who didn't even know where Japan was. They were torturers and tyrants—historical fact—and we helped set things right. I hated them then and I hate them now and if there's such a place as the hereafter I'll hate them there as well."

George's hands were clenched and rigid on the wheel. For the first time Ella felt scared of him. She didn't think for a second he would harm her but she felt fear just the same. It was the rage and bitterness—so suddenly bright and blazing—that she feared. She didn't want it to be in him.

"George, you're not a hateful man. I won't believe you."

"You think you could spray a flamethrower over twenty screaming men trapped in a bunker—then go find more and do it again—without hatred in your belly? I couldn't. You think those yellow maggots committed suicide by the hundred for their honor?" He snorted with contempt. "No. They were terrified—and broken—by a hatred they hadn't imagined could exist, coming at them one inch at a time through everything they could fling against us. It seeped across the sand and through their pillboxes and into their little yellow minds till it cracked them apart. They were one of the great warrior races of the earth. We didn't out soldier them, we out-hated them. And then we slaughtered them. Wasn't courage or Uncle Sam or love for the folks back home that drove us up those beaches. Through massed machine-gun fire? And the spilled-out innard workings of our buddies? No. It was hatred, black and pure and bloody as ever there's been."

Ella felt bombarded, battered. She grabbed at a thought and blurted it out.

"But there's too much hatred, isn't there? All around."

George looked at her and something in her face wiped the fury from his eyes. His features twitched with confusion and regret. He looked shaken and gray. He took a deep breath and blew it out slowly.

"I'm sorry if I upset you, Ella," said George. "That wasn't my intention."

"I know it wasn't. And you didn't, I'm fine."

For a moment he was alone with his memories, of sacrifices made and horrors witnessed that she could never imagine.

"You're right," he said. "There's too much hatred all around. But if we didn't have a use for it, it wouldn't be in us in the first place."

She'd never thought about hatred that way before. It made sense.

"Maybe you're right too," she said. "I just wish you weren't."

"Yes," said George. "So do I."

They sat in silence for a while, listening to the drone of the engine and the hum of the tires on the blacktop and watching the semis rolling by. The Colt .45 in Ella's lap didn't feel so seductive anymore and she was glad. Maybe she'd learned more than just a piece of history from Tarawa. Maybe she could now make more sense of Charlie's letter. Or Clarence Jefferson's, as she was now trying to think of him. George had given her the letter and she'd read it as best she could in the street light of the City without making any comment and without George asking her any questions. Instinctively, she liked that about him, that he didn't ask her much about herself. It made her feel like what he saw in her was what he got and that that was all he needed. It made a change from vapid bullshit and having to put on a show and make out she was more interesting than she felt herself to be. She pulled her bag up from between her feet. She hadn't had a cigarette since getting in the car and throwing up. Now that she thought about it the craving swept through her.

"You mind if I smoke?" she said.

"Feel free," said George.

She rolled down the window. The wind was cool, nice. She lit a Camel. The letter from Jefferson was folded in her jacket pocket. George hadn't asked for it back. She needed to read it again.

"Can we put the light on?" she asked.

In the City George had said no, they didn't want to draw the attention of some cop. Now he said, "Best wait until we're off the highway."

He bent forward to look past her at a road sign. She turned to read it but the sign was gone.

"Just a few minutes," said George.

Ella sat back and smoked the cigarette and let her mind go drifty and blank. She was bone-tired. Exhausted. George was wrong about her: she would never have made a U.S. Marine. Could she have hated enough? Maybe she flattered herself but she just couldn't see it. Or maybe it was because she hadn't seen innard workings of her friends spilled at her feet. Who was she supposed to hate now? Anyone? Did she have to, or would George handle that side? She leaned her head against the doorpost. George turned the car off the highway and swung onto a country road.

Ella stared through the open window at a night landscape full of nothing. She dragged on her cigarette. She felt lonely. She tried to think of somebody she would really rather be with instead of driving around Alabama's answer to the middle of nowhere. She couldn't. She couldn't think of anywhere she'd rather be. She wasn't in this situation by chance. It was predestined. It was in her stars. It didn't matter that she didn't know what the fuck it was all about or that no one seemed able to tell her: if it wasn't somehow a part of her then it just wouldn't be happening. George thought this was his gig, she could tell, but he was wrong. It was really hers. She couldn't explain how she knew it, but she was at the center of all that was going down.

She heard him say, from her left, "Ella? You still want I should put the light on?"

Ella shook her head vaguely, without looking at him, and the light stayed off. She would read the letter again later, when she had some brain worth using, maybe tomorrow. She let the wind whisk the butt of the cigarette from her fingers. The stuff in the letter about the apocalypse and the *corpus delicti* wasn't her business anyway; it was bullshit; it wasn't what it was all about. She was here for some other reason. And Charlie wasn't Charlie; he was Jefferson. Clarence Jefferson. She realized that was why she felt lonely. Charlie wasn't who she'd believed him to be for all these years.

Ella couldn't remember a time when she hadn't known Charlie. He'd been a constant, since childhood. And he'd loved her, she'd always known that, never doubted it. He'd loved her singing too; and he'd made her feel safe, always. Safe. There'd never been any reason to be afraid of anything with Charlie on her side. He'd told her that she could be whoever she needed to be and do whatever she needed to do; all she had to do was be herself, no more—but no less—than that. *"Ella, if you don't have the courage to follow your dreams, why should they ever come true?"* And that had been so simple, and so true, it had amazed her. That was how he'd made her feel. He'd loved her, she knew that, though he'd never said so in so many words; not even in his last letter—which he hadn't sent to her.

And now he was dead. And he wasn't who she'd believed him to be through all the years of her life.

With the soft night wind in her hair, and feeling as lonely and as sad as she dared, Ella MacDaniels rested one hand on the unloaded gun in her lap and fell asleep.

TWELVE

Filmore Faroe spent the early hours—his first hours of liberty—walking around his Arcadia. His Arcadia repossessed. He toured the rooms of the mansion and found it almost unchanged. Even his clothes were still there, almost as if she had expected him to return someday. He went out into the gardens he had loved. And as he walked step by step, alone, he left the safety of the graveled and spot-lit ambulatories and lost his way. And in his lostness he wandered far, then farther still.

He needed, desperately, to be outside, to breathe free air and feel nothing above his head but the sky. The craving had come upon him as a cringing Rufus Atwater had found him in his study and related a story about Clarence Jefferson and a hidden store of incriminating material. Faroe had taken the information in but had not reacted and had given no decision. His world had just turned upside down. Until an hour ago he'd been as helpless as any human being alive. Now men died at his command. A forgotten empire had dropped into his lap. His mind teemed so rapidly he had no time to formulate one thought before the next came crowding forward, itself in its turn to be shoved from his awareness, incomplete, by a successor. But as he wandered through the gardens his thoughts, such as they were, were silenced by the rising floodtide of his senses, senses made hyperresponsive by methedrine and by the eternity he had endured without using them at all. Like a man from the barrenlands withered by thirst, who bolts down water only to find himself vomiting and cramped, he found himself reeling from smell to sight and from touch to sound, from sky to earth, and from flower to fountain, in a mounting delirium of glutted perception.

From out of the night loomed a bush of ghostly lilac, which seized his eyes and pulled him—a speed-charged noctambulant—across grass so soft and yielding to feet that had known only stone that he staggered as if in mire. A memory: he had planted this tree himself. The blossom's perfume sent him dizzy as he approached. Then, as he blundered into leaves and branches, the scent rammed up through his sinuses like thumbs and wrenched his head and dropped him blinded to the ground. His fingers squirmed in soil—erotic, moist—then, groping, found the trunk.

Its thickness spiked his heart. Through the wrinkled bark that filled his palms he felt another trunk, buried inside of the slim sapling— almost a reed—that he'd touched and held in another time. While he had shriveled in his cage in one unbroken, fogbound dream, the tree had grown and marked its years and seasons in the bole his hands now squeezed with uncontainable pain. To him those years and seasons were lost. Fundamentally lost. Without existence. He had even been denied the bitterness of the prisoner: the agony of hope and of fantasy, of the despair and self-pity of scratching the passage of days on the wall of his cell. She had taken not merely his liberty but his imprisonment too: his very being had been unknown to himself for thirteen years. The calibration appalled him with its meaninglessness: it could as well have been thirteen months or thirteen decades: he wouldn't have known the difference. Amid that formless and infinite indifference he remembered—in gouts of shame and rage—her insults and her taunts, her perfect face shining with the primal triumph of revenge. But those moments too could have been both one or one million. They slithered through the oceanic emptiness of his memory like a shoal of voracious eels. She had robbed him of more than just pride and pleasure and power, she had robbed him of experience itself. He had lost a quarter of his life.

For an instant his mind was clear and he saw and felt his loss in all its flawless cruelty: crueler now, by far, than all the indignities he had endured.

The instant snapped shut on him, and Filmore Faroe broke.

He battered his face into the lilac's mocking trunk. He bloodied his fingers to their quicks against its bark. He wept and roared in random bursts of emotion. His mouth filled with a bitter cud of blossom and leaves. A drumming of cold wet blows, tiny and innumerable, fell upon his back and neck and merged into the rivulets on his cheeks. The soil

144

beneath him shifted and slid as a rain as heavy as grief fell upon him, and in it Faroe ranted and crawled, until he could no longer hear his own voice, and he slumped on his belly and lay.

Sometime later they picked him up and half carried him over the lawn and across the gravel toward the wide steps of the portico. His great wandering had taken him, he now saw, no more than a few hundred pitiful yards. The sights and sounds that had earlier provoked him to such strange ecstasy were now a dead landscape that barely penetrated his mind at all. His thoughts assumed a manageable form. He was aware of the falling rain, of the men, whose faces he'd avoided, supporting his arms, and of the grand facade of the mansion resplendent before him. He cared for none of it. If they had dragged him back to the Stone House he would not have resisted, could not have. He realized that the intense, excruciating weariness of his bones, a tiredness that excluded sleep, was familiar to him. Sitting strapped and soiled in his plastic chair, he had felt it before, many times it seemed. Yes. The injection his retarded keepers had given him that morning was wearing off—the methedrine—the artifical high now giving way to black depression. He found himself yearning for the tranquilizers that would normally return him to the fog. A sudden cold seized him and he began to shiver uncontrollably. In place of the lost experience he'd wept for stood an icy and implacable mountain: the future he must reclaim.

"I can't do it," he heard himself say. "I can't."

They were at the foot of the steps to the house. A face slick with rain hovered over his right shoulder. Rufus Atwater.

Atwater smiled at him as if he were a child or a dement.

"Sure you can do it, Mr. Faroe," said Atwater. "Just a few steps now and we're home and dry."

Faroe clenched his teeth against the shivers racking his body. There was no point correcting Atwater but even in this state Faroe was humiliated that they thought he could not climb the steps. He shook their arms away.

"Let me go."

Atwater let go of his right arm and nodded across Faroe to whoever was holding his left. Faroe looked up and saw the letters: ARCADIA— carved into the stone as he had once carved the letters of his name across the world. His shivering vanished. He felt a great power flow into him and with the power a rage and a resolution. He could—and would—do it. He would take his destiny by the throat and any who

145

stood in his way would be destroyed. All this was his again, and more. He had come back from the dead. There was nothing he might not dare. He was Filmore Faroe.

It was time to take charge. Faroe could feel them all around him, waiting on his ordinance. He was, no doubt, a wretched sight: bent beyond his years, etiolated in strength, caked in the filth of his groveling and as ignorant as a nigger fieldhand. He didn't even know who was president of the United States. Yet these men stood waiting for his word. And Faroe knew they were right. He was the man. His mind hummed. The depression of minutes before had vanished; but the physical exhaustion remained. He had to get rid of it. He needed a revitalizer. He turned to Atwater.

"Mr. Atwater, I want you to return to the Stone House."

"Sir?" said Atwater.

"Search the Jessups' place, their home. Somewhere in there you'll find a collection of medications. It's important. Bring them all."

Faroe thought: the Jessups. He'd kicked the corpse of Woodrow in the head, twice, where it had lain on the ground. The feeling had been intense. The killing of Harvill had been even better. But he'd allowed emotion to bury his thinking. The preparations had to be made now for his smooth return to power.

"Bring Woodrow Jessup's body too," said Faroe. "I want both of them preserved."

Atwater smiled nervously.

"Preserved?" said Atwater.

It was clear that Atwater doubted his sanity.

"Put them in the freezer. When you come back I'll want a full rundown of the state of things. I've been out of touch, Mr. Atwater." Faroe smiled. "I'm assuming you are the man I need to talk to."

The doubt evaporated. Atwater grinned. "Yes, sir. I am your man."

"Good," said Faroe. "I want to hear more about Captain Jefferson. We've got a lot to do."

He was giving orders again. The power of it filled him. There would be more orders, thousands, great and small. This was what he needed, not fresh air and lilac blossoms. This was what he was born to. He put a hand on Atwater's shoulder.

Faroe repeated, "We've got a lot to do."

Atwater beamed. "We're ready and waiting, Mr. Faroe."

"These men"—he nodded at the Latinos behind Atwater—"where did you get them?"

"Jack Seed recruited them through a man called Herrera, was some kind of colonel in the Cuban air force. They're safe, see, like illegal immigrants."

Faroe was pleased. He had had many business dealings with the Latin American military. Being unburdened by the tepid ethics of democracy, they possessed the admirable quality, in contrast to their American counterparts, that once they were bought they stayed bought.

"Get Herrera on the phone. I want to speak to him in person."

Atwater bobbed his head.

"The lilac tree where you found me," said Faroe. "You remember it?"

Atwater, puzzled this time, nodded again.

"I want it uprooted and burned. Not cut down: uprooted. Is that clear?"

"Clear as day, Mr. Faroe," said Atwater.

Faroe nodded. "Good. Now let's all be about our business."

THIRTEEN

LENNA PARILLAUD'S family boasted that their name had been a mercantile presence in New Orleans since the days of Louis Napoleon. Their original wealth had been founded on the importation of slaves. After they were ruined during the Civil War the family had started importing furniture and furnishings instead of captive flesh. This had allowed them to regain a toehold on the fringe of wealthy society from which to bow and scrape a sycophantic but comfortable living. By Lenna's father's time the Louisiana oil boom had given the family business a boost, and he expanded into a large warehouse and an elegant showroom on three floors in the Garden District.

When Filmore Faroe had officially "died," one of Lenna's first acts on succeeding to his wealth had been anonymously to purchase her father's business and all rights in perpetuity to any use of the company name, at almost twice the market price. This was not motivated by benevolence. After the deal was signed, Lenna had burned every stick of furniture, every wall hanging, every carpet in the company's inventory. She'd had both sites bulldozed to dust and turned into gardens, which she donated to the city, and the family name was never seen again on the masthead of any public enterprise. She'd paid them a visit then, her father and mother, and listened to their outrage and complaints: to her mother's mealy-mouthed cooing about "the way things were these days" and about disrespect for property and beauty, and to her father's bitter and vainglorious boast that if only he had known then what was going to happen no amount of money could have bought him out. Lenna told them who the true buyer was and watched the pain and incomprehension on their faces. Then she left them to grow old with their "Why?" forever unanswered. She hadn't seen or spoken to either of them since. It was one of the debts that Lenna had felt compelled to pay in full.

When she was seven years old her parents had sent her to an exclusive Catholic convent for her education. There she was schooled in the many complex and exquisite hypocrisies whose mastery was deemed important for those destined to represent the flower of Southern Catholic womanhood. To her later, adult, shame she never rebelled against either her family or the swollen, cawing and loathsome celibates who had instructed her. While some, at least, of her classmates had masturbated and smoked pot, Lenna had been a good girl; the perfect daughter. She had achieved all that had been asked of her. And when, without any thought for her, her socially starstruck parents had promoted her marriage to Filmore Faroe—with frantic urgings that brushed aside her teenage doubts and fears unheard—she had lacked the conviction to resist that too.

Those men for whom money was a true passion—a discipline, a commitment, an inevitability—and for whom the trappings and spending of it were therefore by-products of meager significance, were rare, as were all true men; but Filmore Faroe was one of them. For Faroe, as for many of his kind, socializing was at best an occasional and tedious necessity. Any conversation not spent in the service of the deal he considered a triviality. His business often took him abroad, to Latin America and Africa, where moderately generous bribes secured immoderately profitable returns. He was a racist, though no more committedly so than most men of his wealth and generation. His father had been active in the Klan but Filmore didn't have the time, though he made regular contributions.

While Faroe pursued his passion, Lenna found herself trapped in the splendid incarceration of Arcadia. Faroe didn't want her to go to college and so she didn't go; he didn't want her to work so she didn't; he didn't want her to go into the City alone and so she stayed on the plantation and rode horses and read books and ran the house and its staff. When she tried to discuss these things with her mother, she was reminded that her sworn duty was to love, honor and obey in the same way that she had done. She was married to one of the finest men in Louisiana: what more could she ask for? After two years of what had come to feel solitary confinement, Lenna found the lure of suicide stalking her mind.

· · ·

Grimes listened without interrupting and without asking any questions. Lenna made no excuses for herself; in fact she was careful to tell her story in a way that made clear the contempt she felt for her fidelity to the rules of her upbringing, her lack of spirit, her cowardice. Grimes knew better than to underestimate the psychological power of that elite socialization. The Louisiana governing class she'd inhabited was small, unto itself and—not just twenty years ago but to this day—deeply anachronistic. Grimes recalled one youngster who, on the occasion of his family's lavish annual garden party, had appeared in the branches of a tree and blown his brains out in front of the guests. The gossip columnists had drooled with glee. And Grimes had known others who had plunged into addiction and other vengeful self-mutilations. The payoff for conformity had lost its value; and Lenna, like the others, had felt betrayed. Her own act of rebellion was poignantly banal—the desire to walk a busy street and feel its heartbeat, just for once—but it set in motion a tragedy that couldn't be stopped.

On the evening of her twenty-first birthday Lenna finally broke out. She threw twenty-one red roses and a new emerald necklace into the trash can. She dressed in her tightest jeans and T-shirt and a denim jacket. Then she took herself off to the City. In her pocket was a telegram from Zaire—from Faroe—wishing her much love and a happy day.

The journey to town charged her with intense excitement, with forbidden and unknown possibility. She had no idea where she was going or what she would do when she got there. During those few miles alone at the wheel, a lifetime's eagerness to please was left behind; as it turned out, forever. She'd flipped the coin of an unbroken conformity and discovered on its hidden face a defiance she hadn't imagined was there. The defiance took her over with the force of a drug, a liberating spell that could only be denied at a price she'd spend the rest of her days repaying.

When she reached the City she wandered on foot: through a smoky, sighing dusk and down languidly teeming streets whose names she did not know; past blowsy women in hot pants and heels and the brassy exteriors of neon-lit bars. It was scary and forbidden and she almost went home. But his music called her in. No, both less than music and more: a single last note, aching and impossibly held in the hazy night until it spiraled away into silence. Lenna stepped down from the sidewalk into the applause of a basement jazz club.

He stood, loose and lean and without acknowledging the applause, at the front of a five-piece band. In his hands he held the trumpet whose sound had drawn her down. He looked up and across the room and she saw his eyes. She couldn't tell if he could see hers; but with a quickening in her stomach she hoped he could. Then he turned his face away and began another ballad. He didn't look her way again, not a single glance. Lenna took a table and drank white wine. She watched him while he played and even while he didn't; while the others took their solos, she watched him still. His big hands and long limbs, his strong chin and broad mouth. Lenna stayed for the second set and again, as far as she could tell, she didn't exist for him. When the encore had been played and the patrons drifted home, Lenna came to as if from a trance. She wondered if she was sober enough to drive home. Just as she concluded that she didn't care, he appeared from nowhere, and smiled, and invited her for a drink with the band.

She saw, in his eyes, that he knew it would be as easy as that. The fact that he knew—that that was the way he saw her—made her weak with raw excitement. A voice in her head that she'd never let herself hear before said, *You're going to be fucked.* And she shouted back. *Yes, I'm going to be fucked. I want to be fucked. I want him. And I don't have to answer to anyone.* When she said, "Sure," and he said, "Cool," Lenna trembled.

His name was Wes Clay.

Jammed in the back of a taxi, surrounded by jokes she couldn't catch but that she laughed at just the same, Lenna smoked her first joint. The streets of the City glided past the windows and she soared, she felt right, she was where she wanted to be and doing what she wanted to do. At a second club they slapped hands with other musicians and drank and smoked some more. Now Wes Clay looked at her all the time and she turned to liquid in the darkness of his gaze. He asked her what she thought about this and that and when she answered he listened. He was beautiful. And when he learned that she'd studied piano, he made her play and they taught her some things, and they jammed and fooled around until dawn. Then Wes Clay took her home with him and they made love. And it was making love, and not being fucked, because by then Lenna was in love with him and Wes was in love with her.

· · ·

Grimes remembered the feeling he'd picked up in Lenna earlier on that night: of youth frozen in time. Now, watching her face, he saw it thaw and come alive, saw the vitality and sweetness, the wonder and the passion, the many fragile treasures that she'd locked away and held on ice lest they should die. Though he didn't yet know why, though the joy of her long-ago love was right there in front of him—in the unguarded shine of her eyes and the sudden flash of her smiles—Grimes felt an unbearable sadness creep up inside him. He listened on.

Sex with Filmore Faroe had been unremarkable. It hadn't been traumatic, as she'd been led to believe, but neither was it a transport of delight. Faroe was considerate but conventional and she imagined she was much the same for him. If he hadn't wanted more, then neither had she. Wes Clay wanted her flesh—her juice, her sounds. He wanted her nude and she stripped off her clothes. He wanted her tongue and she sucked his mouth. He wanted her skin and she gave herself to his hands, his fingers gliding, snaring her wrist to her ankle, pulling her face down, splaying her open as he bit her shoulder and whispered "Baby" in her ear. And for a million reasons or none at all—drunk or stoned or crazy out of her mind—she trusted him to want something good and whatever that good was she wanted it too. She asked him to be inside her. She felt his cock part her and push against that initial resistance that she couldn't control and that dizzied her and through which she wanted him to break. He retreated, exquisitely, then pushed again and almost entered and could have but didn't, he waited, he pulled back. She heard his voice—"Baby"—and she made a noise. She lifted her hips hard and this time he slid into her and after that she remembered nothing: of what she uttered or what she did. Just the weight of his maleness, wrapping her around and pinning her down and filling her pelvis, her throat, her face with a liquid rhythm that smothered her from inside and pounded her from out, and in which she would have drowned and died if she could.

Afterward, with her head in his arm and squeezing on his come inside her, she stroked his chest while he slept. Then she slept too and dreamed of things she would never recall.

When she awoke and realized where she was she wanted to roar until the building fell down and snarl at the world so they'd know she was here: here and unrepentant, a hundred feet tall and stronger than the sea. Wes was still sleeping, sprawled on the sheet with a shaft of sun-light on his face. From the street below came the clatter of traffic and the working day. Lenna knew now what it was she wanted: all that she wasn't meant to want. The wasn't-meant-to-want was a fluid in her muscles and veins, a pleasure thick as oil and sweetly nauseous on her tongue. She closed her eyes and pulled her fingers through her hair and arched her back. She looked at him, breathing quietly in the morning light. She brushed her cheek down his ribs, his flank, across his thigh. His tight curled hair touched her face. His skin was sleek and warm. She licked his belly, tasted salt and perhaps herself. She watched his cock grow hard and swallowed the oil in her throat and the sweetness of it sent a spin to her skull. She licked his thigh, then his balls. He stirred. She didn't look at this face. She didn't want to. She wanted this to herself. She didn't want to know his thoughts, she didn't care if she pleased him. She knelt—not looking at his face—then bent and closed her eyes and sucked his cock. She moved in a spiraling dark, just her and her taking and giving. His fingers entered her cunt and she reached back and guided his fingers. She got there quicker than she imagined possible and waited and hovered, balancing on a wire taut and thin. Then he came in her mouth and she let herself fall, drinking and spas-ming as she dropped. As she lay there caked and wet she heard him say "Baby."

Lenna stayed with him for three days. They ate from bags and car-tons in his room, and sometimes in cafés. In a bar they watched a fight on TV and drank shots of Jack Daniel's without ice. At nights she watched him play. In the dawns and afternoons and early evenings they made love. She didn't tell him that she loved him, because she knew it was so, and because all that she was loved and all that she did loved. She was fearless and cool and out on a limb and the words were for those who were scared. She didn't even know whether he treated her badly or well, or her him. She had no maps or markers. Those too were for the scared. Nothing existed out there for Lenna to be scared of. There was only him and her and what they did from one moment to the next and she had no care or thought for how it might end.

On the fourth night it did end. By then there was a statewide hunt for her, missing, presumed kidnapped, concentrated on the City, where they finally found her car. Faroe was on an early plane home and wait-ing for a ransom demand. Her name was on the news channels she hadn't watched and in the papers she hadn't read.

A black street cop found her in the club, sitting with her wine at her table. The cop went over and spoke to Wes. Lenna immediately understood the score. Wes just came over to her and smiled. He wouldn't let his heart break here and neither would she. They were too fearless. They were too cool. Wes said, "You have to go now, Baby." They were too cool to kiss each other goodbye. It was right, she knew. Then Wes walked back to the stage and played for her one last time.

It was the cop whose face contained such fear.

"Don't ever tell anyone his name, you understand?" he told her. "You never met him, you were never here."

As he led her up to the street she heard it again: the aching note, impossibly held, as the cop car drove her away.

Grimes tried to picture Wes Clay in his mind. Beyond a certain point it was difficult. Lenna had known him for four glorious days. Her memory of him was the idealized image that any lover constructs of the beloved in the early days. That didn't mean it wasn't a real image—he didn't question the truth of their love—merely that it was difficult for a third party like Grimes to put much flesh on those radiant bones. Yet it occurred to him that the brief and flawless bliss of her affair had doomed Lenna to the memory of a perfection that she could never regain. She hadn't known Wes Clay long enough to discover his failings, as small or as large as they might have been; she never saw him tainted by anger or bad habit or by any of the petty and manifold weaknesses that afflict all men. Even if Wes had demonstrated such inadequacies in the time she had known him, they would have been either invisible to her or merely further proof of his charm. For he was her beloved and therefore perfect for that while.

When she got back to Arcadia, Lenna lied and excused herself and was understood, and maybe even believed, for there were no marks on her body to tell the tale and Wes Clay did not exist. She was sent to a psychiatrist, to whom she also lied, and was pronounced depressed, neglected and confused. Lenna didn't have a very clear memory of Faroe's reaction to all this, partly because she didn't care, partly because she was indeed depressed and confused. Within two weeks her body began to feel something else—vague but pervasive—and by three weeks after that she was a month late.

Lenna thought about an abortion and knew it was the only option for anyone in their right mind. In all truth she didn't know who the father was; as far as she could calculate he could have been either Wes or Faroe. If it was Wes she was doomed to scandal; if Faroe she was doomed to a life's connection to him that she no longer wanted. If she ran away again they would catch her. She was an adult and in principle she was free to go and do whatever she might choose; but she knew without any doubt that Faroe would have her brought back.

Perhaps, then, she wasn't in her right mind, for she was gripped by a resolution, a paralysis, an inertia—in the end it didn't matter what it was—to see the pregnancy through. She was nauseous and sick; she was drained; she was anemic and weak; she ate little and lost weight—all the normal trials of a secret pregnancy intensified by crippling bouts of terror. But her essential conviction, which she could not have explained to anyone even if she'd chosen to share it, never wavered. Come what may, she would have her child.

Her child.

By four months into the pregnancy she felt bloated beyond belief; yet by the bathroom scales she'd gained barely two pounds. No one noticed, or if any of the servants did they dared not say. During this period Faroe went about his life. He tried with some patience to penetrate her moods and she developed a savage temper she had not known before. Faroe sent her again to the psychiatrist, who also did not notice her gravidity. By five months she was taking her meals to her room and refusing to sleep with Faroe or even to see him. Despite her own conviction that she was going insane, she refused any further psychiatric help. Finally, after frantic scenes involving a locksmith and the dismantling of a barricade, Lenna found herself alone in her room with Faroe, the bulge in her belly no longer disguisable.

The pressure of twenty-three weeks of silence, of secrecy, of mounting paranoia and fear, burst the walls of her resolution. She told Faroe everything and he listened in white-lipped silence. At the end of her confession Faroe left without saying a word.

The lock was replaced on her door, only now she did not have the key, and her life of exile continued. She was supplied with the necessary supplements of iron and vitamins. Faroe came to see her each evening and took her for a walk around his gardens. He never spoke a word of whatever it was he was feeling. Her parents were excluded—by her choice as much as Faroe's—and she saw no one else except a Guatemalan nurse, who brought her food and helped her bathe and who spoke no English. Despite these conditions Lenna's heart lifted. She knew—or rather she thought she knew—what it meant to such a man that, in his terms, his wife might be incubating a nigger's child. Perhaps the torment of doubt that she had passed on to Faroe somehow lessened her own. Her health and strength improved. She gained weight steadily. Her commitment to her child grew more intense. The child had asked for nothing and knew nothing of the world that awaited its birth. It knew nothing of its paternity or its race. Through these last months she speculated on the future. If the father of the child was Wes, she knew, she came to realize, that Faroe would never let her keep it. It would vanish without trace into a family she would never know and would never be able to find. She did not underestimate Faroe's power. If it was his child? She did not know. Was it in him to forgive and forget? He said nothing and she dared not ask for fear of provoking him. He would want the child brought up as his own, that she did not doubt, but would she be allowed any part in it? Or would she be banished from their lives? She could not know.

And she could not know either that Filmore Faroe had already made his deal with a devil called Clarence Jefferson.

Grimes might rather not have heard what was to come next. Lenna had already begun to hold her hand against her belly and rub as though it ached. As she continued her story, her fingers hooked and dug into her, and she rocked to and fro as internal cramps, genuine and severe, bent her forward over her knees. Grimes knew she was in physical pain but he restrained an impulse to reach out. The best he could do for her was sit and listen, for he knew that this was a tale that had never been told before and that her pain was necessary to its delivery.

When Lenna's water broke, Faroe brought a Vietnamese doctor, whose name she never knew. The doctor gave her an injection and Lenna woke up in a one-room shack with a tin roof. Where it was, she didn't know. Her mind spiraled through a twisting tunnel of drugs and pain and dread, and she clung to and focused on her task of delivering the child. Faroe was there, stony-faced and grim, and the Latina nurse and the Vietnamese doctor. Hours passed and Lenna focused and clung. Toward the end, rain started to drum on the shack's tin roof. When the girl child was born and Lenna heard her cries and looked, Lenna cried too. She cried for her beauty. She cried for her puckered, squalling face. She cried for her trembling, fist-clenched energy, tiny yet boundless in its innocent rage. And she cried for her pale brown skin, though at that moment she would not have changed it for the world.

The murmuring, smiling nurse took the baby aside and the doctor bent over Lenna and she barely felt the sting of another needle. Lenna asked to have the girl child back. She could not see her. She had not even held her in her arms. She asked again. She demanded and was ignored. Her consciousness started to fade and drain. She remembered the needle and fought it, sliding, sliding. She demanded yet again, her words a blur in her ears.

Give me my child.

She heard the door open on a gust of rain, and a massive form—a burly shadow in a Panama hat, a pervading essence of disciplined evil—entered the room. There was a muffled groan and the clink of chains.

Lenna's mind mounted a resistance that defied all science against the chemicals crushing her down. She knew. She tried to scream but her vocal cords were numbed. Gunshots thundered, relentless in the squalid space now smoking with bloody execution. She raised herself from the mattress.

At the foot of the bed knelt Wes Clay.

His face, once beautiful—beautiful, even now—was so damaged that she doubted he could see her eyes. Lenna's throat still wouldn't move. She couldn't speak. She couldn't scream. She struggled not to black out. A dull thump. Wes Clay gasped and doubled forward, out of her sight. She saw Filmore Faroe, his face a bright mask of bigotry as something vile blurted from his mouth. He raised both arms above his head. There was a flash of steel in the lamplight and the confusion of her senses was swamped by a single desperate question: where was her child? Lenna struggled for the edge of the bed. She saw her—her baby daughter—there: nestled with innocent contentment in the crook of a thick and bulging arm, the security of a massive hand. Lenna tried to move her arms, to take and stroke and hold. But before she could reach she was frozen by the image of her own ultimate horror.

Dripping and swaying in the air before her hung Wes Clay's head, suspended by the hair from Filmore Faroe's bloodstained fist.

Still Lenna could not scream. She looked at Faroe's face.

Faroe blinked twice. Then he lowered his prize and turned his back and walked away without a word.

Lenna tumbled from the mattress to the rough plank floor. *Her baby.*

She hauled herself to her knees, head swimming, her veins and limbs drugged with liquid rubber. The slam of a door pierced the fog. She raised her head.

The room was empty.

The burly essence of evil—and the swaddled innocence nestled in the bulging arm, the massive hand—was of an instant gone. And with that sudden vanishment Lenna's soul vanished too and her heart was turned to stone.

And now she screamed: with a pain too wide and deep for human knowing.

She crawled through blood. Past the blade of a shining machete; past bodies, one and two; past a third she dared not see. The door swam before her. Disembodied fingers, bloodstained and numb, found the handle, turned and pulled.

A gust of rain.

A bolt of jagged lightning.

She crawled on, into the drenching wind of an infinite night.

Finally she fell.

And as she fell, and in a voice more ancient than her own, she launched across the midnight field a cry that was as vast and bottomless as the darkness itself.

FOURTEEN

A LIFE IN MEDICINE had acquainted Grimes with the infinite variety of human suffering, most of it random and without discernible meaning. Even so, Lenna's tale left him feeling numb. Faroe's crime was so extreme that for any ordinary individual it would have been an act of psychosis. But Faroe had not been insane. He had been justified and informed within his deepest fiber by an entire subculture, by an entire history living still, which murdered black men for far smaller infractions than Wes Clay's, and finally by his own line; a line that deserved to end.

Lenna sat on the sofa. The cramps seemed to have subsided. She was no longer crying and she seemed spent. There were things Grimes could have said but they would have been platitudes sucked empty by the scale of what she had suffered. His words would not have been to help her but to ease his own desire to be useful. He kept his mouth shut, and his tears inside, and let her finish.

Later, on the night that Lenna gave birth, Filmore Faroe found her unconscious body and took her back to Arcadia. When she came around he told her that "the baby of the nigger" had been killed. Throughout all the years that followed Faroe never gave any sign that he believed this not to be true. Lenna remained in a state of near catatonia—of total psychic collapse—for many months. Then the player of games, the burly essence—Clarence Jefferson—reappeared, secretly, before her and offered his irresistible gift.

Grimes could imagine his caramel voice, his bright and shameless eyes, the force of his logic, as he bore down on the traumatized woman and lured her in.

She could, Jefferson told her, win back Faroe's heart. Yes indeed, for such a monstrous crime could leave even Faroe vulnerable to the weakness, the virus, of guilt. Jefferson knew Faroe better than Faroe knew himself; more than that, he understood the way of things human. Faroe had loved Lenna: and rare was the lover betrayed who did not, in the secret heart of his jealousy and shame, love his faithless one even more, and even as he hated her, Faroe would accept her contrite return, Jefferson promised her. If Lenna would have the revenge that would restore her to life, she had to trust him. Then, once she'd regained Faroe's affection, whatever she wanted for his punishment, Clarence Jefferson would bring it to pass.

There was no doubt in Grimes's mind that Jefferson had talked Filmore Faroe into the fateful and murderous course that he'd taken with similarly unctuous words.

Grimes knew that most of what passed for evil in the world was in fact the product of stupidity and other human failings such as self-delusion, avarice and rage. Clarence Jefferson floated above such emotional and intellectual pitfalls. He had set himself the task of ripping aside the mask behind which, as he saw it, all of human life cowered in unforgivable ignorance of its true nature. The cosmos was amoral and cared nothing for its contents. All men—all women—were at their core violent and depraved. Everything that civilization had erected—law, religion, art—was nothing more than a flimsy dike, repeatedly breached, with only a single purpose: to hold back the violent sea of depravity within. The only redemption, the only absolute truth, lay in embracing that depravity and living it out to the utmost possible degree. This was his *raison d'être*. He was the bad man's Calvin, a philosopher-king of vileness.

So in her mental desert Lenna had listened to and heard the fatman's words. The idea appalled Grimes, but it was probably true: hatred had been her only way out, the only lifeline strong enough by which to haul herself out of madness. What other emotion could have given her life meaning? The bought love of therapy? The sublime balm of forgiveness? He could hear Jefferson chortling at the thought from his grave. From hatred alone had Lenna found the strength to reconstruct her sanity and her self. She had steeled herself to the self-abasement she knew she'd have to endure and, over years, she had won back Faroe's forgiveness, and then his love, and finally even his trust.

Then she'd told the fatman what she'd wanted; and even he had been impressed.

Jefferson faked Faroe's death in the car wreck, using a skid-row vagrant of similar appearance and build. He substituted the appropriate X rays and medical records, chose the appropriate coroner and guided the legal process through to a moving and tearful cremation ceremony, after which Faroe's ashes were scattered on the garden he had cultivated himself. The real Filmore Faroe was meanwhile a drugged prisoner, unknowingly awaiting the construction of the Stone House and the recruitment of the Jessups.

Grimes listened to what she'd done to Faroe without comment. The apt and perfect sadism of her revenge astonished him with its precision and scale, its sustained longevity. He would have given in to something far more primitive and brief, something that employed a dull knife. Lenna didn't chronicle the years she'd kept him in there. She just related, without emotion, Filmore Faroe's escape from the Stone House and his sending her there to be raped by Jack Seed. Then she sat hunched on the sofa and stared into space.

It dawned on Grimes that they were in even worse trouble than he'd thought. Filmore Faroe, at this moment, had to be a very angry man; and he would realize that with Lenna free and hunting for Jefferson's hoard, he wasn't yet out of danger himself. The power that Lenna had wielded was now in Faroe's hands and that power stood against them. Against George and Ella, too. Grimes looked at Lenna again and didn't know what to do. For a moment he wished that she would vanish before his eyes. Then he felt ashamed of himself.

He said, "It was Jefferson's letter that told you your daughter was still alive."

Lenna, still staring, nodded.

"And that I knew all the rest."

"You did, didn't you?" she said.

"Yes," said Grimes, "I knew everything. Why didn't you tell me all this before?"

"I couldn't trust you. Not with Ella out there. I didn't know who to believe. And Jefferson told me not to push you. He told me to wait."

Lenna looked into his eyes. Then the tone of her voice changed slightly and she quoted without hesitation.

" 'Put that to him, Lenna, and only that, then have patience and wait . . . For Grimes, as you see him, is a clown—a true clown, a fool—and so he has the heart of a clown, and in his own time, which will be the fool's time and not that which might best fit his purpose, he will come to you with his clown's courage and his fool's strength, and he will stand at your side and show you the way, the way that he does not even know himself.' "

Grimes looked into her harrowed face for as long as he could. Then he swallowed and stood up.

Grimes walked over to the door and pulled it open and looked out. The rain had eased off to a drizzle. Gul loped past him and disappeared into the predawn dark. Grimes lit a Pall Mall and thought about Jefferson. Grimes hated him. The fatman had spun his poisoned web across a vast arc of space and time, and yet his genius lay in the fact that he himself did not eat of the people trapped within it. He let them eat each other while he stood back and laughed. He fed on the strife and pain of their feeding. Everything Grimes had learned tonight confirmed his original theory that the only way to deal with this was, simply, to stay out of the web. But Jefferson had foreseen even that and with a cordial sentence—*"Give my regards to your daddy"*—he had snared Grimes too. The taunt of the airline ticket had just made it more certain that Grimes, the fool, would do the wrong thing. If the letter had arrived alone Grimes would have burned it on the spot and packed his bags and headed for Montana. But he hadn't—he'd given Jefferson's regards to his father—and now he and George and Ella and ultimately Christ knew who else were diligently engaged in the fatman's work. Hatred. Jefferson had taught Grimes some lessons of his own about hatred. The airline ticket had been more than just a taunt: it was a reminder that forced him to acknowledge that he could still—even now—walk away from all this if he wanted to. He could leave them all to it. His chances of survival would be a hell of a lot better than they were at the moment.

He flicked his cigarette out into the dew and turned from the door. Without looking at Lenna he went over to the dryer and took out his suit. It was still a little damp but he wasn't in the mood to care. Gul trotted back inside, wet again and dourly vigilant, and followed Grimes as he took the suit into his bedroom, found a clean shirt and changed. Grimes tied his black tie in front of the mirror without catching his eyes. His shoes were still soaked and cold but there wasn't much he could do about that; he was goddamned if he was going to die wearing sneakers. He finished the necktie and turned around to Gul, who sat on his haunches and looked up at him with blind devotion.

"We are fucked, man, do you know that?" said Grimes.

Gul stood up and came over and Grimes squatted down. Gul licked his throat and Grimes put his hand in the dog's mouth. Gul chewed his fingers without inflicting any wounds.

"You know what Clarence Jefferson said to me before he died?" said Grimes.

Gul let go of his fingers and looked at him, waiting.

"He said, 'Tell me you don't hate me.' "

Gul blinked.

"Now he calls me a clown."

Grimes smiled and rubbed the dog's dewy flanks until he felt the hatred dissolve from his heart. If he could do it without hate, maybe it would be a thing worth doing after all. And, for all that he was a belligerent old bastard, Grimes did want to see his father again. Grimes glanced over to the table where he'd emptied his pockets: wallet, keys, revolver, passport, ticket to Argentina. He walked across and put the things in his pockets. He went over to the window: the rain had stopped. He clicked his tongue at Gul and went back next door. Lenna sat where he'd left her on the sofa. She was still staring into space and looked lost.

"Better get ready," said Grimes.

Lenna didn't react.

"Lenna?" said Grimes.

She looked up at him.

"Get dressed," said Grimes. "We're going to Baton Rouge."

Lenna said, "I thought we were going to Georgia."

"We need an airport," he said. "I've got a ticket we can use."

FIFTEEN

RUFUS ATWATER sat in Filmore Faroe's study and yearned to light up a Kool without finding the courage to ask if he could. Opposite him, Faroe sat behind the leather-topped desk and stared at him with lizard eyes.

While Atwater had gone to the Stone House and made the bowel-loosening trip back with his cargo of drugs, corpses and bad news, Faroe had changed his appearance. The disheveled wreck with gray hair plastered across his cheeks that Atwater had left on the steps was now dressed in a gray suit and blue silk necktie. Faroe had also shaved his head as bald as a stone and looked as menacing as anyone Atwater had ever seen. This effect was enhanced by the presence of the Cuban, Roberto Herrera, standing in the shadows behind Faroe's right shoulder. Occasionally Faroe would say something to Herrera in rapid Spanish and Herrera would nod without speaking, and Atwater would feel even more worthless and out of his depth. Faroe was putting the vise grips on him: the spic cocksucker could speak English. Atwater was wet and miserable. Jack Seed, whom Atwater now missed and loathed in equal measure, was wrapped in a sheet in the Dodge Tradesman panel van with half his skull missing and his dick and balls chewed off. But there was no going back. Icing Bobby Frechette had been a turning point. When Atwater had gone through that door blasting, he'd changed forever. He was no longer a prosecutor: he was a killer. Wet and miserable or not, he'd best start acting like one.

Atwater had told Faroe all he knew, about Parillaud, about Jefferson and about the investigation that had led to them springing Faroe from the Stone House. Almost as an afterthought, and for the sake of completeness, he told him about Dr. Grimes. Faroe had employed Jefferson years back and the idea of the hidden stash that Parillaud and the other parties were looking for had set him thinking. He'd now been pondering in silence for what felt like an hour. No one had interrupted and Atwater had decided it wasn't going to be him.

Finally, Faroe half turned his head toward Herrera and uttered what sounded like instructions, again in Spanish. Herrera listened carefully—his lean features were shrewd, Atwater conceded, maybe even intelligent—then saluted—saluted, for Chrissakes—and left the room with a crisp, military gait. When the door closed behind him Faroe rubbed a hand over his smooth white scalp and looked at Atwater.

"Don't be disturbed by Colonel Herrera," said Faroe. "His interests in no way conflict with your own. This is a team effort."

Atwater let his breath out in what he hoped didn't sound like relief. So he wasn't going to be buried somewhere on the plantation with Jack. He was still needed. He was still a part of the team. His confidence started to return.

"I didn't know he was a colonel, Mr. Faroe," he said.

"Cuban air force. He defected with one of their MiGs. Our government was grateful, but not as grateful as Colonel Herrera would have liked. He understands that I shall not be nearly so niggardly."

"Whichever way he swings, you can count on me," said Atwater.

"It's important you know what's at stake here, Mr. Atwater. My return here is a more delicate endeavor than you might think. It will take time for me to reacquaint myself. I am, after all, dead. But that state is not without its advantages, as I'm sure you can imagine."

Atwater could only imagine this in the vaguest possible terms but he wanted to let Faroe know that he was with the program. "Absolutely," he said.

"Fundamental to the successful outcome of my return is that we get Magdalena back alive. Do you understand that?"

Atwater's mind floundered. "I think so, sir," he said.

"You are a prosecuting attorney, I've no doubt a very expert one. I'm sure you could list much more readily than I can the crimes Magdalena has committed, and of which I am the principal victim."

Now Atwater caught on. He nodded and smiled.

"I think she'd be looking at some hard time."

"I'm sure, also, that it could be arranged so that she would never come to trial at all," said Faroe. "Suicide in prison isn't uncommon, after all."

"It happens, sure," said Atwater.

"I don't want to be seen in the public eye right now. If we have Magdalena I can prepare my affairs at leisure. Then my escape from the Stone House can be reconstructed at a convenient date."

Atwater raised one eyebrow. "So that's why you want the Jessups kept in the freezer."

Faroe nodded. "This breathing space—as a dead man—is even more important now that we are so close to Captain Jefferson's legacy. You are clearly a man of considerable intelligence, Mr. Atwater. You can probably imagine as well as I can the kind of material he might have put away. But you cannot imagine the use to which I will be able to put it."

Atwater had admitted it to himself long ago. It seemed politic to do so in front of his new master. "You're right about that, sir. I wouldn't know what to do with it."

"It will more than simply smooth my return to the arena; it will give me more leverage than any other figure, elected or otherwise, in the whole state. Perhaps even in the South."

"We've been searching for that stash for months," said Atwater. "I don't know that we're as close to it as you'd like. Or to finding Miss Parillaud either, come to that. Even when all the law enforcement agencies work together, a manhunt's as much about luck as anything else."

"Most luck stems from someone else's mistake," said Faroe. "It's clear that Dr. Grimes was plunged into this affair unprepared. The chances are huge that he's made a mistake."

"Grimes?" said Atwater, puzzled. "Where does he fit in?"

"Are you familiar with Occam's razor?" asked Faroe.

"I'm afraid I'm not," replied Atwater.

"It's a medieval scholastic stratagem for solving problems of causality. It states that when there is a choice between, on the one hand, a single plausible reason for a phenomenon and, on the other, several separate reasons, equally plausible when taken together but related only by their common synergistic outcome, then the correct solution is most likely to be found in the one rather than the several."

This sort of bullshit took Atwater back to law school. He could follow it.

"What you mean is that Grimes must be the key to both Miss Parillaud's escape and to Jefferson's stash."

"Very good. You know where Grimes lives?"

"Yes, sir," said Atwater.

"Go and search his home, his office, whatever. Find me something."

"I've already got two men watching his father. Name of George. Grimes saw him last night, seems they had some kind of fight."

"You see? You'd already worked all this out for yourself," said Faroe.

Atwater had a suspicion that this was a roundabout way of calling him an asshole. Okay. He'd show Faroe he needed more than a bunch of spic pilots to help him out. Then he'd be due some loyalty payments of his own. Atwater stood up.

"I'll get on to it," said Atwater.

"No police," said Faroe. "Not until I'm ready."

"Of course," said Atwater.

He was irritated enough to ask the question that had bugged him all night.

"You'll have to forgive my curiosity, but I must ask. Why did Miss Parillaud keep you locked up in that place?"

"It is to your curiosity that I owe my freedom, Mr. Atwater," said Faroe. "And so I do forgive it." He leaned forward and his voice dropped half an octave. "But if you ever ask that question again, of me or of anyone else, our relationship will be terminated as abruptly as I am able to bring it about."

Atwater said, "I guess that's all I needed to know."

He turned and walked to the door, his hand already reaching into his pocket for his Kools, but something still didn't sit right in his gut. He was working for Faroe, no question, but he didn't like being made to feel like an errand boy. As he opened the door he turned.

"Where did Herrera go, Mr. Faroe?" said Atwater. "I think I should be told."

"The Colonel will provide the brawn to your brains," said Faroe. "He's gone to procure essential equipment and more men."

"Equipment?" said Atwater.

"I've authorized him to assemble whatever firepower he thinks necessary," said Faroe. "Including a helicopter."

For some reason this, more than anything, made Atwater realize just how heavy was the shit he was getting into. Then he saw Faroe's lizard eyes boring into him. He didn't want Faroe to think he was having second thoughts. Atwater held the lizard eyes and smiled what he thought of as his Clarence Jefferson smile.

"A helicopter sounds like just what the doctor ordered."

After all, someone had to take the Captain's place now that he was gone.

Rufus Atwater left the room and fired up a Kool and went to nail Cicero Grimes.

SIXTEEN

IT WAS DAWN when they hit the outskirts of Baton Rouge and swung northwest toward Ryan Airport. Grimes felt light-headed. He was so tired he was no longer able to summon up much of a sense of urgency for the miles they had to cover, but he was putting his body through the motions. They were moving. He was starving too. He needed coffee and hotcakes. He assumed that Lenna, sitting beside him with circles under her eyes, felt the same way. She, at least, had managed to sleep a good part of the way.

"You want to stop, get something to eat?" said Grimes.

Lenna shook her head. "I'm not hungry."

Grimes lit a cigarette instead. It tasted pretty bad. A few minutes later he saw the exit for the airport and took it. Lenna glanced over the back of her seat at Gul.

"Does this mean we're leaving your new friend behind?" she said.

"You must be kidding," said Grimes. "You think I could handle any of this on my own? We're going to hire ourselves a plane."

"Have you got the cash?" asked Lenna.

"No. You haven't carried cash in years, right?"

"Right. Yesterday I could've bought the airline."

Grimes pulled into the parking lot.

He said, "Maybe flying with the tourists will be an experience for you."

He slotted the car into a space and Lenna got out and shut the door. Grimes turned to look at Gul, who had raised his head from the back seat and was looking at him as if to say, "Where's the action?" Grimes opened his door and Gul reared up on all fours, his bulk slamming into the roof.

"Okay, asshole," said Grimes. "Let's go and find us some dough."

Grimes got out and Gul clambered after him. They walked over to the terminal. As the electric doors swished shut behind them Grimes spotted their first problem. A security guard was waddling toward them, the type who had taken the job just so he could tell people they couldn't smoke or walk around in bare feet. His eyes were fixed on Gul. Grimes felt the vibration of a low growl by his leg. He spoke quietly without looking downward.

"I'd like to kill him too, pal, but we've got to stay cool. *Cool.* Remember this motto: Cool Breeze, Silent Death."

It seemed to work. The vibration disappeared. Grimes gave the security guard a false smile. The guard didn't smile back.

"I'm afraid you can't bring your dog in here, sir," said the guard.

"I don't own a dog," said Grimes.

The guard seemed stunned by the baldness of this disclaimer. He stared at Gul, who stared back. Grimes hoped that the guard didn't maintain the eye contact for longer than was wise. The guard sensed this and looked back at Grimes.

"You brought the dog in with you, sir," said the guard. "I saw you. Now I must ask you to remove him from the building."

Grimes felt all the pissed-off-ness that he'd been keeping under control rise up in his thorax.

"Listen, sporto," said Grimes. "My wife and I," he inclined his head toward Lenna, "parked our car in your lot and walked in here with the intention of conducting some business at the American desk over there. This fine animal followed us through the doors of his own accord. All I can say is he has done us no harm. You, on the other hand, are getting on my tits. If you want to get rid of him that's your business, go ahead and try, but don't ask me to do your job. Now, earn your fucking pay and get out of my face."

By this time the guard's cheeks were bright red. He didn't step any closer but his hands made a vague gesture in Gul's direction. Gul showed the guard a narrow wedge of fangs and let him have the low-pitched bowel-trembler. The guard's hand drifted reflexively toward the revolver clipped into a belt holster. Gul's hips dropped and his shoulders bunched.

"If I was going to reach for that gun," said Grimes, "I'd make sure I had a decent hand surgeon nearby."

The guard diverted the hand from his waist to his face, which had turned from red to white in a matter of seconds. He rubbed his jaw.

"Look, friend," said Grimes. "This is none of my business, as I say, but as a neutral observer it seems to me that if you let this creature go his way he'll let you go yours, and we can all get on with our lives."

With that Grimes smiled and walked past the guard toward the American Airlines desk. Lenna and Gul came with him. The guard was left stranded on a plinth of humiliation and indecision. Behind the ticket counter sat a woman with a badge pinned to her blouse that identified her as Jeannie.

"Good morning, sir. How can I help you?" said Jeannie.

"Hi," said Grimes. "I'd like a cash refund on this ticket, please."

Grimes took the ticket Jefferson had sent him from his pocket and handed it to Jeannie. He took out his driver's license and handed her that too.

"My ID," he said.

Jeannie studied the ticket. Her brow furrowed.

"This is over four thousand dollars," said Jeannie.

"When your company sold the ticket you were happy enough to take the money—in cash you'll notice. Now, I'd like my money back. If there's a percentage to pay for the cancellation then by all means deduct it."

"We can make the refund, sir, but we'll have to mail you the balance by check." Jeannie, sensing that this wasn't going to please him, smiled her trained smile.

Grimes smiled back. "I know you don't make these policies and you are just doing your job, so I don't want to argue with you," said Grimes. "Please get me your supervisor."

Jeannie thought about this and decided it was a good idea. She picked up a phone and dialed. Grimes turned his back to the desk while they waited.

"So this is life in the real world," said Lenna.

"Yup," said Grimes. He nodded toward the dog. "I guess it's all new to him, too."

Gul lay on the floor surveying his surroundings with contemptuous indifference. In the distance the security guard was engaged in an intense conversation with a colleague, who was looking across in their direction. The supervisor arrived and introduced himself as Russell Beakes, a portly fellow with the air of self-importance appropriate to a minor corporate bureaucrat.

"I'm afraid our operative has informed you correctly, Dr. Grimes," said Beakes. "You are entitled to your refund but you'll have to go through the regular channels."

"I want my money," said Grimes.

"I don't think you understand," said Beakes.

Grimes said, "Do you have the authority to give me my money or not, and if not who does?"

"I could, in principle, authorize . . ." began Beakes.

"Then do it."

"It would be most irregular to issue a cash refund for such an amount. I'm sure you'll . . ."

"I want my money," said Grimes.

Beakes licked his lips and glanced into the distance over Grimes's shoulder, Grimes presumed toward the security guards. It occurred to Grimes to brandish the gun from his pocket and steal his money back. Gul, he was confident, could take out the two guards. Lenna interrupted this train of thought by reaching across the desk and picking up the telephone. She smiled at Russell Beakes.

"Excuse me," she said. "Do you know the name of the president of your company, Mr. Beakes?"

"Naturally. Mr. Stephen J. Cochrane." Beakes looked bewildered.

To Jeannie, Lenna said, "Can I get long distance on this?"

Jeannie, wide eyed, nodded. Lenna started to punch in a number.

"I own a six percent shareholding in American, Mr. Beakes. Steve and I ski together every winter in Vail. That's in Colorado."

She finished dialing and listened. Beakes's hands fluttered. He looked at Grimes for help.

"Steve won't mind getting out of bed on a Saturday morning to authorize this transaction," said Lenna, "but you might have difficulty finding yourself another job."

Beakes's fluttering hands reached out and extracted the receiver from Lenna's grip as if it were an unexploded bomb. He placed it down with a sickly smile.

"If you don't mind waiting a few moments," said Beakes, "the doctor will have his money."

Beakes disappeared and Lenna turned to Grimes.

"Maybe I should get out more often."

Minutes later, with his pocket padded out with currency, Grimes felt better. He thanked Beakes and Jeannie and bent down to Gul and looked him in the eye.

"Stay," said Grimes.

Gul blinked. Grimes and Lenna walked across the concourse toward the exit. On the way they passed the two security guards, their faces now twitching.

"It's only a goddamn dog," Grimes overheard one say.

"You didn't see its eyes," said the other.

Grimes nodded to them. "Have a nice day."

At the exit doors Grimes stopped and turned. Behind the American desk Russell Beakes was waving his arms at the security guards while peering over the counter at Gul. Gul hadn't budged but his gaze was fixed on Grimes. Grimes nodded and slapped his thigh.

Gul came straight across the concourse in a disdainful, broad-shouldered lope. In the Stone House Grimes had seen him move at three times the speed, but the lope was fast just the same. The security guards staggered backward out of Gul's path. When he arrived Grimes opened his arms and Gul went up on his hind legs and threw his paws on his shoulders. Grimes just managed not to fall over backward. He rubbed Gul's flanks.

"You are a good man," said Grimes.

They left and piled back into the Olds and drove the mile or so to the adjoining airfield, which was used by freight companies and private planes. Grimes slipped the man on the gate fifty dollars and explained that they needed to do some traveling with a dog. The man scratched his head and directed them to a jerry-built cabin to the rear and at the far end of a long row of offices. On the gable end of the cabin was an enameled sheet of aluminum, thick with oily dirt. Beneath the dirt was a painted legend:

Titus Oates

The Last of The Independants

The World Is Your Oyster

Grimes left Lenna and Gul in the Olds and walked over to the cabin. There was no sign of life. He banged on the door, which rattled on its hinges. There was no reply. Grimes shrugged and walked back to the car. As he got there the hinges rattled again and the door swung open.

"What the fuck is your problem, man?"

Grimes turned. A large, aggressively bearded man, about Grimes's age, stared at him from the doorway with bleary eyes. He wore a TEXAS LONGHORNS baseball cap with a deep-curved good-ole-boy peak and a striped flannel nightshirt that reached his knees. The shirt hung beautifully from the dense equator of his belly. Below the shirt his calves were hairy and white, and the approximate size and shape of fire extinguishers. His feet were bare and solidly planted.

"Do you know what time it is?" said the big man.

Grimes looked at his watch. "A little before seven," he said.

"Hey, buddy, I needed an answer like I need a bullet through my fucking peanut." He slid a hand under his cap and rubbed his head. "Which, most probably, I do."

"I'm looking for Mr. Titus Oates," said Grimes.

"Oates is dead," said the big man.

"I'm sorry to hear that," said Grimes.

"Whaddya want him for, anyway?"

"I'd like to put some business his way."

The big man pulled his hand from under his cap and ran a pair of shrewd, rapid eyes over Grimes and the Olds 88 behind him.

"What kind of business?"

"The oyster business," said Grimes. "We want to go on a plane ride."

"Where to?"

"About six, seven hundred miles' worth."

The big man's eyes narrowed. "Mexico?"

"No," said Grimes.

"Mmm. What're you carryin'?"

"Just me and a lady and a dog. I'll pay cash."

The big man snorted. "Do I look like I take American Express?" He peered at the Olds.

"Let me see this dog. I'm particular when it comes to animals."

Grimes's heart sank. "Sure," he said.

He walked over to the Olds, opened the door and stuck his head in.

"Who is that guy?" said Lenna.

"I don't know," replied Grimes.

He turned to Gul. Gul opened his jaws and let his tongue loll out.

"Listen, pal, I want you to meet a friend of mine and I want you to be nice to him, okay? Be cool, right? Be good."

Gul's tongue lolled out a little further. Grimes felt Lenna looking at him as if he were an idiot.

"Come on then," said Grimes. "And heel."

Gul clambered out onto the tarmac and walked beside Grimes toward the cabin. The big man pulled his cap off and slapped it against his thigh.

"Jesus Christ," he said. "That is one full-on fucking pooch, man."
Gul kept his cool.

"He's pretty harmless," said Grimes.

"He'd better fucking not be," said the big man. He crouched on one knee and grinned and held out his hand. "Here, boy."

Gul looked up at Grimes.

"One-man dog, eh?" said the big man. "I like that. Yes I do."

Grimes nodded to Gul. "Go on. Remember what I said."

Gul trotted over to the big man and sniffed his hand and then his bare feet and the big man laughed.

"You are the original son of a bitch that fucked his mother, are you not?" He noticed the stitched wound on Gul's scalp. "Mmm. Been gettin' into trouble, eh, boy?"

The big man looked up at Grimes with his shrewd eyes. Grimes didn't speak. He heard a car door slam behind him. The big man's eyes flickered.

"You having another problem, Doctor?" said Lenna's voice.

"Goddamn," said the big man. "And a blonde too, in an Olds 88. You know what, Doctor? You have almost made up for waking me at this ungodly hour."

Gul returned to stand at Grimes's heel and the big man straightened up.

"Pity it's not Mexico," he said. "I could've made a stopover, maybe picked up some merchandise and paid my way back. But if your dog wants to go somewheres else I guess we could come to an arrangement."

"How much?" said Grimes.

The big man squinted thoughtfully. "Five hundred apiece."

Grimes glanced at Gul. "Does that mean a thousand or fifteen hundred?"

The big man put his fists on his lips and stuck his belly out and grinned.

"Are you tryin' to *haggle* with me, Doc?"

"You ought to be on a wanted poster."

Grimes reached into his pocket and counted off the money. He walked over and pressed it into the big man's palm.

"What do I call you?"

"I guess Titus will do for now. Or Oates if you prefer." Titus Oates pointed at the dog. "What do I call him?"

"Gul," said Grimes.

"Cool name."

Grimes half turned. "That's Lenna."

"Lenna's cool too." Oates waved to her. "I got time for breakfast?"

"We didn't," said Grimes.

"Mmm," said Oates. "As bad as that."

He turned and ambled back into the cabin.

"Put the Olds out back. You'll find a tarp there if you need it. I'll be out in five."

Grimes walked back to the car and smiled at Lenna. "Well, we've got our ride," he said.

Lenna glared at him and said, "I can't believe you just gave that man our money."

Lenna climbed into the passenger seat. Grimes shrugged and let Gul jump in the back of the car and got behind the wheel. Without speaking he started the engine, drove around the back of Oates's office and pulled in next to a sky-blue Cadillac with disastrous bodywork. He turned to Lenna.

"You really own six percent of American Airlines and go skiing in Vail with 'Steve'?" he asked.

"No," said Lenna. "But I could if I wanted to, that's the difference. I could also have gotten this guy for eight hundred bucks, max. I mean, you're pretty good with that dog, but in the future just leave the fine stuff to me, okay?"

Grimes looked at her. Her hair caught the sun and turned to gold. So what if she was sullen and bad-tempered and occasionally insulting? Maybe he liked that. Lenna turned to face him and with the gold hair and her eyes looking the way they did she looked, well, lovely. Lenna looked back at him without smiling. She leaned her face toward him across the gap between them. Grimes looked at her lips, then at her eyes.

"Doctor?" said Lenna. "I, well, I'm not feeling too good about myself at the moment. I mean . . ." She stopped, rubbed her forehead. "I don't know what I mean. I just need something, you understand? I've no right to ask, I know, but I just need something to make me feel like I'm not the lowest piece of shit in God's creation."

"You're not," said Grimes.

"You know, when Jack Seed had me tied in that chair last night, I wasn't scared. Not really. You know why?"

Grimes could have made an educated guess but he had to let her say it.

He shook his head. "No."

"Because I felt I deserved anything he could do to me."

Her eyes were steady on his. She waited.

"I can understand that," said Grimes.

"You can?"

"Yeah." He cleared his throat. "Look, I can't change your opinion of yourself, but for what mine's worth I think maybe you deserve a little better."

Lenna closed her eyes and they kissed. Their lips met lightly and Grimes closed his eyes too. Her breath was sweet and warm on his face. They held the kiss, lightly, for a long moment and Grimes realized from a feeling in his chest of a space filling up that he hadn't known was empty that he'd needed that something too. He lifted his fingers to her cheek and touched it and stroked her hair. He opened his mouth, just a little, and she opened hers and they held it like that until she dug her fingers into his scalp. He had a hard-on. He opened his eyes and found her eyes open too, the pupils enormous and black, rimmed with green. They looked at each other while they kissed and Grimes found his hand beneath her jacket, sliding up her belly. His fingers took a fold of flesh and he pulled on it and she breathed into his mouth. He moved his hand onto her breast. Its skin, at the edge, was slack, and sweet to the touch. He rolled the slack skin between his finger and thumb and pinched, still looking into the green-rimmed blackness, and she breathed into him again. He cupped her breast and it shifted in his palm, again slack, but also full, and again sweet to his touch as he stretched it tight. Her nipple was caught in the web of his thumb and he found himself pulling on it and wanting to twist it until it hurt her. He stopped. He wanted to hurt her—not badly, but a little—and he knew that something in her was calling that desire from him, and that in that unspoken exchange lurked an intense eroticism. But he knew too much, and too recently, of the horror she had known in her past. Against his will his mind showed him the bloody interior of the shack— the original Stone House—and he heard her screams. He felt his hard-on starting to fade. Their lips were still touching but lightly now. The doubt that had to be in his eyes was reflected back from hers. The hunger and the violence in them—and maybe in his too—was suddenly chased by bewilderment. Lenna closed her eyes and he was glad. He took his hand from her breast and pulled her face away from his and into his chest.

They sat breathing for a while and Grimes tried not to think of anything at all. Then he was jolted by a great crash on the roof and a savage roar from Gul. As Lenna jerked upright Grimes saw a wide, bearded face grinning at him through the window.

"Drop your cocks and grab your socks," bellowed Titus Oates.

Grimes turned around. "Gul," he said.

Gul fell silent but remained vigilant.

"Good boy," said Grimes.

Until they were airborne Grimes didn't believe they were going to make it. Titus Oates flew an old single-propeller De Havilland Beaver, which was the aeronautical equivalent of his office: the plane rattled as if a sneeze would blow it apart. Lenna sat in the cockpit, apparently unconcerned, and while she talked and Titus Oates laughed and swore a lot, Grimes sat strapped to a seat in the empty cargo hold and held Gul between his thighs. Gul brought to the raging noise of the engine and the juddering of the fuselage the same steely aplomb that he'd brought to the rest of his odyssey through the outside world. Once they were flying at a steady speed and the noise had become a constant Grimes was sufficiently shattered to fall asleep in his seat belt.

He awoke to the jolt of the undercarriage hitting the ground. Titus Oates seemed to fly his plane as if daring it to kill him. Grimes gave thanks that he didn't have any breakfast in him to throw up and clung to Gul for reassurance. When they finally stopped Oates leaned into the hold from his seat and grinned.

"How about that, Doc? The Devil went down to Georgia, eh?"

"Where are we?" asked Grimes.

"Well, Lenna here told me your de-sired destination and I got on the waves and found us this little down-home airfield—cropdusting outfit not thirty miles south of where you want to be. Jordan's Crossroads, right?"

"Well done," said Grimes.

He unlocked his seat belt and stood up unsteadily. Grimes walked to the loading door and slid it open and jumped down with Gul. The sun was bright and the sky was blue. They were on a short strip of tarmac in the middle of open fields. At varying distances in every direction the fields were hemmed in by green forest. To one side of the tarmac strip was another aircraft that Grimes took to be the cropduster. Beyond it was a small single-story building painted white and, beside it, another the size of a barn, outside of which was a stack of barrels. A man in olive-green overalls came out of the white building and started walking toward them. Oates and Lenna joined Grimes.

"Give me a coupla hundred bucks and I'll see this guy straight," said Oates.

"Give him eighty," said Lenna.

Grimes obediently looked for the right amount and couldn't find it. He gave Oates a hundred. Oates scribbled something on a card.

"You guys want a return flight, I'll be hanging around these parts awhile. This part of the country, they make some of the finest sippin' whiskey money can't usually buy. I figure to reinvest some of my profits."

He handed the card over. On it was a number. Grimes looked at Oates, and Oates pointed a thumb at a flexible metal spiral protruding from the breast pocket of his denim jacket.

"Cell phone," said Oates. "See, if you wanna compete in a modern entrepreneurial culture, you gotta have the technology. By the way, I figure old Gul there would make a good business partner. I could go maybe four hundred bucks, you wanted to sell him to a good home."

Grimes was no longer surprised by Titus Oates's gall.

"Gul goes his own way. He isn't mine to sell," said Grimes. He turned to Lenna. "Let's go."

Oates called after them, "You change your mind, you know how to find me."

The cropduster's nephew gave them a ride north in his pickup truck. The town wasn't much more than a main street and two churches. The nephew told them that the nearest motel was another thirty miles away but that a widow called Stapleton sometimes rented rooms to fishermen during the season. If they could show her a wedding ring they'd like as not be okay, but he couldn't speak for the dog. Grimes reckoned that they were now at least five hours ahead of his father. Even an hour of decent sleep—in a bed—was something he couldn't put a price on. They got out of the pickup a mile the other side of town and climbed up onto Mrs. Stapleton's porch.

Grimes said to Lenna, "I'll leave this to you."

While Lenna rang the bell Grimes looked out from the porch with gritty eyes. The house was set a good way back from the road and as the pickup disappeared all he could hear was the song of birds. Within his sight the trees he couldn't name were blossomed with a dozen different colors. There was a soft, fragrant breeze. Grimes felt his head spin as the burgeoning peace of it suddenly struck him. He felt like he'd arrived on another planet, where danger was far away. And he thought: Holden Daggett had been right. If these were the Ohoopee River bottomlands, in spring they were kind of fine.

SEVENTEEN

THE DAY started badly for Rufus Atwater. He dragged his ass back into the City and broke into Grimes's apartment only to find a garbage dump of such proportions that he thought he was in the wrong building. But, no, the place did belong to Dr. Eugene Grimes. What a fucking weirdo. The prospect of searching the place for clues filled Atwater with such despair that when he found a bed in one of the upstairs rooms he threw himself on it with the intention of sobbing and instead fell asleep. He woke up in a panic, then discovered that it wasn't yet nine A.M. Not good, but not terrible either.

The terrible part came when he pulled out his cell phone and made some calls and discovered that Dusty and Hank, the two operatives he'd hired to shadow George Grimes, had been gunned down by an unknown assailant. Dusty had died on the table after four hours in surgery. What the fuck was going on? Was it possible that the old guy had killed them? Atwater decided that there was nothing to be gained by revealing any of this to Faroe. He pulled himself together and flung himself around Grimes's apartment, emptying drawers and cupboards, flicking through books and papers, searching the pockets of all the clothes he could find. After an hour of fruitless and destructive rummaging the place didn't look any worse off than it had before and Atwater was none the wiser.

He cursed Grimes, Faroe and Jefferson, each more bitterly than the last, and stumbled down the staircase to the front door. The Cuban cocksucker Herrera was no doubt at this moment discharging his duties to perfection, insinuating himself deeper into Faroe's trust and affections while he, Atwater, was moving from one fuckup to the next. Atwater decided to go get some breakfast and work out what to do next. He dragged the front door open, kicking at the unopened junk mail carpeting the hallway door. As the door scraped the mail up into a heap it got jammed.

He hadn't checked the mail.

Atwater stopped kicking, slammed the door shut again and fell to his knees. In a frenzy he scraped the mail into random stacks and then started sifting through them. The junk stuff and a bunch of medical magazines he threw aside. The bank and credit card statements he placed together unopened, reserving the tedium of going through them until later. Anything on which the address was handwritten he sorted into another pile. There were a few postcards from ex-patients and friends. Atwater read them without illumination and added them to the junk pile. He started opening letters on which the address was typed. Anonymous pitches from insurance companies and financial advisers, invitations to lectures and conferences, some IRS shit, something from a lawyer in Georgia asking for an appointment in person, utilities bills, a request to submit a paper to an addiction journal on detoxification of opiate addicts . . . another letter from the lawyer in Georgia.

Atwater's gut squirmed with hope.

He sat back on the floor and lit one of his Kools and reread the two letters from one Holden Daggett of Jordan's Crossroads, Georgia. There was no specific reference at all to the nature of Daggett's business with Grimes, just Daggett's regret that Grimes had not replied and had proved uncontactable by telephone. The second letter indicated that unless Daggett heard anything to the contrary he planned to call on Grimes in person to try to conclude the matter in hand.

On the surface it didn't seem like much, but two things set Atwater's heart beating. First, the letters combined an implied urgency with a total lack of concrete subject matter, which was strange. Second, the date on which Daggett said he planned to call on Grimes in person was yesterday—the same day on which Lenna Parillaud had received *her* letter and all hell had broken loose.

Atwater didn't have time to put the picture together piece by piece; he just knew it was there. He ran back upstairs and found an atlas. On the map of Georgia he located Jordan's Crossroads. He hit the cell phone again and made a call to Gough Lovett, a private eye out of Savannah. He gave him a description of Grimes and Parillaud—they'd stick out like cold sores—and told him to get on down to Jordan's

Crossroads ASAP. Atwater could've called Filmore Faroe, too, to let him know what he'd found, but he didn't like the idea of any plans being made out there at Arcadia without him being present. He'd tell Faroe in person. Then maybe Faroe would understand what kind of an operator he was dealing with in Rufus Atwater.

Atwater left Grimes's apartment and sped back through light traffic. The size of Faroe's plantation always misled him. He'd driven out there a score of times but Arcadia was always that much bigger than he remembered. The route to the house didn't take him past the Stone House—that was buried miles away—and Atwater was glad. If he never saw that place again he'd be happy. Atwater was a straight guy; he didn't like weirdness, and that was as weird a setup as he'd ever seen. And that was before the terror of his life—when he'd found Jack Seed's nude and butchered corpse in the silent cage. Atwater shivered and headed through the wrought-iron gates to the mansion.

When he got there, there was a helicopter sitting on Faroe's lawn. Atwater knew nothing about choppers but the machine on the lawn was big and looked like the ones he'd seen in Vietnam War pictures, except it was painted matte black and wasn't sporting any machine guns. On the other hand the spics who seemed to be everywhere were. On his way to Faroe's office Atwater must've passed at least a dozen of them. Most of the Cubans were wearing combat fatigues and carrying either M16s—or maybe Armalites—or shotguns. He spotted one Kalashnikov. Jesus. Herrera had let the "Colonel" business go to his head.

Atwater was worried—for Mr. Faroe's sake—that it was all getting out of hand. He'd been happy enough for Jack Seed to round up a few wetbacks to do their dirty work for them. And he didn't blame Faroe for calling in Herrera—the guy was out of touch; he had no contacts. But this second phase of reinforcements was over the top. There was Atwater doing the fine stuff—finding clues and hiring PIs—and meanwhile Arcadia was turning into a fucking boot camp. Maybe Herrera was preparing some kind of *coup d'état*.

Sure enough, when he entered Faroe's study Herrera was there, greasy as a loose turd. Atwater made like Herrera didn't exist and marched up to the desk. Filmore Faroe, with his shaved skull and snake eyes, looked as bright as a button. Atwater thought about the dry ampules of speed he'd brought back for Faroe from the hillbillies' place. The boss man was jacked up high as all Jesus. Atwater had heard that speed could do strange things to people. Plus, he'd been locked inside that fucking weird cage for thirteen years. Maybe that accounted for the overkill on the mercenaries. Fuck it. Atwater stopped at the desk. Faroe looked up.

"You were right," said Atwater. "I got something."

"Sit down," said Faroe.

Atwater sat and told him about the letters from Holden Daggett. As he spoke he took the letters from his pocket. Faroe read them without speaking. He looked up at Atwater.

"Jordan's Crossroads is a hayseed town deep in moonshine country," said Atwater. "I've got a private eye on his way there from Savannah. He'll be there before noon. He'll keep an eye on this Daggett guy and he's got descriptions of your wife and Dr. Grimes. He reckons in a place that size they won't be hard to spot. That's if they show up."

"And if they do?" said Faroe.

"He'll let us know and await instructions."

Faroe frowned. "We're dealing with desperate individuals, Mr. Atwater. I remind you what happened to Jack Seed."

Atwater felt like saying, "Look, buster, it wasn't my idea to send old Jack off to stick his pecker up your wife's ass." Instead he said, "So what do you want me to do?"

"We're playing for high stakes," said Faroe. "That can never be done safely."

Faroe retreated into himself, thinking. After a respectful pause Herrera said something in Spanish. Faroe grunted and nodded his shaven head. Atwater waited.

"I want them alive," said Faroe. "They can always be killed later."

"Sir," said Atwater.

"Colonel, how soon can your force be ready?" said Faroe.

"They are ready now, sir," replied Herrera.

"Good. Tell them they're leaving in ten minutes."

Herrera saluted and strode from the room.

Atwater leaned forward. "You're sending them up to Georgia?"

"If we wait for your Savannah gumshoe to spot them we'll lose the hours it will take to get there. By then they may be gone."

"What if Grimes and Parillaud aren't there?"

"Then all we've lost is a few gallons of aviation fuel. Do you question my judgment?"

"No, sir. It's just that, with all due respect, sir, I'm not sure I'd trust these guys one hundred percent. If I didn't say so I wouldn't be doing my job."

"I appreciate that, Mr. Atwater. What's more I agree with you," said Faroe. "That's why you're going to go with them. You'll be in charge on my behalf."

"You mean I'm in the catbird seat?"

"Colonel Herrera will answer to you."

Rufus Atwater tingled all over. He was more than just a killer. He was going straight to the top at last.

EIGHTEEN

I N HIS DREAM Lenna Parillaud was sitting on the sofa in Grimes's cabin with her blue dress hitched around her waist while Grimes knelt between her legs and fucked her. Lenna looked at him with her green eyes, her thighs taut as she pushed the tips of her toes into the floor and lifted herself into him. Her sullen mouth was open and she made quiet, intense sounds in the back of her throat. With her right hand she masturbated. With her left she kept reaching out and putting her palm against his chest. Just as Grimes was about to come, in what he knew would be the single most gratifying orgasm of his life, he woke up with a crippling hard-on and blinked in despair at the wallpaper of Mrs. Stapleton's guest room. The hard-on remained to torment him but the contents of the dream rapidly faded away to leave a haunting space, never to be filled, in the pit of his stomach.

There were two beds in the room. Grimes rolled over and looked toward the second. Lenna, fully clothed in her black suit, lay in what looked like a deep sleep. She was lying on her stomach, her eyes shaded by the crook of her arm. She had one leg bent, the effect of which was to tighten the cloth of her pants into the crack of her ass. The word *voluptuous* sprang to Grimes's mind, followed by several others, shorter and less elegant. He rubbed his eyes and prayed to God, as he had so often before, to neuter once and for all whatever glands, chromosomes and neural tracts conspired to afflict him with the burden of lust.

As his mind struggled toward a more useful level of consciousness Grimes realized that though sex with Lenna was a nice idea, the reality of it would carry a greater price than he was prepared to pay. She was fucked-up, so was he and they were in a fucked-up place. He liked her and he cared what happened to her but he didn't love her. He didn't want to love her; or anyone else for that matter. In his experience it was rare for sex to be truly casual for both parties at the same moment; it was inconceivable to him that this now might constitute one such moment. Either he would fall for her or she for him and there would be difficulty and heartache all around. He now regretted kissing her in the car. He'd been exhausted and crazed; so, probably, had she. Now he was rested. He looked at his watch. It was after three P.M. Instead of the two hours he'd promised himself, he'd slept for almost four. He swung off the mattress and stood up. From the floor at the foot of the bed Gul sprang up and came to him. Grimes crouched down and rubbed his flanks.

"Shhh," said Grimes.

Lenna didn't stir. Grimes went to the bathroom and splashed cold water on his face and rinsed his mouth. He was starving. He went back into the room. Lenna was still flat out. If he could go and get Jefferson's suitcases alone it would save him a certain amount of worry. However he cut it, he was still a couple of hours ahead of his father. He scribbled a note for Lenna on the pad on the table, left some money in case she woke up hungry, then stuck the Colt in the back of his pants and trod softly from the room with Gul at his heels.

Downstairs, the excellent Mrs. Stapleton, in memory of her dog-loving husband, gave Gul a bowl of milk and water and Grimes made a call to Holden Daggett. He reached the office and got an answering machine. Grimes hung up without speaking. By the telephone was a directory. Grimes flipped through it and found Daggett's home number. He rang. After three rings it was answered.

A calm, dry voice said, "Holden Daggett speaking."

"Afternoon, Mr. Daggett," said Grimes. "This is Eugene Grimes."

"Dr. Grimes," said Daggett evenly. "How are you?"

"Fine," said Grimes. "I need to see you."

"Let me give you directions to my office," said Daggett.

"You don't sound very surprised," said Grimes.

'When one of your patients tells you he thinks he's Napoleon Bonaparte I don't imagine you sound very surprised either."

This was a fair point, though Grimes wasn't very comfortable with its implications. He listened to Daggett's instructions, then collected Gul and strolled a pleasant mile west into the center of Jordan's Crossroads.

The walk did him good. At the local diner he left Gul sitting outside and went in and bought two cheeseburgers to go, a coffee, black with sugar, some juice and a raw sixteen-ounce T-bone. Further down the street he found a bench and sat down to eat the burgers while Gul wolfed down the steak. There was a light Saturday afternoon traffic up and down Main, folks, mostly white, wandering and shopping, small trucks parked with shotgun racks in their cabins. The coffee didn't do an awful lot for Grimes, but it was a start. He was halfway through the second cheeseburger when a florid-faced local in jeans, sneakers and a green FALCONS windbreaker ambled by and smiled at him affably from beneath his baseball cap.

"Afternoon," said the Falcons fan.

Gul growled unpleasantly. Grimes, fearing the random mutilation of an innocent man, put his fingers under Gul's collar and whispered in his ear.

"Hey, be civil," said Grimes. He looked at the man. "Good afternoon."

"Handsome dog," said the man. His voice was long and wide and syrupy.

With his growling black German shepherd dog and his limp half-burger Grimes suddenly felt horribly exposed. He felt like he had the word *stranger* tattooed on his forehead. He calmed himself. The guy was just being friendly: it was nice. Lots of people liked to go up to dogs. Give the guy a smile before he calls the cops.

Grimes smiled as best he could. "Thanks," he said.

"My brother-in-law's got a shepherd bitch. You wanted to breed from this beauty, I reckon he'd be interested."

There didn't seem any point in lying.

Grimes said, "I'm just passing through."

"Well, good luck to you. You all take care of each other, now," said the man.

"We will," said Grimes.

The man clicked his tongue at Gul, smiled at the dour lack of response and ambled away without looking back. Grimes dropped his garbage in a can and walked on. Further down Main he found the neat red-brick building that Daggett had described. On it was a brass plaque engraved with Daggett's name. He rang the bell and Holden Daggett appeared in pressed gray slacks and a white short-sleeve shirt. His eyes flickered over Grimes's beardless face and clean shirt.

"This time I put some shoes on," said Grimes.

Daggett smiled and they shook hands.

"This is Gul."

"Charmed," said Daggett. "Come on in."

Daggett's office was neat and shelved, paneled and furnished with old wood. A sense of honest industry. On the wall, among various diplomas, was a black-and-white photo of a group of young marines in full-dress uniform. Daggett was an emaciated-looking youth in the front row. It was captioned *Parris Island 1951. Graduation day.*

"What can I do for you?" asked Daggett.

Grimes sat down.

"Mr. Daggett," said Grimes. "The letter you brought me yesterday has kind of turned things upside down for me. It was from a man called Clarence Jefferson. I presume he was your client."

Daggett's face remained neutral. "Go on, Doctor."

"Maybe you don't know who Clarence Jefferson really was, it doesn't matter. But I need to know where I can find what Jefferson called 'the Old Place.' "

"The Old Place," said Daggett in a flat tone.

"Jefferson asked me to go to the Old Place. He told me how to find it but I lost the letter. My father, George, has it. For reasons of his own he's trying to carry out Jefferson's instructions himself. I'm pretty sure I'm ahead of him and it's important to me that it stays that way. I want to keep him out of danger."

Daggett's expression didn't change.

Grimes said, "I'm hoping that if you handled Jefferson's affairs you might know where this Old Place is. I give you my word you wouldn't be telling me anything Jefferson didn't want me to know."

Daggett frowned and turned to stare through the window. Grimes waited for him to say something but he didn't. Grimes sensed he'd be wasting his time trying to cajole an old horse trader like Daggett into doing something he didn't want to do. And he wasn't going to threaten him. After a few moments Grimes stood up.

"I understand you're bound by confidentiality," said Grimes. "That's a sacred trust, especially to a dead client."

Daggett turned back to look at him.

"But I'd be grateful if you'd think about it," said Grimes. "If you change your mind you can leave a message for me at Mrs. Stapleton's."

Grimes stood up and turned toward the door, hoping that Daggett would stop him. He didn't.

"Come on, pal," said Grimes to Gul.

On his way across the office Grimes's eye caught the old photograph again, of the young marines at Parris Island. He stopped. It was worth a shot.

"Which division were you with?" asked Grimes.

Daggett glanced across the room at the photo, then at Grimes.

"The First," answered Daggett.

Grimes looked at him. "You held the Chosin Reservoir."

A ghost flitted across Daggett's eyes. Grimes glanced again at the gaunt youth in the photo and wondered what he must have felt facing the endless massed wave attacks of the Chinese infantry.

"You're well informed," said Daggett.

"My father was with the Sixth," said Grimes. "First Battalion. In the Pacific."

Daggett pursed his lips. "Those boys did some things," he said.

"So I'm told," said Grimes.

Daggett nodded slowly. He swallowed.

"Would you excuse me for a moment, Dr. Grimes?"

"Sure," said Grimes.

Grimes went into the reception room and sat down. The room was hot. There was a fan in the ceiling but it wasn't moving. Grimes thought about taking his jacket off, then remembered the Colt sticking into the small of his back. For a moment, beneath the ticking of the fan, he thought he could hear Daggett speaking. Then Daggett emerged from his office wearing his straw boater.

"Come along," said Daggett.

Daggett drove them in a tan Lincoln Town Car, over a decade old but well preserved. They didn't pass back through the center of town but headed west. Daggett seemed preoccupied and didn't speak and Grimes didn't ask any questions. As the miles rolled by they left behind the light industry and cultivated fields that occupied the outskirts of the town, and wound through hills deeply forested with cedars, cottonwoods and pines. For a while other vehicles would approach and pass them every half a mile; then the cars became fewer until there were none at all and it felt to Grimes like they were the only travelers in the land.

Gul sat between Grimes's knees, peering through the window and occasionally looking up at his face. Grimes winked at him. Maybe things aren't going to be so bad as we thought, pal. If he could collect the goddamn suitcases from the Old Place at least his father would have nothing to do except lie low. What about Ella MacDaniels and Lenna? And Faroe? The shit was still flowing deep and fast. Grimes cursed Jefferson's black soul. One step at a time, he told himself, that's all you can do. Just grab the suitcases and take it from there.

The Lincoln topped the crest of a hill and started to descend. The trees shading the road from either side gradually thinned out and the landscape opened into a broad valley. To their left—the south—the valley's meadowed floor sloped down a shallow gradient toward a winding thread of water, golden in the late afternoon sun.

"The Ohoopee River," said Daggett.

Grimes figured that the land had been cleared for agricultural purposes, but now it was rampant with wildflowers. That reminded him of Lenna's plantation, but these bottomlands were much prettier. In the center of the spreading fields, set half a mile back from the river, stood a farmhouse and barn. Grimes felt his heart thumping. Daggett turned off the road and bumped along hard-packed dirt, lined here and there with trees. As they got closer Grimes saw that the barn was missing half of its roof. The farmhouse was paint-peeled and leaning, canted over with age and rot. Some of the windows had cracked under the strain. There was no sign of life. Daggett drove around to the back of the farmhouse into a cobblestoned yard facing down to the river. He turned the Lincoln in a circle until it pointed toward the road again and stopped. He looked at Grimes.

Grimes could have been mistaken but Daggett looked a shade paler than before.

"This is the Old Place," said Daggett. "I'll wait here for you."

"Okay," said Grimes.

He opened the door. Gul lunged eagerly outward. Grimes grabbed his collar and held him back. A disturbing wariness clogged his throat. He glanced back over his shoulder at Daggett.

"You're not in any danger," said Daggett.

Grimes let Gul climb out and followed him. He closed the car door. Gul reconnoitered the yard, his long nose close to the ground, shoulders bunched low. Grimes stepped up onto the back porch. The boards creaked under his feet. Behind a screen the inner door stood open. Gul joined him, eyes sharp, ears moving in small twitches. Grimes pushed open the screen door and stepped inside.

They were in a large kitchen with a flagstone floor. It was fitted out with what looked like quality 1950s appliances: stove, refrigerator, toaster, percolator, a table and six chairs. On the table was a mildewed checked tablecloth. There was a layer of dust over everything, fuzzy in the warm yellow light that filtered through the dirty windows. Two open doors led off the kitchen, one onto what looked like a laundry room, the other into a hallway. At the far end of the hall, angling back up toward the second floor, was the handrail of a banister. On first glance it all seemed frozen in time, as deserted as it was neglected; then Gul started his low growl, so low it was almost silent.

Grimes crouched at his side and put a hand on his back. Gul's muscles were coiled. He didn't look at Grimes. His black eyes, gleaming with the primitive violence Grimes had seen the night before, were fixed on the hallway.

"Steady, pal," said Grimes. "Stay cool."

Gul twitched his ear, then suddenly moved across the room with intense and soundless speed. On the threshold of the hallway he stopped and glanced back, waiting. Grimes followed. He thought about pulling out the revolver and decided against it. It seemed overdramatic and he wasn't confident in its use. He entered the hallway corridor at Gul's shoulder.

Just beyond the kitchen door and to the left gaped a set of stairs, going down into the basement. The steps were dark. According to Jefferson's letter the suitcases were down there. Grimes looked for a light switch. Just as he found it, Gul left him and stalked with silent purpose down the hall.

"Gul," said Grimes. For some reason his voice came out as a whisper.

Gul stopped outside a closed door. He snuffled at the crack at the bottom, glanced at Grimes, then stood pointing his nose at whatever was in the room on the other side. After a moment he looked at Grimes again, but he didn't move from his position. Reluctantly, Grimes followed him and stopped at the door. He could feel the dog almost quivering at his side. Grimes felt drenched with fear and, at the same time, ridiculous. Should he knock or just go in? How should he go in: fast, slow, on his knees? He wasn't used to this stuff. Grimes wiped his brow and stood against the wall to one side of the door. If a bullet came through it would pass over Gul's head. Grimes reached out and turned the door handle. Nothing happened. He pushed the door and let it swing open.

Gul bared his teeth and made his sound. He looked ready to do his thunderbolt rush if he needed to, but he didn't enter the room. Grimes stepped away from the wall and looked in on a cobwebbed parlor.

For a moment Grimes lost all sensation below the neck.

Sitting facing him, in a winged chintz armchair, among the shadows on the far side of the room, was a massive figure in a blue Hawaiian shirt and a Panama hat. Beneath the brim of the hat, Grimes saw the warm smile and inscrutable eyes of his own most sweat-drenched dream.

Grimes said, "You fat son of a bitch."

NINETEEN

SOMEWHERE in Alabama—she didn't know where—Ella MacDaniels and George Grimes awoke at dawn and let Mitch Kerrigan fuss over them while he prepared a large breakfast and tried to persuade them to take him with them on the road. Mitch didn't know where they were going or why; George wouldn't tell him any details; but Mitch wanted to come anyway and Ella found that it made her sad.

Mitch was in his mid-fifties and wasn't anybody's idea of a loser. He ran an auto bodyshop with one of his sons; he had a wife, Alicia, whom he loved, and he had no diseases or debts. Yet the presence of George inflamed him. They talked about the battles they'd fought over thirty years before, and although Ella got lost among the quick-fire references to the AFL-CIO and the Meatcutters and the ACWU and Taft-Hartley and "that bastard Meany," she felt awed by the depth of their passion and by the sense that during this strange and bygone age of which they spoke, their lives and actions had been inspired by ideals more grand and more urgent than any she had ever known. They missed it and they hungered for it and therein lay the sadness that she felt for them. And maybe she felt sad for herself, too, for not really knowing what it was that they missed. Ella knew that there was no shortage of suffering and strife in the world but she couldn't get a handle on it. No one she knew could. It was hard to care that much, or rather there didn't seem to be anywhere to put the caring and so it shrugged its shoulders and went on home. It was like a lyric without a tune to carry it. After breakfast Mitch took them out to the woods to shoot some guns.

After much discussion about the relative merits of autopistols and wheelguns, at the end of which they left the choice to her, Ella swapped George's Colt .45 for a Smith & Wesson Model 15 Combat Masterpiece loaded with Black Hills wadcutters. It was like listening to the guys in the band arguing about amplifiers and effects pedals. The trigger action of the wheelgun was heavier than the .45 but she preferred it to the snapping slide and flying brass of the auto. It had a two-inch barrel but since they insisted that she would not be using it at more than ten-foot range that didn't matter. Mitch set up some targets—flattened cardboard boxes tacked to wooden stakes—and she used up thirty rounds at ten and six feet. Six feet—when she forced herself to imagine the cardboard as a man's body—was frighteningly close. Again she felt the siren song of the weapon's power and again she told herself not to trust it. Then Mitch gave them the use of his Jeep Cherokee and made one last pitch to be taken along. George turned him down.

Just before they set off Mitch shook George's hand and said: "In our youths, our hearts were touched with fire."

Something in the way Mitch said it, and something in George's face as he heard it, told Ella that the younger man had learned the words from the elder, a long time ago.

They drove all day under cloudless skies, taking turns at the wheel every two or three hours. The interstate was dreary and ten miles out of Montgomery they took Highway 80, which was pretty all the way, and headed across the Alabama–Georgia line toward Macon.

George talked a lot, as if it was something he didn't get a chance to do very often, and Ella listened without getting bored. In a town called Geneva they bought sandwiches and fruit and milk at a store and stopped for lunch at some picnic tables overlooking the Flint River. There George told her about his sons, Luther and Gene, and about how proud he was of them. She could tell, though he didn't say so and would probably have died before admitting it, that they had caused him great grief and that made her wonder about the worry she had caused her parents with her singing in dives and what they saw as wild ways. Reading between the lines, it seemed that George's boys had gone a little further than that. The elder brother, Luther, who had been a soldier—in George's words "a soldier's soldier"—was dead; George avoided saying how or why. Gene, the younger, was a doctor and the original recipient of the letter from Charlie. Although George adored him, almost desperately, he was clearly bewildered by Gene and, for all his articulateness when talking politics and war, words seemed to fail him when it came to saying why.

Ella wanted to meet Gene, badly. Gene had known Charlie. Not

Charlie: Clarence Jefferson. It was just a name, she knew, yet when she thought "Clarence Jefferson" she couldn't see a face or hear a voice; Charlie disappeared. Why hadn't he told her his real name? Maybe because he was a cop. A bad cop. Charlie had treated her well. He'd supported her, always, in her ambition to sing; he hadn't told her she was a dreamer and a fool like some others had. In a way that had sometimes shamed her, she'd loved Charlie more than her mother and father.

Ella had no brothers or sisters. Her parents, Sam and Tina Mac-Daniels, had been—and still were—the best anyone could wish for. She loved them but she'd never felt that she was *like* them. Then, most of her friends thought that about their folks. But with Charlie there'd been something else. It wasn't a sexual thing. Charlie had never laid a finger on her or even looked like he wanted to. Her father, Sam, had passed Charlie off as an old friend, yet he'd always been nervous around him and they never seemed to spend any time together. With Charlie having been around for as long as she could remember Ella had never much dwelt on this before, but the letter he'd written to Grimes had turned all she thought she knew about him upside down. Two lines from the letter repeated themselves in her head: "Besides you she's the only person in the world I give a shit for . . . she's no part of this, except that she's a part of me."

Ella looked at George across the picnic table and asked him the question that had come to her in her sleep.

"George?" she said. "Do you think Clarence Jefferson is my father?"

George squinted at her in the sun. She could tell that the thought had occurred to him as well.

"I don't know," he said. "I guess it's possible."

With the question out in the open it took on a greater force. She looked at her arms. Her skin was paler than either of her parents'. In itself that didn't mean anything, or it never had until now. She tried to listen to her body: the truth of who she was was buried somewhere inside her. Half of her had come from her father: surely that half could make itself heard. She closed her eyes and felt the vibration of her energy. She thought of her parents and couldn't hear them within her at all. This she suddenly knew with total conviction: she was not born of her parents. They resided in her heart but not in her fabric. To her surprise this new knowledge didn't shock her as much as she would've expected; but then on some level it wasn't new: she'd known it all her life. She concentrated again, intensely and long. She couldn't feel Charlie inside her either. She wanted to. The thought of not knowing at all was terrifying, though she didn't know why. She tried again; but she still couldn't feel him. It was different with her parents. They definitely weren't there. With Charlie there was doubt: she couldn't hear him, but at the same time she couldn't feel with the same certainty that he wasn't there. It was possible. He might be. She wanted him to be.

"Ella?" said George.

Ella opened her eyes and blinked. There were tears clinging to her eyelashes she hadn't been aware of. She felt foolish and brushed them away with the back of her hand.

"Family's always difficult business, one way or another," said George. "I don't know what else I can tell you. We don't choose them, and they don't choose us." He smiled. "Not like you and me."

His words seemed to reach out to enfold her and Ella realized just how stranded she had felt.

She said, "I would choose you anytime. Always. Always."

Then she looked up at his eyes—his old and gray and crazy eyes—and a massive sadness rolled up, sobbing, from her chest. She bent her face down, wishing he couldn't see her, but she couldn't stop the sadness and the sobs, which were for George and his oldness and the sons who had caused him grief, and for her parents who weren't her parents but had been the best of all time, and for Mitch and his rekindled fire, and for all the world and all its souls, struggling and mystified and lost; and for Charlie, whoever and whatever he had been, and for herself, Ella MacDaniels, whoever and whatever she was.

She felt George put his hand on the back of hers without speaking. The sadness waned. She collected herself. She was fine.

"I don't often cry," she said. She looked at him.

"I know," said George. "Me neither."

"Will Gene know if Clarence Jefferson was my father?"

"Maybe. He has a way of getting to the heart of things. We'll ask him when we get back to the City."

Ella saw his features crease up with concern.

She said, "Will he be in trouble?"

George wiped his concern away.

"No more than we are, if he is." He smiled. "I raised him to take care of himself, least I hope so. He doesn't always hold with my way of thinking, but I guess I wouldn't have it any other way. He'll be sure enough mad at me for taking off with you after these suitcases of dynamite."

"Why?"

"He reckons it's not his business and it won't change anything anyway."

"You think it will."

"I don't expect it will make the lion lay down with the lamb but it'll sure as hell make for some good TV. And maybe it'll make people think twice about who they give their power to."

He nodded across the picnic area toward the Jeep.

"You ready to go?"

"All the way," said Ella.

Ella took the wheel and within ten miles George had fallen asleep. At Macon, Ella skirted the city and continued east on I-16. By the time she turned off onto Route 1 heading south the sun was low in the sky behind them. George woke up from his doze and stretched himself back to life. He blinked through the window at the passing countryside.

"We're almost there," said Ella.

"We've done well," said George.

"The Old Place is out in the backwoods. This town coming up is Jordan's Crossroads. It's our last chance to score a coffee and some food, if you want to."

"Good idea," said George.

When they reached Main Street Ella pulled the Jeep into the parking lot behind the diner and George climbed out stiffly. They went inside and took a table by the window and both ordered steaks, rare, and fries. In her head, as she ate, Ella pictured the route they would take out of town. At the crossroads they'd head west for about fifteen miles. Then there was a turn they had to make, a cutoff to the left that she wasn't sure of. She couldn't remember any landmarks to guide her. She hoped the cutoff would come back to her when she saw it. She looked up from her steak.

In the rear corner of the diner, sitting in a booth, was a woman with blond hair, dressed in a black suit. The woman was staring at her. As Ella caught her gaze the woman immediately looked away. Ella turned back to her meal. It occurred to her that out here an old white man and a young black woman made strange dining partners. Back in the City nothing surprised anybody anymore but this was deep in the boondocks, as George would say. Klan country. Aryan Nation and other creeps. The blonde didn't have a country look to her, though. Ella threw another glance toward the booth.

The woman was watching her again. Ella suddenly felt weak inside, a strange vibration she'd never felt before. She didn't know what to do: the blond woman watching her had tears streaming down her face.

TWENTY

W HEN Lenna Parillaud woke up in Mrs. Stapleton's guest room she experienced a moment of disorientation and fear. She'd been in the sort of leaden, ultradeep sleep that left the pillow damp with drool and her limbs barely responsive to her instructions to move. Between the top of her shoulders and the base of her skull her spine felt like a piece of rubber tubing. She struggled up to sit on the edge of the bed and used her hands to lift her head and massage some life back into her neck. Grimes and his dog were gone. There were just some bills left on his bed and a note on the table. The note said:

> Dear Lenna,
> I've gone to find Jefferson's bullshit suitcases; it'll take me a cou-
> ple of hours. There's a diner in town; if you're not here when I get
> back I'll look for you there. Don't get too mad at me.
>
> Yours, Grimes

Lenna did feel mad. Her brain cleared. Grimes was such an asshole that he hadn't said what time he'd written the note so she didn't know what "a couple of hours" meant. She had the fleeting thought that he'd abandoned her altogether. She recalled his gaunt, wide-boned face and his steady pale blue eyes, and decided that she was being more paranoid than was necessary. She was hungry too. Lenna brushed her hands over her sleep-crumpled clothes, went downstairs and walked into town through hazy late-afternoon sunshine.

She went to the diner as Grimes had suggested and found a booth at the rear. She ordered coffee and, with reluctance, a tuna salad. When the salad came it was too big and the dressing was sugary sweet and she pushed it aside after two mouthfuls. She looked at some of the families in the diner: eating, squabbling, laughing, correcting each other's manners and talking about the weather, baseball, which new movies were at the multiplex; lavishing upon each other in a hundred hidden ways, some helpful and some not, their unquestioning affection and concern. Good people, in a good country, in which she herself felt like an alien. That was probably because they were basically happy. If she ever found happiness she wouldn't know what to do with it.

Lenna had never been inside a multiplex or sat in the bleachers. She'd never been in a diner like this before. When she didn't eat alone she ate in the eerily overcontrolled environment of expensive restaurants, served by handsome waiters with fake smiles and in the company of business partners whose smiles were even more fake, the kind of places where it was compulsory to find at least one tiny fault with the food or the wine and send it back to the kitchen for rectification. It wasn't that she exactly liked this diner; she felt too out of place here; but it spoke of a mundane warmth and stability she'd never known and which she envied. Then she remembered that she had known this world: for three days and three nights, two decades and a thousand years ago, in the arms of Wes Clay.

All she'd ever done was wrong except for that. All else she regretted; all else seemed beyond any possibility of redemption. She was a contagion to all who touched her: Wes Clay, Filmore Faroe, Bobby Frechette, Cicero Grimes, Ella MacDaniels, her own parents. They all staggered out of her malignant orbit bearing infected wounds or worse. She thought of the desperation with which she had accepted Grimes's embrace. His strong fingers on her body, his tobacco-stained breath upon her lips, had brought her into the world and she had wanted him. For those moments she had loved him, as she hadn't loved for twenty years, but Grimes deserved better. For Lenna only Clarence Jefferson had been fit company, and her for him: a pact of erotic humiliation and self-punishment. The crucified saints and bleeding martyrs of her childhood had taught her that secret: the only cure for guilt was punishment. And what better punishment than that she allow her body to be fucked and soiled by the murderer of her child?

Except that hadn't worked, either. She had only poisoned herself more. She should have killed Clarence Jefferson on the hundred occasions when she had the chance. And Faroe too. Killed them both and thrown herself upon the law. There might at least have been some self-respect in that. The truth was that everything she'd done had been a sustained shriek of self-pity. She had kept Faroe alive, she had kept Jefferson in her bed, just so she could scream at them: *"Look what you have done to me."* She thought: look what you have done to yourself.

It was too late to change very much but, maybe, she could change a little. A fragment from the Bible stole into her mind: "If not the Lord of Hosts had left unto us a very small remnant . . ." Yesterday she'd commanded all the power that millions could buy. All she had now was this body, this brain, this soul, sitting here at this table. A very small remnant. But maybe her powerlessness in the world gave her back her power over herself. She could still do one thing rather than another.

She would cut herself off from Cicero Grimes. He was a good man. She would protect him from her contagion; she owed him at least that much. She would leave him a note and disappear. What mattered most was that Ella MacDaniels be safe and stay safe; and that demanded that Faroe die. If he ever found out Ella was alive there was no knowing what he would do. Lenna had to return to Arcadia and kill him. With luck, she would die in the attempt; for beyond the moment of Faroe's death she could see no profit in existence. Yet she couldn't stop her heart from asking: but don't you want to know Ella? Don't you want to help her? Don't you want to love her?

Lenna took her heart and squeezed its selfish yearnings to death. To wish her love on anyone was second only in horror to wishing them her hate. Ella had lived her life in freedom. If it became known—if Ella came to know—that she was Lenna's child, then her freedom would be destroyed forever. Even if Faroe were dead, Ella would be dragged down into a swamp of publicity and filth. Ella must never know where she came from.

With that decision, Lenna felt better. She'd been struggling in quicksand. Now she knew what to do. For the first time since she'd grown Ella in her womb she had a purpose worth having. Not vengeance or hatred or masochism, but the protection of a freedom infinitely more precious than her own. She picked up her coffee cup and drained it. As she set it down she looked across the room.

In a warp of time so brief it was eternity the ache inside her pelvis radiated outward through all that she felt herself to be, and the yearnings she thought she'd squeezed to death came back to life, and not screaming or shouting, but singing: with the voices of angels and a music so sweet it melted every nerve and every cell of the very small remnant she yet possessed.

The woman sitting by the window was beautiful and strong. In the bones of her face and the fullness of her mouth was the imprint of Wes Clay. Her limbs were long and her fingers graceful. Her eyes were long-lashed and gentle and her skin a lustrous brown. Her hair was a cascade of shining braids. In her nose was a diamond stud.

Lenna felt and saw all this in an instant, and in that instant she remembered with perfect clarity why she had lost her heart so gladly to Wes Clay; her man; her star-crossed lover. But more than that Lenna understood, fully and at last, why a bewildered girl those twenty years ago had endured, with such senseless and stubborn resolution, the terror of her lonely pregnancy.

For here was her daughter: Ella, grown well and tall and proud, and so inexpressibly fine.

Ella smiled at the old man eating with her; and Lenna lost her hold and fell.

Ella's smile was of such loveliness that Lenna heard the world crack open beneath her and felt herself falling, wheeling, into whatever lay below and she prayed: let it happen. Let me vanish now with this picture painted on my soul and I will keep it alive and beauteous, even in the darkest fiery pit, and others will come and gaze on it and be comforted in their burning. I want no more. I want no more. Everything has been paid for. All debts are settled, all my trials and more I offer, free and full, for this one moment. Let me go now.

Then Ella looked at her directly across the room.

Lenna turned away.

She didn't want to. She wanted to sit here and stare forever; but instead she turned away. Because beneath her feet was the floor of a diner and not the abyss she'd prayed for; because her stare was the stare of contagion and death; and because she was ashamed. She was ashamed that she, and not some other, better, woman, was the mother of this lovely girl. She could not look her daughter in the eye and have to tell her, even in the wordlessness of a silent gaze: I am your birthright. Lenna felt tears running down her neck. Confusion seized her, panic. Leave. *Leave.* Just leave, now. Then: *please, just one more look; just one more glance.* The choir of yearnings dragged her eyes across the room.

She saw Ella looking down at her plate.

Ella lifting a fork to her mouth.

One more picture, one more glimpse.

Ella putting the fork down, untouched.

202

Then: Ella looking directly at her, again.

Lenna turned away.

She blanked her mind. She stood up. She threw some money on the table. She saw the napkin by her plate, picked it up, wiped her face. The door. The sidewalk. The road away. Go. She turned and stared at the exit. The room was a tunnel, a blur. Walk. She moved down the aisle, her eyes on the door. An awareness as strong as the heat of an open furnace flared and roared just ahead to her left: Ella, her table. Lenna kept walking, reeled through the blast, she was through it, she was past, she was gone, the door still there ahead. Then a voice.

"Excuse me, Miss?"

Against her will Lenna's legs stopped moving. She felt her shoulders shaking. Her body was lost in a flood of sensations, intensely physical. Gut, head, muscles. She couldn't breathe. I will not cry. I will not cry. The voice again: a simple and incomprehensible compassion.

"I just wondered if you were okay."

Lenna's mind swam. Say something and go. No, just go. The door: there. *Just a couple of words. Let me speak to her just once.* She gave in. She turned and looked at the huge and gentle eyes a few inches away.

"Thank you," choked Lenna. "I'm fine."

She felt a spasm bubble up through her throat and clamped down on it. She felt herself shaking with the effort. Ella took her arm.

Ella touched her.

Ella said, "Please, come and sit with us for a while."

"No. I mustn't. I have to." Lenna ran out of breath and didn't dare take another. "I have to . . ."

The old man wiped his mouth and threw down his napkin and stood up.

He said to Ella, "Take her outside. I'll get the check."

Lenna looked at him for safety. He had gray eyes, worried but strong. He nodded to her and smiled a kindly smile. With the smile he turned, for an instant, into Cicero Grimes and she realized this was his father, George. The nod and the smile poured strength into her. She turned and walked to the door, feeling Ella's steps behind her. By the time she reached the sidewalk she was breathing again. She turned and looked at the notch in Ella's throat. She didn't dare look at her face.

"Forgive me," said Lenna, "but would you hold me for a moment?"

Ella hesitated. "Sure."

Ella's arms opened and Lenna stepped between them and the arms folded around her. Lenna closed her eyes as the skin of Ella's neck touched her cheek. She felt their bodies press together, felt gentle hands upon her back. It was the softest place she'd ever been, the loveliest, the deepest. She put her arms around Ella. She thought nothing, she didn't ask to know what it was she felt, she just accepted this gift as it was given, out of the freedom and innocence of a stranger. She lost track of time and within whatever time it was she recovered herself, so that when she sensed George Grimes walk up and heard him cough she was able to let go and stand back feeling okay. She was even able to look Ella in the eye.

"You're very kind," said Lenna. "I'm sorry if I embarrassed you."

"You didn't," replied Ella. "I'm fine. It was nothing. God, you should see me on my bad days."

Lenna swallowed another urge to sob and wrested her wits back into place. She made herself think: only Cicero Grimes knew that Ella was her daughter. That was how it had to stay. She mustn't let emotion sway the clear decision she had made to protect Ella from her origins.

George Grimes said, "You're Lenna Parillaud."

She looked at him and nodded. "That's right. And you're George Grimes."

Lenna held out her hand and George shook it. In George's eyes was a veiled suspicion. She was glad. She didn't want Ella hanging out with a fool.

"This is my friend Ella MacDaniels," said George.

Lenna's voice was close to a whisper. "Ella."

George looked up and down the street. "Let's go around to the Jeep."

As they crossed the parking lot George fell in between Ella and Lenna. His brow furrowed.

"You traveling alone?" he asked her.

"No," Lenna replied. "I came with your son, Gene."

"Where is Gene?"

Lenna glanced across him at Ella, who was listening. She didn't want to expose Ella to any more than was necessary. The less she knew the better. George read the glance.

"Ella gets to know everything I do," said George. "That's the deal between us."

Lenna looked at him. "Gene's gone to find Jefferson's papers."

George grunted. "Anyone else know why you're here?"

Lenna saw no reason to mention Daggett. "No. At least I don't think so."

They reached a red-and-black Jeep Cherokee and stopped. George rubbed a thumb along the side of his chin and stared into the western sky.

"Be dark within the hour."

He looked back at Lenna.

"You don't mind, Miss Parillaud, Ella and me need a word in private."

Lenna nodded and walked to the other side of the Jeep, out of earshot. George's evident concern for Ella was comforting. She clung to her resolution to go it alone from here, to keep herself away from anyone she didn't want to hurt. Now it seemed a better idea than ever.

"Miss Parillaud?" called George.

She turned and walked back to them.

George coughed and said, "Miss Parillaud . . ."

"Lenna, please," she said.

"Lenna, then. Now, I know this might not sound friendly but you've got to understand we're in a situation here that might get dangerous. I appreciate you're with Gene, but he's not here. We don't know you, or what your end is, and to be frank, well, we'd be foolish to completely trust you."

George paused to look at Ella. She nodded.

"We're pretty well armed," continued George, "and we're ready to protect ourselves, whichever way we have to and against anyone as takes up against us. We don't mean to frighten you or cause unpleasantness, you understand, but we can't leave you to, well, run around and maybe cause us a problem. The upshot is, you're coming with us."

Ella added, "George doesn't mean we'd shoot you or anything like that, Lenna . . ."

"Of course not," said George.

". . . it's just we think it would be better if we all stuck together until we find Gene. We'll look after you."

"Right," said George. "That's what I meant. Anyone comes against you, they come against us."

Lenna looked at them both standing there, grimly heroic and at the same time terribly frail, and she realized that she loved them. It was as simple and as painful as that. She'd lived so long inside herself—inside her prison of hatred and loss—that she didn't know how to deal with it. She felt the flood welling up again and this time the tears were filled with something more haunting than all her pain: she was happy. She was happy just to stand and breathe, here in the lot with these two people she'd never even met before.

Ella said, "All you have to do is ride with us."

And Lenna Parillaud blinked and smiled and said, to Ella, "I would love to."

TWENTY-ONE

T HE GOOD DOCTOR'S appearance was haggard and changed. Within the shimmering light and shadow of his pale blue eyes and the hollows of his face were the stigmata—clear and yet invisible— of the time they two had spent together. Yet in spite of that Grimes was the man that he had been, and the man that he was and always would be: a clown in the midst of an incomprehensible adventure, yearning for that which he had lost but could not name, searching not even for an answer but merely for a question that was worthy of the asking: the latest, but not the last, of an ancient line.

All this Jefferson saw in the shadows of the pale blue eyes and he felt his heart move with an unaccustomed pity, an inexplicable love. What was this love, this stirring that had haunted him in his fastness? Of what strange stuff was it wrought? And by what strange hand?

In the green-wood burning of his exile, in the Ohoopee River bottomlands, Jefferson had considered this matter long but without profit. If desire was an amoral savagery that he'd embraced without apology or regret, then love was a degradation and a crime, a plunge into gutters randomly chosen, a futile unmaking, an imbecile's gargling laughter at the joke he did not understand. If there had been an erotic element to his love it would have been simpler: he would have fucked Grimes in the ass and the mouth while he'd had the chance; and there, most likely, it would have ended. Instead he had tortured him to the twitching brink of collapse and beyond; he had charred his nervous system to wires of blackened ash; and yet in search of what? He had not known. Integrity's only resting place was that of silence and of pain, and Grimes had known them both. In such a place it had been that Jefferson had loved. And like a shuttered window opened of a sudden onto blazing day, love had opened onto death.

His mind had become an abattoir of unsolved riddles, the architecture of his intellect a roofless and gutted ruin, its skeleton walls tilting in the smoke. Confined to his chair by blistered flesh and ankylosing joints, he had wandered nevertheless, here, across the bottomlands, in search of the silent core. In search of his discipline.

Nothing must be wanted.

Violence must be without justification.

Suffering must be futile.

These were his tools. They could not be questioned. They could not be blunted and disabled by pedestrian reason, for their power, their occult meanings, were seated in unreason. Justification was a scourge—the vapid convalescent home of the civilized, the cowardly and the weak. He would not be justified. "Why?" was the bleating battle cry of the pitifully stupid. He would not ask "Why?" Did they really think they could explain it? They who had only possessed language for four miserable millennia and had groped at the apron strings of thought for less than three? Their trillion words of exegesis and insight, of analysis and explication, had penetrated the miles-deep mystery not an inch. Frightened scum, masturbating over the faded, cum-stained photos of a truth they dared not fuck in the ripe and rotten flesh. "Why?" He choked on the word. The rich horror of human existence was wasted on them. They were the flies who ate shit as happily as they ate chocolate cake.

His discipline had been of a more exacting order. His discipline had been to do away with everything in which others located their humanity: trust, friendship, progress, loyalty, devotion; and, most especially, all traces of anything that approached the treacherous bliss of tenderness. He stumbled back over fragments of remembered atrocity: of men executed for crimes they did not commit, of the healthy crippled in spine and bone, of screaming penitents devoured by beasts, of a shack's wooden planking sprayed wide with gore. Of men and women separated from the ones they loved. Of mothers from their daughters. Of fathers from their sons.

As he had separated himself.

His bleak and futile compulsion—and knowingly thus—had condemned him to a desert—an austerity—of inarticulate longings; yet he had ground those longings into dirt. He had banished from his life all that was comforting, all that might bring pleasure. He had even denied himself the inverted solace of despair. He had destituted his humanity:

without reason, without justification, without "Why?" He had wanted nothing: neither love nor knowledge, neither power nor beauty. These things he had accumulated, and exploited and spent, but he had not wanted them. He had attempted to free himself, short of death, from all the clanking chains of his wretched human being: a blind voyage into whatever lay beyond, without expectation or need of anything he might find.

And he had failed.

In a squalling bundle of swaddled rags, he had failed.

In a man who would not hate him, he had failed.

And in the Ohoopee River bottomlands he had come to know the extremity of his failure, the falsity of his solitude, the rank and disgraceful inevitability of his humanness.

He had needed to see them again, to feel them near.

He had summoned them to this meeting place.

The grain of wood.

The cleavature of stone.

The heart of the atom.

Buried secrets, only revealed to the eye of man by violent forces randomly applied.

If there was indeed a purpose to his summons—for he himself knew it not—then only by such application would it be revealed.

And when the revelation came, if come it would, it would take its place with all the others—grain of wood, cleavature of stone, heart of atom—and disappear from sight: trampled granules of sand washed by the vast ocean of all that was unintelligible.

In the end, he thought, nothing that was true had ever made sense.

Clarence Jefferson smiled across the musty parlor and said:

"You've lost weight, Grimes, I'm concerned."

TWENTY-TWO

CLARENCE SEYMOUR JEFFERSON, seated like an ailing suzerain upon a blighted throne, did not look well; but he was most irrefutably alive.

Grimes stood on the threshold of the parlor and reassured himself that if he uttered the appropriate order then Gul would tear Jefferson apart, without a qualm and probably with some enjoyment. Gul stalked slowly across the moth-eaten carpet, his hips hunched low, ready to spring in an instant at the deformed figure hulking in the winged chintz armchair. The dog's primeval basso made the mote-filled air tremble.

"Gul," said Grimes. "Stay cool."

Gul stopped. His eyes did not waver from Jefferson, who sat for all the world like a pagan idol cast in bronze and did not blink. Gul settled his muscled haunches on the carpet, still poised and ready to go, and waited.

"Good man," said Grimes. He looked at Jefferson. "This is Gul."

Jefferson glanced at the great black dog and nodded.

"I know Gulbudeen," he said.

Somehow Grimes was not surprised.

"You know 'em all, don't you, Clarence?"

Jefferson shook his huge head. "Nobody knows them all," he replied. "Sit down, why don't you? You're among friends after all."

Jefferson lifted his right arm and pointed at a second chair. The arm ended at the wrist in a thick black stump of what looked like a hard matte-black resin. Grimes glanced from the stump, whose origin he knew well, to Jefferson's eyes. Jefferson knew too; he smiled. Grimes looked away and walked over to the second chair and sat down. The butt of the Colt revolver in his belt jammed into his kidney and he shifted on his seat.

"You can put the gun on your lap, Grimes," said Jefferson. "I won't be offended."

Grimes pulled the Colt out, stuck it in the front of his belt and considered his situation. The first sight of Jefferson had made him feel sick. Initially it was with shock and an amorphous residue of the fear Jefferson had inspired on their previous encounter: when they had pushed each other, blow for blow, to the outer limits of existence and when Grimes had survived even if he had not won. This residue Grimes wiped aside. He would not be drawn into another game, not of that kind. He would not fear him; he would not hate him. Whether knowingly or not, Jefferson had taught him the folly of hatred, in the tunnel of pain they had crawled together; but now was not the time to dwell on that darkness. He would not be sucked into the past. All around Grimes there tossed a sea of rampant emotion: Jefferson's torment, George's lust for glory, the rage of Filmore Faroe. He could not afford that luxury. He had to mount the power of his will and his reason against the tides of feeling shifting within himself; otherwise he was lost.

With his mind at least temporarily under control Grimes found his nausea sustained by a different source: the peculiar odor that pervaded the room. He was familiar with the smell for once known it was never forgotten. It was the smell of field hospitals in the killing fields and of limbs awaiting amputation. It always provoked in him a strange blend of disgust and pity, for it was the smell of bacteria toiling ceaselessly, and innocently, at their life's work of consuming human tissue. *Pseudomonas*. Gangrene. Grimes swallowed the nausea and oriented himself.

This side of the farmhouse faced north. The light from the casement windows was soft and pale. In the apple trees outside the window nameless birds flung profligate harmonies to the breeze, indifferent to they who listened inside. Grimes thought: bacteria, birds, dogs, men. He wondered if they all of them existed within themselves, as he did. He couldn't see how they could not. And, if so, he wondered by what leaps infinitely large, and infinitesimally small, and by what alchemy and over what eons the toiling microbes had transformed their inner existence, whatever form it took, into birdsong and the stoutness of Gul's heart and the fevered brightness of Jefferson's eyes. And then he wondered what random and ephemeral forces had brought them all here together, on this late and fading afternoon in this dusty parlor, perfumed with gangrene, in the Ohoopee River bottomlands.

Grimes recognized in the drift of his thoughts the hypnotic influence of Clarence Jefferson. The Captain sat there watching Grimes wonder as if ensconced among barren crags, waiting in abject serenity for a long predestined outcome. Against the back of his chair was propped a long wooden crutch. On the floor beside him, where he could reach it with his left hand, was an automatic shotgun with a sawed-down barrel.

The fatman was no longer fat. If Grimes had shed pounds, Jefferson had shed all but the thread of life. His body was shriveled in the baggy wrapping of his skin. If Grimes had not known so well the gargantuan origin of the strength—the psychopathic strength—from which Jefferson's spending of himself had begun, he would not have believed it possible that a pulse might still beat in this frame. But beat it did: in the bowed and sensuous mouth, in the shining eyes, in the insolent bluntness of the resinous stump. Six-feet-six and as wide as God, his blond skull a marble boulder gracefully hacked, Clarence Jefferson still defied his Maker even as he stank. His face, its classical lines clearer now that he was wasted, glistened with a thin, unhealthy sweat. His left leg was propped on a worn red leather footstool, whose stuffing bulged from a gash in the side. The leg of his tan cotton slacks had been slit as far as the knee to accommodate the grossly edematous limb. The naked foot was also swollen. Over the lateral aspect of both leg and foot the skin was grotesquely deformed by the unmistakable scar tissue of a full-thickness burn. Under one edge of the scar, on the warped fullness of the calf, was a livid purple-black disc, moist at the center and angry red at the edges. *Ecthyma gangrenosum.* The lesion was in shadow and Grimes couldn't see it properly, but he knew that it was from there that the sweet smell emanated.

The last time Grimes had seen him, Jefferson had been flat on his back and surrounded by flames with almost a foot of steel in his belly.

Grimes said, "How did you survive?"

Jefferson said, "It was something I decided to do."

"You were well fucked and far from home."

"The fire, Grimes. You remember. The fire brought me around, the fire took out the wall. All I had to do was pull out the blade and crawl."

Grimes glanced at the swollen, gangrenous leg.

He said, "You're dying now, you know."

"Maybe," said Jefferson.

"May I take a look?" asked Grimes.

Jefferson hesitated, then smiled a smile that chilled Grimes's blood.

"Why, I'm touched, Grimes. By all means."

Grimes stood up and walked over. As he got closer he saw that in the moist center of the black discoid lesion there was a pale and tiny movement. He squatted at a safe distance from Jefferson's good hand. The forearm seemed the only part of Jefferson that had not withered: it was still the diameter of Grimes's thigh and as dense as ironwood. Grimes knew Gul would take the Captain out before he reached the shotgun, but if that meaty hand—its veins and tendons buried muscle-deep— closed around Grimes's throat, then it would be *adios muchacho* for him, Gul or not. Grimes looked more carefully at the ulcerating wound. As experienced as he was, he swallowed.

The pale and tiny movement at its center was a live maggot.

Grimes said, "That's a little old-fashioned, isn't it?"

Jefferson laughed. "You know, Grimes? You don't disappoint me."

"You put it in there yourself."

"Don't knock it. That little feller's keeping me alive."

"Maybe for a while," said Grimes, "but he won't help the infection in your blood. You need a couple of heavy-duty antibiotics."

The names Tobramycin and Ciprofloxacin flashed through his mind. It didn't seem worth mentioning them.

"You didn't come all this way to write me a prescription," said Jefferson.

Grimes squinted and inwardly sighed at himself. This man, this Captain of Vice, was the origin of all his woes; and yet Grimes was bizarrely glad to see him. He was glad Jefferson was not dead. He almost said so but didn't. Grimes admired guts more than just about anything else. Clarence Jefferson might have been a cocksucker but guts he had in plenty.

Grimes said, "Then why did I come?"

"Because I asked you to. I knew you wouldn't refuse an old friend."

"So why me?"

Jefferson gazed at the ceiling for a moment, then looked down at him.

"Because you deserved another chance," he said.

"Thank you," said Grimes.

Jefferson raised his eyebrows. "Will you deny that you needed me, rotting in your hole as Daggett found you? As I knew he would find you?"

Grimes didn't feel like answering.

Jefferson said, "I've brought pain into your life, Grimes. Past and present."

"I'm not complaining."

Clarence Jefferson smiled. "Your stoicism is already beyond question."

"Fuck off."

"But as our mutual friend Seneca said, while God is *beyond* suffering, the true Stoic is *above* it."

"One day," said Grimes, "I'm going to work out why it is that so many people want to tell me how I should live my goddamn life."

"You're a much-loved man, Grimes. That's why you're here."

"I just want to keep my father out of trouble."

Jefferson said, "You delude yourself. You are here, as are we all, to sup on anguish. If it is so, as our Seneca implies, that suffering contradicts the very nature of God, then by the same token it defines ours. That is why, in the end, we so resolutely desire the anguish which imperils our life. Or rather, not anguish alone but anguish transcended. The man who thereby conquers the scalding anguish of desire, hatred and fear 'surpasses God himself.' Is that not our project?"

"It isn't mine," said Grimes. "I just want to go back to my hole."

"Come now, Grimes, cynicism is a boy's game. We are men, are we not? You must acknowledge that an extremity of anguish is the precious possession of an infinitely small elite."

"That's the primest bullshit I've ever heard." Grimes felt himself heating up. This was stupid. He stood up from his squat. "I won't argue with you."

Jefferson looked up at him. "As you will, but at least hear me out. Surely you wouldn't cheat Fate of the immense labor she has invested in bringing us together again?"

Grimes walked over to the window and looked out on the first glimmerings of dusk. He ought to leave, yet couldn't. He listened without turning.

"You know you don't have to be here any more than I do, Grimes. Don't tell me you 'had to come,' that your conscience forced you. The Stoic does not spend his energies on the despair of guilt any more than on the frivolity of joy. You chose to make this journey, as did I, and for one reason only: because we both know in our hearts that it is only by dancing, cheek to cheek, with ruination and death that we can overcome them and take our rightful place among the stars."

"And Lenna Parillaud and my father," said Grimes, still facing the window pane. "Are they dancing too?"

"The invitation to the dance excludes no one."

"So this elite of yours isn't so small after all."

There was a pause.

"I retract that indulgence," said Jefferson. "It was vain. And yet I meant it. For if our overcoming is to be more than abject submission to the random hostility of the cosmos, one condition—and one only— must be met in full. And it is this: that our anguish be a fit measure of the spirit of the man—or the woman—who desires it."

Grimes turned to look at him. There was an eagerness, an invitation, in Jefferson's eyes that he had seen before, and had refused.

"So you've got what you wanted," said Grimes. "Sitting on the throne of God and measuring our fitness for eternity while the rest of us run around like assholes."

"No right man wants to be a god. A king, perhaps, but not a god."

"Maybe I don't want to be a king, either," said Grimes.

"Not even of yourself?" asked Jefferson.

Grimes heard the slap of a gauntlet hitting the floor. He said nothing.

Jefferson nodded.

"That kingdom is the hardest conquest of all," said Jefferson. "To keep it is harder still. Both endeavors insist upon the spilling of blood: whether blood of vein or blood of soul; your own and that of others, too."

So there was the nub of all that the Captain had summoned him to hear.

Grimes didn't want to see things the way Jefferson did; the burden was too grave. Yet he had accepted this summons; he was here. Maybe the Captain was right, then; but Grimes suspected that Jefferson was driven by the same mysterious undercurrents as he was, and as were they all, and that Jefferson's speculations were no more than a thin garment hastily thrown over his fear of the inner unknown. As Grimes held his gaze, the feverish tinge to Jefferson's eyes grew more intense. Grimes would deal with his own unknown in his own way. He decided it was time to go.

"Okay," said Grimes. "I've heard you out. You wrote me about two suitcases. Where are they?"

"You mean the anvil of justice," said Jefferson.

"If you insist," said Grimes. "Do they exist? Or was that just a part of the great game?"

"Look behind me," said Jefferson.

Grimes stepped away from the window and looked behind Jefferson's armchair. In the shadows between the chair and the wall stood two large suitcases in brown leather, bound by straps. Grimes bent down and picked one up. He almost dislocated a disc.

"It feels like it's full of gold bars," said Grimes.

"More than gold, Grimes, much more."

Grimes said, "Well, this is what I came for."

Grimes picked up both cases. He reckoned he could just about make it to Daggett's car. He carried the cases into the center of the room and set them down. Gul looked up at him and showed him his tongue. Gul, at least, knew the score. Grimes cast a glance around the decaying room. The Old Place. It felt like a tomb.

As if reading his thoughts, Jefferson said, "I was born in this house."

The words, though flatly stated, reached Grimes's ears with the desperation of a plea. He turned back to the gangrenous carcass sweating away the last of his strength in the winged chair, and with those words and in that moment the legend of Clarence Jefferson died in front of him. Grimes saw only a man, putrefying in his own skin, a man who had sat here for a thousand crawling hours with nothing to keep him company but the memory of the lives he'd blighted, his attempt to squeeze some bitter drops of meaning from what he had done, and the maggot in his leg. That Jefferson had held on to the thread of sanity at all was a measure of his demonic will. Grimes hesitated to credit him with a great mind. Could greatness devote itself to evil and remain great? There were those who spoke readily enough of the glory of transgression; Jefferson had lived it. Had he, then, known glory? His body was being slowly and hideously poisoned, as he had poisoned the lives of Lenna, and of Faroe, of those whose own crimes were crammed into the cases on the floor and of many more now dead and gone. And yet it seemed to Grimes that there was no justice in Jefferson's slow putrefaction, but only more suffering.

Jefferson sat staring at him in silence, as if waiting for the shroud of isolation to fall once more around his shoulders, and Grimes felt an intense pity for him. He would have preferred something else, triumph maybe, or gladness or relief. But pity was all he could come up with. There was nothing left to say.

"Goodbye, Clarence," said Grimes.

Without waiting for an answer Grimes bent and picked up the suitcases.

"Gul," he said. "Let's go."

As Gul rose majestically to his feet Jefferson swung his leg from the footstool. Gul displayed some teeth and growled.

"Easy," said Grimes.

Grimes had some small inkling of the extraordinary pain Jefferson had to be in, yet the Captain hoisted himself to his feet without flinching. He grabbed his crutch.

"I'll see you to the door."

"Thanks."

Grimes headed down the corridor toward the backdoor. At his heel Gul kept an eye on the towering figure stumping along behind them. They passed through the gloomy kitchen and went out onto the porch and Grimes set the cases down. Across the cobblestoned yard Daggett was sitting in his Lincoln. Beyond the car was spread the splendor of the valley and the river's winding gold.

Behind him Jefferson said, "You ought to stick around awhile. At sundown, if you're lucky, the bottomlands can seem like they're bathed in blood."

Grimes turned and looked up into the fatman's face, no longer fat.

Jefferson said, "I reckon it's as good a place to die as any other."

Grimes said, "When I see your head on a pole, I'll believe it."

"Before you go, I have something I wanted to give to Ella."

Jefferson shifted his weight from the crutch and leaned his right shoulder against the timber supporting the porch roof. He put his left hand into his pocket.

"I was hoping you might bring her, for a last visit."

"I figure she's with my father," replied Grimes. "I never met her."

"Are you telling me they're coming here?"

"Probably. I showed George your letter," said Grimes. "He got to her first."

A curious light came into Jefferson's eyes. He had looked at Grimes the same way when he'd first entered the parlor. Jefferson pulled his hand out empty; whatever he meant to give Ella he left in his pocket.

Grimes said, "If they do show, tell them to stay out of trouble until I get back home. And don't rile George. He's armed and paranoid and he doesn't have my patience. He'll also be disappointed not to get these." He nodded at the cases. "Is there anything in them could hurt Lenna?"

"Nothing."

"I guess there's not much more you could do to her anyway."

Jefferson's gaze did not flicker.

Grimes said, "Until I met Lenna I thought Ella was your daughter."

Jefferson said, "Ella is mine. I made her so."

It was as well Grimes hadn't brought Lenna along. He couldn't imagine her not beating Gul to Jefferson's throat. He wondered what kind of a man it was that could steal a babe still screaming for the first embrace of her mother's arms. In a sense he already knew, for he knew Jefferson; not in any way he could articulate, but deeply just the same. More mysterious to him was why Jefferson had not fulfilled his brief to kill the child; that he could have done so without blinking, Grimes didn't doubt.

"You were meant to kill Ella," said Grimes. "Why didn't you?"

Jefferson's lips curved in a totemic smile.

"Because something in the earth called upon me not to."

Grimes turned away from the smile.

Jefferson said, "Afterwards, you know, Lenna and I became lovers."

Grimes hoped that the lurch in his guts didn't show on his face.

"Didn't she tell you?" said Jefferson.

"Why would she?" said Grimes.

He could imagine why Lenna had surrendered herself to the perverse comfort of Jefferson's arms, why she might need it; it was a fitting punishment for the guilt that had scourged her and scourged her still. The unremitting extremity of that guilt, on the other hand, Grimes could not imagine.

"Don't think badly of her, Grimes."

"I don't," said Grimes. "Nor would I, ever."

"As you said, she is a dancer."

"Yes," said Grimes. "She is."

Jefferson held his left hand out.

"Good luck in Washington. You'll be a hero at last."

"Not if I can help it."

Grimes took the massive hand with his right and squeezed it.

Jefferson said, "Wrap up warm, Grimes."

And in Jefferson's face Grimes saw things, and in his own chest he felt things, that he would rather not have seen or felt. He let go of the hand, grabbed the cases and walked across the yard toward the Lincoln without looking back. Gul trotted by his side. The dog looked up at him with his sad eyes.

"Cheer up," said Grimes. "We get this stuff to D.C., it's over, man, we're gone. Wyoming. Just you and me."

Gul barked gruffly.

"No. Lenna can look out for herself. What the fuck can a pair of clowns like us do?"

Gul barked again.

"Okay," said Grimes. "You're right. One step at a time, like before."

Grimes loaded the cases into Daggett's car. In an hour it would be dark. He tried not to but he couldn't help it: as he opened the passenger door and let Gul clamber in, Grimes looked back toward the Old Place.

The porch was empty. Clarence Jefferson had gone.

Grimes climbed in the car and Holden Daggett drove them back through the impending dusk.

TWENTY-THREE

GRIMES AND DAGGETT didn't speak much on their way back to town. Grimes told Daggett that Jefferson needed medical treatment and Daggett said he knew, but Jefferson wasn't a man to be argued with once his mind was made up. Then Grimes asked Daggett how long he'd known the Captain.

"As a client—boy and man—nearly forty years," replied Daggett. "Clarence was ten years old. His father died in, well, circumstances. His mother sent him away, down South, didn't want anyone to know where he came from. I arranged it all. Before me, my own father represented the family. That's the way things tend to go around here."

Grimes asked, "You know what's in the suitcases in the trunk?"

"That may or may not be my affair," said Daggett. "Either way it isn't my place to discuss it."

"I just didn't want you to be at risk without your knowing it," said Grimes.

"Let's say I know as much as I need to know, no more, no less. Nobody's holding a gun to my head and I'm not breaking any laws or ethics, nor would I, for anyone. But I appreciate your concern."

When they reached Mrs. Stapleton's place Grimes got out of the car with Gul and went around to Daggett's window.

"Am I good for one last favor?" asked Grimes.

"You can try," replied Daggett.

"Those suitcases weigh a ton. Can I leave them in your car until I arrange some transport out of town?"

Daggett removed his straw boater, took a handkerchief from his pocket and wiped the leather brim.

"We are but slaves to fate, chance, kings and desperate men," he said.

"Fellow travelers, maybe," said Grimes, "but not slaves."

"That makes it harder," said Daggett.

"I guess," said Grimes.

Daggett sighed and put his straw hat back on.

"I'll be at my office for a couple of hours. Any later than that, you'll find me at home."

"I'm obliged," said Grimes.

"Funny thing," mused Daggett, "the way some folk can get beneath your skin."

Grimes knew that he meant Clarence Jefferson.

"Yes," he replied. "It is."

"I'll be seeing you," said Daggett.

"Thanks."

Daggett drove away and Grimes felt some of the pressure lift from his shoulders. He had the suitcases. At least George wouldn't be running around with them. Just before he went indoors he remembered to transfer his revolver to the back of his pants.

Inside he talked with Mrs. Stapleton for a few minutes while she fussed over Gul and how beautiful his eyes were and how much her husband would have liked him. As she fed Gul water and scraps she told Grimes that his wife, Lenna, had gone into town and Grimes was neither worried nor surprised. She'd be in the diner. He went to check their room and found it empty and his note gone, then he told Mrs. Stapleton that they'd be moving on that evening. He reassured her that the room had been fine and her hospitality wonderful and paid her more than she asked him. Then he went into the parlor, took from his pocket the card that Titus Oates had given him and called the number.

The phone rang several times before it was answered and Grimes almost gave up. Then there was a click and a large voice boomed into Grimes's ear.

"Who the fuck is this?" Oates sounded disturbed.

"It's Grimes," said Grimes.

"What the fuck, man? I've got four shotguns pointing at my fucking balls and one of them, I've just been reminded, is loaded with deer slugs. These guys already got me working for the AT&F. What the fuck you tryin' to do to me?"

Grimes realized he'd interrupted Oates in the middle of his expedition to purchase bootleg whiskey in the backwoods. He thought he could hear a second man breathing near the receiver. It seemed to Grimes that it was best to play it straight.

"I just wanted to give you some more flying business."

"Jesus," said Oates, heavily.

"When can you get back to the airfield?" asked Grimes.

"Listen, cousin, I've been driven around half the afternoon in a fucking blindfold. I'm not even sure what state I'm in. You any idea how easy it is to lose a corpse out here?"

"Don't get overexcited," said Grimes. He thought of the second listener. "Those guys are just exercising their constitutional right to keep and bear arms, same as the rest of us. I'm sure they're men of honor."

"Of course they're fucking men of honor. That's why they lost the Civil War."

"How soon can you get back?"

There was a pause and Grimes heard a distant murmur of conversation.

"An hour, maybe more, depending on how long we're down to haggling," said Oates.

"Don't let me down," said Grimes. "And watch out for the deer slugs."

"Ten-four and fuck your mother."

The line went dead.

Grimes sorted a schedule in his mind. He'd go and find Lenna, then Daggett could drive them out to the airfield. It was now around the time that George and Ella could be expected to turn up, assuming they'd made good time. Grimes decided not to wait or look for them. Traveling alone made everything simpler. He would even have preferred to leave Lenna somewhere safe, but he knew she wouldn't agree to that. He was satisfied that if George and Ella did make it to the Old Place, then Jefferson wouldn't harm them. So Grimes fetched Gul, let Mrs. Stapleton kiss him goodbye and walked the road into town for the second time that day.

All in all things were working out as well as he could have hoped. He was confident that he could get Jefferson's anvil of justice to Washington, D.C., and unload the cases, anonymously, on some hotshot journalist who would go on to win the Pulitzer Prize and be played by Tom Cruise in the movie. Maybe they could get Bob Hope out of retirement to play Cicero Grimes; except that Grimes had no intention of letting his name be known. He discovered that he had no curiosity at all as to what exactly the cases contained. The less he knew the better.

Lenna's problem with Faroe was another matter. Right now Faroe seemed, thankfully, a long way away. Lenna would have to deal with it later. Probably her best option would be to throw herself on the mercy of the law. She could afford the lawyers and it would be a hard-hearted jury that would find against her. As for Filmore Faroe, his arm was long and his pockets were deep, but even if he could manipulate the law he couldn't survive a thousand hours' exposure on TV. Maybe George was right, thought Grimes. Maybe this was a great country after all.

Grimes reached the diner on Main and peered through the windows. He saw nobody he recognized but he couldn't see all the tables. He told Gul to sit outside and stay cool and then popped in. He described Lenna to the waitress and the waitress remembered her because she'd left a ninety-dollar tip, which the waitress assured him she was prepared to return if the lady had made a mistake. The waitress told him that Lenna had left with an older man and a young Negro woman. For a moment Grimes's heart went out to Lenna. Seeing Ella for the first time must have been an ordeal. That explained the mistaken tip; he told the waitress to keep it and left.

Gul stood up and looked at him.

"I figure they've gone out to the Old Place," said Grimes. "I guess we'll have to go get them."

They walked down Main toward Daggett's office. The sun had disappeared behind the buildings. Things were less good than before but still fair to middling. There was no need to panic. Daggett's car was parked outside his office, sixty yards away. As they passed the entrance to a bank, the door to Daggett's office opened and Daggett stepped out. Grimes was about to call to Daggett when a second man emerged behind him. Before he'd worked out why, an instinctive paranoia made Grimes dodge sideways and out of sight into the wide granite doorway of the bank.

"Gul."

Gul followed him.

"Good man. Sit."

Grimes peered cautiously down the street. The guy with Daggett was wearing a baseball cap and a green FALCONS windbreaker with a satin finish. It was the same guy who had spoken to Grimes and Gul on the bench. His right hand was bunched in his pocket and pointed, awkwardly, at Daggett. Daggett's stiff body language, as he opened the Lincoln's trunk, suggested that he was not doing so voluntarily. The Falcons fan looked in the trunk and nodded and said something. Daggett slammed the lid and got into the car. The Falcons guy glanced briefly up and down the street then climbed into the passenger seat. Daggett's Lincoln started up and moved off.

Grimes stepped out into the street.

He had no idea exactly what the fuck was going on but it was bad. He didn't know where the Falcons guy was taking Daggett. The suitcases were gone. The Falcon was only one man, but he changed the picture. George and Lenna and Ella were now in danger. Grimes had to get to the Old Place and pull everyone out, get them to the cropduster's field and Titus Oates's plane. Grimes needed a car.

He looked up and down Main. At the far end, in the direction Daggett had taken, was a gas station.

"Come on," said Grimes.

He ran, with Gul loping without effort a foot to his right. Within a hundred yards, too many Pall Malls and the months he'd spent on the floor eating junk started to get to him. He told himself he deserved it and pushed on. By the time he lumbered into the gas station and past the pumps his lungs felt as if someone were tearing strips of adhesive tape from their inner surface. To one side of the glass-fronted office he was relieved to see a Ford pickup. He walked the last few yards, opened the office door and barged in.

Behind the counter was a young guy wearing a faded BLACK CROWES T-shirt and some kind of Stetson decorated with a Stars and Bars badge. The guy ignored Grimes and looked down at Gul with wide eyes.

"Hey, cool animal," said the guy.

"Thanks," said Grimes.

"You wanna sell him?"

"He's not mine to sell. But I'd like to rent your truck for a couple of hours."

"Sorry, friend, it's not mine to rent."

"It's urgent," said Grimes. "Very urgent. I can pay you a hundred bucks."

"Hey. I'm not trying to jerk you around. The truck belongs to my boss. I can't do it."

"Two hundred," said Grimes.

"If it were mine you'd already have a deal. It's that urgent I can call the cops for ya."

"No," said Grimes. He fumbled for his money. "Three hundred."

"I've got a motorcycle out back," said the guy. He pronounced it "motorsickle."

"A motorcycle?" said Grimes.

"Genuine Electra Glide. 1973. Sucks up the curves like it's working for the Lord hisself."

Grimes hadn't ridden a motorcycle in nearly twenty years.

"You don't understand," said Grimes. "I need a car. I need to take the dog with me."

"So?" said the guy. "I told you, that's a cool animal."

On the lot behind the office, the young guy started the Harley for him and Grimes gave him three hundred dollars.

"Obliged," said the guy.

Grimes swung into the saddle and took the handgrips. Despite his raw lungs and the fear for George and Lenna he couldn't deny a thrill of pleasure. Then he remembered Gul. The dog was looking up at him with mild curiosity. Grimes slid back as far as he could, then slapped the saddle in front of him.

"What are you waiting for?" said Grimes.

Without hesitation Gul leapt up onto the saddle in front of Grimes and settled himself down across the wide gas tank as if it were a favorite spot in the sun.

"Just forget he's there," advised the guy, "and he'll be fine."

Grimes twisted a few revs through the engine and kicked away the stand.

"You take care of him, now," said the young guy cheerily.

"I'll try," said Grimes.

"I was talking to the dog."

Gul barked.

Cicero Grimes shrugged, engaged the clutch and roared off west toward the Ohoopee River bottomlands.

TWENTY-FOUR

ELLA DROVE ON for three miles beyond the cutoff to the west before she decided that she'd missed it. The last time she'd been out to the Old Place it had been winter and the landscape had looked different. Now it was heavy and green. She pulled the Jeep over, hung a U and headed back. It didn't cost them more than ten minutes. Once they'd turned onto the cutoff she still wasn't sure it was the right road until they crested the hill and the valley opened before them. The sun was a red disc sliced in half by the far horizon and the meadows rolling down toward the river were wild with flowers. It was prettier than she'd ever seen it. In the midst of the meadows stood the black silhouette of the Old Place. The silhouette brought a sadness to her throat, the thought of Charlie dead and the times he'd brought her here. She looked at George.

"That's it," she said. "That's the Old Place."

"You done good," said George.

From the backseat Lenna said, "How come you know this place?"

Ella glanced over her shoulder. Lenna had the deepest eyes she'd ever seen; there was something in the way they looked at her that scared Ella a little. It wasn't that she thought Lenna meant her any harm, but the look made her think of starvation, of a desperate hunger. At the same time Ella felt pulled in as if by a silent voice calling out from a dark cave. She would've liked to hang out with Lenna somewhere safe and ordinary, where they could relax a little more and talk, but that would have to wait. She looked back at the road and spoke over her shoulder.

"I've been out here before, with Charlie," answered Ella.

"Charlie?" said Lenna.

"Sorry, I mean Clarence Jefferson," said Ella. "I always knew him as Charlie."

There was a dense silence from behind and Ella glanced into the rearview mirror. She could only see Lenna's rosebud mouth. Ella thought she was beautiful. Lenna was biting her lip.

"Did you know him a long time?" asked Lenna.

"All my life I guess," replied Ella. "I guess he was kind of an uncle to me."

The question hadn't really left Ella's mind all day: was Charlie her father? More than anything, more than getting the suitcases and going to Washington, she wanted to meet George's son, Gene, and find out the truth.

Lenna said, "Was he a nice uncle?"

"Oh yeah," said Ella. "Charlie was the best."

In the mirror she saw the lower half of Lenna's face flinch. She ducked her head to get a glimpse of Lenna's eyes but George interrupted her. They were almost at the track that led from the road to the Old Place.

"Take the farm road nice and slow," said George. "See them bushes and trees about thirty yards short?"

Ella slowed and turned onto the bumpy dirt track. Toward the far end was an overgrown clump of bushes spilling over the edge of the field onto the track.

"I see them," she said.

"I'm going to slip outa the car and recce the place. Don't stop. Just pull around the yard so you're facing back onto the track. Keep the engine running and wait in the car for me."

"Okay."

"You got your piece?"

Ella put her hand on the bag by her side.

"Locked down and loaded," she said.

George looked back at Lenna. Ella couldn't see her face.

"She's picking up my lingo," said George. "But don't be alarmed. We're not expecting any trouble."

George turned his eyes back on Ella: they were intense.

"If you do hear trouble or if I'm not out in five minutes, I want you to pull out."

Ella opened her mouth.

"Promise me," said George. "We've got a responsibility to Lenna too."

Ella was horrified at the thought of George not being around, but she owed it to him to be cool. She nodded. "Okay."

"You just go straight back into town there and call the cops. You've done nothing wrong; you can tell 'em everything."

George cast a hard glance at Lenna. "You got that too?"

"We'll do as you say," said Lenna.

"Good."

George slid down in his seat. As they approached the clump of bushes that would shelter them from the house for a few yards, Ella looked at the speedometer and slowed to five miles an hour.

"Close the door after me," said George.

Ella nodded. As the bushes drew level George swung his door open and dropped from sight. Ella reached across and grabbed the handle and pulled the door closed. In the mirror she saw George pick himself up and stalk toward the house. Ella glanced at her watch—five minutes. She carried on at the same speed.

The Old Place cast a deep shadow across the ground before them. It was just as she remembered it except that its tilt had gotten a little worse and another window was broken. It had always held for her the tingle of a mysterious castle. Now that tingle was heightened. She and Lenna were alone together for the first time and somehow it added to the strangeness. In the parking lot behind the diner George had told her that Lenna was a powerful woman, "richer than Croesus." He figured she was after the suitcases for purposes of her own. George had made Lenna sound like someone dangerous; Ella had found her sad and lost. She hoped Lenna wasn't too scared.

"George is just being cautious," said Ella. "He knows what he's doing."

"I'm sure," said Lenna.

"George was on Tarawa," said Ella. "And it doesn't get any tougher than that."

Lenna didn't answer and Ella guessed that she didn't know where Tarawa was, same as she hadn't. The Jeep pulled around the shadowy hulk of the building into the cobblestoned yard, where the light was strongest. She'd always liked that here, being able to sit on the porch and watch the sunset. She turned the Jeep in a semicircle and left the engine running as George had said. She picked her bag up and slipped her hand inside. The butt of the Smith & Wesson filled her palm. She kept her hand in the bag so as not to alarm Lenna, and turned to face her.

"This won't take long," said Ella, and smiled.

"You've been very kind to me," said Lenna. The starved look was still there.

"All we have to do is pick up a couple of suitcases. Nothing to it."

Ella looked at her watch. Two minutes to go. She wondered if she could do it, if she could drive off and leave George. Her stomach clutched into a ball at the thought of it. She'd promised. It wasn't going to happen, she told herself. George would show up. But if he didn't? Ella couldn't do it. If there were gunshots, maybe, but if all she got was silence, then no. She'd just have to wait a while longer. Ten minutes. But what if there was still nothing? Then she would have to go in and check it out. At least she knew the lay of the place. Then she thought, What if there are shots and *then* silence? Could she just drive off and maybe leave George wounded? George wouldn't ever leave her behind. They were supposed to be partners, right down the line. She couldn't leave him. But she had a responsibility to Lenna too. George had said so. Ella looked at her watch again in disbelief: only thirty seconds had passed.

"Are you okay?" asked Lenna.

Ella realized her face must be giving her away. She smiled.

"Sure," said Ella. "I'm just stiff from driving all day." She fell on the idea with relief. "I'm just going to stretch a little."

She opened the door and got out with her bag over her shoulder and her hand still inside. She immediately felt better. The rear porch was empty. Beyond the throb of the car engine she could hear birds and insects but nothing else. She looked at her watch. One minute left. She could wait that long. She heard Lenna open her door and get out. Ella turned.

"I'm stiff too," said Lenna.

Ella was just about to tell her to get back in the car when Lenna looked beyond Ella's shoulder toward the porch. Her face was paralyzed with horror. As Ella started to turn to see what it was she'd seen she felt Lenna seize her right arm.

"Give me your gun," said Lenna.

Her voice was low and urgent and her green eyes were wild.

"Lenna, no," said Ella.

She wrenched her arm away and stepped back. Her hand came free of the bag, holding the gun. She was panicked now. She swung the gun up and pointed it at the porch as she turned. She froze.

Out on the porch beneath the overhang of the second story a huge shadow of a man stood leaning on a crutch. So wasted was the great shadow's silhouette that the crutch might have been one of its bones. The shadow was topped by a Panama hat. As she watched, the shadow raised an arm and took the hat off. A few fine strands of blond hair lifted palely on the evening breeze. He pitched his molasses voice across the yard.

"Hello, Ella."

The sound brought a welling of soft fire to Ella's eyes.

"Charlie?" she said.

"Let me embrace you," said the shadow.

"Charlie," she repeated.

She started across the yard, her paces getting faster. As she got closer she saw his face: the same face, the familiar face, and yet so carved with excavated hollows that she almost didn't want it to be. Then she saw the swollen leg enflapped by stinking rags—and inhaled the smell that caught her even at this distance—and the foot twisted by what looked like melted slabs of pink plastic. Her whole body rocked with the knowledge that enormous agony had caused this change, for it was him: it was Charlie. Charlie changed. And Charlie was smiling, despite the agony, smiling from hollowed bones, smiling at her.

Five feet behind Charlie the screen door swung open and a shotgun barrel speared out from the darkness, aimed square and steady at the back of Charlie's skull.

"George!" shouted Ella. "It's all right!"

The memory of the men gunned down so swiftly last night was upon her. George had to see that she was okay. Ella stopped three feet short of the porch steps and dragged the right name from her memory.

"It's Clarence Jefferson!" she said.

The shotgun barrel didn't waver. Charlie hadn't moved a muscle. George's dry voice drifted out from the kitchen.

"I'll agree with you on this much, Mr. Jefferson: when it comes to shotguns, I'll choose an autoloader over a pump every time."

Charlie had not stopped smiling at her. He looked at the revolver in her hand and the smile turned into a grin.

"Looks like I'm out-gunned for sure. It's your call, Mr. Grimes."

"The belt gun under your shirt," said George. "Hand it to the lady there. You know how."

Charlie put his hat back on and Ella's eyes dropped to his right hand. The arm ended short in a black stump as thick and brutal as a drain-

230

pipe. Ella swallowed. With his left hand Charlie reached under the back of his blue Hawaiian shirt and produced a heavy, blued revolver. He tossed it and caught it by the ventilated barrel and held it out to her. Ella stepped forward. As she took the gun Charlie stared across the yard at Lenna with a look in his eyes that Ella could not penetrate. Ella looked back over her shoulder.

Lenna stood by the Jeep, staring right back at Charlie.

The look told Ella that they knew each other. They knew each other well. It made her feel strange, she didn't know how. Jealous. She felt the guns weighing heavy in her hands. She turned back to the porch and looked at Charlie.

"I knew you weren't dead," she said. "I knew."

"It's selfish of me, I know, but I'm glad you could come," he replied.

Without haste Charlie lumbered a couple more places from the kitchen doorway on his crutch. He still moved with the huge but relaxed power she'd always found so comforting. George was an old mountain lion, dangerous but not invulnerable. Charlie, even a shadowy and mutilated Charlie, was a mountain.

"Will you join us, Mr. Grimes?" said Charlie.

George emerged from the doorway with the shotgun at his shoulder. He lowered it to his hip but kept the muzzle trained on Charlie's middle. Ella looked at George and she could see him read that she wanted to go to Charlie. His steely caution melted a little.

"Go ahead," said George.

Ella put both guns down on the planks of the porch and ran up the steps. Jefferson held wide his stumped arm and she hugged him. Beneath his shirt he was still enormously wide but there were bones sticking from his back that hadn't been there before.

"How's my beauty?" he said, softly.

"She's fine," said Ella.

She closed her eyes for a moment. She had experienced a lot of strange things since the show at the Factory—less than twenty-four hours ago—but now she felt more confused than ever. Bits of the letter that Charlie had written, that she'd struggled to work out all day, tumbled through her head. *"He did his share, and more, of killing and of torture, and of other evils as vile as any a man might set his hand to."* Was Charlie really that man? She stepped back. The smell coming from him was sickening but she didn't let it show.

"Can we talk, I mean you and me?" she asked.

"Surely," said Charlie. "We'll find us some time."

Charlie looked past her and Ella turned. Lenna had come up to the porch. In her face Ella was shocked to see anger. No, pain too. Both. Ella's gut told her something she found hard to understand: Lenna was jealous. It was unmistakable; another woman's jealousy always was. She couldn't get her mind around it.

"Ella?" said George.

Ella looked at him. His face calmed her: no jealousy there.

"It wouldn't be wise to get ourselves stuck out here in the dark," said George. "I reckon we should get what we came for and press on."

"Can we take Charlie with us?"

The answer came from the cobbled yard to Ella's right.

"No, we can't."

It was Lenna. Her face was a grim mask. She walked the two paces toward the steps. Charlie stared at her.

"Lenna, don't," said Charlie. "This isn't the time."

Lenna ignored him and picked up Charlie's revolver from the porch. She cocked back the hammer and pointed it at Charlie's face.

Lenna said, "You're not coming with anyone."

Ella saw in Lenna's glittering eyes that she was about to shoot him.

Ella stepped in front of the gun muzzle and walked toward her. Lenna blinked and tried to speak, but couldn't. Whatever it was she was feeling Ella knew it was terrible, and she felt for her, but she couldn't let her shoot Charlie. Everything around Ella seemed frozen still. She stopped in front of Lenna.

"Lenna, me and George told you that anyone who comes against you comes against us too, remember?"

The torment in Lenna's face became worse. The gun in her hand was now a few bare inches from the center of Ella's chest. She didn't seem able to answer.

"Well, the same goes for Charlie," said Ella.

Lenna's eyes seemed to lose focus, then she looked at the gun and where it was pointed.

"Oh God," said Lenna. The sound seemed torn from her. "Oh God."

Lenna raised the gun until it was pointing harmlessly into the sky. She closed her eyes, trembling.

"Please," she said. "Will you take this away from me?"

Ella reached out and carefully took hold of the gun. Lenna unclenched her fist. Ella took the gun away, kept the barrel pointing at the sky and lowered the hammer safely. She bent quickly and picked up her own gun. Then she handed the first to George. George nodded at her. There was a silence.

Lenna opened her eyes long enough to gauge where the kitchen doorway was, then she closed them again and lunged across the porch and disappeared inside. The screen door slammed behind her. Ella heard muffled sobs. She felt totally bewildered; but she knew that for whatever reason, Lenna needed someone close. The reason wasn't important; all that mattered was the need. She started across the porch to follow her.

"Ella, better give her a minute alone," said George.

Ella almost ignored him, then realized he was right. She stopped. She'd wait for a minute but then she would go to Lenna. She would hold her again as Ella sensed that only she could. And then she would solve this mystery that was suddenly exploding all around her.

"We'll take Charlie with us, if he wants to come," said George. "Lenna too. But my water tells me we should get on our way soon as we can."

"You're right," said Charlie. "But what you came for has gone. The good doctor beat you to it. Your son. He asked me to tell you to stay out of trouble until he gets back home."

George's eyes narrowed with distrust.

Charlie said, "He also told me that you don't have his patience and I'm not to rile you. We can pick him up in town. If that's what you decide you want to do."

George looked at Ella. "What do you reckon?"

Ella nodded. "Let's go. I'll go get Lenna."

George nodded. As Ella started forward she stopped and listened. There was no sound coming from the dark kitchen. Lenna had fallen silent. But there was something else, something far away. She looked from George to Charlie. Neither of them seemed aware of it.

"Can't you hear it?" asked Ella.

The two men concentrated. Ella went back to the edge of the porch and scanned the valley. It seemed as peaceful as before; but the sound was getting louder. A low, fluttering drone.

"Now can you hear it?" she said, and turned.

George had crossed the porch and was already handing the big blue revolver back to Charlie. Their faces were grim as they spoke to each other.

George said, "If we can make it up the hill we'll have tree cover nearly all the way back to Jordan's Crossroads. If they catch us on the open road then we're a beer can sitting on a fence."

Charlie avoided Ella's eyes and looked out to the sky above her head.

"You're right, Mr. Grimes. But we're too late." He pointed with his stump. "We'll have to stand them off here."

Ella followed his gaze. For a moment she saw nothing; the sky above the far rim of hills was empty. Then there it was, beneath the rim: a black helicopter swooping across the valley toward them.

Ella kept her face out to the yard for a moment. She didn't want them to see the pulsing liquid fear that had suddenly washed through her body like a drug and paralyzed her limbs.

Behind her, George said, "What's this thing loaded with?"

"Double-aughts," replied Charlie. "Six rounds."

"If the women get in the Jeep and we wait here till the chopper sets down . . ." began George.

"They can drop men off without setting down," said Charlie.

"Well, if it does, then we could keep them busy while Ella and Lenna make a run for the hill."

Ella wanted her limbs back. She wanted to tell them, no, she wasn't going anywhere without them. She heard the screen door slam. The sound restored her power to move. She turned. Lenna stood on the porch, looking at the approaching chopper.

"I'm not running anywhere," said Lenna.

Ella said, "Why not?"

Lenna looked down at her. For the first time since they'd met Lenna's eyes, though rimmed with red, were utterly calm. Ella shivered.

Lenna said, "Because I'm the one they've come for. I'm the only one they want."

234

TWENTY-FIVE

RUFUS ATWATER had never flown in a chopper before. His ass was aching and his stomach still pitched unexpectedly from time to time and his ears were numb from the pounding flutter of the rotor blades, but he was wired just the same. The chopper—a Sikorsky, he'd learned—got into your nervous system and juiced it up whether you liked it or not. The tops of the trees had been skimming beneath their shadow for what seemed like a thousand square miles and Atwater just hoped that spic boy up in the cockpit there could find his way to the right spot. The sun was behind them so at least the pilot could see where he was going. And there were charts and compasses and other stuff that Atwater knew nothing about. He didn't like having to leave it all up to others, especially Roberto Herrera, but he had no choice. Even though he was officially in command it was hard for Atwater to feel that way surrounded as he was by a dozen armed men speaking a foreign language. They could speak English, too, of course; they just didn't, in order to make him paranoid.

Paranoid or not he was exhilarated. Filmore Faroe had been right to send them up here on a wing and a prayer; Cicero Grimes had arrived in Jordan's Crossroads and had made contact with Holden Daggett. But it was Rufus Atwater who had found that lead to Daggett, and Atwater who'd had the foresight to get Gough Lovett over there from Savannah. Atwater had met Lovett over too many beers with Jack Seed one time, when Lovett had been in the City for a snoopers' convention. Lovett had called Atwater back about forty minutes ago and told him that he'd tailed Grimes and Daggett to some kind of derelict farmhouse and that Grimes had gone inside. There'd been no sign of Parillaud. Lovett had located the position of the farmhouse for them in a triangle between a pair of county roads and the Ohoopee River and Herrera had pegged out the area on his charts. Atwater felt a faint trembling in his hand and looked down.

His phone was ringing again.

Atwater cursed the noise of the rotors and switched the phone on and jammed a finger in his left ear.

"Yeah?" he shouted.

"Atwater?" Lovett's voice was crackly and faint but recognizable.

"Yeah it's me."

"I got the suitcases," crackled Lovett.

"You got the suitcases? What suitcases?"

"Grimes brought two suitcases out of the farmhouse. Got to a point where I had to make a choice: the guy or the goods. I figured Grimes wasn't going nowhere fast, so I nailed the goods. That okay?"

Atwater's stomach pitched again, though not from the flight. It was too good to be true, man. He crouched forward in his seat. The suitcases? The goods? Jefferson's hoard? What the fuck else would Grimes be picking up? The sly cocksucker. Atwater jammed his finger in deeper.

"Yeah, that's good, that's perfect. You got a bonus coming. Where are ya?"

"I'm in lawyer Daggett's office," said Lovett. "What do you want me to do?"

Atwater looked around the cramped interior of the chopper and its sullen crew. They couldn't land in the middle of Jordan's Crossroads, that was for sure.

"Can we land a chopper out at this farm place?"

"No problem. Quiet as . . ."

The voice crackled inaudibly.

"Gough? You still there? I didn't hear ya!"

"I said the farm is as quiet as a grave!"

"Good. Bring the goods out to the farm," said Atwater. "We'll meet you there."

"Okay. What about Daggett?"

"Bring him, too. We can set up base at the farm and go find Grimes and the woman later. You got that?"

"I got it."

"We'll be there in . . . Hang on." Atwater leaned forward toward Herrera in the copilot's seat and yelled, "Roberto? How much farther, *amigo*?"

236

Herrera jabbed his index finger at the floor.

"We've just located the river. Now we'll follow it to the farm. I don't know, say ten minutes, more or less."

Atwater bent over the phone again. "Ten minutes more or less."

"I'll see you there," said Lovett.

"Ten-four."

Atwater switched off the phone. He could hardly swallow. He could hardly breathe. Before the night was over he'd have Mr. Filmore Faroe licking clean the ginger hairs on his ass. They had to find Parillaud, but she was somewhere close by, Grimes too, both of 'em just waiting to be scooped up. Why, Atwater even began to feel more kindly toward Herrera; the guy had gotten them here after all. Herrera was a cold fish for a Cuban. Atwater had learned that after Herrera had defected with the MiG, the communists had put his parents and sister in some kind of military prison and they'd never been heard of since. Maybe that's why he didn't seem to have any nerves. But that was okay too; that's what you wanted in a hired gun.

Atwater peered out at the landscape rushing by below. The light was fading but the river was there, snaking through the thinning trees. He watched and waited, watched and waited as the minutes crawled and the miles flew. As he stared his concentration kept slipping and all his eyes would take in was a green blur while his mind roved wildly across fantasy landscapes of power and wealth, of mistresses in slinky gowns and maître d's snapping their fingers for the best tables in restaurants he'd never even heard of. Herrera's voice broke through into his reverie.

"There it is," said Herrera.

Atwater's eyes reeled for focus. He scanned the countryside in the direction of Herrera's pointing finger. He couldn't see a fucking thing. Then there it was: in the middle of the open fields spreading up from the river was a black cluster, resolving as they got closer into two separate boxes. Buildings, no doubt about it. A farmhouse and barn.

Rufus Atwater jiggled in his seat and thought, This is it, man. This time this is really fucking it.

TWENTY-SIX

A S THE BLACK CHOPPER made a wide turn over the valley, searching for a landing spot, George pulled Ella from the edge of the porch to the kitchen door. He motioned to Lenna with his head. "We'd better get inside."

Ella looked at Charlie, stumping toward them on his crutch. He nodded to her. She still found it hard to think of him as Clarence Jefferson; Jefferson was the man of whom she knew nothing, the man of many evils who so many feared. She didn't want him to be Jefferson. Charlie put his blunt, handless arm across her shoulder and followed her through the screen door. Inside the kitchen the clatter of the chopper seemed closer than ever. Ella felt useless and scared. She didn't know what she was supposed to do. She became aware of the Smith & Wesson in her hand, the one she'd carried so blithely all that day. Suddenly its weight felt real. She swallowed a lilting surge of nausea. She also felt caught between Charlie and Lenna in some strange way that she didn't understand. She watched George take up a position by one of the windows with his shotgun and squint out. She decided to stick with George. George turned from the window to Charlie.

"This place is too big to defend," said George. He pointed. "And they'll have all the cover they need from the barn and those outbuildings."

Charlie said, "A man with the right kind of nerve would let 'em come inside before starting the ball."

George looked at him, then cast his eye around the room, down the hallway to the front door and back to Charlie.

"Suits me," said George. "You watch the front, I'll take them in here. From the hallway." He turned back to the window. "There's no markings on that machine. Any idea who these guys are?"

"No," replied Charlie.

"I'm no friend to the G man, God knows," said George, "but that don't mean I want to cut 'em down without a call, if that's who they are."

"Listen to me!"

Ella turned. Lenna stood in the dusty twilight, her hands clasped together in front of her. Her face was white. Her eyes bored into Charlie.

"Last night Faroe got out of the Stone House."

George said, "Filmore Faroe? I thought he was dead."

Without taking her eyes off Charlie, Lenna shook her head. Ella looked at Charlie too.

Lenna said, "The chopper must be Faroe's people."

It wasn't in Charlie's nature to show fear but Ella could tell he thought this was as bad as the news could get. His face was covered with an oily sweat she hadn't noticed outside and she realized he was ill, very ill. He didn't answer Lenna.

Lenna said, "If I turn myself in there'll be no trouble."

"Don't be naïve, Lenna," said Charlie.

"Faroe wants to settle with me."

"Faroe wants to settle with the world."

From the window George said, "They're unloading."

George turned and looked at Lenna, and Ella knew from the set of his jaw that he wasn't going to give up anyone without a fight.

George said, "Dead or not, this guy wants you pretty bad."

Ella ran across and looked over George's shoulder. In the middle of the meadow beyond the cobblestoned yard the black chopper hovered a few feet above the flattened grass as what looked to her like soldiers jumped out carrying rifles.

"Four, six, eight," said George. "And you were right, Mr. Jefferson. They're taking off again."

As the chopper rose back up into the air Ella watched the eight soldiers fan away to left and right in two groups of four, and run, crouched low, toward the yard and the barn.

Charlie said, "Does Faroe know?"

Ella turned and found Lenna staring at her with dread, as if Charlie's question had something to do with her. Who was Faroe? And what did he know?

"No," said Lenna. "He knows nothing. No one knows but you and me."

"And the good doctor Grimes," said Charlie.

Lenna blinked. "Yes."

Ella was convinced they were talking about her. "Who is Faroe?" she said.

Lenna looked at her in a way she couldn't read. Charlie stuck his revolver in his belt and walked toward Ella. Neither of them answered her question. From his pocket Charlie pulled a brown paper packet and slipped it into the bag slung from her shoulder.

"For later," he said.

Before she could ask what it was George said: "It's zero hour."

George stepped back from the window and herded them all into the hallway. Charlie went to the far end and stood by the door to the parlor with his revolver poised. Behind him was the bigger door that led to the front stoop. The house shook around them as the chopper roared low overhead. Ella felt George's left hand close tightly on her shoulder. His old hawk's face was stretched with tension.

"Look at me," he said.

Ella looked at him.

George said, "Like it or not, Ella, you are the priority here."

Ella suddenly felt hugely alone.

"Say, 'I understand,' " instructed George.

"I understand." Her voice scraped in her throat.

"If you don't accept that, you will bring us down. Say, 'I understand.' "

A whisper. "I understand."

"Will you do as I ask you?"

George's eyes were brimming. For her. This time her voice was strong.

"Anything. Anything you want."

"Okay." George turned to Charlie. "Tell her where to hide."

Charlie looked at her from the end of the hall and pointed his stump up the stairs.

"The attic," he said. "You remember?"

Ella nodded.

"The cold water tank next to the boiler is empty. Take the lid off, get inside, close the lid. Wait. Anyone opens it without declaring themselves: kill them. Then you come up, look around. You see anyone else, you keep shooting."

Ella nodded again.

Suddenly Lenna lunged desperately past Ella and George toward the kitchen. George blocked her across the chest with his arm and slammed her against the wall.

"Lenna, I know what you're doing, and it's brave and it's right," said George. "But if we give up without a fight they'll be over this place like ants. They will find Ella. If we at least bloody their noses before surrendering, they'll be more inclined to believe they've got what they want. Trust me."

Lenna's shoulders relaxed. What George said made sense. She nodded.

"You take Ella upstairs," said George. "Then wait on the landing there till the shooting stops."

George turned back to Ella. Unexpectedly, he grabbed her around the waist, pulled her into him and kissed her on the cheek. He whispered in her ear.

"God bless you, girl."

As suddenly as he'd taken her George shoved her away down the hall.

"Now, go. Go on!"

He turned his back and Lenna caught Ella's hand and pulled her toward the stairs.

Charlie was no longer by the front door. Ella heard him moving around inside the parlor. She was desperate to say goodbye to him but she owed it to them all to be cool. As she started up the stairs behind Lenna she saw George lay himself down full length on the floor of the dark corridor. He and his shotgun were hidden from the kitchen by the half-open door. Why was the terror of leaving him so much greater than the terror of dying? She couldn't understand it. Lenna pulled her on and they reached the landing, where the stairs doubled back on themselves toward the second floor. They stopped. Ella looked up. The second-floor corridor was almost dark. At one end she knew she'd find a retractable ladder up to the trapdoor into the roof space. The thought of the water tank filled her with dread. Her resolve weakened.

"Ella?" said Lenna.

Ella looked at Lenna.

"When it's quiet here, go back into town and find Grimes. Wait for him at the diner where we met. He'll know what to do."

"How will I recognize him?"

"He'll have a black dog with him."

"Okay."

Lenna took a deep breath and when she spoke her voice was tremulous and her words jerked out as if forced past some intense constriction in her chest.

Lenna said, "Ella, I'll never see you again, and this won't make any kind of sense to you. But there's something I want you to take away from here, for me. Will you do that?"

Ella nodded. "What is it?"

"I love you," said Lenna.

Lenna's eyes held on to hers and all Ella could see in her face was that it was true. It was desperate and terrible but it was true; utterly true. And as Ella felt its truth she also felt, somehow, that it was she herself—and not Lenna or Charlie's hoard—that stood at the very center of all that was happening around them. Ella was at the center, she and the terrible love in Lenna's eyes.

Lenna said, "Will you take that away for me?"

"Yes," said Ella. "I'll take it away for you. And I will make it mine."

Lenna threw her arms around Ella and Ella held her.

Then, from below, came a roar of gunfire.

Shotgun blasts: one blending into the other, too fast for Ella to count them. Machine guns exploded in reply. At the foot of the stairs below them wood splinters and plaster erupted from the walls. The boom of a revolver. Screams of pain, voices shouting in Spanish. Again the shotgun. Then a savage cry, the rage of a human bent on death.

It was George.

Ella broke away from Lenna's arms. Lenna grabbed at her, caught the strap of her bag. Ella struggled free, left the bag behind, leapt down the stairs two, three at a time. The hallway was swirling with bitter gray gunsmoke. From the parlor came the slam of Charlie's magnum. Ella plowed toward the kitchen, where the shooting had stopped, her marrow frozen by the berserk battle cries of George Grimes as they echoed through the sudden silence of the guns. Ella stopped by the kitchen doorway and looked inside.

The flagstones were awash with blood. Fallen bodies sprawled bleeding and twitching amid the cordite smoke. In the middle of the floor George was on his back, grappling hand to hand with the soldier kneeling astride him. George's right fist clutched his .45 but it was pinned to the ground by the soldier's left hand. The soldier slammed wild, flailing punches into George's face. George roared at him through the blows, his left hand fingers clawing into the center of the soldier's throat, crushing the Adam's apple and windpipe.

Ella wanted to move but couldn't. She couldn't step out into the blood.

Suddenly George slipped his hand from the soldier's throat and around his face instead, jamming his thumb deep into the man's right eye, gouging and burrowing to dislodge it. The soldier writhed in panic and pain; but he wouldn't let go of George's gun hand; he stopped punching and scrabbled at the back of his belt. Ella saw the hilt of a sheathed knife, the soldier's frantic fingers closing around it.

Ella pushed herself across the room, into the blood and smoke.

As the soldier pulled the knife free, Ella rammed the stubby barrel of the .38 into his left armpit and pumped two wadcutters through his thorax. The soldier wheezed a red sigh and was lifted sideways; as he slumped down, George snapped his wrist free, crammed the .45's muzzle into the soldier's neck and shot him again.

Ella staggered back, sickened and trembling, her eyes stinging.

"Go away!"

Ella blinked. George had struggled up to a sitting position, the dead man across his lap. There was a moist black hole torn through George's upper right chest and his face was spattered with gore. He yelled at her again.

"Go! I don't want to see you!"

Hands seized her shoulders from behind and pulled her back into the hallway.

It was Lenna. Ella didn't resist as she was bundled down the corridor to the stairs. From the parlor came the sound of tinkling glass and gunshots ripping into walls. Lenna pushed Ella up onto the steps without speaking, then turned to the front door. She wrenched it open.

"Lenna!" Ella cried.

Lenna stepped out onto the stoop and disappeared from sight.

Ella heard shouts outside. The shooting stopped.

She turned and ran up the stairs. At the landing she collected her bag, went up the next flight and climbed the ladder into the roof. She unhooked the ladder, pulled it up behind her and closed the trapdoor. Set into one gable end of the attic was a small window that allowed in enough light to see by. Under the eaves stood the copper boiler and, beside it, the cold water tank. She went over and slid off the wooden lid. Inside the tank was lined with stained gray metal. She would only get in there if she had to. Outside she heard the sound of the helicopter close by, very close. She hadn't heard any more shots since Lenna had walked outside. Ella slung her bag over her head and went to the window. It was twelve inches too high to see out. Nearby was a sealed wooden chest layered with dust. Ella climbed onto it. She was high enough now but still couldn't see anything but sky. She reached up and grabbed hold of one of the timber struts between the rafters. Holding on to that, she leaned forward on her tiptoes.

A section of the meadow to this side of the bumpy track came into view. The helicopter was on the ground, its rotors still thrashing, flattening the grass in a wide circle. Ella watched and waited. In the doorway of the chopper crouched a gangly man with a long, thin head and ginger hair. He waved his arm, beckoning. He grinned. Then Lenna, George and Charlie were escorted to the chopper by a group of armed men. George and Lenna were in handcuffs. The gangly man moved back and the prisoners were bundled inside. The soldiers climbed in after them.

A moment later the chopper took off and disappeared; and Ella MacDaniels was alone.

TWENTY-SEVEN

WITH THE WIND battering into his face and Gul's black bulk pressed against his belly and chest, Cicero Grimes barreled through the fading dusk toward the Ohoopee River bottomlands.

He was traveling the empty blacktop under a dense canopy of trees and the '73 Harley glided around the curves with the grace and ease he had been promised. Framed between the handlebars before him, Gul's skull seemed like an ebony figurehead on the prow of a pagan vessel of war. Gul was a dog among dogs; Grimes was proud to be riding with him. He needed that feeling, needed something to hold on to. He and Gul would get the others to safety; they had to.

When they reached the left-hand turn that would take them to the Old Place, Grimes slowed down and let his foot skim the pavement, for the corner was sharp and he didn't want to lose the bike. As he straightened up he opened the throttle wide and in doing so felt a great anger rise in his chest.

Too many people were doing their best to fuck him up and he was beginning to tire of it. He'd held the center as best he could; he'd eaten their shit by the pound without losing his cool—Jefferson, George, Atwater, Lenna, the assholes at the airport; and now some redneck football fan whom he'd never done wrong was ramming a blunt instrument up his ass. Grimes felt his teeth grinding. He didn't want this. He wanted to take Gul to Wyoming and stand under the Sweetwater Rim, he wanted to smoke more cigarettes than was good for him and not care, he wanted to drink whiskey in a cheap hotel and make love to a long-legged woman he'd never met before and watch her eat pancakes in the morning and never see any one of these son of a bitches again.

But he could do none of these things. He ground his teeth harder. Then he reminded himself of his resolution to see this thing through without hate.

Fuck the resolution. He would show them hatred. He would show them rage.

Gul half turned his head and barked.

Further up the hill ahead, flickering under the branches and leaves, was Holden Daggett's tan Lincoln Town Car.

So the scum-sucking pig in the green satin jacket was heading for the Old Place too. Why? They had their fucking suitcases; what more did they want? Another twist in Jefferson's game? Grimes had been insane to trust him, to leave him alive. He urged the Harley forward. If he remembered right they weren't more than a mile and a half from the valley. Soon the trees would give way to pasture. Daggett wasn't going much over thirty miles an hour, and even with Gul on board Grimes figured he could overhaul the Lincoln if he wanted to. What would that achieve? He briefly thought of pulling out his gun and shooting the Falcons fan through the window: but even if he didn't hit Daggett instead, and if Mr. Falcon didn't shoot him first, he would almost certainly end up in a tangle of twisted steel by the side of the road. Grimes kept his distance. The Lincoln couldn't reach the farm without alerting George, and George was more than a match for the Falcon. Maybe it would work out, then: George would recover the suitcases and they could all get out together. But the questions still grated on his nerves: why was Falcon going to the Old Place, and from whom was he taking orders?

Up ahead the Lincoln topped the hill and disappeared. Then, further over to his left, Grimes saw a bulky black shape rise up slowly above the thinning tree line. Through the roar of the Harley's exhausts he heard the puttering of rotor blades. The chopper paused in its vertical ascent and turned in their direction.

The hand of Filmore Faroe had reached out across three states to close around them.

Grimes abandoned caution and blasted after the Lincoln. The din of the bike engine and the whistling wind in his ears drowned out the sound of the chopper's blades. Grimes felt the revolver pressing against his spine. If he reached for it at this speed they'd go down. He felt Gul's muscles coiling beneath him, and a primeval power surged through his belly. He had no idea what he was doing; he could not see what good he might do; yet every cell within him that bore the reckless imprint of life pushed him on toward the paradox of death. He felt no courage; he felt no fear to give courage its substance. He felt only an atavistic delirium scoured of all morality and thought. He wanted to fuck someone up; he wanted to feel his fist pounding through the bones of someone's face. Grimes opened his mouth and let out a shout that was lost on the wind.

Grimes crested the hill and swooped down the grade toward the western sky.

In the sky the chopper floated toward the road.

On the road Daggett's Lincoln was approaching the fringed edge of the forest. Grimes could see the two silhouettes of their heads and shoulders.

At the last moment Holden Daggett deliberately spun the wheel and swerved the Lincoln leftward across the blacktop. He drove the car point-blank into the bole of a cottonwood tree.

A hollow bang. Shattering matter. A bulky green blur hurtled through the windshield in a spray of pulverized glass and falling leaves and vanished into the meadow. The rear of the mangled Lincoln skewed sideways across the road. Grimes's way was blocked.

Grimes pumped the brakes and tried not to lock the wheels, fought to control the skittering trajectory of the bike. The wreck loomed closer. Squealing rubber. The bike was slowing, slowing. Gul, steady. There was still a gap, a strip of blacktop to one side of the wreck; he could squeeze through. Then with fifty feet to go Grimes felt the rear wheel lock and in his gut he knew he was going to lose the bike.

Grimes threw his weight backward and to his left. The Harley, still moving, started to tilt and fall. Grimes let go of the left grip, threw his hand across Gul's right shoulder and heaved him off the saddle. As Gul disappeared Grimes felt the rear wheel slew forward in a smoking arc. He let go and closed his eyes and heaved himself away. He clamped his elbows around his skull and hauled his knees toward his chest. He landed on his back. A power wave jounced through his skeleton. A blackness splashed with yellow and red spiraled around him. His brain tossed among violent sounds. The juddering vertigo abruptly ceased.

Gasoline in his nostrils. He opened his eyes. Smoke. Through the smoke: green grass scattered with wildflowers. His body was still clenched. He pushed out an arm; a leg. He could move. He couldn't feel anything yet; but he could move. He scrambled to his hands and knees. Something warm and wet lashed his cheek and ear. Gul's face thrust itself into his. Grimes shook his head and looked up.

The driver's door of the smoking Lincoln rattled open. The car had hit the tree off-center and the right side of the hood was crumpled back into the fender. Holden Daggett unfastened his seat belt, reeled out, dizzy, and caught his balance. He peered beyond the car and staggered forward.

"Daggett!"

Grimes struggled to his feet. Pain stabbed his body in too many places to identify. In his ears were implosive thuds, getting louder. In the grass beyond the road he saw a bloody face rise into view, a green jacket splashed with dark stains, saw Daggett lunge toward it on unsteady legs. Somewhere near the lacerated face he saw a brandished gun. An automatic.

"Gul!" Grimes threw out his arm. "Go!"

As Gul charged, Grimes ran after him. His view was blocked by Daggett. The gun-cracks came in a rapid, random shower but Daggett didn't stop. As his hands reached out for Falcon's throat Daggett convulsed and spun and fell as the back of his shirt tugged and billowed red with the exit of the slugs. As the line of fire cleared Grimes saw Gul leave the ground and clamp his jaws around Falcon's gun hand and drag him screaming across the grass. Grimes hurdled Daggett's body and put all his momentum into a bladder kick, the ball of his foot driving through Falcon's pubic bone with a sick crunch. Falcon left the ground and landed among the flowers. Grimes moved in to stomp him some more but by the time he got there Gul was already astride the green-jacketed body, his snarls gargling in the spillage from the opened blood vessels of the neck.

Grimes picked up the fallen automatic and turned. Holden Daggett was splayed on his back, his wiry torso punctured and drenched. Daggett coughed and scarlet phlegm sprayed over his lips and chin. Grimes dropped the automatic and knelt beside him and rolled him onto his side so he wouldn't choke. Daggett blinked and looked up at him.

"What the fuck did you do that for?" said Grimes.

Daggett pushed out a mouthful of bloody drool with his tongue.

"I never did like being told what to do," he said.

His pierced lungs spasmed in another bout of coughs.

Grimes began to tear open Daggett's shirt. "You got a first-aid kit in the car?"

Daggett fought back the cough. "Don't make me laugh."

The battering of the chopper penetrated Grimes's awareness. He looked over his shoulder. The chopper was slowing as it swooped down above the road and angled toward the meadow, its tail section swinging for stability.

Daggett reached out and took the automatic.

"Put me on my belly, where I can see them coming," he said.

"We can make it to the trees," said Grimes.

The skin on Daggett's face looked paper-thin, but his eyes were clear.

"You see your father, tell him you and me talked old times together."

The Chosin Reservoir. Grimes felt a flame of guilt. He had gotten Daggett into this. But that was an insult to Daggett; he put the guilt aside.

"I will," said Grimes.

He maneuvered Daggett into the position he wanted. Daggett rested his head on his forearm. He was weakening fast. Grimes looked up at the chopper. In its side, a door slid open and a rifleman appeared. Grimes squeezed Daggett's bony shoulder and stood up.

"Gul," called Grimes.

Grimes turned and ran for the trees. His left knee clicked and wobbled with each pace but held up. Gul bounded beside him. As he passed the Lincoln a spray of bullets rattled through the metal bodywork and chewed a shower of bark from the tree; but Grimes was through, into the twilight shadows of the forest. He threw out his arm and grabbed a trunk and his momentum jerked him around and slammed his chest into the far side. Pain stabbed his ribs. He heaved for breath.

"Gul, here. Down. Stay."

Gul crouched, poised, at his feet. Grimes peered out from behind the trunk.

The chopper was descending toward the ground at a safe distance from the trees. Through the opened door Grimes could see the rifleman; beyond him lurked dark figures. Grimes reached under his jacket and pulled out his Colt. His hands were shaking and he had to guide his finger onto the trigger. One side of the cylinder was bloody and smeared with a skein of peeled flesh from Grimes's back where he had skidded on the road. He looked up. As the chopper settled onto the meadow, three riflemen jumped from the door and ran toward the Lincoln. They looked like soldiers. Grimes was about twenty feet from the wreck. In the doorway of the helicopter a fourth rifleman covered the trees. Daggett lay motionless in the grass. As the soldiers got closer Daggett started shooting.

His first shot cracked and one of the soldiers stumbled, clutching his hip, and fell sideways. The gunner in the chopper opened up with a long burst. The two soldiers added their fire. If Daggett got off any more rounds Grimes didn't hear it; but he saw the bullets churn Daggett's body into rags. The guns fell silent. The two soldiers crouched low and changed clips. The wounded one got to his feet and drew level with them. The soldiers moved toward the Lincoln.

Grimes pulled his head back behind the tree and squeezed the butt of the Colt. If these bastards wanted his blood they'd have to mix it with their own. He thought of Daggett and the Chosin Reservoir. His father. He asked himself how George would handle it. Close range. Grimes would let them get within six feet. No, three feet. Charge in among them so they'd be confused, afraid to shoot each other, their rifles cumbersome, jam the Colt into their guts one at a time. And there was Gul, too: he could take one, scare the others. It was a fighting chance; but only if they came to him.

They never did. Grimes heard a clank. He risked a look. Two of the soldiers were behind the Lincoln, rifles sweeping the forest, while the third hauled Jefferson's suitcases from the trunk. They'd known they were there. Grimes pulled back, waited. He could hear only the chopper. Another look; the three men were moving back toward the chopper, two of them walking backward to cover the third man, who was staggering on the soft ground under the weight of the cases.

Grimes rested his forehead against the tree trunk. They weren't coming in to flush him out: they had the suitcases and he wasn't worth the risk. His gut rolled over with a sudden release of tension; then once again with anxiety: where was George? And Lenna and Ella? And Clarence Jefferson?

They were either dead in the farmhouse or prisoners in the chopper. Was there any mileage in turning himself in? Grimes couldn't see it. He had nothing to bargain with. He heard the tone and volume of the chopper blades rise in intensity. It was taking off. He looked.

The chopper rose from a flattened disc of grass. The side door was still open but empty. At about forty feet the chopper stopped and hovered. Above the noise of the blades came an amplified voice.

"Dr. Grimes? You remember me?"

Grimes's mouth curdled. Rufus Atwater. Atwater appeared in the doorway with a handset held to his mouth.

"Rufus Atwater, yeah? Well, we got your pa, Grimes," said Atwater. "Lenna and Jefferson too. But your pa, he's hurt. He's hurt bad. If I had the know-how, I'd help him, you know? But I don't. Do you wanna come try?"

Grimes felt all the fight drain from his body. The Colt almost slipped from his hand. Just as he was about to step out from the tree a voice in his head said, *"Do it, but remember it's for you, not for him."* Grimes didn't move. The voice was right. He imagined what his father was going through right now: praying that his son wouldn't add to his pain by giving up. Grimes squeezed the revolver. He wouldn't betray his blood. He held his ground.

"Listen!" said Atwater. "He wants to talk to you. I tell ya, Doc, he needs you bad."

In the chopper doorway a broad figure with iron-gray hair stepped unsteadily into view. His wrists were handcuffed before him. He seemed hunched forward with pain. Then he placed his feet wide and pulled his shoulders back, pushed his jaw out and looked out over the trees.

Grimes felt himself shaking, a sudden sting in his eyes. They had no right to treat this man this way. This man was his father. Grimes ground his teeth. This man was his father. But the dread that filled him was not just fear of his father's death. George could throw his arm around Death's shoulder with the best of them and it seemed to Grimes that he owed it to him not to be afraid on his part. It was the last thing George would have wanted. Grimes's dread stemmed from guilt at his failure as a son, the truth of which now bore down on him without pity. Grimes remembered the times he had fought with George and hurt him; the times he had avoided seeing him when he might have transformed barren hours into gold; the precious tales he had been told but had forgotten; the memories he had of George—mopping up his gravy—so pitifully few when there might have been—when there should have been—so many more. All these thoughts and more invaded Grimes's every cell and synapse, demanding that he answer for himself, yet knowing all the while that his destiny was lost already, and he was condemned.

Grimes tried to see his way out. He had to find the still point of the cyclone. George, he knew, would never find him wanting. Although George was the man upon the gallows, it was Grimes who stood now before the judge that was himself. Down the years he'd been ashamed of his love for his father. He didn't know why. Now the shame of that shame paralyzed him. This was his last chance to renounce it, but he didn't know how. His gut said, *Let him see you.*

Grimes stepped out from behind the tree and walked forward into the field. When he thought George could see him he stopped. He felt Gul brush against his leg. He looked up.

Although he could not see George's eyes, Grimes could feel them looking back into his, and he felt an intense pride that cracked his heart. Grimes held the crack together and pulled his own shoulders back, for at this moment, if it was possible, he wanted his father to feel proud of him too. And into the eyes that he could not see but which were staring into the center of all that he was, Grimes poured his heart that it might be healed. He couldn't help his father, but even now his father could help him. Grimes thought: I'm with you, goddamn you, old man. I cursed you and defied you. I hated you and hurt you, but I'm with you. I always was. And I won't be ashamed to love you anymore.

Up in the chopper, George Grimes smiled.

It was the hardest thing he'd ever done; but Cicero Grimes smiled back.

Rufus Atwater stretched out his arm and held the handmike to George's mouth.

Grimes waited.

George's voice was steady and fierce.

"Gene? You'll do what you have to, like you always did, and so will I, like I always did." He paused. "Just tell Ella I was proud to ride with her. And remember that work we talked on, you and me."

Then George smiled again and the words came back in Grimes's head: "Some work of noble note may yet be done, not unbecoming men that strove with Gods."

Rufus Atwater scowled and made a gesture and a crouching figure suddenly appeared and a rifle barrel jutted down from the doorway.

George Grimes, still smiling, stooped as if to lift a crate and snared his handcuffed arms around the figure's neck. The rifle fell. Then George threw himself from the chopper, dragged the struggling figure with him and plunged them both down into the earth.

Grimes raised the Colt at arm's length and Atwater dived from view. Grimes almost fired, almost pumped the cylinder empty, but Lenna was in there. Grimes held back. The chopper dipped and wheeled and soared away into the safety of the sky. Grimes lowered his gun and watched the chopper disappear. There was a breeze. Grimes's face felt cool and wet. He wiped it on his torn sleeve. Then in the silence he walked across the field to where his father lay.

Gul got there ahead of him and sat on his haunches to guard and wait. At three paces Grimes saw his father's shoulders slowly rise and fall. He was tangled with the soldier. Grimes knelt down beside them. The soldier's neck had been snapped like a gamebird's by the encircling chain. Grimes unlooped George's arms and pulled the two men apart.

For the first time in his life Grimes's clinical instincts deserted him. His father was unconscious, his body was broken, but Grimes had no thought for how he might put it back together. The tools were there in his mind: he could have examined the positions of the fractured bones and the angle of the bullet wound in the chest; he could have made a judgment as to where his father was bleeding from, and how fast, and how it might be staunched; he could have fallen upon him and tried to keep him alive; but Grimes did none of these things. Instead he loosened the red Slim Jim tie around his father's neck and straightened his twisted limbs.

Then he pulled a white handkerchief from his pocket and wiped the blood from his father's face. In places the blood was fresh, in others tenaciously caked, and Grimes had to dampen the handkerchief with spit, the way George had sometimes done when Grimes was a boy. George's face looked like it was chopped from Indiana limestone, yet to the touch the skin felt fragile, and Grimes was afraid that if he rubbed too hard he would tear it; but he didn't, and eventually the face was clean and gaunt and handsome again. George's breathing had slowed now and between each brief rise and fall of his chest there was a long pause in which he did not move at all. The pauses got progressively longer. George didn't open his eyes and Grimes didn't try to rouse him. In the midst of this pain-strewn field George had found himself some peace, and Grimes sat within it and took it into himself. He watched the pale face, the papery eyelids, the stern lips and bristled iron jaw. At first he struggled for thoughts, words, but they weren't there; neither were the guilt and shame. So Grimes did without words and let the moment be what it was, and himself and the twilit valley with it: a quiet valediction to a man and his last passage.

George's chest had not moved now for a long time and his lips were dark blue; but Grimes knew he hadn't yet gone. He waited. Abruptly, George inhaled—a deep breath, deeper than any that had gone before—then let it go in a great sigh. With the sigh his spirit left him and Grimes felt it passing by. And, as he had known in his inmost heart, the music of that dying breath was sweet, and worth the listening.

Grimes stood up. For a moment he closed his eyes. He looked down.

In death, George Grimes looked like a bloodstained king.

There was a sound nearby and Grimes turned. Gul was already alert but had stayed by Grimes and had made no sound. Standing a few yards away was a young woman, black and striking in looks, with tears on her face. Ella MacDaniels, the child conceived in abandon and born into darkness and pain. Grimes looked into her eyes: they were bottomless with grief. In them he could see Lenna Parillaud. He turned back to his father. He knelt down again and slipped one hand under George's shoulders and another under his knees and scooped him up and folded him into his arms. He stood up and walked toward Ella.

"Ella?" said Grimes.

Ella pulled her eyes away from George and nodded. She seemed unable to speak.

"George asked me to tell you he was proud to ride with you."

Ella started crying again.

Grimes had to put his mind to things practical. He looked up at the road. The Lincoln was finished. The Harley looked okay. He'd have to return it so that the kid wouldn't call the cops. Then they had to get to the airfield and Titus Oates. He turned back to Ella.

"Ella? Do we have a car we can use?"

Ella wiped her face and nodded again.

"I'm going after Lenna. I want you to stay with a friend, Titus Oates. He'll take you somewhere safe."

Ella stared at him with an anger that took him aback.

"George and me were partners, all the way down the line," she said. "He let me make my own choices. That was George's way."

Grimes realized this was an argument he wasn't likely to win. It didn't seem worth insulting her intelligence by pointing out the dangers. He nodded.

"Yes, that was his way," he said.

"Where are you going?" she said.

And then Grimes realized that even though she didn't know that it existed—still less what it meant—Ella would have to go back to the site of her own darkest moment.

"There's a place," said Grimes, "called the Stone House. That's where we're going."

A question passed across her face, but she saved it. Ella turned and started back across the field toward the farm. After a few yards she started to run.

Grimes walked back to the road with his father still in his arms. His muscles ached with the weight but he wouldn't put him down. The ache felt proper. The blacktop ran due west, and here it was almost dark, but above the far horizon the indigo clouds were gashed by the scarlet pandemonium of the dying light.

And Grimes remembered the way Jefferson had put it.

The Ohoopee River bottomlands were as good a place to die as any other. And at sundown, if you were lucky, they seemed like they were bathed in blood.

Part Three
THE STONE
HOUSE

The fatman thirsts.

His tongue is parched, his throat is dry.

Yet his thirst is not for water alone; nor even for blood. The fatman thirsts for life; just a few drops more, a mouthful; that is all. And here he detects a paradox, an inconsistency that troubles him. All around he senses the tremble and the beat of well-forged steel: the toiling blades of the hovering machine. The fatman lies upon its floor and he has been beaten too: by the boots he glimpses through swollen eyes, by rifle butts and fists; by the outrage of defeat. For hours they have hammered on his carcass and their blows have brought him close to death—he feels it— and thence to the paradox. For the fatman admits no contenders in the arena of intellectual virility and he has long known—and long argued— that death is but life's most luxurious indulgence. Why, then, should he crave one last gulp of gruel when the banquet itself awaits him?

The hovering machine descends and settles and he is chained, left hand to right ankle, and dragged, and heaped before a gray house of stone.

The fatman lies there, broken and weak; the man of strength, his strength now gone. Only his thirst remains strong, yet still it confounds him. Death is the youth of the world; this he knows well. It is a truth so fundamental as to defy the blindest ignorance: the simplest law of nature. Life is the unrestrained utterance that consumes itself, a perpetual tumult whose freedom is contracted upon one condition alone: that the spent and ruined organism make way, in its time, for the new— for new organisms, new effusions of uncontrollable turbulence, who will enter the dance with new steps and new partners, and with new forces, as yet unimagined.

The fatman was born to such a dance. To a life of luxurious expenditure—of excess in all things, and of anguish most of all; and here, at the last pinnacle of reckless extravagance, he knew that death—his own death—was the ultimate, ruinous refinement of all that he had worked. It was ungracious to refuse it. The thought offended him. And yet he craved just one more swallow. He demanded, in defiance of his honor, one more card of fate, dextrously dealt from the bottom of the deck.

And then he understood why.

For while the fatman was willing to spend the last of himself, he was not alone. Another demanded its own share of luxurious consumption: and the fatman could not deny the justice of that claim. There were yet others, it was true: Ella and Lenna; and the good doctor Grimes; but they were not present in his flesh to press their suit. The other was. It had kept him alive; and it would hold the fatman to the bargain he had struck.

He opened his eyes and saw the booted foot that would usher him—for a while—into oblivion. And as the boot descended he promised his companion that their thirst would be slaked and their card would be dealt. For the fatman could not break his word.

To the maggot, living in his leg.

TWENTY-EIGHT

THE DE HAVILLAND BEAVER named *The Last of the Independents* flew south-southwest in a cloudless sky across a land enshrouded by night. Grimes sat with Gul in the cargo hold as before and kept vigil over the body of George Grimes, which lay wrapped in a tarp on the floor. In the rear of the hold were crates of moonshine, heavily roped down. The crates rattled constantly, as did the plane itself, and the noise of both vibrations counterpointed the muted drone of the big propeller at the nose. Ella sat up in the cockpit with Titus Oates, and Grimes was glad: he didn't feel like making the effort conversation would require.

Against a generalized ache that mapped out the whole of Grimes's body, the pains from his left knee, left ribs and lower back stood out with particular prominence. If he could have afforded the luxury, he would have been depressed; instead he settled for exhaustion. For a while he closed his eyes and tried to rest but fell into that nether state of consciousness where he didn't know whether he slept or not. After a while he opened his eyes and rubbed his face and considered what exactly he should do next.

On basic principles Grimes believed civilization to be a good thing. It pleased him that, within certain wide boundaries, no one had the right to walk up to him and shoot his balls off, and that if such an unfortunate event were to take place there would be some possibility of redress under the law. But in the final analysis law was merely the threat or actuality of being at the mercy of a violent power greater than oneself—men with guns. If there was a power greater than the law—more men with more guns—then the law was of scant comfort or utility. By the same token law demanded that the crime in question be brought to its attention, otherwise the crime effectively didn't exist. Filmore Faroe was not, ultimately, more powerful than the law; but he certainly had the resources to keep a great deal from falling under its gaze. In Faroe's shoes Grimes would have wanted Ella, Lenna, Jefferson and Grimes himself to be dead: maybe not immediately but certainly before any of them could open their mouths.

Grimes made himself consider going to the police to report the events of the last twenty-four hours. Even if the cops believed him and went to investigate, they would be so retarded by legal red tape that Faroe would have plenty of time to tidy up before they found anything. It took six months to indict someone for pissing on the sidewalk and Faroe would have a dozen lawyers plugged into his millions in ten minutes. Meanwhile his mercenaries, unhampered by the Bill of Rights, would be dropping Lenna's body parts into the Gulf of Mexico in weighted sacks. Grimes concluded that Filmore Faroe had to be killed and that it was basically up to him to do it.

Rufus Atwater would have to go down too.

All he had to do now was figure out how to do it.

Ella climbed back into the hold from the cockpit. Gul awoke and stood up and shook himself down. Ella sat beside Grimes and looked at the holes in his suit.

"You okay?" she said.

"As right as rain."

Gul shouldered his way between Grimes's legs and he stroked him.

"I'm sorry about George," said Ella.

"Yeah," said Grimes.

"I didn't know him long." She hesitated. "It was long enough to know him."

"Thanks for that," said Grimes.

Ella didn't speak for a while.

"I know this is a hard time for you, but if you can stand it there's some things I need to ask," said Ella.

Grimes had been expecting this, though he hadn't been looking forward to it.

"Go ahead," he said.

"Is Charlie—I mean, is Clarence Jefferson my father?"

"No," said Grimes.

He wasn't sure whether what he saw in her face was disappointment or relief. Perhaps it was a mixture of both. He wondered how much she knew about the Captain's life. Probably very little. It was clear that she had a lot of affection for him. Grimes didn't see any sense in taking that away from her. He wasn't entirely immune himself.

"Jefferson took care of you as best he could, but he isn't your father."

"Is he a bad man or a good man?" asked Ella.

For a moment Grimes was stumped by her bluntness.

"I don't know," he answered. "Jefferson has an unorthodox take on those concepts."

"Are you his friend?"

"Let's say we're close."

Grimes felt in his pockets and found a crumpled pack of Pall Malls. He extracted one that had survived and lit it. Ella was thoughtful. He could see her trying to deal with a sadness she didn't understand.

"If Clarence isn't my father . . ." Ella hesitated. She looked at Grimes full-on. "Then Lenna must be my mother."

"Yes," said Grimes. "She is."

Ella looked away and the sadness grew deeper. A tiny rim of liquid gathered and glistened around her eyelids.

"How did you figure it out?" he asked.

Ella swallowed, pulled in a deep breath. "Before we split up, she told me she loved me."

Ella covered her emotion by reaching into her bag. She searched around, came up empty.

"Can I take one of your cigarettes?"

"Sure."

Ella lit up. She stared at the steel plating of the floor between her feet.

"I know this sounds kind of a weak thing to say, but," she paused, struggled, "but why didn't Lenna want me? I mean, you know, I can make a guess, but it's, I mean . . ."

"Lenna did want you," said Grimes. "Nobody ever wanted anyone more."

"Is it silly to want to know where I came from?"

"No," said Grimes. "It's your birthright."

He took a drag on his cigarette and tried to figure out how to tell it. Ella seemed like the kind who'd want to hear it straight up, but even so. The whole truth had been tough even for him to listen to. He blew out the smoke.

"When Lenna was about your age she married a man called Filmore Faroe, a rich man, and she went to live at his plantation. It's called Arcadia."

"Did she love him?" interrupted Ella.

"That's not for me to say," said Grimes. "Anyhow, Lenna didn't have much of an existence at Arcadia. Faroe didn't abuse her, the way she tells it, but he wouldn't let her live her own life. After a couple of years Lenna's life was running through her fingers and she was cracking up. She'd spent too much time trying to please other people. So she went into town. It was there she fell in love without question."

Ella looked up from the floor into Grimes's eyes. He wanted to look away but didn't. He saw how much she needed this, and more than that, she needed that he tell it one way rather than another. He went on.

"It was a great passion and a true one, a whirlwind, a fateful spell. The passion of her life. Her lover's name was Wes Clay."

Ella blinked. The cigarette between her fingers trembled. She dropped it to the floor and crushed it under her boot.

Grimes said, "Wes was a musician, a trumpet player . . ."

At this, tears started to roll down Ella's cheeks. Grimes blinked himself. He was afraid his words would dry up on him and he didn't want to let her down. He remembered Ella's face on the poster of the club and realized what the details of Wes being a musician might mean to her. He pushed on.

"It was a summer's night, and it was his music that called out to her and pulled her in, off the street and into a small basement juke joint. Lenna had never been to such a place before. Wes Clay played like a man among men, which I figure is what he must have been. The moment they set eyes on each other, man, that was all she wrote. Lenna abandoned everything that she had in order to be what she was. And for three days they laughed and made love and shared their dreams. It was during those days that they conceived you."

Ella's breath shuddered in her throat. She closed her eyes and drops squeezed out and clung to her lashes. Grimes waited. He wanted her to hold on to whatever she was seeing in her mind for as long as she wanted to.

Ella said, *"In our youths, our hearts were touched with fire."*

Grimes's own heart ached as he recognized the voice of his father.

"Yes," said Grimes. "Their hearts were touched with fire."

264

Ella took the time she needed, controlled her breathing, opened her eyes again. She nodded for him to go on.

"By that time Lenna had been reported missing, presumed kidnapped. The police found her in the nightclub and took her home."

Grimes saw Ella flinch with disappointment. He could see her asking herself why Lenna hadn't stayed.

"Lenna had to go. She didn't have a choice. For herself she would have risked anything, but she couldn't risk Wes Clay. She knew that if she stayed with him it would cost him his life. An old-style grandee like Faroe would never tolerate the humiliation of his wife leaving him for a black man."

"But she kept . . ." Ella hesitated. "But Lenna kept the child."

"Lenna told me that for all the grief it brought her, she never regretted loving Wes Clay. Ever. And she never regretted giving birth to you."

Ella said. "The grief?"

Grimes swallowed.

"When it became clear that Lenna was pregnant, she let Faroe believe that he was the father. That was possible, but Faroe knew more than she realized. He must have found out about Clay. When Lenna went into labor, Faroe had her secluded in a secret place." Grimes paused. "When you were born, and you weren't Faroe's child, you were taken away from her. Lenna wasn't given any choice."

"You mean they just took me away from her, I mean, physically?"

"Yes."

Ella looked away. Grimes could see her imagining what it had been like for Lenna. He saw a question cross her face and saw her decide not to ask it. Grimes took a guess at what the question might have been.

Grimes said, "Lenna never looked for you because she thought you were dead. Faroe ordered that you be killed."

"As a baby?"

Ella asked as if this were inconceivable. Grimes knew she wouldn't have been the first child to die for that reason; he didn't say so. He nodded.

"Faroe believed that you had been killed. So did Lenna. It wasn't until yesterday she found out you were still alive."

Ella took this in and thought about it amid the roar of the propeller for a long time. Then, unconsciously, she wrapped her arms around herself.

"It was Charlie—Clarence Jefferson—who took me away, wasn't it?"

Grimes nodded.

"Was it him that was meant to kill me?"

"Yes."

Ella stared at the floor, hugging herself, as she put the picture together.

Then she asked, "So Jefferson never told Lenna that I was alive."

"No, he didn't," replied Grimes. "I can't tell you why. Clarence Jefferson marches to a different drum than the rest of us."

"And the secret place where I was born, where was it?"

Grimes felt a sudden dread of telling her. She saw it in his eyes.

"I have a right to know, don't I?" said Ella.

"You were born in what Lenna calls the Stone House."

"Where we're going now."

"I figure that's where Faroe will hold Lenna."

"How do you know that?"

"Because Lenna turned it into a jail and kept him prisoner there for thirteen years."

Ella searched his eyes. She seemed bewildered. Then, as if seeing something open out before her, she said, "It's like a tiger chasing its tail, on and on until it eats itself."

Grimes nodded. He had no right to judge any of them, and he did not.

"Can we stop it?" asked Ella.

"Faroe's got a lot of hate inside him," said Grimes. "It won't be over until he's dead. That's down to us."

"Won't that make us part of the tiger too?"

"When I got into this deal I told myself I wouldn't do anything out of hatred, that I'd only do what needed to be done."

He looked down at the tarp-wrapped body on the floor.

"That's the only answer I can give you."

They sat in silence for a moment and Grimes waited for the question she hadn't asked yet but would have to.

"My father—Wes Clay . . ." It was hard for her. "He's dead, right?"

"Yes."

"Did Clarence Jefferson kill him?"

"No." Grimes shook his head. It wasn't that simple, but what did it matter? "No. Faroe killed Wes Clay himself."

Ella said, "Thank you for telling me."

Grimes sensed that she wanted to be alone. He stood up.

"I better go talk to Oates, figure out how to get to Lenna," said Grimes. "Will you look after Gul for me?"

Ella put her arms out to Gul and he went to her.

Grimes climbed forward into the copilot's seat. Titus Oates sat massively at the controls, as if this was where he most liked to be.

"Did I happen to tell you, Doc, that I'm thinking of converting to Islam?"

Grimes sat down next to him. "No, I don't think you did."

"I've been studying the Koran. It's one fuck-off heavy-duty religion, man. And, you know, you get to wear those neat hats and choose a cool name for yourself."

"I wish you luck," said Grimes. He tried to broach the issue at hand. "How far are we from New Orleans?"

"Twenty-five minutes."

Grimes said, "I'm already in your debt, Titus . . ."

"Balls, man."

"I'm going to ask you for something more."

"Shoot."

"The people who killed my father," began Grimes. He swallowed. "They've got Lenna and they're going to hurt her, badly. Ella is Lenna's daughter."

Titus Oates turned his hairy, beefed-up face toward him. Behind the beard his face was that of a deranged cherub. He twisted in his seat and looked back at Ella where she sat listening to them. His expression darkened.

"Mmm," said Oates.

From the breast pocket of his jacket Oates pulled out a thick joint. He put it in his mouth, lit it with a Zippo and inhaled deeply. He held it in until his face started to turn purple, then let out his breath with a gasp.

"Christ. Alaskan hydroponic. I'd tell you guys to toke it up but I wouldn't want to be responsible."

Oates inhaled again and spoke without letting any of the smoke escape.

"You got any large-caliber firearms?"

"We've got two pistols," said Grimes.

Oates grunted as if this was unlikely to fit the bill.

"So pitch me the bottom line," said Oates.

"The bottom line," said Grimes, "is that I need to know if you have an especially deep attachment to this plane of yours."

"This is a 1967 De Havilland Beaver, man. The last of the independents."

"I know."

"Mmm," said Titus Oates.

This time he sounded like Gul. He took another toke of his joint.

"Maybe you guys better tell me exactly what's involved."

TWENTY-NINE

THE SQUAT GRAY BOX stood brooding against a landscape of unimpaired blackness. Its walls were bare of windows or any other feature. From the glass panes set into its roof two broad shafts of blue-white light struck upward into the sky. Paradoxically, the effect of the roof lights was to heighten the sense that this was a place of mystery, where acts private, or obscene, might occur in perfect concealment.

Lenna had never seen the Stone House in darkness before; only in daylight. It was she who had built it, this place of concealment—for acts both private and obscene—and perhaps it was that thought more than any other that chilled her now.

"Here we are, Magdalena," said Filmore Faroe, behind her. "Welcome home."

Lenna didn't turn. Whatever was inscribed on her face, she didn't want Faroe to see it. She stood with her back to the chopper, and to Faroe and Herrera and his men. Lying motionless in the yard before her—his left wrist shackled to his right ankle by a length of chain—lay Clarence Jefferson. Lenna's handcuffs had been removed. She looked down at Jefferson.

At regular intervals, beginning with his capture at the farm, Jefferson had been beaten, by the rifle butts and boots of Atwater's thugs, into a sack of raw meat. Jefferson had borne it without a sound. Lenna could not see him breathing. As she looked at his mutilated form she no longer felt the malice—or the self-disgust—that had bound her to him for so long. She felt pity. Suddenly the blade of her pity pierced her to the hilt, and its sharpness shocked her and she gasped, and she realized that amid all the torment she had carried on the shoulders of her hate, she had felt nothing so agonizing, or so welcome, as this pain—this pity—lancing through her now. For it freed her.

Her hate was gone.

She searched inside and she couldn't find it.

It was gone. It had slipped away without her knowing. Since giving herself up to Atwater she had been filled only with one sense, one feeling, one all-fulfilling image: Ella's face looking into her eyes and saying *"I will take it away for you. And I'll make it mine."* That was when her chains had melted into air. Her heart was no longer of stone; it felt as fragile and open as a newborn child's. She was able to look upon Clarence Jefferson with pity and more than that—she made herself admit it even though it shamed her—she looked on him with love, architect though he was of so much that had harmed her.

She heard Herrera say, "What do you want us to do with that one?"

Faroe replied, "Put him where his stink won't bother anyone."

Two of Herrera's men stepped past her, rifles slung. Each grabbed one of Jefferson's feet and dragged him away across the tarmacadamed yard toward the Jessups' place. Faroe appeared beside her. She didn't look at him. He held his forearm out.

"May I?" said Faroe.

Still avoiding his face, Lenna put her hand on his arm. Together they walked to the damaged steel doors of the Stone House and went inside.

As they passed among the crates and through the antechamber Lenna felt a rising thud in her chest. Inside the main chamber the fluorescent lights were white and lifeless. Beyond the wall of steel bars stood the original Stone House, the true Stone House: the wooden shack that she had transplanted so perfectly, and so eerily, into this enclosing jail. They entered the cage. Their footsteps clacked on the tiled floor. When Lenna stopped before the age-warped doorway of the shack, she discovered, here at the last, that she was no longer afraid to walk inside.

Inside the single room of the shack no lights burned. Three steps led up from where she stood to the platform upon which the shack was lodged. At the top of the steps a door hung open from its leather hinges onto the shadows within. Lenna had not been inside the shack since the night, twenty years before, when she had dragged herself from its bloody interior and screamed herself unconscious in the rain. Only in her dreams had she dared go back inside, and then always unwillingly, and always to lose herself in a blur of horror too unbearable to remember. Faroe, in bringing her here, no doubt imagined he inflicted on her something of that horror; but he was wrong. Now it was just a sharecropper's tin-roofed shack, where she would finally complete the circle around whose circumference she had toiled for so long. She wanted to go inside.

She turned and looked into the eyes of Filmore Faroe.

He stood at her right elbow, and as he saw the look on her face he smiled. Probably, he thought he saw fear. But Lenna wasn't afraid. Death she did not fear; she had wished for it too many times. Anything Faroe could do to her she could endure, now that she had that image in her mind. Ella was safe and Faroe knew nothing of her existence. And Ella knew that Lenna loved her. Nothing else mattered. Let Faroe believe what he would.

So Lenna looked at him: and felt nothing.

She saw a bloated, spindle-limbed wretch who had shaved his head to impress his mercenaries. She saw the specter of a man once fine, now grinding his teeth behind his smile, infected by the rage that would torture and enslave him forever. She saw a broken king, scrabbling amid the ruins for a worthless crown. She felt no pity for him; and certainly not the love she had never known before; but neither did she hate him anymore. She knew, now, that something in her wiser than herself had waited for this moment. That was why she'd never killed him. If she had she would never have been free. His death would have condemned her hatred to an eternal life; as Faroe would now condemn himself.

Lenna said, "What would you like to do, Fil?"

The calmness in her voice seemed to disappoint him. He held his hand out toward the shack.

"We're going inside, Magdalena. Just you and I."

Lenna mounted the steps. At the doorway she paused and listened. She heard rain falling on the roof. She heard her own panting cries. She felt a contraction in her belly. Then she heard sounds she'd been too afraid to remember since first she'd heard them: the first cries of a life. The cries had been exiled to a lost territorium whose ground she had not dared tread; now they returned. Along with the face of Ella the young woman—and her eyes and the touch of her hand—the remembered cries of Ella the baby would keep Lenna company throughout whatever was to come. Lenna stepped through the door into the shack.

By the light falling through the door and windows she could see that the shack was just as she remembered it. A bed covered with crumpled sheets, a dresser, a table and chairs, even, at one end, an iron stove. The bloodstains were still there too, dashed across the walls and floor, drained by age to a faded pallor, yet at the same time dark as sin. Lenna walked over and sat at the table. Faroe stepped tentatively through the door. He saw her watching him and blinked and then he sneered and walked toward her.

"Did you ever come in here, Fil?" she asked. "When you were resident?"

"I don't remember," said Faroe.

He sat down opposite her.

"So, are you going to keep me here forever, Fil?" she said.

"No," said Faroe. "Only until the trial."

"The trial?"

Faroe said, "When I'm stronger, when I'm ready to take my place again, I'm going to turn you over to the authorities. You'll be tried by the law for all that you did to me. A woman who joined forces with a corrupt police captain to steal her husband's fortune. I don't think the jury will have too much difficulty reaching a verdict."

"And the murders you're guilty of?" said Lenna.

"You mean the nurse and the doctor? There were never any records of their existence. And Wes Clay? That sorry tap-dancing nigger? Magdalena, please."

He smiled at the pain she must have shown him.

"No, no. I don't think there need be any public discussion of those regrettable events. Do you?"

"I'll take whatever I've got coming," said Lenna, "but when the questions are asked I'll tell the truth."

"That would cause me an embarrassment I could live with but which I'd rather avoid. I believe that you would too. After all, don't you have your daughter's feelings to protect?"

Lenna felt her throat and face go numb.

"You might consider her safety, too," added Faroe.

Lenna stared at him without speaking. Her mind seemed blank. All she could think was: he knows about Ella.

"You look unwell," said Faroe.

From his pocket he took a sheet of paper. As he unfolded it, she saw what it was. Clarence Jefferson's letter. Lenna felt nauseous. She closed her eyes. The night before. The conversation with Grimes. The blue dress. The sleeping pills. Bobby Frechette waking her. The black suit. Then Bobby dead, Faroe coming through the door. She'd left the letter in her bedroom, in the dress. There'd been too much confusion, she'd . . . She stopped the shrieking excuses. The letter. Jefferson hadn't mentioned Ella's name. She'd had to ask Grimes for Ella's name. She was certain of that. She remembered. She opened her eyes. Faroe sat across the table savoring her distress.

"I have to hand it to the Captain," said Faroe. "He is a piece of work."

He waved the letter.

"He doesn't mention the name of this black nigger offspring of yours, but if we made a public appeal at the trial, I'm sure she's the sort of person who would come forward to help her mother."

Lenna found herself overbreathing. Her body felt rigid. She forced herself to take a single deep breath. She found her voice.

"I'll do and say anything you want," she said.

"Of course you will."

Faroe carefully folded the letter back into his pocket.

"You know, my memory is not quite my own at the moment," he said. "In here I lived with fantasies and dreams. So tell me, did I ever strike you, Magdalena, that is, physically? The truth, now."

Lenna shook her head. "No. You never did."

"I often imagined, here in your Stone House, that it might be satisfying to do so."

Lenna said, "Then why don't you?"

Faroe punched her in the mouth. Her head spun but the punch was weak. She felt her lip swelling. She was stronger than him, she knew. She could probably overpower him. Could she strangle him before his bodyguards arrived? Probably not. She would have to take it. Until she knew more she would have to take it. She sat in the chair and looked at him with disgust.

"I was right," said Faroe. "It feels good."

The sound of feet mounting the steps came through the door. Herrera appeared, holding a phone in his hand.

"Mr. Faroe, sir?"

Faroe turned and snapped, "What?"

Herrera raised the phone. "It's Atwater. Some kind of trouble at the house."

"Trouble?" said Faroe.

Lenna's nerves screamed. She tried to calm herself. It wasn't possible that the trouble had anything to do with Ella. She was too far away. She was safe. Lenna's only function was to keep her that way, to keep her from harm. She couldn't let her daughter be killed again.

Herrera said. "Mr. Atwater insists he talk with you. He sounds hysterical. Or maybe drunk."

"Deal with it," said Faroe.

"Sir?"

Faroe stood up. "Deal with it. I want you here. Send the helicopter with some men. Do your job."

Herrera saluted and disappeared.

Filmore Faroe turned back to Lenna.

"Stand up," he said.

Lenna stood up.

Faroe said, "It's strange, you know, the things one clings to, to keep oneself alive. Do you remember, Magdalena, the rhyme that kept me company during my exile? That little child's nursery rhyme?"

Lenna saw in his watery eyes, swimming about and containing the inner core of malice and anger, the massive horror she had inflicted on him and which Faroe had endured. She did not look away from it. She had done what she had done.

Faroe said, "For want of a nail, the shoe was lost."

Faroe punched her in the stomach and she jackknifed forward. This blow was stronger, more confident than the first. Faroe pulled her back upright. This time he whispered.

"For want of a shoe, the horse was lost."

Faroe doubled his fist and hit her, again in the belly. Lenna fell to her knees. She heard his voice above her. This time he screamed.

"For want of a horse the rider was lost."

THIRTY

RUFUS ATWATER was mildly drunk. He was sitting in Filmore Faroe's study in the CEO's chair with his feet crossed on the desk and a glass of champagne in his hand and the bottle in an ice bucket on the floor. The champagne was old and French, and for the first time in his life Atwater understood why people made such a fuss over it and paid through the nose. He took another sip. He had also learned that you drank the stuff from tall, curvy, narrow glasses, not from those wide flat-topped deals they always used in Cary Grant movies. From now on this was the way it was going to be. No more stinking junkies vomiting on his shoes and begging for the methadone program. No more rape victims changing their minds about testifying a day before trial and fucking up his case. No more listening to the D.A. chew him out. He had brought home the grand slam: Lenna Parillaud, the suitcases of political plutonium and, as a little bonus, Captain Clarence Jefferson himself. Mr. Filmore Faroe was mightily pleased. Only Dr. Grimes had escaped the net, but Faroe's arm was long. No: Rufus Atwater's arm was long. Now, Atwater was Faroe's right hand. Grimes was a dead pigeon, like his psycho old man. Atwater took another slug of bubbly.

He was an *éminence grise* at last.

On the other side of the desk were the two brown leather suitcases. They hadn't yet been opened. Faroe had been so eager to get Parillaud over to the concrete hangar that he'd said the cases could wait until later. Herrera and most of his boys were with Faroe. Atwater had Arcadia more or less to himself. He was aching to see inside the cases— he had high hopes that he'd find something especially damaging on his boss, the D.A., like maybe a snapshot of him being fucked in the ass by a donkey—but he hadn't dared sneak a look. He didn't trust Jefferson not to have planted some kind of booby trap in them and didn't want to be blamed if anything went wrong.

As to what the hell Faroe was doing to Parillaud in the Stone House, Atwater wasn't interested. He was too cool to get involved in emotional disputes; that was why Faroe had fucked himself up in the first place; that was why Atwater had succeeded so spectacularly. He was the ice man. Others could fuck up their judgment with emotions, but not him. Filmore Faroe was half-crazy with amphetamine shots and rage. Atwater was concerned for him, but what the hell, the guy had been caged up for a decade and it was early days. He had a right to blow off some steam. He would calm down soon enough. Then Atwater would ease "Colonel" Herrera out of the frame. Herrera had had his uses, true, but the gunplay was over now and guys like him were a liability. Atwater was the number-one shithammer now: there was a new marshal in town and the sooner people got used to the idea the happier their lives would be.

A plane buzzed overhead and Atwater frowned. They weren't on any flight paths here. He listened more closely. It wasn't a jet engine. Some weekend flier. Hey, maybe he would get a pilot's license for himself. He would have to spend the money he was going to make on something. He emptied his glass and put it down and walked around the table and squatted down by the two bulging suitcases. They looked ordinary enough, but then they would. He was sorely tempted. Maybe there was a little something in there he could take for himself without telling Faroe, for personal insurance. He had a sudden image of himself with his arm blown off, or drenched with wash-proof dye. No. He'd played his hand to perfection so far. Let Faroe open the cases; later there would be an opportunity to sneak something away.

The airplane came over again. This time it was so low the windows shook in their frames.

"What the fuck?" muttered Atwater.

He stood up and walked over to the window and looked out across the great lawns of the esplanade. He felt the color drain from his face.

"Jesus Christ," he said.

Rufus Atwater ran over to the desk and grabbed for the phone.

THIRTY-ONE

LLA wanted to take a blast on Titus Oates's joint but she feared that if she did she wouldn't be able to do what was required of her. A madman like Oates could probably conduct a gun battle while stoned but she doubted that she could. Even so, the grass would have been soothing. She was confident that she looked cool enough on the outside—she was used to brassing it out onstage—but inside she was mush. It felt like all her bones had dissolved.

Yet somewhere inside the mush there was something hard, hard and strong and yet warm. All her life there'd been an unasked question in her heart, not something that had troubled her, just a vapor of uncertainty. It seemed like it shouldn't make any difference where she came from or how or why. She was who she was, wasn't she? But in the course of a single conversation with Grimes she had changed; she was different; she was still her and yet at the same time someone else. And the someone else was filled with an aching sadness and a violent love for Lenna. Could love be violent? Yes. Its energy was so great that it had to be so—an elemental violence like a powerful wind or a crashing sea. It was a violence without malice or hate and she hoped that Grimes was right and George had been wrong. She didn't want to have to hate anyone in order to do what was right. And no matter how frightened she was, she knew it was right to go to Lenna. If she didn't at least try then the identity that had given her the strong warmth inside would never truly be hers. The wind and the sea didn't make deals; and neither would she. In the cockpit she heard Titus Oates call out to her.

"Ella?"

She turned and looked at the smoke-wreathed beard and the pulled-down cap. Beneath the cap were a pair of big, crazy eyes that she could not read. She sensed that Oates could kill you on a Monday if he wasn't on your side, and die for you on a Tuesday if he was. What determined whether he was or not was probably unknown even to Oates himself, and perhaps to him most of all.

"Ella, you're a smart chick," said Oates. He jutted his beard toward Grimes. "But you've thrown in with this asshole, right?"

Grimes prodded at a graze on his face.

"To the end of the line," replied Ella.

Oates looked at Grimes as if her answer implied some deep mystery.

"So, in a nutshell," said Oates, "you're asking me to get myself killed and destroy my livelihood—*and* a whole fuckload of the finest sipping whiskey I ever even seen—for no gain whatsoever."

"What should it profit a man," said Grimes, "if he should gain the whole world but lose his immortal soul?"

Oates laughed like a psychopathic Santa Claus.

"I told you, Doc, I'm having serious doubts about Christianity."

Ella said, "I can pay you."

Oates stopped laughing. He and Grimes turned toward her together. Ella reached in her bag and pulled out the envelope Jefferson had given her. For some reason, since Grimes had told her Lenna's story—and hers—it was no longer difficult to think of Charlie as Jefferson. From the envelope she pulled out two thin plastic wallets and some papers. She'd opened the packet earlier but with so much else going on they hadn't seemed worth mentioning. She handed the wallets over to Grimes. They were bankbooks.

"Jefferson gave them to me," said Ella.

Grimes flicked through them impassively, then handed them to Oates. Oates's eyes bulged.

The wallets contained two bank deposit books, one of them in the Bahamas, the other in the Cayman Islands. They were in her name and contained a total of two and three-quarter million dollars, a figure so unimaginable to her as to be meaningless. Grimes took the wallets from Oates and handed them back to Ella. She put them away.

"Do we have a deal?" asked Ella.

Oates said, "The Koran instructs us that 'persecution is more griev-ous than slaying.' Seems to me this big-shot scumbag Faroe is guilty of both."

He pulled on his beard.

"The book goes on to say: 'but fight them not by the holy mosque until they fight you there, then, if they fight you, slay them.' "

He looked at Grimes from under the brim of his cap.

" 'Such is the recompense of unbelievers.' "

"Fuckin' A," said Ella.

Grimes glanced at her as if he thought she was losing it.

Oates nodded. He fumbled in his pocket.

"I figure those backwoodsmen musta given me this little souvenir for something."

Oates opened his palm to reveal a huge cartridge with a bullet as thick as the end of his thumb.

"Deer slug," he said. "Under that seat I got a Remington 870 cut down to seventeen inches. Security." He put the slug back in his pocket. "Anyhow, I never could resist a God-given opportunity to kick ass. How're we going to get in?"

Grimes peered out of the cockpit and put his hand on Oates's arm.

"There," said Grimes. "That's Arcadia."

Oates looked. "You telling me that's our landing zone, Doc?"

Ella stuck her head into the cockpit and followed their gaze. Below them was a vast flat blackness. Standing bright in the middle of it was a pool of yellow light. As she looked harder and they got closer she saw a building, a mansion that looked like a courthouse or a bank, with its front facade illuminated. In front of the mansion stretched a thin ribbon of illuminated road.

"You've got light, and the driveway's three or four hundred yards long," Grimes said. "It's the closest we'll get. And there's a fair chance Filmore Faroe's in there right now."

Titus Oates wrinkled his nose. Without speaking he took out a pair of Aviator shades and put them on.

Grimes said, "Where the road looks like it ends, I mean going away from the house, it runs into a bunch of trees."

"Better get in back and batten down, then," said Titus Oates. "And open the cargo door."

"Why?" asked Grimes.

"If it gets jammed we don't wanna be trapped inside."

Grimes climbed into the hold and wrestled open the cargo door and slid it back. The wind was intense. Grimes locked the door in place then buckled himself in next to Ella. His face was pale. Ella almost asked him if he was okay, then decided that it might make him feel worse and he would only say yes anyway.

"Are you okay?" asked Grimes.

"Right as rain," said Ella.

"We can still call this off if you want to," he said.

"Do you want to?" she replied.

"Better not ask," said Grimes. He turned. "Gul!"

Gul trotted from the rear of the hold, where he'd been sniffing around. At the open door he paused and looked out. Ella's heart stopped.

"Gul!" she yelled.

Gul turned, wondering what the fuss was about, and came to Grimes. Grimes pulled him between his thighs and locked his arms around the dog's chest.

The plane took a stomach-churning dip.

"We're going in!" growled Oates.

Ella looked at Grimes. Grimes winked at her. Ella winked back, then bent forward and clasped her elbows to her knees. As she did so she heard Grimes murmur into Gul's ear.

"Hang in with me, pal, and you'll be okay."

Ella closed her eyes.

Titus Oates bellowed, "For *Allah* is Lord! And mighty is his sword!"

THIRTY-TWO

THROUGH the open cargo doorway Cicero Grimes could see the tops of the trees skimming by, inches below the belly of the De Havilland. Over the roar of the propeller and the sucking of the wind he heard Titus Oates hollering oaths to himself in the cockpit. There was a sudden, violent dip and Grimes thought he was going to throw up, then his spine jolted with a massive impact and he knew his seat belt was going to tear away from the wall. He closed his eyes and clung to Gul. Gul, his head over Grimes's shoulder, uttered not a murmur. The seat belt held.

Grimes's head filled with rumbling. His bones registered a different quality of movement. Wheels. The big rubber wheels were grinding along the driveway. They were on the ground. Grimes opened his eyes. Through the open door he saw the lawns of Arcadia speeding past. The whole fuselage trembled with the strain of braking. He saw a gray blur and an instant later a deafening bang stunned his eardrums. The plane bucked and juddered. Screaming metal. The speeding ground loomed toward the door as the plane tipped then righted itself. Slower now. Grimes glanced at Ella: she was huddled beside him, her eyes clenched shut. Grimes twisted forward and looked over Oates's shoulder: through the shell of the cockpit loomed the Doric columns and wide steps of Arcadia.

They were heading straight for the portico.

Grimes pulled back and braced himself. A moment later he left his seat and the belt almost cut him in half as the plane mounted the steps and barreled on. There was a vast, grinding crash of metal and stone. The cabin lights cut out. Grimes felt the breeze of something huge brush past him and splinter against the forward bulkhead. A dense mist of alcohol fumes swept into his nostrils.

Then everything stopped.

Grimes's vision was blurred and it was dark. In his arms Gul was panting.

"Good man," said Grimes. He couldn't hear his own voice.

Grimes let Gul go. He unsnapped his belt and turned to Ella. She was moving but he couldn't make out her features. Her voice reached out faintly to his concussed ears.

"You okay?" she said.

She was fine, then.

"Yes," he replied.

He stood up unsteadily. Ella's face came into focus. From the direction of the cockpit he sensed a bulky rummaging, then heavy feet crunching on broken glass. Titus Oates emerged. His cheeks and brow were speckled with grazes. In one hand was the cut-down Remington. One lens of his Aviators was cracked.

Grimes squatted down by his father's body.

"Leave him," said Oates.

Grimes looked up. Oates took his shades off and threw them away.

"We got a lot of inflammables and a red-hot engine," said Oates. "Sorry, man."

Oates racked a shell into the cut-down and went to the door. Grimes pulled the tarp back from his father's face. The cheeks were sunken and gray.

"Ella," said Oates.

Grimes found Ella looking over his shoulder at George.

"Goodbye," said Ella to George.

She followed Oates. Grimes hung on for a moment. He didn't know why.

"Doc! Goddamnit!"

Grimes pulled the tarp back over George's face and stood up. In the cargo doorway Gul stood waiting for him, flapping his tail. Between the door and the inner portico wall there was a two-foot gap filled with floating dust.

Grimes said, "Let's go, pal."

Gul jumped down and Grimes followed him. To his left, the entrance to Arcadia was blocked by rubble and the twisted blades of the propeller. Along the outer metal skin of the plane was a great gash where the wing had been torn off. Grimes clambered down the steps toward the pillars and lights. Out on the lawns to either side of the drive, both wings of the plane lay amid the rubble of the two marble statues that had shorn them off.

"Over here!"

Twenty yards to his left Titus Oates, with Ella next to him, beckoned Grimes toward one of the elegant floor-to-ceiling windows that fronted the house. Grimes started toward them, after Gul. As he cleared the plane's tail section there was a dull *whoosh* behind him. He looked back and saw a billow of flame flare out from the cargo door. Grimes ran.

He found Oates and Ella stomping the glass and wooden crosspieces from the tall window frame. Oates finished the job with the butt of the Remington, ducked and stepped inside. Gul picked his way through the glass. Grimes and Ella followed. The room was similar to the parlor where he'd first met Lenna. Oates strode over, opened the door and glanced professionally back and forth down the corridor.

"Anyone know where we're going?" said Oates.

As Grimes walked across the room he oriented himself. The study seemed like the best place to start. He led out into the corridor and found his way toward the main hallway. As they approached it smoke drifted toward them. Oates put a hand on Grimes's shoulder and pulled him back.

"There's still a fuckload of aviation fuel in that thing that hasn't blown yet."

Grimes looked. In the main hall the big carved front door lay flat on the tiles where it had been rammed from its hinges by the twisted nose of the plane. The nose itself was wreathed in flames.

"I don't know any other route," said Grimes.

"Then make it fast."

They ran with Grimes through the smoking hall and past the walls of paintings toward the study. Beside him jogged Ella, gun in hand. Grimes's Colt was still in his belt. Gul trotted a yard in front, Oates brought up the rear. They reached the study. The double doors were closed. Gul put his nostrils to the crack and started his soft death growl. From inside came a muffled but audibly panic-stricken voice. Grimes looked at the door handles. He took hold of Gul's collar and pulled him back. Gul strained toward the doors.

Grimes said, "Open it, Titus."

Oates leveled the cut-down at the handles and blew the doors apart.

Grimes let go and Gul went, roaring savagely toward a bleating vibrato of terror. Oates darted after him, shotgun to shoulder. Grimes followed and saw Rufus Atwater make it onto the leather-topped desk in one fear-fueled leap. As he teetered for balance Gul lunged up and snapped his jaws around Atwater's ankle. Atwater's scream drowned out the sound of crunching bone. Gul dragged him from the table with a contemptuous heave. As Atwater smashed, squealing, into the floor, Gul let go and made as if to go in for seconds.

"Gul!" ordered Grimes. "No more."

Gul stopped and hovered over the blubbering prosecutor. Grimes walked over and saw the automatic under Atwater's arm. Grimes un-holstered the gun and tossed it to Oates. He grabbed Atwater by the lapels and hauled him to his feet. Atwater was gagging with terror. His eyes when they locked onto Grimes's contained a desperate plea for mercy. Grimes thought of his father. He remembered to keep his neck loose, for maximum whiplash velocity, then head-butted Atwater in the bridge of the nose. Atwater sagged and groaned pitifully through the blood pouring from his nostrils. Grimes held him up. For a moment he was blind with rage. Half a dozen ways to kill the prosecutor rippled through his mind. He didn't; but he had to do something or his brain would burst. He hawked a mouthful of phlegm and spat in Atwater's face. Atwater cringed. Grimes grabbed Atwater's scrawny throat and pulled him close.

"Do you remember, Mr. Prosecutor, what happened to Jack Seed's balls?"

Atwater nodded. He had stopped breathing. Grimes squeezed some more.

"Answer me."

Atwater croaked, "Yes."

"Good. Where's Lenna?"

Atwater vaguely waved his hand toward the window. Grimes drove his knee into Atwater's crotch and shoved him onto his knees.

"Gul," said Grimes.

Gul bared his teeth and gargled horribly an inch from Atwater's wobbling eyes.

"She's not here!" screamed Atwater. *"The hillbillies. The hillbillies. The Stone House."*

"And Clarence Jefferson?"

"Him too. Faroe too."

"We need a vehicle," said Grimes.

Atwater nodded, drooling and sobbing. Grimes dragged him to his feet and shoved him toward the door. Atwater stumbled, blood pouring over his shoe from his savaged ankle. Gul herded him against the wall. Grimes noticed the two big suitcases on the floor.

Oates nodded toward them and said, "These the ones we're hot for?"

Grimes nodded. Oates stuck Atwater's pistol into his belt and tossed the Remington toward Grimes. As Grimes caught it he sensed a movement in the corridor. Without having to decide he pulled the butt into his hip and pointed the shotgun at the doorway. When a man in combat fatigues sprang into view, Grimes squeezed the trigger and blew him backward into the corridor wall.

As the man crumpled forward into the gush of his own innard workings, footsteps clattered down the corridor, running away. Oates pulled his automatic, checked the corridor, then bent down over the disemboweled figure. He came up with a second automatic.

Grimes realized he'd just killed another man. He realized too that if it was supposed to trouble him, it didn't. He racked another round into the shotgun. It felt good. He looked at Atwater.

"The car," said Grimes.

Atwater limped toward the door and past the dead man. With Gul and Ella, Grimes followed him down the corridor, away from the entrance hall. At the end Atwater peered around the corner.

"It's clear," he said.

Grimes rammed him forward with the shotgun butt. There were no gunshots.

"The others, how many?" said Grimes.

"I don't know," wheezed Atwater. "Nobody tells me a goddamn thing."

Ella said, "Where's Titus?"

Grimes looked back toward the study. Oates emerged, carrying the two suitcases as if they were plastic bags crammed with Twinkies.

"Then, if they fight you, slay them," said Oates, and laughed.

Hastily, Rufus Atwater took them through a huge kitchen and a laundry room to a side exit toward the rear of the building. Grimes opened the door quietly. Outside stood a dark blue panel van, a Dodge Tradesman. To the rear of the driver's seat was a sliding door, closed. Grimes hauled Atwater to the threshold and took him by the throat.

"Open the van," said Grimes. "If you yell, you're dog food."

Atwater nodded.

"Gul," said Grimes. "Go look."

As Gul slid outside, Grimes shoved the prosecutor after him. Atwater hobbled forward in agony and fell against the van for support, biting his lips. Grimes watched Gul rove back and forth. It seemed safe. Atwater slid the side of the van open. It was empty. Grimes turned to Ella. She looked like she was holding up at least as well as he was, maybe better.

Ella said, "Let me drive."

Grimes nodded and crossed to the van. There were no seats in the back and no windows except for one in the single rear door, which looked like it opened upward. Grimes pushed Atwater inside and Oates loaded the suitcases. Ella got behind the wheel. Grimes returned the shotgun to Oates and got in beside Ella. Oates settled himself on one knee to the side of the open door.

"Gul," said Oates.

Gul jumped in the back and sat staring at Rufus Atwater from close range. Atwater stared down at his own belt buckle and sucked on his lips. Ella switched on the engine. They pulled away.

As they drove around the edge of the mansion and onto the gravel esplanade the van's right-hand wheels were lifted from the ground by the concussion wave of an explosion. Grimes ducked his head as the window next to his face cracked with a loud bang but didn't shatter. More debris pelted the windshield, dented the body work, ricocheted through the open side door. Ella swerved left, bounced over a curb onto the lawn, got control. Grimes wound down the cracked window and looked back.

The grand Palladian facade of Arcadia was a mass of oily fire. Black and orange flames scoured and defaced the perfect white stonework and flared away into the darkness above. Heaped around the burning rage of the cargo plane's shell were the shattered remnants of the splendid portico: its slender columns and proud entablature were now a mass of broken masonry and smoking timbers.

Oates said, "Reckon this is as close as I'll ever come to a broken heart."

Grimes turned. Titus Oates knelt in the door watching the self-immolation of his plane. He looked at Grimes.

"At least your pa got the send-off he deserved."

"Yeah," said Grimes. "I guess he wouldn't complain."

Watching the inferno consume Arcadia, Grimes remembered what George had said about the Faroes: a line that deserved to end. But they weren't finished yet.

Ella skirted one shorn wing of the plane where it lay on the lawn and pulled the van back onto the driveway. She picked up speed toward the tunnel of trees.

"Here they come," said Oates.

Grimes swiveled his head. From the opposite side of the burning mansion a four-door sedan came skidding through the gravel and straight toward them across the west lawn. Its windows were down and Grimes could see arms holding pistols, and a pair of rifle barrels, sticking out. There was a muzzle flash and a futile crackle of automatic fire. Then Ella plunged the Dodge beneath the trees and the pursuit car disappeared from view. Grimes turned back to face the windshield. The road hurtled beneath them in the headlights. Wide black trunks, hanging ghosts of Spanish moss. Grimes thought: the gate. The wrought-iron gate.

"Ella," said Grimes. "When these trees end you'll find about a hundred yards of clear road and then a gate."

"What kind of gate?"

"Double wrought-iron gates, twelve feet high, set into a wall. They'll probably be locked."

Ella reached for her seat belt. Grimes followed suit.

"What do I do?" she asked.

"Titus?" said Grimes.

"Ram them. Not too slow, not too fast. Thirty miles an hour," said Oates. "Aim just off-center."

"Okay," said Ella.

"Gul," called Grimes.

Gul clambered forward and Grimes held him tight on his lap. He heard the zing of bullets. The van was untouched.

"Amateurs," sneered Oates. He looked at Rufus Atwater, pushed his beard into his face, and roared at him: *"Amateurs!"*

Atwater covered his bleeding face with both hands. Oates rummaged through Atwater's pockets and produced two spare bullet clips, then grabbed him by the hair and threw him flat on the floor behind the backs of the front seats. Oates sandwiched the prosecutor against the seats with the two suitcases, then sat against them and wedged himself crossways between the van walls.

In the side mirror Grimes saw, in the distant pitch-dark, the lights of the pursuit car. He looked at Ella's face. The tendons of her neck were strung tight and her lips were a clenched line. Her eyes were fixed ahead and totally focused. There was nothing Grimes could say: she was in control. The live oaks lining the road suddenly thinned and disappeared. The road cleared. He looked at the speedometer: the needle was dropping toward thirty. Through the windshield the road curved and at the limit of their beams the headlights swept across a section of red-brick wall. In what seemed like an instant the tall gates loomed ahead. Grimes clamped Gul with his thighs and grabbed two handfuls of his fur.

"Hold on!" shouted Ella.

Grimes's vision turned black and he felt himself kicked in the chest. A shower of glass lashed his face. His head cleared. They had stopped dead. Gul squirmed in his arms. Grimes opened his eyes. Inches from his face the wrought-iron bars of the gate slanted down from above the cabin roof and down across the hood of the van. They were jammed: the lower hinge of the right-hand gate had been smashed free but the upper had held firm. He looked at Ella: she was already gunning the engine back to life. She slammed into reverse. The van creaked and squealed backward.

"No. Everybody *out!*" bellowed Oates. *"Out. Clear the wagon."*

Grimes threw his door open and Gul leapt away. The van stopped. As Grimes ripped off his belt he saw Ella slipping out of the driver's side. Grimes tumbled clear. His knee gave way; he fell. Gunshots were singing from the bricks behind him. He was dazzled by lights. He dived off the road and into the grass, out of the dazzle. He rolled, stopped on his back, dragged the gun from his belt, flipped onto his belly and lay prone.

Twenty yards away the pursuit car slowed amid the wild flashes of its own gunfire. Bullets started slamming into the van. Grimes couldn't see anyone to shoot at. Where was Titus? Through the van's open side Grimes saw Oates's boots, toes splayed down to the floor, soles pointing toward the driver's seat. His body was obscured. Grimes thought: *He's dead.* An urge to charge the pursuit car seized him. *No.* He aimed his Colt and waited. Close range.

As the pursuit car came to a halt the single rear door of the van sprang upward and emitted a rapid fusillade of shotgun blasts punctuated by the meaty clack of the racking slide.

Before Grimes's eyes the pursuit car turned into a writhing slaughter chamber of exploding glass, punctured limbs and screaming faces. The shotgun fell silent. A voice boomed from the van.

"Hold your positions."

The van rocked and Titus Oates jumped from the back, an automatic clamped in either fist. He held the guns out at strange angles, like a huge, drum-chested praying mantis, stepped clear of the headlight beams and walked briskly up to the buckshot-sieved sedan. He poked one of his arms into the reeking interior. There were four irregularly spaced shots. Grimes stood up. He found Gul standing beside him.

"Ella!" called Grimes.

A door slammed.

"Here."

Ella was already back in the driver's seat of the Dodge. She reversed further back from the tangled gates.

Oates called, "Wait."

Grimes walked over and joined him at the rear of the van. Oates reached in and picked up the shotgun. From his pocket he pulled the deer slug. As he shoved it into the magazine Grimes glanced back at the riddled pursuit car. Wisps of gunsmoke drifted from the open windows and curled through the lights. Oates caught the glance.

"Nothing you can do for 'em, Doc."

Oates smiled and racked the deer slug into the chamber. He jerked his head toward the gates and Grimes followed him. From a few inches' distance Oates aimed the muzzle at the upper hinge of the gate where it was mortared into the bricks. He fired and blew the hinge from its moorings. The gates, still fastened together in the center, sagged and wavered uncertainly. Grimes and Oates dragged them aside. They piled back into the Tradesman. Behind the suitcases Grimes heard Rufus Atwater snuffling quietly. Ella drove out through the gates and onto the road.

Titus Oates's head appeared over Grimes's shoulder.

"I just thought I'd tell you that this is one of the few world-class women of her generation, or any goddamn other. The last time I saw driving that cold was Colorado Springs back in 'eighty-six."

"What happened in Colorado Springs?" asked Ella.

"For an objective account you'd have to dig out the newspapers."

Ella looked at Grimes.

She said, "Where's the Stone House?"

"Go straight, I'll tell you when to turn."

They all fell silent for a while and Grimes stared through his window. They drove across the flat and moonlit plantation, through acres of silver marsh grass that waltzed and whispered in the wind. And the whispering dance was eerily serene, as if the tall blades of grass were moving to a melody chanted by the land that said, *"All this too will pass."* Then Grimes heard something else.

"Listen," he said.

Across the great flatness he could hear the thump of an approaching helicopter.

Oates said, "Hey, man. No one mentioned a Sikorsky to me."

THIRTY-THREE

DESPITE HIMSELF. *At all costs.*
Beating, beating.
The blows fell softly now.

A fluttering—no more than that—at the outer perimeter of knowing.

If the blows carried with them some charge of pain he had slipped beyond its appreciation. At this, the final extremity of *continuum,* he felt the ecstasy of supreme definition. Here—amidst the deliriac celebration of the death of God, the death of death, the dissolution of interiority—the psychobiological torment of ages was metamorphosed into a gaping breach between *the one* which was one and *the other* which was all sensate things. And in that breach he danced, with neither witnesses nor partner to share his heady wine, his light and wheeling steps, his dissolute grace. He was sanded to a shadow's ghost, denuded to an impersonal resonation, but a fingernail's scraping from zero.

Despite himself.

At all costs.

Oh yes.

He had brushed his cheek against that greater-than-himself; that greater-than-he-was *despite himself;* that whatever-it-might-be which *at all costs* must not be; that moment toward which he had striven with all his might, and which at the same time he had fought with all his power to repel.

Miracle.

Dissolution.

Extremity.

Joy.

The homes we never write to and the oaths we never keep.

Beating, beating, beating.

He stirred amid the shit of pigs. He could no longer smell his own rotting. He missed it. The beating was against his head; no, against the tiny bones and stretched-taut drumskins of his ears. It was sound that bounced on his sensorium, not rifle butts and feet.

He thought: *The machine that hovers goes aloft.*

The Captain opened his eyes. Swollen slits peered into obscurity. The slithering tiles of a pigpen. The mooch and grunt of fine fat hogs with bristles smooth and dappled hides. The Captain smiled. Was this the best they could do? This faint dribbling of concern too anemic to qualify as fear? Did they think that hogs might erase him from the uncharted wilderness of time? No. The Captain's ripening meat was too tainted by far for the delicate palates of these good beasts. Beauty, laughter and filth claimed no liens on trembling reason, try as it might to throw its net over them. It was in surrender that the supremacy of evil lay. He would not bow before this servile cosmos, still less its scuttling slaves. He would slake himself on their rending. Let the plenitude of horror and that of bliss be one. Let the irreducible collision be commenced. An uncontainable force of eruption cracked wide the fissures of his stasis.

The Captain, clanking, lumbered to his feet.

Constriction.

Through slits he saw a silvery chain, slim-linked but strongly mettled. A fence of wood. A stretched steel triangle: ankle, cross-spar, wrist. He raised his stump and sundered the cross-spar in one. He shuffled forward. The slithering tiles gave way to gravel, softly shifting, then concrete, then plank. He opened a door onto brightness and a fast-turned face, lips gaping in surprise. The lips embraced his resined stump and shed their small white bones. His left hand filled with hair. His blunted right rammed home once more, between the mewling gums, and down. And down. Feeble claws at his chest. And down. The shunting *clack* of a dislocating jaw. Another inch, one more. The stump-clogged throat gave up its spasmic heaving and was done. He probed among the rags. A key. A key then dropped, then found and housed and twisted and clicked. The slim-linked shackle trailed upon the floor. He took a knife, its butcher's blade half-whetstone-scraped away. He touched it to his tongue; the tasty sting of well-keened edge. Into my pocket, beauty. A gun? He scorned it. They think him mad?

Then let them.

For the Captain knows them all.

And *despite himself* and *at all costs,* the midnight campo calls him.

THIRTY-FOUR

ELLA switched off the van's lights and squinted through the frame of the shattered windshield. A bunch of drifting clouds were cutting across the moon. To either side of the blacktop were the darker gashes of deep flood ditches and she was afraid of running into one. The sound of the helicopter was closing in. She briefly dropped her hand to her belly: the Smith & Wesson was there, loaded, tucked into the waist of her leggings. She looked at Grimes.

"We've got to bring the chopper down," said Grimes.

"Can't be done, Doc," replied Oates. "Not with the ordnance we got."

Grimes told her, "At the next crossroads hang a left."

Ella nodded. Grimes climbed over the back of his seat and into the rear. He spoke to Rufus Atwater. Ella half turned her head so she could hear.

"Listen, Rufus," said Grimes, with surprising kindness. "I've got my reasons for being here and so have you. Right?"

A pause.

"Answer the doctor," snarled Titus Oates.

"Right," stuttered Atwater. "Right."

"But do you know why Mr. Oates is here?" asked Grimes.

"No, sir," said Atwater.

Ella decided she didn't know either.

"Tell him, Titus."

"Because," said Oates, "in this country we have the right to keep and bear arms. And that means that to prove that point we can kill any assistant fucking prosecutor we fucking want. And you know something else? That's why the rest of the world is afraid of North America. Are you afraid, Mr. Prosecutor?"

294

Oates paused and Ella glanced over her shoulder. Atwater was actually crying, silently, with bewilderment and fear.

"Okay, Rufus," said Grimes. "Now, I want you to do exactly what Mr. Oates tells you to. Can you do that for me?"

"Yes, sir."

Ella jumped as the first burst of gunfire came from above. The bullets kicked into the road ahead, then battered and rattled into the hood of the van and the roof above her head. She ducked. The battering stopped. Grimes was still talking in back but she couldn't concentrate on his words. The crossroads were on her. She jabbed at the brake pedal and spun the wheel. The road in front of her tilted. She dialed the wheel back. The van righted itself and she stamped on the gas. For a moment the sound of rotor blades diminished as the chopper overshot the turn. She glanced sideways: out above the fields the chopper swooped and wheeled into a wide turn. Grimes's head appeared at her shoulder.

"Ella, I'm going to jump out the back, you understand?"

She nodded.

"The next time their fire hits us I want you to step on the brakes. Halve your speed. But wait until they hit us. Okay?"

She nodded again.

"Good. Then, right after that, I want you to drive like you're losing control. Weave, slow down some more, then put the van into the left-hand ditch."

"The ditch."

"The ditch to the left of the road. Take both your left-hand wheels over the edge. The weight will be right, don't worry. It'll tip it over on its side. Then do what Titus says. You got all that?"

"I got it."

She felt his hand squeeze her shoulder, then he was gone. She focused herself. The road seemed darker than ever but she could see the black strips of the rain ditches racing by on either side. The rotor blades were closing in again. She glanced at the speedometer. They were doing fifty. She heard a dim rattle of gunfire and almost snatched her foot from the gas but the slamming of bullets didn't follow. *Wait till they hit us.* She waited. The road. The ditches. The left-hand wheels. This time she didn't hear the gunfire at all: just a sudden din of hammered aluminum and steel. She crammed on the brakes. There was no need to pretend to lose control: her body jerked forward and the wheel in her hands slipped through her fingers. The black rim of the ditch veered toward her from her right. She squeezed the wheel, heaved, swung back toward the center, whipped her foot off the pedal, bullets kicking dust spots from the surface up ahead. The speedometer: twenty. Another clanging drum roll on the hood. She jacked the wheel left then right, almost off the road, then back again, more brake, slowing—*both left-hand wheels*—and back across, in a shallow diagonal, toward the gaping black stripe of the ditch: *now.*

A bang as the axle beneath her hit the edge of the pavement. Her shoulder slammed into the door. Moving, grinding, squealing underneath her. Only the front wheel was down. She sensed the rear end about to skim rightward and roll them over. She dragged the steering wheel clockwise, still moving, heard a bellow of rageful movement behind her, a weight hurled against the wall—a second bang as the rear end dropped. The wheel slipped from her hands. Then the world tilted before her, still moving, weeds and dirt whipping into her face. She closed her eyes. They stopped. She found herself clenched up in a ball.

"Ella, get back here. Keep your head down."

It was Oates. The van was two-thirds on its side, the right-hand-side door gaping up to the sky, the floor almost perpendicular to the pavement. Through the open rear door she saw a section of road and a few yards of watery ditch. Grimes and Gul were gone. Atwater lay in a tight huddle. Titus Oates stacked the two suitcases one behind the other near the rear exit. Ella crawled over to him.

"Got your gun?" said Oates.

She reached down. The revolver had slipped inside her waistband. She pulled it out, checked it.

"Good," said Oates. "What loads you using?"

"Black Hills wadcutters."

"They'll do the trick. Hunker down behind these cases."

He indicated the barricade he'd made at the backdoor.

"Eyes and ears peeled. Don't mind me. Anyone comes along from this end you play dead until their body blocks the door, then you let them have three of them wadcutters. Can you do that?"

"I can do it."

"I'll handle the rest."

Ella curled behind the cases. It wasn't right. She shifted one of them over four inches so there was a gap between the edge of the case and the rim of the doorframe through which she could look and fire. She focused on the sound of the chopper: it was coming from the far side of the road and the pitch of its rotors had changed. She guessed it was landing in the field. She looked back into the van.

Titus Oates was crouched with his back to the tilted floor, just beneath the gaping hole formed by the open side door. On his knees before him was Rufus Atwater.

"When your buddies show up, Rufus, you are going to talk to them, real friendly, and exactly as I instruct you."

Atwater nodded.

"Then you're going to climb out, real cool, and then there'll be shooting."

Atwater swallowed.

"From now on I want you to repeat everything I say," said Oates.

Atwater nodded and waited.

Suddenly Oates clamped Atwater's head between both hands and jammed his thumbs into the prosecutor's clot-rimmed nostrils. Atwater uttered bewildered grunts of pain.

"Obey me, scum," whispered Oates. "Repeat everything I say."

Atwater said, "Obey me, scum. Repeat everything I say."

Oates, satisfied, nodded and let go. Two automatics appeared in his fists. He checked them rapidly. Ella turned back to the ditch. They waited.

The noise of the chopper was even lower now and at a constant pitch. It had to be on the ground. The seconds ticked by. She kept her mind blank. Then, very close, a blast of gunfire raked the underside of the van. She squeezed down behind the cases. The shooting stopped. Her ears rang. From her angle of vision she could see nothing.

Behind her, Atwater yelled. "*Muchachos!* It's me! Atwater! Don't shoot!"

She couldn't help glancing back. Atwater had raised both hands through the doorway above him and was slowly standing up. Both of Oates's pistols were pointed at his crotch.

Oates said softly, "The others are hurt bad. I think they might be dead."

As Atwater's head and chest cleared the door he piped, "The others are hurt bad! I think they might be dead!"

Ella heard a voice answer, "How many?"

Oates murmured, "Just two. Can I get outa here?"

"Just two. Can I get outa here?" asked Atwater.

She looked out the back again: still nothing but ditch, road and sky.

"Slowly!" came a voice, closer than before.

Oates said, "Am I glad to see you guys."

"Am I glad to see you guys!"

Ella forced herself to keep looking outside as she heard Atwater climbing out. Ditch, road, sky. Suddenly the van echoed to a rage of guns. She snapped her head around.

"Eat the peanuts!" bellowed Titus Oates.

Titus was up on his feet, muzzle blasts blazing from both fists. His body twitched once. He kept firing. Ella's neck prickled. She turned.

A dark shape plunged with a splash into the ditch outside. She pointed and fired twice. The shape jerked. A flutter of flame. Something thumped into the cases in front of her. She pointed and fired twice more. The shape collapsed into the trench and didn't move. The deafening rage had stopped. She looked backward: the guns in Titus Oates's fists were silent. Oates ducked his head down and glanced back beyond her, nodded.

He said, "Nice shooting. Now let's see if the doctor kept up his end."

THIRTY-FIVE

P LAYING DEAD in the middle of the road was the easiest thing Cicero Grimes had done all day. He had crouched in a ball at the back of the Tradesman and waited until the bullets hit and Ella had slowed down, then he just tipped himself out and over the edge. So battered was he already that bouncing on the pavement again hardly made much of an impression on him. When he stopped moving he lay prone for a while. He might have stayed there for good but Gul came up and pushed his tongue into Grimes's left eye. Grimes raised his head in time to see the van teeter into the flood ditch and fall on its side. The Sikorsky was wheeling above the field, to the right of the road, and straightening up to land.

Grimes was behind schedule.

He dragged himself to his feet and started running. He jumped into the right-hand flood ditch to conceal himself and splashed through the mud. Each step as it landed jarred his knee, his spine, his head. Gul loped ahead of him, setting the pace. Grimes stared, trancelike, at the muddy water and thought only about getting air into his lungs. Above the rasp of his breathing he heard the chopper descending. He glanced to his right: above the tops of the marsh grass he saw the black chopper puttering down toward the earth. It would land about twenty yards from the edge of the ditch. Grimes trudged on. He realized, belatedly, that the clinging mud in the ditch was doubling the energy demanded of him. The ditch meant he didn't have to bend forward to conceal himself; but the men in the chopper probably weren't looking at him anyway. He closed up on the van, from which came no sign of life. Another rightward glance: the chopper was out of sight but he could feel its wind. The gunmen would be unloading; at any moment they would appear on the road ahead. Ideally Grimes would reach the Sikorsky after the troops had cleared the field but before Titus had started the ball. Gul suddenly increased his pace and stretched ahead of him.

"Gul," wheezed Grimes.

Gul stopped and looked back at him. From amid the grass—no more than fifty feet away—came a burst of automatic fire directed at the Tradesman. Grimes plunged sideways into the field. He landed on his knees, got up, and waded forward, bent at the waist, through the chest-high blades of grass. The shooting stopped. All he could hear were the rotors. He couldn't see Gul. He felt the downblast getting stronger, the grass now leaning into his face. He reached the edge of a flattened circle in the middle of which sat the Sikorsky, its tail pointing almost toward him. He paused, forearms propped on his knees, and heaved for oxygen. Did the pilot have rearview mirrors? Was there a blind spot? He should've asked Titus Oates. What the fuck difference did it make? He reached for his Colt: it wasn't there. He searched. He must have lost it when he hit the road. Fuck it. He plunged forward across the wind-flattened circle.

The inside of the Sikorsky was dark. Had they left a spare man in there? The fear of what lay inside was countered by the knowledge that come what may, he could soon stop running. Gul appeared to his left. Grimes blessed him.

"Gul."

The dog glanced over. Grimes pointed at the chopper.

"Go."

Gul streaked ahead, jumped, disappeared into the dark doorway. Grimes thought he heard gunfire from the road but he wasn't sure. He staggered against the side of the chopper with his right shoulder, looked inside, saw: the rear of the cockpit, Gul's stiffened tail, nothing more. He darted across the doorway, checked the rear of the interior: nothing. He heard marrow-curdling growls and a wail of terror. He hoped the pilot hadn't done anything rash. Grimes crawled into the chopper and thrust his head into the cockpit.

The pilot was buried beneath his arms, his knees pulled up into a shivering ball. Gul looked up at Grimes and barked, pleased with himself. It was quieter in here than it was outside.

Grimes said, "You, what's your name?"

The pilot didn't answer. Grimes poked his shoulder blade. The pilot showed him one glazed eye and a wedge of face. He looked Hispanic.

"*Su nombre?*" said Grimes.

"Mariano."

Grimes sat in the copilot's seat. It felt so good he doubted he would ever be able to get up again. He pulled Gul back a few inches.

"Mariano, relax," said Grimes in Spanish.

Mariano unwound from his ball. He turned rabbit eyes on Gul.

"It's safer if you don't look at him," said Grimes.

Mariano turned the eyes on Grimes.

"When I tell you to take off, you do it, immediately. Understand?"

Mariano nodded. He put his hands on the controls.

"How many of your companions are at the Stone House?"

"Four, I think. Including Colonel Herrera."

"Is the woman inside?"

Mariano nodded.

"Alone?"

Mariano shook his head. "With the boss man and Colonel Herrera, maybe another, or more, I don't know."

The Stone House was a fortress. Grimes remembered the steel-lined antechamber to the cage. Even one man could hold it till doomsday. Could the pilot talk them in? It seemed unlikely. Could Faroe be bargained with, with Jefferson's suitcases? Grimes guessed Faroe was in too deep to turn back. How could they get inside?

Grimes looked out toward the road. He couldn't see the van. He twisted and scanned the empty cabin behind him. Bolted into the back was some kind of tool chest.

"Do you have a rope?" asked Grimes.

"Yes." Mariano pointed back at the chest.

Grimes looked outside again. A gangly silhouette appeared above the edge of the field. Grimes waited. Another figure: the baseball cap and bulk unmistakable. Then Ella. She waved. Grimes levered himself from the seat and went back and showed himself in the doorway. The others started forward through the grass. Grimes went to the tool chest and unlatched it. Inside he found a coil of nylon climbing rope. He rummaged further and pulled out a pair of oily rawhide gloves. Ella climbed inside. Her face was drawn but she seemed unharmed.

"Go sit up front," said Grimes.

Grimes looked past her. Atwater toiled forward, his legs wobbling under the weight of the suitcases. Behind him came Titus Oates, shotgun in hand. Oates's right hand glistened with a dark sheen. His sleeve was soggy. Grimes looked at him.

"I've been shot before," said Oates.

Grimes went back to the pilot.

In Spanish he said, "Call Colonel Herrera. Tell him you have the prisoners and Mr. Atwater and that you're bringing them in."

Grimes took one half of the headset and listened. When Herrera asked how many prisoners, Mariano looked at Grimes. Grimes jerked his thumb at Ella and himself: he wanted Faroe to feel good.

Mariano said into the mike, "Two. A man and a girl."

Herrera checked out. The muzzle of Oates's shotgun appeared against Mariano's skull.

"You wanna get rid of Paco here, I can fly this bird."

Grimes let Mariano pray for a moment then said, "No, I need you out back."

Oates grunted his disappointment and fell back.

To the pilot Grimes said, *"A la Casa de Piedra."*

THIRTY-SIX

F OR WANT of a rider the battle was lost."

She could take it.

"For want of a battle the kingdom was lost."

She could take it.

There was a pause in the cycle of yells and blows.

Lenna waited.

For all that she had been punished by time and fate, Lenna had never been physically assaulted before. She huddled on her hands and knees as the spasms of her body faded and her breath returned. There was blood in her mouth, but since the first blow Faroe had directed all his kicks and punches, with perverted precision, at her belly. She hadn't fought back. She did not want to stoke his anger any more than he stoked it himself with his chanting rhyme. Her mind floated strangely above the nausea and pain. She had given up her body; she'd made it a commodity to be bargained with. She would sell it in return for Faroe's anger and for a window of time. If he could pour that anger into her perhaps he would have less to direct at Ella; if the window was large enough perhaps an opportunity would arise to ensure her safety. Even so, Faroe's violence revolted her, as did his pale, shaved cranium and gleeful eyes, his watery mouth, his withered arms and shoulders not even strong enough to kill her. Moments before, Faroe had started to unzip his fly when Herrera had called him away. She knew he'd be back.

She could take it.

Her body was no longer hers. With each blow of his fist she had felt herself change, felt some small crumbling of that which remained of herself to herself. It was not the bruising of her flesh. It was as if she were being pushed back step by step down a tunnel, at the end of which she would find a cell in which she would be locked away forever from any possibility of contact and trust. The contact and trust that had ached her bones so deeply, and so briefly, in the arms of Cicero Grimes; and in the arms of Ella. When Faroe took out his penis and jerked off in her face or jammed it inside her, would that cell door clang shut? It didn't matter. As long as outside the cell—far outside—Ella, and Grimes and all the rest of the world were able to find their very small remnant, it wouldn't matter that she'd lost hers. After all, she had taken Faroe's from him. She had no right to pity and she did not claim it. She raised her head as Faroe returned into the room. He looked down at her without smiling.

Lenna became aware of the sound of a helicopter beating overhead.

"I've got her, Magdalena," said Faroe. He raised his eyes briefly to the roof. "I've got your daughter. She's come back home to the Stone House too."

The window had closed and with it the door of her cell. Lenna pulled one foot under her, firm on the floor. Her stomach muscles cramped. She looked at Faroe. Though he held the world in his hands he seemed more wretched than ever. She would not hate him again. She would not die with any trace of his poison, or her own, in her heart. She thought of Ella and loved her.

"Help me," she said, calmly.

Faroe blinked, uncertain. He took a step forward and held out his hand. Lenna took it and climbed to her feet.

She thought of Ella and loved her.

Then she threw herself on Faroe and sank her teeth into his lips. She closed her eyes to his face and her ears to his screams and retreated into a boundless space, which she filled with her love. And somewhere outside that space her teeth clenched and locked and would not let go and her hands groped and found a withered throat and squeezed. She loved and bit and squeezed. There was a sudden flash and an absence. Then she was falling in blackness and she heard a shatter of blurred noise. And she knew it to be the sound of her death and in the silent center of that sound Lenna heard herself cry: *I love her.*

THIRTY-SEVEN

GRIMES SAT in the chopper and stared down at a splash of blood on the floor. In the De Havilland, flying back from the Ohoopee River bottomlands, he had not imagined that so much would have to be spilled or that he would be steeped in it so deep. The stuff itself bothered him not at all; over the operating table he had spent thousands of hours incarnadined to the elbows. But this was different. The pool of cells and plasma at his feet signified something else.

Most of those who had died need not have. Grimes could have left Lenna to the mercy of Jack Seed. He could have left his father to the fate that in the end he had failed to alter. Did it matter that some had died for power and money and others for belief? Would the former always push the latter to that pass? Apart from George and Holden Daggett he did not mourn for the fallen; they had made their choices, as had he. But somehow, through a succession of slithering and unacknowledged moments of decision, he sat here now with more lives yet to be lost weighing in the balance of his say-so. If he told Titus Oates, whose blood it was on the floor, that they were backing off and going home, then Oates would protest but he'd give in. So would Ella. And Lenna, if she was still alive, wouldn't thank him for what he planned to attempt. The suitcases stacked beside him meant no more to him now than they had the day before; Grimes refused to let death give them value. And Clarence Jefferson, the player of games: why did Grimes yearn for him so? Perhaps in order that the wasted fatman weigh the balance for him?

Grimes told himself: you're fucked-up, exhausted and scared. Go back to your pit, your floor of garbage, where you belong.

But he no longer wanted to.

If he was stained with blood now, it was because of his original re-
fusal to weigh the balance that Jefferson had thrust upon him. He
could hear the wheedling argument of civilization, of the safe and
smugly knowing, buzzing around the outer skin of his brain. He cared
nothing for them anymore. There was no longer any logic to be artic-
ulated concerning either the law or the good or even how best to
protect himself from the wrath of Filmore Faroe. There was simply
a primal imbalance demanding redress: a righting of never-to-be-
calibrated scales; a judgment invited from an ancient court. If that represented justice, then fine and comforting; if not—if, rather, something
else, closer to bloodlust—then so it was and would be, comforting or
otherwise.

He wondered how he could claim the right to think in such terms.
In the cool of the morning, civilization would condemn him; and so,
perhaps, would he. But this was not the cool of the morning; it was the
heat of a monstrous night. Here he could no longer shelter beneath the
shady palms of ethical debate. Here he could only act: and throw all
their lives upon the wheel once more; and bear within himself, now and
afterward, the burden of the outcome of its spinning. Or not, as he
chose. *For both endeavors insist upon the spilling of blood: whether blood
of vein or blood of soul; your own and that of others, too.*

Such were the thoughts that turned through the mind of Cicero
Grimes as he stared at the blood on the floor.

"It's sound and ready," said Titus Oates.

Grimes looked up. Oates was swinging his weight from the rope he
had lashed to the rail above the open door. Grimes stood up and bent
forward into the cockpit. Through the glass shell he saw the gray bulk
of the Stone House looming toward them from the lightless plain.

In Spanish Grimes said, "You know what to do?"

Mariano nodded without taking his eyes off the target.

"Grimes?" said Ella. "I don't want you to go."

Ella's face was drained. It was the first time Grimes had seen her look
scared.

"Me neither," he said.

He glanced at Gul, sitting up between her knees.

"Hold on to him," said Grimes. "He's known to be an asshole at
times."

The Stone House was now only a hundred yards distant. Grimes
turned and went back to Oates. Grimes stood close and lowered his
voice.

"Titus? I need another favor."

"Doc?" said Titus. "You've got a lotta nerve for a guy who's done jackshit for me."

"When I'm clear I want you to get Ella out of here."

"No way, man."

"You've got the suitcases. If you really want to kick some ass, take a look inside. Ella knows what to do."

Oates pursed his lips sullenly.

Grimes said, "And because I like to think I'm a guy who pays his way, you can hang on to Gul, too. If he'll have you."

"I guess that would settle all debts."

Oates pulled out one of his automatics and put it in Grimes's jacket pocket.

"Glock. Seventeen rounds. Just pull it out shooting."

The Sikorsky was hovering motionless. Grimes put a hand on the rail and looked straight down into a wide glare of fluorescence. A bare six feet below, on the western slope of the Stone House roof, was a wide, frosted glass skylight. Grimes pulled on the rawhide gloves and looked at Oates.

"Remember," said Grimes. "I want chaos."

Oates glanced menacingly at Atwater. "You'll have it."

Grimes took the rope in his gloved hands.

Behind him, Rufus Atwater said, "You're crazy."

Grimes looked at the prosecutor. "I'm glad you think so," he said. " 'Cause you're coming in there with me."

He turned from Atwater's blanching face and nodded to Titus Oates.

Grimes said, "Such is the recompense of unbelievers."

Titus Oates said, "Amen."

Then Oates threw his shotgun to his shoulder and pumped two loads of double-aught bucks through the skylight.

Grimes jumped through the door and dropped.

Impression: his guts coming up into his throat. Intense heat on his palms. Glaring light. Steel bars. Falling. Too fast. Squeezing. Burning. Look down.

Impression: Corrugated iron speeding toward him. Bend knees. Squeeze. His feet hit the iron, legs buckling. His hip. His shoulder. His breath knocked out of him. The burning eased. Sliding down, twisting onto his back. The edge of the iron loomed. He squeezed the rope with all his might.

Impression: a white bang to the back of his skull. Dangling. Still sliding. The snap of the rope's end. His palms suddenly empty. Grimes dropped six feet onto a wooden platform, crashed knees and shoulder, rolled. The platform disappeared. He tumbled three feet onto hard tiles. Winded. He opened his eyes.

Before him gaped the platform's understructure. He rolled under, lay prone, fought for air. His ears were ringing. From his pocket he dragged the Glock. His fingers were too thick. He ripped his right-hand glove off with his teeth. The sting of the skin that came with it forced some structure on his senses. The rotor noise: diminishing slightly. His position: lying head toward the rear of the building.

Behind him, then, was the cage wall. On the far side of the shack above him was the door into it. He threw a twisting glance back toward the cage wall. His view was blocked by the platform. Floor and concrete wall, nothing else. He looked across the underside of the platform: too many supports and cross-spars, a death trap; he couldn't go that way. He heard wild shouts in Spanish. Running footsteps bounced on the platform. Behind him, at the far end, the cage end. Fear gripped him. Where was his chaos? He wriggled onto his back. *Think.* The footsteps stopped. *They don't know where you are. What would you do?* A picture leapt before him: someone peering around the cage-end corner of the shack. *Let them come softly.* He took his weight on his right elbow, Glock in his fist. With his left hand he grabbed hold of a stave under the platform's outer edge. He gave them a count of three. Don't blink. Point and fire.

Somewhere above, the second skylight imploded in a blast of buckshot.

Grimes heaved on the stave and swung himself out and up. He saw a figure, face upturned to the commotion above. Ten feet away. Grimes pointed and fired—a flash came from the figure's hand—and fired and fired. Five shots. The figure spun into the shack wall and fell to his knees. Grimes wormed out from under the platform, gun pointing at the kneeling man, and climbed to his feet, pointing, pointing. Gunfire blazed from the second skylight. Grimes—pointing—closed on the kneeler on the platform. Beyond: the cage wall; emptiness. The kneeler turned his face and Grimes fired into it once. The head slammed into the shack and fell, leaving bone fragments embedded in the rough timbers. The gunfire above stopped. Grimes looked up at the sound of a penetrating scream.

Limbs flailing, Rufus Atwater plunged shrieking through the roof and crashed from sight on the far side of the shack.

As the rotors pulled away above, Grimes walked backward toward the rear of the room, his gun covering the cage-wall end, stealing glances over his shoulder. At the rear corner of the shack he snatched a glimpse behind it: clear. He moved forward to the opposite rear corner, stopped, listened. Obscure noises, maybe voices. He looked: between where he was and the closed gate of the cage wall there was no sign of life. He paused, uncertain.

Lenna had to be inside the shack; Faroe too.

He waited.

He asked himself: would he let Lenna die, if necessary, in order to kill Faroe? He answered: no. In a different world than this one, she was a woman he could have loved; and would have been honored to love. Maybe he already did. He asked himself: what would Lenna want? Before he could answer for her there was a disturbance inside the shack and Grimes crouched behind the platform's edge. He leveled the Glock at the doorway.

Slowly, Lenna's face appeared. Her head was pulled back by her hair. She couldn't see him. A gun appeared against her left cheek. To her far side a second gun appeared and was pressed against her right cheek. Then, from the same side, a pair of black, intelligent eyes peered at Grimes. Grimes took this to be Colonel Herrera. Lenna stepped out onto the platform. Her arms were jacked up behind her. She was crammed between Herrera to her right and, to her left, Filmore Faroe.

It could only be him: the instant Faroe's eyes met his, Grimes recognized that this was a mind crazed beyond reasoning. One half of his upper lip was missing in a raw, ragged crescent, exposing his teeth. Grimes's eyes met Lenna's.

She said: "Kill him."

Grimes blinked.

"Grimes, kill him now."

Herrera jacked her arm up some more. Lenna clenched her jaw. Grimes looked at Faroe.

"The good doctor Grimes," said Faroe.

Despite the pain he had to be in from his torn mouth, Faroe's voice was steady and clear.

"You know, Doctor, there are a lot of questions I'd like to ask you. About myself. I imagine that the time and conditions I experienced in these accommodations might make me a fascinating case study." His mouth curled in a grotesque smile.

Grimes wondered if a response was worth the breath.

He said, "We can sit down right now if you want."

"Another time, perhaps," said Faroe. "Will you give us the road, Doctor?"

Grimes suddenly realized that his father, George, would have done it: he would have shot Faroe right now and taken a ten percent chance on Lenna surviving. But, for better or worse, Grimes wasn't his father.

Grimes said, "Another time then."

Herrera went down the steps first, pulling Lenna with him, his gun still at her head. Faroe, similarly, followed. As Faroe reached the tiled floor Herrera snapped his gun from Lenna's head.

Grimes, waiting for it, dived behind the shack. The bullet chopped out a cloud of splinters. He waited as he heard their footsteps walk away. As he listened he realized he could still hear the chopper somewhere outside: Oates and Ella hadn't left as he had asked. He stepped out from the shack.

Lenna and her captors were almost at the gate.

Grimes started after them.

From under the platform a pair of arms encircled his legs; but too weakly to bring him down. Grimes staggered. A battered, knobbly face appeared at his waist, babbling incoherently with hatred. Desperate hands clawed their way up his jacket, seeking his throat. Grimes threw his left arm around Atwater's chest and half lifted him and squeezed. Ribs already broken by his fall crunched inward. Crimson drool blurted over Atwater's lower lip and down Grimes's lapels. Grimes looked over Atwater's shoulder toward a clank of the gate.

He saw Herrera unlock the gate and pull it open and Faroe shove Lenna out through the cage wall. As Herrera followed them, he pulled the key from this side of the lock. They were going to seal him in.

"Lenna!" yelled Grimes.

Grimes put the Glock to Atwater's wobbling head and, without letting go of him, blew away the vault of his skull. Atwater's chin flopped over Grimes's left shoulder.

Lenna hurled herself sideways, taking Faroe with her, away from Herrera, out of the line of fire.

Grimes fired twice around the edge of Atwater's body; he missed.

Herrera in the doorway: firing back.

Grimes felt thuds against the body clutched in his left arm.

Grimes sighted carefully on the shape in the gateway, fired twice more.

Herrera's leg jerked out from under him and he dropped to one knee.

Grimes flung Atwater aside and charged, pointing the Glock but holding his fire, his feet clacking brittle echoes from the tiles. Herrera started to bring his gun up again. Grimes waited; another yard; another; he opened up. Running, firing, closing.

Herrera's spleen and ventricles disintegrated in a violent paroxysm. He pitched forward and exsanguinated onto the tiles.

Grimes's gun snapped empty. He threw it aside.

Faroe fired at him once, missed. He thrashed his pistol across Lenna's head, dragged her into the antechamber. They disappeared from view.

Grimes splashed past Herrera's corpse. As he entered the short steel-lined antechamber a bullet ricocheted around its walls. He paused at the outer end; no more shots. He dived out among the stacked crates, wove his way toward the exit: the doorway gaped out onto the night and the yard. He stopped on the threshold, his ears ringing from gunfire, his eyes blinking to recover from the glaring light he'd just left behind.

Outside the door at his feet lay a corpse in combat fatigues, its throat slashed clean to the bone. A few yards to the right was sprawled another, similarly slaughtered. At the left extremity of the yard stood the Jessups' house; between that and the Stone House was a stretch of open field; opposite Grimes was the line of silver birch trees; to his right the dirt road. In the center of the yard sat the black chopper, motionless and, as far as he could see, empty. The night seemed impossibly silent. Then through the silence came the pit-pat-pit of padded feet.

Gul trotted out from the silver birch trees and across the yard toward him. Grimes stepped out of the doorway. Gul stood quietly at his side. Grimes turned to his left and saw them.

Filmore Faroe stood by the edge of the field, the barrel of his gun jammed beneath Lenna's jaw, his left hand threaded under her arm and wrapped around the nape of her neck in a half nelson. His paranoiac eyes flitted here and there; his half-lip trembled. He seemed stranded in an infernal darkness. He turned and looked at Grimes, at Gul, back at Grimes.

Grimes started walking toward him.

Grimes hoped that Titus Oates was out there in the trees. He hoped that Oates had a weapon trained on Faroe's head. He hoped that Faroe would be panicked into aiming a shot at him. Or at Gul. He hoped that Titus Oates's bullet would get there first. But Faroe neither budged nor wavered. He just stared at Grimes, the eyes in his shaven cranium as dead as marbles. As the distance between them closed Grimes wondered what he would do when he got there. There was nothing left that Faroe could be threatened with. The man had nothing left to lose.

When Grimes was ten feet short, a voice rang from among the silver birch trees.

"Mr. Faroe!"

Grimes stopped. Gul stopped too. The voice was Ella's. For a moment there was stillness and silence. Faroe blinked, as if the voice had dragged him, confused, from another world.

Then he said, "Who goes there?"

Ella stepped out from the trees. Her hands were empty. In the moonlight her face was solemn but calm.

She said, "I'm Ella MacDaniels. I'm the reason we're all here."

Faroe's eyes cleared, then shone with an intense curiosity.

Ella said, "I thought we might talk."

Grimes bit his tongue.

Lenna struggled. Faroe wrestled her savagely.

"Lenna, please," said Ella.

Lenna stopped fighting.

Ella walked across the yard toward them. Faroe stared at her as if mesmerized. Ella held his gaze. Three paces short she stopped. For a moment she met Lenna's eyes. Tears began to roll down Lenna's cheeks; she didn't move. Ella turned her dark, open gaze back on Faroe.

Ella said, simply: "Lenna is my mother."

The lines around Faroe's eyes crimped deeper.

"I didn't have a father," said Ella. "But in a way—the way I see it— I had many. Some that I never knew, and some that I did. Some that are living and some that are dead. You're one of them, Mr. Faroe."

The muscles of Faroe's face fluttered with mystery and, within the mystery, dread.

Ella said: "I'm the child you tried to kill."

Grimes felt his spine shiver. Faroe tried to turn away from her eyes; couldn't.

Ella said: "You could have stopped me from being born. But you didn't, did you?"

Faroe didn't answer. In Ella's face was something he could not have seen in anyone's face before: pity. And not that pity which tinged itself with contempt but, rather, with sadness: for the immeasurable anguish that Faroe too had borne.

"You wanted me to be yours," said Ella. "Didn't you? That's why you allowed me to be born."

Faroe opened his mouth but still could not answer. It was as if the malice leaking from his pores were being crammed back inside by Ella's naked innocence. Faroe seemed on the verge of exploding. Grimes dared not move. By his leg he sensed Gul, taut as a bowstring, ready to attack. Grimes dared not speak.

"You wanted me to be yours and you would have loved me. I know that."

Faroe shook his head, numbly, as if trying to deny a truth he couldn't bear to hear.

Ella said, "When I wasn't your child, you wanted me to be killed. Do you still want to kill me, Mr. Faroe?"

Faroe finally choked out some words. "What do you want from me?"

"I want you to go away," replied Ella.

"Go?" said Faroe. His voice was hoarse. "Go where?"

"Wherever you have to," said Ella. "That's your own choice."

Ella glanced at Lenna's tear-stained face; then she looked back at Faroe.

Ella said, "Once upon a time, you loved her too."

Faroe looked at her for a long time. What went through his mind in those moments, Grimes could not guess. The pain of betrayal, the torture of confinement, the slaughter that had ushered Ella into the world. Things terrible, things grievous, things sad: these things unknown and perhaps, even in him, a very small remnant of something else: something more eternal than the rest. Faroe took a sudden heave of breath.

He said: "And all for the want of a horseshoe nail."

Grimes thought Faroe's mind had finally snapped. Do it, he thought. Tell Gul to go and depend on Faroe's basic reflexes to turn the gun away from Lenna.

But suddenly Faroe dropped his arm. The gun fell away from Lenna's throat. He let go of her and stepped back. His gun clattered to the ground. Filmore Faroe looked at Ella one last time, with an expression that Grimes would always remember but would never entirely comprehend; then he turned and fled, stumbling, into the blackness of the midnight field behind him.

Lenna fell into Ella's arms.

Faroe was gone.

Grimes walked over, with Gul, toward where Titus Oates was emerging from the tree line. An M16 rifle hung dejectedly from Oates's hand. He jerked his thumb toward the undergrowth.

"I guess this means I have to give Paco a break too," said Oates.

Grimes nodded. "Seems ungenerous not to."

Oates looked down at Gul. "And into the bargain I lose my fucking pooch too." He glared at Grimes. "You were supposed to get yourself killed, man."

Grimes crouched down and put his fingers in the fur of Gul's neck. He stared into the bottomless black eyes and Gul stared back.

"Listen, pal," said Grimes. "If you want to hang out with me, I'll do my best for you, but I have to tell you that Titus here would make a better partner than I would. You understand?"

Gul blinked once.

"It's up to you," said Grimes.

Gul looked up at Oates. Oates held out his right hand toward him.

"Well?" he said. "What's your problem, man?"

Gul licked Oates's hand. Oates smiled at Grimes.

"Sorry, cousin."

"That's the hand with blood on it," said Grimes.

"Hey, Mrs. Oates didn't raise any of her babies to be assholes."

"Remember, Gul's planning a trip to D.C. with those suitcases."

"Mmm," grunted Titus Oates. "Well, if him and me are going to be partners, I guess it wouldn't do to welsh on our first deal."

"Treat him right," said Grimes.

He walked away toward Lenna and Ella. Gul barked. Grimes turned. Gul looked at him but stayed by Oates's side.

"Be good," said Grimes.

Gul barked again and Grimes swallowed the things he felt and turned his back and walked on.

When he reached the women, Ella said, "Tell her, Grimes. Tell her she's got to come with us."

Lenna looked at him and Grimes knew from her eyes that whatever he might say, it wasn't going to work.

"I'm staying here," said Lenna.

Grimes waited.

"All this is mine," said Lenna. "All this and all that's happened."

Grimes said, "That's not so."

"Most of it is mine," countered Lenna. "I never took care of things the way I should have. This time I will. No one need ever know you or Ella had anything to do with it."

"No one has to take a fall for me," said Grimes.

"It's what I want," said Lenna. "It's what I ask of you."

She looked at Ella.

"It's what I ask of you both."

In Lenna's expression, as she looked at her daughter, Grimes saw that this was her way of being what she'd always wanted most to be: Ella's mother. Perhaps it was the only way she had.

"Good luck, then," said Grimes.

Lenna smiled at him and the smile melted his heart.

"Is that the best you can do?" she said.

Grimes took her in his arms and kissed her. Her lips and skin and hair were soft, and lovely. The kiss tasted of all the things he knew of her, and of all the things he knew not, and wanted to, but never would. In a world of different possibilities, perhaps, but not this one. The limits of this one had been inscribed, and fixed, before they'd ever met.

Not this world then, but some other.

His imagination knew it well.

Grimes pulled away and looked at Ella. She seemed unconvinced. Grimes held his arm out and she came and embraced him. He spoke quietly in her ear.

"George let you make your own choices. I reckon we owe Lenna the same."

Ella looked at him. She nodded. Grimes smiled.

He said, "I'm proud to have rode with you, too."

Then a long and curdling scream arched above them through the night.

It called out to Grimes; and it called him alone.

The yearning that had haunted him and haunted him still.

Grimes turns toward the midnight field and runs. He runs over grass and weeds and clods of clay. He runs on and on, through a hazy dark. And splayed upon the fallow ground he finds a body: with spindled limbs and gaping neck.

The body's shaven head was gone.

Grimes looks to north, and east, and west, and he cannot see him. He strains his eyes. He cannot see him. The sky is bigger than all his sight, and, too, the land; and in the black the land and sky seem one. Grimes cannot see him.

Then a bolt of lightning cleaves the sky and floods the midnight field with incandescent witness: he is there.

And he is running too.

Bestumped and rotting and wasted: he runs. With a maggot in his leg.

And the earth cannot stop him, nor her gods, nor the gone dead souls that grieve upon the wind. And in his arms he holds a ragged bundle, tight.

And as the incandescence fades and a bolt of thunder rolls the darkness home, Grimes imagines that he sees the fatman *smile*.

And Cicero Grimes smiles too. For in his heart he knows: the fatman loves them.

He loves them dear.

EPILOGUE

T ITUS OATES, and his partner, Gul, took the lawman's *corpus delicti,* with which they had been entrusted, to D.C., and Titus divided the *corpus* into two portions. The one he delivered to *The Washington Post* as Cicero Grimes had suggested, and as Gul insisted that he do. But because Titus did not wholly trust the *Post,* tied as they were, at least as he saw it, to certain principles that conflicted with his notion of freedom, he delivered the other portion to *Soldier of Fortune* magazine. Neither organ let them down. The hurly-burly that the lawman had predicted ensued and the anvil of justice rang loud across the land. Oates became a feted and famous man, all the more so when he was tried on a multitude of indictments in the states of Louisiana and Georgia. Though Oates denied nothing—and in fact embellished his deeds in order to take into account those actually performed by Cicero Grimes—so heroic was his tale, and so forthright his defense of the justice of what he had done, that the citizens twelve and true chosen by each court acquitted Oates of all charges, on the grounds that he was constitutionally entitled to defend himself, and the lives of vulnerable others, to the best of his reasonable judgment. After the trial, Titus Oates changed his name to Hajj Dha Bah, which he understands to mean "the pilgrimage of ritual slaughter," and disappeared with Gul into the remote wastes of Canada in order to wander the Northern Roads. To what exact purpose, and in search of what goal, no one knows.

Lenna Parillaud also stood trial and was found guilty of the charges that Filmore Faroe had planned to bring against her concerning his abduction and imprisonment and the defraudment of his wealth. She made no mention of the fact that Ella MacDaniels was still alive, or of

Grimes, and they respected her wish that this be so. She is presently serving twenty-five years in the Louisiana State Correctional Facility for Women, and when Ella visits her, or she writes to Grimes, Lenna insists that she has no complaints. Her appeal, and the complexities of her estate, have yet to be resolved.

Ella MacDaniels returned to the City and changed little of her outer life. She started writing songs, and continues to perform. She refuses to use the deposits Clarence Jefferson bequeathed her, because she figured that the cash was accumulated out of injustice, of which she wants no part. She too corresponds with Grimes and he has learned that she is presently negotiating a recording contract with an independent outfit based in the City, and that she's taken herself a lover, who, she says, treats her well.

Cicero Grimes went back to his hole and dwelt for a while upon the death of his father, George. When he finally decided that he was bound to the Orphic wheel along with the rest of them, and that in the end he had earned the right, in front of himself, to stand alongside his father's bloodstained ghost, he settled his affairs, which were few, and left the City for good. He packed his Olds 88 with the things he needed, and a few of the things he wanted, and drove south, deep into Mexico, where the air was dry and the days were long and where he could speak Spanish and be thought of as strange because he was a gringo and not because strange was how he was.

There, in the mountain town in which he has chosen to live, he has started to practice medicine again and his hands have come back to life. And maybe he makes a difference and maybe he does not, but he feels, and he hopes, that it is work of noble note and in it he believes he has rediscovered something of that which was most precious to him and which for a time he thought he had lost.

And often in the heat of the night, and sometimes in the cool of the morning, Grimes dreams of Clarence Jefferson. And in those dreams the fatman too is stained with blood. And this is right and fitting. For though he is a demon he is also a king: of a realm whose mysteries are without resolve, a dominion whose wilderness is without end. And the fatman is running. He is running still. Through the eternal darkness of a midnight field. To a crossing of roads which he will not shun. To a congress—and a confrontation—with the shades of bloodstained kings.

ABOUT THE AUTHOR

TIM WILLOCKS is a novelist, screenwriter, and doctor
of medicine specializing in addiction.

ABOUT THE TYPE

This book was set in Galliard, a typeface designed by
Matthew Carter for the Merganthaler Linotype Company
in 1978. Galliard is based on the sixteenth-century
typefaces of Robert Granjon.